# SERVANTS OF STONE

## SEAN EADS AND JOSHUA VIOLA

Crystal Lake Publishing
Where Stories Come Alive!

www.crystallakepub.com

# WELCOME
## TO ANOTHER

# CRYSTAL LAKE PUBLISHING
## CREATION

Join today at www.crystallakepub.com & www.patreon.com/CLP

# PROLOGUE

## October 1818

*I wasn't going to kill him. Bullheaded fool just wouldn't stay down.*

Evan Vines's hands shook as he tried to steady his grip on the reins. The cold, stinging rain had him gritting his teeth whenever he tried to look ahead. The coal-black stallion that pulled the cart all but disappeared into the darkness. The road had become nothing but suctioning mud, but the horse somehow triumphed. The Devil only knew where the beast was taking him.

*I told him to stay down. He'd be alive if he'd listened. He forced my hand.*

Vines spat into the rain and the gusting winds dashed it back against his face.

*Why didn't he listen? It's like he was desperate. What do fat men like him know about desperation? They've never starved. They've never sat in hunger's classroom or learned its sums. But he got his education tonight, didn't he?*

"But I only meant to rob him!" Evan Vines shouted at the horse before settling back and tucking his chin against his chest to brave the storm. He should have known the fat man would fight back. Greed and gluttony always danced together, and their minuet didn't begrudge so much as a crumb to the needy.

The rain didn't seem to be washing the blood away. Then he realized it was his own blood. The knuckles on his right hand had split open when he hit the driver in the mouth after wresting him off the cart. The blow crumpled the man, putting him on his hands and knees and making him spit teeth into the mud. That *should* have been enough. He *should* have surrendered. He'd still be alive. But instead, he got up and Evan Vines kicked him in the side. *"Quit trying!"* Why wouldn't he stay down? What was so important to him? Vines had looked at the ox cart, its back covered by a fraying white tarp, and became excited. The man started to push himself up a final time, and Vines screamed and began kicking him in the face. He kicked until the man's breath came out like the last dregs of a wine skin, and then he went on kicking, the savageness increasing until the final kick missed the man and caused Vines to fall backward into the mud.

The horse pulled the cart forward and stood over him. Vines squinted to make out its fierce black shape against the backdrop of the storm, and when a flash of lightning revealed its magnificence, he got to his feet. Then he looked around as if someone might have seen his crime.

He knew better. He'd been wandering along the road for two days and the last farm he'd passed was half a day's walk behind him. Maybe the fat man lived there.

Vines climbed into the cart. He tugged the reins but the horse didn't move. The animal seemed to be staring at the body.

"He brought it on himself. Best be obedient to me. You're mine now."

The horse craned its neck to glance back at him and snorted. It strained against the traces, working the cart's wheels out of the slippery mud. It was slow going for half a minute, and Vines didn't see how it'd be possible to get the cart free. Then the horse bolted forward with a power that almost sent Vines falling out of his seat. He clutched the reins just to keep from falling out of the cart.

But after thirty minutes at an impossible speed, and with the body many miles behind him, Vines began to assert himself. He pulled on the reins. The horse *would* yield to him. He *was* its master now.

"Stop, damn you!"

He searched around for a whip but found nothing. The cart began to slow.

"Easy," Vines said. "Pull off the road and stop under those trees."

The horse did just that.

"Ah, good. You're recognizing your master."

In the summer season, the full trees would make a decent shelter, but the stripped branches did little to blunt the storm's assault. Nevertheless, Vines left the seat and turned to pull back the tarp.

"Now let's see why the fat man kept getting up."

Expecting a revelation of gold, Vines found nothing in the cart except a covered wicker basket. As the rain began to strike it, Vines heard a baby's cries.

It took him several moments to accept the reality of the sound. He removed the lid and the baby's wailing reached a fever pitch.

"Good God," he said. From its size, he judged the child to be little more than a few months old.

*The fool should have said something. Why didn't he?*

He went to stand next to the horse. Thick, long locks of soaked black hair stuck to his cheeks like plump leeches.

"I bet his mother's dead. And now his father. I know the orphan's life. We're going to do this child a kindness."

He repeated those last two words, whispering them against the battering rain.

But how to bestow that kindness?

Maybe the best thing was to leave the basket out in the road uncovered and let the weather seal its fate. Some other improbable traveler might come along and give the baby a reprieve. It had already been a night for strange chances.

Vines went back to the cart bed. As he reached for the bassinet, however, the horse pulled forward. "*Stop*," he commanded. The horse ignored him and took the cart back to the road.

He seized the horse by the bridle.

"You have other plans? Is this to be a contest of wills?"

The horse and cart lurched forward. Vines scrambled up into the driver's seat and pulled the reins with little effect. Vines found himself mesmerized by the horse's unflagging strength as it veered off the path and began careering across the sodden, rutted land. Vines was pitched back into the cart and clung to the basket as if it could anchor him.

Vines clawed his way back to the seat, taking forth the bassinet with him. The cart bumped and rocked, reaching a speed its parts couldn't sustain. The left back wheel broke off and the cart skipped and sputtered. The horse kept pulling until the right wheel shattered and the dangling cart dragged like the mouldboard of a plow as they cut a trough through the land. Evan Vines shouted without shame, but his pleading seemed to encourage the horse. To Vines's horror, they were moving straight toward the bank of a river, its waters swollen by the storm, its currents making a fearsome dash through the darkness.

"Goddamn you! Stop, or we'll both die!"

He was about to jump when he saw a light shining from overhead. There seemed to be a cliff face rising from across the river, though he couldn't measure how far away. The light flickered like a campfire but had the brightness of a coastal lighthouse. Vines gaped at it even as the cart careened into the water. It should have sunk, would have sunk, except the horse moved so fast and battled so hard that neither raging undertows nor wind nor water depth defeated it. The river seemed at least half a mile wide, though, and nothing could prevent the swollen waters from taking their toll. The battens broke away, and then the tongue splintered. The horse was in danger of pulling itself free of the cart altogether, and in the moment's urgency, Vines called out to it.

"We're going to drown if you keep this up!"

But the horse would not relent. They reached the other side with only a minimal semblance of a cart. Vines fell onto the rocky shore, almost crushing the basket beneath him.

"What the hell are you, beast?"

The horse, now free, came around to him.

"You're going to go up there to that light, aren't you? That's where you want to take the baby."

The horse snorted as Vines staggered up clutching the basket. Wind gusted into his face.

"What if I don't give him to you?"

The horse reared back, jolting Vines to the ground. He whipped the basket in front of him like a shield and the horse settled down.

Vines grinned. "You're a smart beast, aren't you? I'm not sure I like smart beasts. You're determined to take the baby up to that light, but you'll need my help and you know it."

He felt a burst of heat from the horse as if its fiery heart had just exploded. Vines laughed.

"You're just brimming with pride, aren't you? You've no saddle. How can I mount you without stirrups and hold tight to a baby in weather like this? Bow down so I can get my legs across your back."

The horse stood still for a few seconds as if deliberating. Then it lowered itself and Vines smirked.

"Much better. Not so tall now, are you?"

He cast the basket's lid aside and took the infant into his arms. The baby was cold, wet, and silent.

But still alive.

Vines got into position.

"Very well," he said as the horse rose. He cradled the little body against his chest. The horse began following a side trail. "The child's fate rests with that light up there, for good or ill. Once we reach it, we leave the baby and depart. You belong to me now."

The wind had been cold before, but it carried more than a hint of winter as they braved the steep and winding path.

"How much higher can it be? I swear, beast, I'll throw the baby down and be done with it if we don't reach–"

The path leveled off. Vines confronted a bright, almost perfect sphere of light ahead of him. A silhouette moved inside it, looking for all the world like a woman in labor. The figure was on its back, with legs bent and splayed. Its back arched and writhed.

"What the hell is this? Turn around, beast. We're leaving."

Lacking spurs, he drove his heels into the horse's sides for emphasis. The horse had the upper hand, though, and reared back halfway, throwing him onto a landscape of gravel and larger rocks.

"Not a wise move, beast. If I'd landed the wrong way, the baby would be dead."

He got up still clutching the infant.

From the sphere of light, a wan and weary voice said, "Deliver me my child."

Vines looked at the baby and then forward into the light. The silhouette had not changed position. It still seemed to be mimicking the thralls of labor, though he heard no cries, no screams of pain.

"I'll place it right here," he said. "Come and get it."

The horse stomped its front hooves and pivoted toward him. Vines retreated two steps.

"Do as thou were bid, husband," the voice said.

*"Husband?"*

The silhouette's movements calmed. The figure rose and waited as the horse walked toward it. As the woman reached out to touch him, a sharp flash of lightning transformed the entire sky. The dark clouds all seemed to be a hundred enraged faces. He shut his eyes from a reflex of shock. When he opened them again, he found himself standing in a large stone hallway lined with statues and busts. The hallway extended onward and out of sight to his left. To the right, it ended in an altar just ten feet away.

A woman knelt there. She seemed very old, and her naked body looked thin and frail.

"Thou are not he who answered my summoning song. Nightcamp has shown me what transpired."

"Nightcamp? Is that the horse's name?"

"The dead man had a bargain with me thou must now fulfill."

Vines looked down at the baby in his arms. "The child?"

The old woman rose and nodded.

"Why should I give him to you? Maybe I've always wanted a son of my own."

She laughed. "Men such as thou seek to father far greater things."

They circled each other. Vines saw the woman struggle to take her attention off the baby and look him in the eyes.

"Where are we? Where did the cliff go?"

She waved her right hand and Vines found himself at the mercy of the storm again. The horse stood to his right and the woman was before him, naked, unfazed by the wind and rain.

"Give me my child, husband."

"I'm no husband to you or anyone else!"

She held out her arms.

"Place the baby in my hands."

Vines cocked his head. For all the woman's strangeness and air of dread, there was a touch of helplessness about her. He'd spent too many years among people in desperate need not to recognize its face.

"Here," he said, holding the baby forth. "Just take it."

"Thou must give it unto me."

"Why?"

She waved her hand, and they were back in the stone hallway. The transformation happened with all the quickness of stepping from one room to another, though his feet hadn't moved.

The woman went to the altar and took up a dagger. The blade was black with an uneven, glistening bevel. She turned to the nearest row of busts. In the room's low light, the busts were so lifelike Vines could imagine each was a living person kneeling behind a pedestal.

She lifted one of the busts and dragged the blade across it. The stone yielded to the dagger as flesh would. Vines held his breath as he watched her deftly remove the original face and carve a hideous replacement. A low and persistent hum filled the air. It seemed a tune sung between the blade and the bust, and it did not stop until she withdrew the knife in satisfaction.  The result would have satisfied any Gothic craftsman from the Middle Ages. She put the new bust back and turned to him.

"You have talent," Vines said after a long moment of silence. The woman laughed.

"A trifling art to while away impatient hours."

"Is that meant to be a gift for me? Something to give me in exchange for the child?"

"The gift of warning," she said, and her voice was like the slowing drip of water as it begins to freeze.

"You want something I have. Very well. You talk of bargains. What can you give that's equal to your want—and mine?"

She waved her hand and they were back on the rocky plateau of the cliff in the driving rain.

"I give thee Nightcamp to do with as thou wilt."

Evan Vines forced a smile. "I need more than some nag. What did you offer the man I killed? It must have been pretty big, considering how he fought. Anything you were prepared to give him you can give me."

There was a second when he thought he'd pushed too hard. She still had the stone knife in her grip, and she pointed it at him. He almost broke and threw the baby at her, but she then directed the blade toward the edge of the cliff and walked in that direction. He followed, keeping several steps behind her.

"I will not insult the scope of thy ambition by offering thou the same bargain. Behold my covenant with thee."

She pointed the blade outward, and in a flash the rain stopped, and they stood looking down at the river on a sunny day. On the other side lay impressive, almost boundless tracts of forest.

"Place the child into my hands, and this shall be thy kingdom."

She gestured with the blade like someone conducting a symphony. Vines struggled to believe the changes taking place across the river. The trees fell and a town rose on the cleared land. A town, a city, an entire state. Greater than that, he realized as the buildings kept on spreading. It was all dominated by a tower rising in the center. He'd never seen a building so tall. It cast a westward shadow too long for his sight to follow.

"The limit of the shadow alone shall mark the extent of thy sovereignty if you give me the child."

Evan Vines shifted the baby into the crook of his left arm and moved past the woman to stand on the very edge of the cliff. He stared out for several minutes, trying to gather in the majesty of it all. He heard his name rising into the air, chanted from thousands of prayerful lips. He was their king.

Their god.

At last, he turned back to the woman and said, "Is this real?"

She showed a humorless smile and lowered the blade. At once they were back in the stone corridor, standing close to the altar.

"Place the child into my arms, and tomorrow I will place a kingdom into yours."

The baby began to cry. Vines held it out.

The infant squalled with all its waning energy as Vines gave it to the old woman. She took it to the altar at once and he turned his back, cringing in expectation. The cries ceased a moment later, and he let out a long sigh. Then he heard the cooing.

The old woman was sitting on the altar with the baby against her left breast. The teat was far too old and withered to produce milk, yet the baby was suckling *something* from it.

"At last, it is done. Thou proved a difficult labor, but now the task is accomplished. Thy wriggling form pleases me. So like a tadpole thou are, therefore, Toad I name thee."

She stood up and took the baby from her teat and placed it on the altar. Her right hand held the black dagger again.

"Come, husband. Gaze upon thy son as I perfect him."

"Send me back to the cliff," Vines said. "I don't want to see any more."

She drew the blade through the air and began to sing. Vines didn't understand a word of the chant, but just hearing it made his skin itch. Atop the altar, the infant's body began to harden. Its legs froze mid-kick.

The old woman started carving.

The horror of the deed carried Evan Vines into unconsciousness. His dream was plagued by the leering expressions of sinister gargoyles. When he woke, he found himself on the rocky plateau, his skin and clothes dry. He stood up to a glorious sunrise.

The sound of a snort sent him turning around. The dark stallion was there, saddled, waiting.

He remembered what the woman had called it and said, "Nightcamp. Looks like you've been thrown in as part of the deal. This pleases me. There are many things I'll not forget about last night, including the way you treated me. Brace yourself for long retribution."

Evan Vines climbed into the saddle and set the horse on the downward path.

# PART ONE

# FLESH

# Chapter One

## June 1830

Lily Hobbs couldn't wait any longer. The *Witchhand* would be tapping at the window any minute, like it had every night for the last week, starting on the night of her 10^th birthday, the first of June.

It seemed to grow stronger with each visit. Last night, the *Witchhand*'s ghost-like fingers nearly got the latch open.

Tonight, it was going to get her. She just knew it.

Lily got out of bed and knelt as if to pray. Instead, she thrust her right hand under the mattress, groping for Mouse. She wished she could have snuck all of Papa's tiny stone animals into her room and lined them up facing the window like an army. Papa said he made the sculptures to protect her. They might not be able to move, but they could keep her safe.

Somehow.

*Where's Mouse? I'm sure I didn't shove him so far under—*

Scritch. Scritch. Scritch.

She whimpered and gave a grim stare toward the window and its four little panes.

Smoky white fingernails scratched up and down the upper right pane.

*The Witchhand!*

Gasping, Lily fell away from the bed and kicked herself against the far wall.

*Just scream,* she thought. *Mama and Papa will come if I scream. But if I scream, the Witchhand will get them, too.*

The *Witchhand* moved from pane to pane, pressing against each one. Lily heard the subtle complaint of the glass and bunched up her shoulders, anticipating the break. Almost breathless now, she lunged back to the bed and reached under the mattress as far as she could.

No Mouse.

No hope.

The *Witchhand* slapped at the panes. The whole window shook.

The glass would shatter any moment.

The clawing and the slapping stopped. Lily held her breath and stared at the white hand. It had always seemed larger than the whole window, but now she realized it wasn't much bigger than her own.

But it wasn't human. The nails were hooked like claws, and there was ghostly webbing between the fingers.

*Go away,* she thought. *Please just go away.*

The *Witchhand* began to tap on the pane. Lily cringed again, expecting the worst. But the tapping was light.

There was a rhythm to it.

As she listened, she felt herself responding to the melody. Her heart seemed to beat to its pattern.

She stood up, forgetting Mouse and everything else.

The *Witchhand*'s tapping seemed to say: *Come and open the window.*

Lily stepped forward.

*This is wrong. I shouldn't. I mustn't open the window.*

The tapping had become a song with a single, insistent lyric: *Open. Open. Open.*

She kept coming forward, so close her nose nearly touched the glass.

*No, no,* she thought. *Turn away.*

Lily closed her eyes and covered her ears. The *Witchhand*'s song still held sway. It wanted her to obey, and it wouldn't stop until she did. The song filled her imagination with scenes of joy. She saw herself letting the *Witchhand* whisk her away and show her the glories of the night. She'd be carried through the sky, higher and higher.

She opened her eyes and put her right hand to the pane. Only thin, perilous glass kept their palms from touching.

*Open open open*

Lily's left hand went to the brass latch.

*I shouldn't, but—*

Nothing would save her this time.

Just as she swiveled the latch open, a high-pitched, drawn-out cry filled the air like a burst of light. The sharp noise drove the *Witchhand* away as if it'd been scalded. Old Ben, the family rooster, crowed again, pulling Lily from her trance. She shook herself alert, saw the open latch, and raced to close it. Then she scrambled back to the safety of her bed.

Mouse was there, somehow, right in the middle of the mattress. The little statue was positioned to stare straight at the window. Lily grabbed the sculpture and tucked it beneath her pillow, then crawled under her top sheet, pulling it to her chin as the wild pace of her pulse began to settle.

"Thank you, Old Ben," she whispered.

# Chapter Two

At the first hint of sunlight, Lily got out of bed, dressed, and made her way to the chicken coop. Old Ben stood tall, proud, and red.

"Thank you for saving me," she said, and the rooster lowered his head both in acknowledgment and to receive a pet from Lily. She was glad to ruffle her fingers through his soft plumage.

There was something wrong about the air, a sense that the *Witchhand* was somehow still around. She retreated nearer to the farmhouse, moving to what Papa called his *stone menagerie*. It was a funny word that meant a group of animals. Papa had carved 30 of them for her. Mouse and Fox, Racoon and Skunk and so many others. Lily liked placing them all together so they could be friends.

The animals were all looking toward the river. That's not right, she told herself. She'd put them in a circle. Who would have moved them?

*A face, a face,*
*With open eyes,*
*Spare my life*
*From Mama's pies!*

The joy of the song turned her thoughts from trouble and her face to the cornfield. Fat Jack was up early!

Lily ran through the crops, moving through the early summer plantings of corn and kale, cabbage and carrots, and beets. In another month or so, the corn would be tall enough to hide Fat Jack from view, but for now, she saw his massive orange shell rising from the middle of the field like a drowsy king. She threw herself against Fat Jack. The pumpkin had gotten so round even Papa couldn't wrap his arms around it.

A hearty bellow came from inside the gourd.

*Who's that I feel against me?*

*A bird, the wind, the leaf of a tree?*

*Why are you there? Tell me who can it be?*

*This flower! This girl!*

*This beautiful Lily!*

His song was stronger than anything else on the farm. Greater than the squirrels or the birds. Not even the choir of pigs singing their sloppy mud song could overcome Fat Jack's boisterous trilling.

The pumpkin had been a little larger than Papa's fist when she found it four years ago and sat down to stroke it as she would a cat. He answered with a song she had to strain to hear. Fat Jack was Little Jack back then.

"How strange," Papa had said. "I've never planted pumpkins."

He bent to take it.

"Don't!"

Lily threw herself over the little gourd and pleaded into her parents' questioning eyes.

"He's so tiny," she said. "Please don't hurt him."

"We could let it grow and make it into a pie," Mama said.

"I won't let you make Jack into a pie!" Lily shouted.

"Jack?" Papa said.

"Little Jack."

"Our Lily's named everything around here down to the last ear of corn. Adam could have used you when he was tasked with labeling the creatures of the Earth."

"Oh, Papa, please let Little Jack stay. And Mama, you must promise not to make him into a pie!"

"I pledge to keep him here in the field and away from your mother's oven. But Lily, every gourd will rot on the vine sooner or later. When that time comes, Jack will have to go."

Lily nodded. In her heart, she knew Little Jack wouldn't rot. And she was proven right. Year after year, the pumpkin grew, becoming a bright and fiery orange. Papa shook his head and laughed whenever the time came to sow new crops.

A new song interrupted her remembering.

*I sing for sun*
*I sing for rain*
*But songs for Lily*
*Are my favorite refrain!*

Lily clapped and gave his shell a little pat.

"I have so much to tell you! The *Witchhand* came again last night, but Old Ben scared it off. Did you see it? Oh, I know you didn't. You're always sleeping!"

Before Fat Jack answered, Lily heard Mama shouting.

"Lily! Where are you, child?"

"Here, Mama!" she cried and gave the pumpkin a little kiss before running back to the house. Mama was in the kitchen, and Lily grabbed the basket beside the table, knowing Mama must be cross because she hadn't started her chores.

Mama took the basket away.

"But I have to get the eggs."

"I'll collect them, Lily. Today is a special day. Your father wants you to go with him to New Vineland."

# Chapter Three

A day without chores? A trip with Papa to New Vineland?

Any remaining dread of the *Witchhand* evaporated like a bit of spilled milk. Lily couldn't believe the news and ran out the door toward the river before Mama could say another word. She sprinted past the crops and down to the river, where Papa had his workshop. Papa was at the dock, hitching one end of a towline to a simple flat raft. The other end was tied to the farm's two horses, Bandit and Ruffian.

She jumped up and down, clapped her hands, and said, "When are we leaving?"

Papa looked up and laughed. "In your mind, we've already left."

Lily tried to get on the raft, but Papa grew serious and ordered her back. "Not just yet," he said. "There are still things that need doing."

She watched Papa finish with the towline and then followed him back to his workshop, about 50 yards from the waterline. Papa was a stonemason and Lily couldn't remember a day when he wasn't in the shop. Her chores seldom let her visit him, but when she could he at first only allowed her to stand at the door and watch him work. After a few minutes, he would always grin and say, "Don't speak of this to Mama," and motion her inside. Then he'd show her objects called *mallets* and *mason chippers* and many other strange, heavy tools. Papa would put his hand over hers around the handle of a hammer and demonstrate how striking it against a chisel could make a rock break a certain way.

He had shown Lily several things now, and she was familiar enough to recognize the tools by the sounds they made. Hammers went *chunk, chunk, chunk*. Finer tools went *tink, tink, tink*. He made many sculptures for people who lived along the river, but the stone animals were for her alone even though many had offered money for them.

Today there was large rock slab on the table. Lily stood tiptoe to see it better and realized it was a gravestone. It was shaped with a rounded top and engraved with angels blowing long trumpets toward the sky. A name and a year seemed to rise from the divine bugling.

## ANNA
1830

She reached to touch the smooth rock, her fingertips tracing the grooves of the simple engraving. So many things sang to her—the animals, the trees, Fat Jack, and the water. But rock never had. Seeing the tombstone made her glad rock didn't sing. She could only imagine its sad melody.

"Who was she, Papa?"

There was a brief pause before he spoke.

"I'm not sure."

"What was her last name? How old was she?"

"Sometimes those things aren't known."

"Oh," she said. Many questions came to mind, but she didn't know how to ask them. Then she gasped, seeing Papa take up the heavy stone without any effort. He carried it outside and she followed.

"Are we taking it to New Vineland?"

"Yes," he said. "That's the reason for the trip. Mr. Goodman needs it for a funeral."

Lily's heart warmed at the thought of Mr. Goodman. It had been two weeks since he last visited the farm.

"Will we see him there?"

"Oh, I don't think so. He's very busy. Pastors always are."

He placed the tombstone in the exact center of the raft and motioned for Lily to get on. As she did, she spied Mama coming down the path with a covered basket. Papa met her on the dock and they kissed, which made Lily smile. Papa was a handsome man with his dark hair and beard, his shoulders were broad, and his eyes were a warm brown. Mama was just as pretty, with braided plaits of hair the same caramel color as Lily's.

"Some of yesterday's biscuits and butter for the trip, since you're determined to set off without a proper breakfast."

"You're truly good to us, Katherine."

They kissed again. This time Lily noticed it was much shorter, and that Mama stepped away from Papa's embrace. Lily heard her say, "It will be hard, but it's for the best. He's very old, and if he can't tell midnight from dawn then he's not of much use."

Lily's brow furrowed. She started to leave the raft. "What are you talking about, Mama?"

"Nothing, child."

"Stay on the raft, Lily. We're leaving."

Nothing else was said. Papa took up a push pole and whistled to the horses, who moved forward.

"We'll be back by evening," he said.

Lily looked back at Mama and saw she was already moving back to the farmhouse, her footsteps not at all quick as if they were taking her toward a task she had no desire to do.

# Chapter Four

## October 1826

*Father would call this town a monument to blasphemy*, Harold Goodman thought as he moved out of the sunlight and into the tower's shadow. He lowered the wide brim of his straw hat and headed into a cobblestone alley, stepping between puddles along the way. They were fresh reminders of last night's rainstorm, though a stink rose from the water as it might from a stagnant pond.

The alleyway was unoccupied and Goodman thought it a great location to spy on the people who were coming and going everywhere else. Sunlight glinted off their finery, coats of dyed silk and cotton, leather shoes with silver buckles, golden bonnets, and fur caps. He looked for familiar faces—not an easy task with thousands of people milling about, but he expected to remember at least one man or woman after weeks of exploring and observing. These people all seemed recent arrivals, fresh from the dock and already certain about their future here.

New Vineland seemed a chaos of movement, but Goodman had come to see there were two distinct patterns at play: a stream of newcomers in their poorer clothes heading toward the tower, and the growing flow of people in glorious attire sweeping forever clockwise with the tower as the axis of their motion.

Bored with watching, Goodman headed to the outskirts of New Vineland. He'd taken this walk multiple times now, always starting at the same spot, and each time the walk took just a little bit longer than the time before. How could the town's boundaries expand overnight? How were there new dwellings appearing with no evidence of construction?

If the people kept coming, how long would it be before New Vineland surpassed Philadelphia and New York for city supremacy on the continent?

Just inside New Vineland's latest perimeter, Goodman sought out a fence post that had itself only appeared three days ago. At that time, the post *was* the town limit. The next day, a house existed five paces north of it.

He found the post and began walking and counting.

There was no doubt.

New Vineland's northern boundary had expanded 100 paces since the post appeared.

For all the steady migration and new miracle buildings, New Vineland still didn't have a single church. No absence was more conspicuous, but it was not the town's sole irregularity. There was but a single inn and Goodman was its single resident. The inn was run by an unwelcoming man named Watkins whose constant goal was encouraging Goodman to enter the tower. Indeed, it was impossible to live long in New Vineland and not go there. If you sought a barber-surgeon, you'd find it in the tower. Nor could you seek out a blacksmith or get a saddle repaired, without going through one of the four gaping entrances at the tower's base. These entrances had neither doors nor gates, and a bright, interior glow welcomed all commerce regardless of the hour.

Of course, no one came to New Vineland in search of a barber-surgeon or a blacksmith. Rather than get a saddle repaired, they acquired a brand-new replacement—inside the tower.

Goodman returned to the inn and found Watkins wiping the dining room table. His attempt to sneak past Watkins proved fruitless and confirmed his whole cleaning act was nothing but theater.

"Ah, Mr. Goodman," he said. "You've been exploring again."

"Many new faces out there today. I'm surprised no one besides me ever lodges here."

"Perhaps the question should be, how is it you're the only visitor who insists on *remaining* a visitor? More than a month now, is it?"

"I'm particular about where I choose to live."

"A British trait, perhaps?"

"Perhaps," Goodman said. "I suppose I'm so British that England itself wasn't quite good enough for me. We must hope I recognize the right place when I find it."

"I believe you have," Watkins said. "New Vineland has something for everyone. Houses waiting to be owned, beautiful women waiting to be married. This is a town unlike any other, the fruit of a new nation."

Watkins smiled with no trace of mirth. He didn't have all his teeth and the teeth he did have seemed broken. In fact, now that Goodman thought about it, everything about the man's face reminded him of something that had been shattered and pieced together. There weren't any obvious scars or seams, but the sense of disorder persisted beneath the skin.

"I'm curious, Mr. Watkins, what brought you to New Vineland?"

"Same as everyone else, I suppose. Opportunity."

"To run an inn in a town that doesn't need one?"

"How could I know that at the time? I was among the first who heard about New Vineland and made the trip. In those days, all newcomers—"

"Those days? Mr. Watkins, I was led to believe the town was founded in 1818."

"Yes."

"It's only 1826. 1818 shouldn't be spoken of as ancient times."

"Is that so? It seems so much longer. Life, I mean. My life."

His voice trailed off with a touch of sadness. Why was it that the first hint of humanity in so many people had to be some display of regret and sorrow?

"I keep hoping to meet the town's founder on my walks. What's his name again?"

"Mr. Evan Vines."

"Would I be able to meet him?"

"He is a very busy man. So much to administer and oversee, so much happiness to guarantee."

Goodman smiled. "Perhaps he could use an assistant. I have a fair hand at keeping things in order. Learned it from my father."

"Was he in the Army?"

"No, sir. He's a pastor."

A hint of sourness entered the innkeeper's expression. "Oh, I don't think Mr. Vines has much use for religion around here. No one in New Vineland does."

"Perhaps I'll find I belong here after all," Goodman said and hurried up to his room.

# Chapter Five

*October 19, 1826*

*Father,*

*I remember well your disapproval of my wanderlust and how you admonished me to settle into a useful life. This you expressed even on the day of my departure, and with regret, I remember my arch and impudent response.* "How can a man of God claim to know anything if he's seen no more than twenty square miles of the world God made?"

*I have written to you from many strange places and sought to convey both their wonder and terror as I have observed them. How strange it is that I encounter something in America that makes me think of setting sail and returning to the safety of your parish. This continent has been called the New World for centuries, yet it is as old as every other place on Earth and harbors many of the same dark forces you and every other pastor, priest, and saint believe to have expelled from the forests of England and Europe. Perhaps they all fled here to wait and bide their time. Perhaps for some of them, that time is now.*

Goodman looked up from the letter with a measure of self-disgust for the childish notions he'd allowed himself to confess. Dark forces biding their time? No pastor or priest had expelled anything from England.

Locke, Montesquieu, and Rousseau were the great exorcists of the human mind, not Catholics or Anglicans.

He wanted to tear up the letter but couldn't bring himself to do it. He folded the two pages and slipped them into a brown satchel on the bed behind him. The bag contained three more letters for his father. One was composed just before he heard of New Vineland and the other two expressed a far more favorable opinion of the town, words enthused by first impressions of the evident wealth and happiness he found when his boat docked here on September 1st. The very streets had a pleasant yellow hue like rays of sunshine.

He told the boatman he would not be continuing to the Sound, where he was to embark on another ship that would sail him along the coast to Florida. He had his travel trunk disembarked and then watched his transport go. Strange, it was only then that he noticed the inescapable presence of the craggy cliff face rising from the opposite riverbank. It reminded him of the White Cliffs of Dover, though the rock was black and no more than a third the height. The geology did not fit at all and may have stirred a hint of disquiet. But he was too impatient to explore New Vineland to admit dread.

Even the tower raised no alarm at first, though its architecture was out of sorts with the surrounding buildings. It was dull and featureless, the brainchild of a dull draughtsman. What was its purpose, its point? His questions became feverish as he set off toward it, following the steps of about two hundred people.

Oh, the disappointment, to reach the tower and see the placard—

*All Needs Met*

His shoulders sagged and he remembered that Americans were, after all, British in all but name. Just the sort of people to build a massive, unconventional structure to house a general store.

Who was he to refuse commerce? Goodman walked forward, joining the throng, and passed through the open doorway. As soon as he crossed the threshold, however, his mild bemusement turned to confusion. All at once, he found himself standing among vast rows of shelves stocked with every kind of imaginable goods. He'd never seen so many varieties of tobacco, accompanied by displays of pipes that looked like they'd been carved of cherry and maple, their bowls rimmed with gilt or encrusted with jewels. Moving forward, the offerings changed to bolts of cloth made of cotton, satin, and silk, accompanied by sewing notions and accessories of dazzling ribbon, gossamer thread, and buttons resembling pearls. Advancing still further, he encountered shelves of clothing: shirts, tailored suits and dresses, stockings, and all manner of hats and shoes.

Goodman had walked through the bazaars of many ancient cities, places of great wealth, and never encountered so much opulence under one roof. Looking back, he realized the entrance was gone. How far had he progressed? How large could this single room be? These and other questions were dismissed by the next spectacle ahead, a butcher and a vegetable market operating alongside each other in a space too large for the tower to contain.

"The sign certainly lived up to its promise," he said, scratching his head. A couple brushed past him; their arms bundled with new clothes. The clothes they wore seemed little better than rags, and a natural curiosity overcame him. He'd already noticed the absence of any prices on the shelves. He started to follow the couple, trailing them for what felt like a mile. The store's layout must have involved some sort of optical illusion and maze to accommodate so much variety, but Goodman felt he'd been walking a straight line.

At last, the couple came to a clerk's desk, occupied by a little man with rounded shoulders. As Goodman got closer, he saw the man seemed rounded *everywhere*, shoulders and stomach, face; even his hands at first glance seemed like uniform ovals of flesh rather than individual fingers. The clerk rose as the couple arrived. To Goodman's astonishment, the couple shed their old clothes until they stood naked in front of the clerk. They handed over their rags and then dressed on the spot in their new clothes. Goodman watched the last buckle secured; the last button fastened. They moved toward an exit Goodman hadn't even noticed.

"Next," the clerk said as he looked down and wrote something on a piece of paper. Goodman stepped forward and cleared his throat.

"Your clothes, please," the clerk said, then gave a startled grunt when he realized Goodman had made no selection.

"I have some questions."

"This is not a place of questions."

"The sign promised all needs would be met."

Goodman thought the clerk flashed an appreciative smile.

"Very well."

"Why aren't there prices on anything? It's like you operate on a barter system."

"Indeed we do."

"What will you do with what they gave you?"

The clerk smiled. "They go into the furnace as pointless scraps of past lives. New Vineland is a place of beginnings, as our esteemed founder Mr. Evan Vines says. Isn't that why you're here?"

"I'm only after adventure. I want to see the world while I'm young enough to enjoy it."

"Perhaps New Vineland is as much of the world as you need witness," the clerk said. "Now, what is it you want, and what is it you'll give?"

Goodman was unnerved by the sudden, pressing intensity in the man's tone and found his way out. Returning to the inn, he set out to record as much of the conversation as he could, ignoring the parts that left him shaken. Then he put a positive account in the letter to his father to demonstrate there were other modes of living besides dogmatic Christian schemes. In that heady moment, New Vineland really did seem like an answer to every social disease that infested England. Soon the letter took on the quality of a treatise. New Vineland was the promise of American potential, the example of how freedom from want liberated the greater spirit and mind of man. Let his father go on wagging his finger and whispering, *"Robespierre"* at him. The Reign of Terror ended 30 years ago and wasn't going to start here. The store clerk was right: No other place on Earth could equal what he'd found in this wonderous new community. Sir Thomas More's *Utopia* was manifested here. *All Needs Met!* indeed.

He went downstairs on the third morning intending to ask Mr. Watkins about posting his letters. The innkeeper was not present, however, so Goodman set off toward the tower, hoping to encounter the clerk he'd met on the previous visit. Considering everything else the store offered, Goodman would not be surprised if it also acted as a post office.

As he neared the tower, he stopped out of a peculiar certainty that the landscape had changed. The tower was just as featureless as before, but could it somehow be taller than he remembered? The notion was absurd, of course, but as Goodman stared up at it, he felt sure he was craning his neck more than before.

He moved on, once again content to join the masses. Goodman made sure to go in the same entrance as last time, but when he found himself facing row after row of stationery supplies, he thought he must have gotten turned around. The paper colors alternated between bright white, soft cream, and beige, and came in sizes for both letters and short notes. He saw stationery for business transactions, and mourning and condolence. Goodman picked up a few sheets and found they had a pleasing weight and texture. The envelopes were just as fine, but what drew his attention most were the sealing wax stamps. He picked one up and studied the design.

His hand shook.

"But how?"

"Those can be made to order," a voice called from behind. Goodman recognized it and turned to find the rounded little clerk from his first visit.

"In my case, it seems to have been made in advance," Goodman said. "The stamp contains my initials."

"Indeed? HG? Don't tell me your name is Holy Ghost."

"No, it's Harold Goodman."

"Is that what you are, the herald of the good man's news?"

"I don't believe I've come to announce anything, sir. Not even myself. I do need some more answers from you, though. Where can I send letters?"

"Ah, letters," the clerk said. "Then you do need stationery, envelopes, and a seal."

"I have those things already."

"But if you're staying, you'll be writing more letters. Perhaps even invitations to your friends to join you here."

"I only intend a stopover. My plan is to go much further down the river and then head Westward."

The clerk gave a dismissive wave. "Stay here and save yourself the journey. Sooner or later the West will be brought here. New Vineland will be everywhere you want to go."

Goodman cocked his head at this arrogance but decided not to challenge it. "How can I post a letter?"

"You can give your letters to me, and I will see them placed on the next mail barge. One pulls up to the docks at least every other week. How many do you have?"

"Just these to send to my father in England."

"Perhaps you'd write more if you had a higher quality of paper upon which to record your thoughts," the clerk said, gesturing to the shelves.

Goodman grunted. "What's the price for a stationery set? The shirt off my back?"

This brought a roar of laughter from the clerk. "Oh, no, it's always *like for like* here whenever possible. Bring me all your old paper, your seal and wax, and your pens. Bring me your unsent letters and any tedious diary you've been keeping. Trade them in. I'll burn them all, and you can begin writing fresh thoughts on fresh pages."

Goodman retreated a few steps. "I think I'll see about the mail barge myself. But I do appreciate the offer and advice, Mister..."

"Wormwood," the clerk said.

"Mr. Wormwood, I—"

"Just Wormwood. Do take care, Mr. Goodman, and come again. Soon."

# Chapter Six

Goodman went straight back to the inn. Mr. Watkins still wasn't present. He went up to his room and opened his travel trunk, sifting through layers of folded clothes until he found the one book he'd bothered to bring on his journey. Jostling had caused it to slip toward the bottom of the trunk.

The book was a novel called *Wieland* and it was by an American named Charles Brockden Brown. Goodman was fifteen when his uncle gifted it to him. He knew little of the author's life except that he'd died in Philadelphia in 1810, and when Goodman's travels brought him to America, he vowed to visit the man's grave. A man of such fearsome imagination deserved paid respects, and he intended to see Philadelphia regardless. He found the cemetery and then a breathtaking stone cenotaph, complete with a carved urn and shield. He was struck at once by the precise listing of Brown's age at death—39 years, 1 month, and 8 days. Why such specificity? For a moment, he had no answer. Then Goodman touched the rock and closed his eyes. Somberness stole over him. He thought of the novel's importance to his youth. He thought of his uncle, now dead.

*In seventeen years, I will reach his age. What if that's also the limit of my life? What purpose will there be between then and now? What does seeing the world matter if I'm always just passing through? From now on, every day must be counted and measured.*

He had this vow in mind when he decided to stay and investigate New Vineland. The town's strangeness felt like it belonged in *Wieland*, but Goodman couldn't pinpoint the exact reason until now, as he leafed through the book and found a favorite passage.

*At the distance of three hundred yards from his house, on the top of a rock whose sides were steep, rugged, and encumbered with dwarf cedars and stony asperities, he built what to a common eye would have seemed a summer house. The eastern verge of this precipice was sixty feet above the river which flowed at its foot. The view before it consisted of a transparent current, fluctuating and rippling in a rocky channel, and bounded by a rising scene of cornfields and orchards. The edifice was slight and airy. It was no more than a circular area, twelve feet in diameter, whose flooring was the rock, cleared of moss and shrubs, and exactly levelled, edged by twelve Tuscan columns, and covered by an undulating dome. My father furnished the dimensions and outlines but allowed the artist whom he employed to complete the structure on his own plan. It was without seat, table, or ornament of any kind.*

*This was the temple of his Deity.*

He carried the book out into the street and headed toward the docks. The river verged on being blockaded by the boat traffic. Goodman stared across at the cliff face before rereading the passage. In the novel, a German man created his own religion and came to America to convert the natives, building a temple upon a high rock before he burst into flames as he worshiped alone. It was one of many morbid curiosities in the story that captured Goodman's imagination, but now he felt something like a fever chill as he contemplated certain similarities between the novel and this town.

*Wieland, New Vineland, Wieland...Evan Vines.*

Goodman squinted toward the top of the cliff. What if there *were* some kind of temple up there, built to a god unknown?

He chuckled and shook his head. Why even entertain such a piece of juvenile fancy? It was madness.

*But I'm in command of my mind*, he thought. *I'm not crazy. I'm a rational Englishman.*

He walked the docks, searching for a captain he might hire to take him across. Few would even acknowledge him. But one sailor took a keen and immediate interest. He wore simple broadfall trousers and a wool sweater and stood a little over six feet. Bright white hair was cropped close to his skull, and his cheeks were salted with stubble just as white.

"Sounds like you're interested in the cliff," he said.

"More about what's on top of it."

"Who'd build something up there?"

But his tone wasn't as skeptical as the question suggested. He gestured for Goodman to follow him, and they went to a moored keelboat.

"Pardon me for saying, but you sound like you know something about the cliff you're not letting on."

"I've no wish to be mistaken for a madman."

"After what I've seen of New Vineland so far, my credence is becoming flexible."

They shook hands and introduced themselves. The sailor's name was Pike. "I lost an entire crew to this place the first time I encountered it. I'd captained many vessels up and down this river and never noticed the docks or the town before. Then—one day—there it all was. Like it'd all sprung up overnight. But then some of my trips can last a few months, and sometimes I can go a year without coming this far downriver. It's easy to lose track of time, and things change faster than you realize."

"What do you mean you lost your crew?"

"It was about a year and a half ago. We saw the docks and all the bustle and decided to pull in. Truth be told, I think my crew would have mutinied on me if I hadn't. Every one of them looked ready to jump overboard and swim if I'd decided to keep going. I gave them permission to leave and they never came back."

"Never?"

"Aye," Pike said. "I tried to track them down. I made inquiries, though no one would give me the time of day. What can I say? Six grown men can handle themselves, so I couldn't suspect mischief there. But it seemed to be everywhere else. Men came to invite me to stay in town, but I felt suspicious. I cast off alone and didn't pull into another dock until I reached the Sound."

Goodman looked at the keelboat. "Is this yours?"

"My pride, if not always my joy. Mind you it's not the same boat I was talking about before."

"Were you bringing in goods?"

Pike laughed. "Passengers, I'm sad to say. Two men and a woman. Picked them up in Hamilton. That's six days upstream from here. They spent the entire trip bunched at the prow, looking straight ahead. Didn't eat, drink, or sleep the whole time. How's that for strange?"

Goodman looked toward the cliff again.

"It bothers you, doesn't it?"

Goodman nodded.

"Maybe you've got a sailor's intuition, Harry. I'll tell you one more thing I think you'll find interesting. Maybe half a year before the trip that cost me my crew, I was coming downriver this way during a bad storm. It was a new moon anyway, so it would have been dark even without the weather. The current had become swift. The boat felt like it was sledding down a hill. I was at the wheel trying to enjoy a pipe under the protection of a makeshift tarp. Do you see yonder bend?"

Goodman followed Pike's pointing hand to a spot a considerable distance up the river.

"Yes," he said.

"We were just about there when I saw the light."

Pike pointed to the top of the cliff.

"It was like a fire, but not a fire. Bright as any lighthouse that ever steered a ship to safety, but I didn't get a safe feeling from it at all. It made me feel cold. What could it have been? How did it survive the wind and the rain?"

"Did you stop?"

"Lord, no," Pike said. "It was a storm, remember? We were going down this river like a shooting star. But I could still see that light a few miles downriver. When I was younger, I shipped out to sea and saw many things that helped hasten the color out of my hair. But maybe there's something even more haunting about certain rivers on certain nights. Laugh at me if you will."

"You'll get no mockery from me. In fact, I'd like to hire you to take me across to the cliff. What's the cost for such a trip? It looks to be half a mile."

"More like three-quarters here. The river gets wider further downstream. But there's no charge. An adventure with a new friend is payment enough, Harry. I'm ready now if you are."

"Then we can go at once," Goodman said, grinning.

"You need nothing else?"

Goodman raised the novel. Pike nodded and said, "True enough, a man armed with the Bible needs but little."

"That may be so," Goodman said. "But Charles Brockden Brown is *my* shepherd, and I have no want."

# Chapter Seven

"What's the name of this river, anyway?" Goodman said as they pushed away from the dock. Pike gave him a pole and he imitated the old sailor's actions, stabbing into the water and bearing down with his weight.

"Its proper name might be Styx, but I've always heard it called Saint Julian, named after the patron saint of wanderers. I don't approve. Rivers aren't wanderers. They all know just where they're going."

"How far does it run?"

"A couple of hundred miles all the way down to Long Island Sound. Until New Vineland sprang up, there wasn't much to catch the eye between Hamilton and Preston Harbor. Just scattered hamlets and small villages, family farms, and the like."

Goodman pushed against the pole, grinning as sweat formed on his brow. His pulse thrummed. The cliff face grew nearer, taller.

"Is it strange I should be enjoying this?"

"Enjoying what?" Pike asked.

"The work of getting across. And the sense of mystery, though there might not be one at all."

"There's a bit of the philosopher about you, Harry."

"My father would say more fool than philosopher."

"One and the same to those who labor," Pike said, straightening his back a moment. "There's much to savor about an active life. I've always preferred visible goals, going from one point to another on a map."

Pike started whistling. Goodman didn't know the tune, but he liked it and soon picked it up. They worked their push poles and steered the boat against the soft current as the cliff face loomed overhead.

Then Goodman realized he whistled alone. Pike stood very quiet and still, his head cocked a little to the right. He held his push pole entirely out of the water, its length cradled in both hands like a lance.

"What is it?"

"Listen, Harry."

Pike spoke in hushed, warning tones.

It took Goodman a moment to understand. The tune they'd commenced was continuing from a third party they couldn't see.

"It's coming from the water," Pike whispered.

Goodman pulled his push pole out of the river and Pike moved back and forth in quiet steps, inspecting both sides of the boat.

"Maybe a swimmer who needs help?" Goodman said.

"I've never known a man in fear of drowning to be musical. It's not quite a whistle, is it? There's a quavering. Or a warble. I'm not even sure how I'm hearing it. It's in my head but not my ears. You get my meaning?"

Goodman nodded. He touched his forehead as if the sound was seeping in through a crack.

"I still think I can track where it's coming from," Pike said. He scanned the river, back and forth, then looked straight down and muttered, "My God."

Goodman tensed. The push pole was becoming slippery in his grip and he wiped his right palm against his trousers. The river was so brown that sunlight didn't seem to penetrate past an inch.

And something—someone—was staring up at them from an inch and a half.

The whistling became a call and he followed it to the starboard side with only a dim understanding of his actions. He raised up his right foot and planted it on the gunwale. The water rocked the boat with such tenderness. The cliff face was getting further away as the boat moved with the current. The whistling grew louder. He bent forward. He should jump overboard. Someone waited to welcome him in the river. To answer all questions. He could almost see it, a face, round and white like the full moon. But black eyes. Lidless midnight eyes.

"Yes," Goodman whispered. "You summon and I come."

He was about to jump. Before that happened, Pike made a sideward thrust with the long pole, swearing a blue streak as he stabbed into the water. His pole struck meat and a black substance bubbled up from the water as the whistling became a shriek.

Goodman shook himself to his senses as Pike went on stabbing into the river like some spear fisherman. Goodman heard—*felt*—another scream as somewhere below soft flesh tore open like a wet sack. The water around the boat had become black and putrid.

"Damn the thing!" Pike said as the boat shook them both to the floor. Some force tore a plank from the hull, and water gushed into the opening. Another plank was ripped away and Pike stabbed through the space, swearing again. Goodman could see Pike had given up any hope of saving the boat or himself and only wished to hurt the creature as much as possible before they sank.

Goodman looked toward the cliff. They weren't within practical swimming distance but what choice was there? They might escape if their attacker's rage stayed focused on the boat.

"Come with me, Pike! We can make it!"

Pike gnashed his teeth. No flame could have burned as hot as the fire showing in his eyes. Goodman saw no hope of reasoning with him and dove off the gunwale. He made furious strokes toward the riverbank and didn't dare look back until the water became shallow and he could stand up and stagger his way onto the rocky shore. He collapsed there, panting and wiping his eyes as he looked back at the river. The water moved at its old tranquil pace, with no sign of trouble.

Or the boat.

*Poor Pike—*

The sailor coughed and hacked up water as he crawled ashore about twenty yards upstream. Goodman limped over to meet him. After several gulped breaths, Pike said, "I take back what I said about the active life. An armchair and a full pipe suit me just fine now."

"What the hell attacked us?"

"I don't know," Pike said. "But, just in case it can come up on land, let's see about getting to higher ground. *Up there* will suit me just fine."

They headed off.

# Chapter Eight
## June 1830

Lily found herself drowsy from the gentle song of the river. Its tune was much like the water itself, flowing, ceaseless, and subtle, a bedrock melody underlying every other sound. She stretched out on the raft and hummed the song while staring at the brilliant blue sky. The clouds overhead seemed ready to bend to the will of her imagination. What if the clouds were just soft rocks she could sculpt with the chisel of her mind? She could make sculptures in the air! But what image should she carve? She thought of the fish in the river, their songs gurgling from their bright red gills. She saw them with great clarity in her mind and the clouds became the image in an instant. Schools of white fish swam back and forth overhead, and she hummed in delight.

"That's a lovely melody you're humming," Papa said. "Perhaps you'll become a musician."

Lily went on with the tune, though it was different now. It wasn't the river's song anymore. She had changed it without understanding how, and all the shapes she imagined rode the melody into the sky and became true in the clouds. The schools of fish became butterflies. The butterflies became Ruffian and Bandit pulling the boat. Lily concentrated, thinking of her and Papa on the raft. The cloud horses became a misty reflection of the boat. Lily smiled at her cloud-self looking back at her.

Darkness was creeping along the edge of the clouds, poisoning their bright whiteness with an ashy gray that soon gave way to a grim, scary purple. Lily sat up. A new song came from the water. She looked around, trying to hide her startlement. The melody was familiar and quickened her pulse.

The *Witchhand* was here.

*Under the water, find me there,*
*Weaving delight for you alone.*
*Stone to flesh, and flesh to stone,*
*Venture, venture to my home.*

The singing voice was boyish and not at all scary. Was she mistaken? Was this *not* the *Witchhand* after all?

*I am he who watches thee*
*And summon with my summoning song.*
*Come to me now*
*Do not linger*
*Follow the song*
*And find the singer.*

The voice came from under the raft. She felt the slightest bump as if they had run over something in the river. There were little openings between the floorboards. She looked through them and stifled a gasp.

There was a white face looking right up at her.

It darted away, but the song continued. She heard it from her right now and turned to stare in that direction. What little of the face she could see breaching the water was terrible and misshapen. It *couldn't* belong to the singer. How could something so ugly have such a beautiful voice?

The song became louder, more insistent. Hearing it stole the breath out of her lungs. She got to her knees and inched toward the lip of the raft. Somewhere beneath the song she heard Papa telling her not to get so close to the edge. But how could she not? The song and its singer *needed* her.

She dipped her fingers into the water. At once, she knew she was touching a submerged hand reaching up to her. Lily held her breath. Papa called out but he seemed far away. There was no song now. Even the river and every living thing along the banks had fallen into hushed expectation. *Who are you?* Lily thought, staring hard at the brown water. *Are you the Witchhand?* Her entire arm was submerged. A bracing cold enveloped her wrist. It could pull her overboard in an instant. She found she wanted that to happen. Someone was *right there*, just a fraction out of view but looking right at her.

*"Lily, I said get back!"*

Papa grabbed her shoulder and pulled. Not even the *Witchhand* could stand against his strength. The spell broke and Lily fell against his legs. She looked up to see his puzzled, worried expression.

"What happened?" she said, looking about. Her sight took in the tombstone and the girl's engraved name. For a second, the letters there seemed to spell out her own, and she began to cry.

# Chapter Nine

Papa directed the raft to the shore and carried Lily over to a fallen log. He unwrapped the parcel of biscuits and sat down next to her.

"Time for these."

Lily took a small bite and glanced at the water. She glimpsed the top of a bald white head darting under just as she looked. Even the thought of its ugliness gave the biscuit a bad taste and her chewing slowed.

"Don't you like it?"

Lily found Papa was staring at her. His look of concern turned his features into a stern, cold, and graven image.

"I like it, Papa."

A black beetle crawled from a crevice in the tree trunk, its shell gleaming like a piece of polished onyx. Lily flinched when she saw it and Papa brushed the beetle aside and it crawled away.

"Unusual for you to be afraid of a bug. What's wrong?"

"Nothing, Papa."

"It hurts when you don't trust me, Lily."

She looked down at her feet. "I trust you, Papa," she said, her voice small.

"You were very close to the edge of the raft, and you ignored me when I told you to move back. Did you not hear me?"

"I don't know, Papa."

"Were you daydreaming?"

She repeated the question to herself, thinking Papa was trying to give her the very answers he wanted her to say. Wasn't it best if she did?

"I must have been, Papa. I'm sorry."

He grunted and bit into a biscuit. "Your mother's baking gets better and better every day, doesn't it?"

Lily nodded.

"She won my heart with bread and butter. Maybe you'd like to hear that story now."

"Do we have time? How far away are we from New Vineland?"

"Many miles yet. Yes, we have time. And the horses should like a rest, I think."

She leaned against him, and he draped his right arm around her shoulders.

"Do you know what a Lodge is, Lily?"

"A place to stay?"

"It can mean that. Lodge is one of those funny words that somehow has a lot of meanings and none of them are related. Lodge can mean a place to stay, or to fix something in place. It can also mean to make an appeal. It means many other things too, Lily."

"I thought you were going to talk about you and Mama."

He laughed. "Be patient. Lodge can also mean a group or gathering of specific people. Once upon a time, just before your mother came into my life, I belonged to what's called a Masonic Lodge. The men of my Lodge were all inspired designers and builders. Some had worked on cathedrals and palaces in Europe, while others used their influence in other ways during the Revolutionary War and the rough years that followed. But I knew little of all that. You see, I was the youngest of them by a good thirty years."

"Did Mama belong to the Lodge?"

"Women can't be Masons."

"Is that the reason I can't make an animal like you can? Because girls just can't?"

He brushed the hair away from her eyes. "Would I bother showing you my tools or letting you hold them if I believed that? No, Lily. It's just a very old notion, and old notions have a way of lingering when they should be discarded. The ones that stay around too long get called traditions, and there are many traditions we'd be better off without."

"What if Mama is an even better Mason than you are, but she doesn't know it because she was never allowed?"

"It's possible."

"What if you're an even better baker than Mama, but you don't know it because—"

Papa laughed and smoothed her hair. "Have another biscuit and let me continue."

Lily nodded, took up a fresh one, and chewed it.

"There are many Masonic Lodges in the world, but mine was different than the rest. We were committed to rediscovering the most ancient secrets of stone and architecture. Have you heard of geology and geometry, Lily?"

She shook her head.

"Pretty words for pretty subjects, and there's a reason the words sound a bit alike. Geology is the study of the Earth, and geometry is the study of shapes and design, among other things. Understanding the deeper connections between the two was the ambition of my Lodge and a personal obsession for myself."

"But what does Mama have to do with this if she wasn't allowed to be a Mason?"

"Oh, Lily, I owe your mother so much. When I say I was obsessed with the secrets of stone, I don't want you to think I'm calling this a good thing. An obsession begins by occupying your mind. Then, it occupies your heart. The world fades away from you. You forget hunger, you forget thirst. You don't even realize how you're wasting away. Thanks to your mother, this didn't happen to me."

Lily dipped her head to get a better look into Papa's eyes. His stare seemed very distant.

"Your mother was seventeen and I was twenty-two when our paths crossed. I was traveling to Washington to meet the Elders of my Lodge and reveal a discovery I'd made, a breakthrough of such importance I almost trembled at the thought of showing it."

"What was it, Papa?"

He held up a cautioning finger. "I can't answer that question. You see, I'm speaking of a past I abandoned in favor of the life I live now with you and your mother. So there I was on the road to the Capitol. A storm came up toward evening, one of the most violent I've ever seen. Lightning strikes and thunder so deep I felt in my bones. My horse almost threw me off, but I got it settled and we found an inn. It belonged to your mother's uncle, who was away for the night. I sheltered my horse in the stable and then I came in, dripping water everywhere. There were plenty of oil lamps lit, but the room still seemed dim. I called out for anyone. Your mother came out from some back room. She had a handful of towels for me. I'd never been so welcomed. I felt cared for in an instant, and when she asked me what I was doing on the road and where I'd been going, I truly forgot the answer. It was so strange to feel her presence in my chest. After so much time studying stone, my heart remembered it was flesh after all."

Lily stared at Papa, fascinated by his dreamy look and a smile she'd never seen before. A smile of memory, maybe. She could just *see* a younger version of Mama fussing over Papa's wet hair.

"I fell in love with her that night, and I turned my back on the past."

"But you still make things from stone, Papa."

"Yes," he said in a quiet voice. He looked at the ground a moment, then offered a smile. "Feel like trying the river again? If we don't set off soon, we won't be home before evening."

She looked at the water and neither heard nor saw any hint of the creature that had sung to her. But it was there, somewhere.

"I wish Old Ben was with us."

Papa laughed. "Why in the *world* would we bring the rooster along?"

Lily blushed and offered a slight shrug.

"I don't know, Papa."

Papa frowned and scratched the back of his head. "Lily, about Old Ben—"

But Lily left the log in a sprint and started for the raft.

# Chapter Ten

Close to noon, and about a mile out from New Vineland, the cliff face came into view, dark and looming.

Lily heard the *Witchhand*'s song again.

The sound was like an endless black cloud dripping notes of menace overhead, a steady pitter-patter beat of rain that tapped the top of her skull until she couldn't think of anything else. Lily looked to Papa, wondering how he could ignore it. But it was clear he didn't hear it at all.

*Why do I? What does the* Witchhand *want with me?*

By reflex, she began to hum a counter-tune in her mind, an echo of the song she'd used to shape the clouds. It was like putting up an umbrella, and she felt steadier as they came around the final bend. New Vineland appeared in a burst of activity, with curls of smoke rising from chimneys on every peaked roof.

She saw the tower, too. Tall and dark. Lily stood up.

"Impressed?" Papa said.

"I think it's awful," she answered, unable to help her instinctual dread. She could just make out the top of it, though it seemed unfinished. The *Witchhand's* melody extended across the sky from the tip of the tower to the heights of the cliff. Lily could not comprehend the meaning of it, but she knew something was very wrong.

She looked at Papa. From his expression, she guessed he believed the same thing.

"It's a hundred feet tall by my estimate. Which makes it the tallest structure in the country."

"Who built it?"

Papa's silence puzzled her. Didn't he know? Or had the tower always been here, like the river, like the cliff face?

"Evan Vines," he said.

She looked back and forth between the tower and the cliff. Sometimes the tower seemed taller, sometimes the cliff. Both made her feel smaller and smaller as they drew closer.

"The Dockmaster."

"What, Papa?"

"*Damn* me."

His soft curse startled her. All at once he cast the push pole down and began taking off his shirt. New Vineland's docks were up ahead, extending halfway across the river and crowded with so many boats Lily didn't see where their raft would fit.

"What's wrong, Papa?"

He ignored her, draping his shirt over the tombstone. Then he ordered Lily to sit on it.

"But why?"

"Quit asking questions and obey!"

Nothing could bring Lily near tears like a scolding from Papa. She couldn't imagine why he was mad at her, but she did as he said. Papa meanwhile picked up the pole again and began working the raft toward the docks.

A man stood there watching them. He had the sourest expression she'd ever seen.

"What's your business in New Vineland?" the Dockmaster said.

"Supplies, sir," and Papa named several things Lily knew Mama had plenty of at home.

*Why is Papa lying?*

Her heart was beating even faster than last night. Who was this Dockmaster? Why did Papa sound afraid of him?

There must have been a hundred people milling around behind him, but the Dockmaster kept his cold stare right on Lily as Papa moored the raft. He had short white hair and his cheeks looked rough. Not a beard, but not shaven either. His shoulders were as broad as Papa's. Was he as strong? Could he hurt Papa?

"I'll send my daughter to fetch them. Then we'll be on our way."

"Be quick about it," the Dockmaster said, giving a contemptuous sneer. "New Vineland's docks can't be occupied with trifling matters."

After he moved off, Lily whispered, "Papa, why did you say—"

He got down on one knee in front of her. "Listen now, Lily. I need you to be brave."

"But lying isn't right."

"It was this time."

"But Mama says—"

"We can talk about that later. Right now, you have a task. I didn't mean for you to have it, but there's no choice and I believe you can do it."

He placed several heavy coins into her right palm. She'd never held money before. The coins seemed strange.

"Hold on to these tight. I want you to go to the tower. There's a store inside it. You're to enter and buy sugar."

"But doesn't Mama still have—"

Papa grabbed her arm and shook it. He'd never done anything like that before. Lily felt like he'd just shaken every thought out of her head.

"I have to stay here. I'm not going to explain why, but I need you to obey me. You're ten now and mature for your age."

She squared her shoulders at the praise and nodded.

"Go to the tower. You'll see a man at a counter," he continued. "Show him the sugar and give him the coins. Then hurry back to me. Understand?"

"Yes, Papa," she said as a nervous thrill built in her stomach. Papa kissed the top of her head and directed her to a short ladder mounted to the side of the dock. Her knees trembled. It was only four rungs to reach the top of the pier, but she felt like she'd climbed a thousand feet. Papa looked so small on the raft.

The gruff Dockmaster was returning. Lily hated the idea of leaving Papa alone with him. What if he forced Papa to leave while Lily was getting the sugar?

*Then I'll walk back, alone or with the horses*, she thought. *The path along the river will take me straight home.*

"*Go, Lily.*"

She set off and noticed the *Witchhand's* song was everywhere. Every man, woman, and child in the dense crowds seemed to exhale it. Could this be where the *Witchhand* lived? If so, why was it visiting her window at night? What did it want from her?

Lily had never seen so many people. She felt suffocated and darted through every little opening in the crowd to move ahead. It took her fifteen minutes to reach the tower, and once she did, she stopped to stare up its length. The tower was made of some dark stone that seemed to move just a little, like the whole thing pulsed with the *Witchhand's* melody. The subtlety of the movement was more pronounced near the top. She'd almost swear the upper reaches were swaying like the branches of a tree.

The Dockmaster's gruff voice sounded from behind her.

"Didn't your father tell you to get sugar?"

Startled, Lily turned. The man's expression wasn't as harsh as she expected, but his presence spurred her forward. The tower entrance was just a broad opening four or five people could walk through side-by-side and had no visible door. She only just remembered the sugar as she passed through, but her mind was full of the other things she saw on the people around her, flashes of jewelry and gloves, hats, dolls. She inhaled rich aromas of strange spices and cured meats, the pungent sharpness of the great hoops of cheese and tubs of salt fish, and barrels of soda crackers and pickles swimming in brine. Fruity smells of dried apples and peaches and pears.

Everything any heart could desire—plus the sugar.

It sat at eye level in front of her on a shelf that hadn't been there a moment earlier. The sugarloaf was wrapped in colorful paper cinched by a pretty yellow ribbon. She reached for it by instinct, expecting the crowd to want it with equal desire.

But no one was there.

Somehow, she had a vast room of treasure to herself.

Lily squeezed the coins in her left palm and reached for the sugar. Her hand ended up touching a doll sitting right beside it. The doll was something she'd always imagined for herself, a friend even better than Fat Jack, though Lily winced to admit it. She held the doll and smiled. A floral scent came off its light blue dress. Its hair was dark and felt real, not threads or string. Lily began rocking the doll against her chest as she spied other treasures. Marbles, whirligigs, jackstraws.

*Wouldn't you like to live here in New Vineland with me?*

Lily held the doll out in front of her. "Did you say that?"

*You and your whole family could stay here with me, and everyone would be so happy.*

The doll began to throb in the rhythm of the *Witchhand*.

She all but threw it back on the shelf and grabbed the sugar. The doll pleaded with Lily to take her.

"I want to, but...Papa..."

*Bring him, Lily. You'll see how much he likes it here.*

The coins became slippery in her sweating palm.

"I can't. I'm sorry, but—"

*Lily don't leave me. I'm your best friend. I always have been. You came all this way so we could meet. Stay with me in New Vineland so we can be together forever.*

Lily backed away. *The* Witchhand, she told herself. *Its song is everywhere. It's trying to get me.*

She took the sugar and ran down the aisle until the doll's voice couldn't be heard anymore. The shelves kept going and going. She saw a heavy glass jar filled with the cherished peppermint sticks she only got on Christmas morning. Boiled sweets!

*Papa won't mind if I—*

She snatched up a stick without completing the thought and moved forward.

The next aisle boasted bolts of bright fabrics and spools of yarn, smaller spools of thread, and needles and jars of buttons of different sizes. Ready-made clothes and shoes! Dresses and hats fancier than in any drawing she'd seen. She touched the soft lacework of a bonnet and imagined wearing it in front of Fat Jack. How he'd sing!

The bonnet was perfect and spoke to her of its perfection in a voice identical to the doll's.

She rubbed the coins together in her left hand and took the hat.

# Chapter Eleven

Papa said there'd be a man to give the coins to, but Lily was still shocked when she saw him. His head was round, bald and white, and it made her think of the creature she'd glimpsed in the river. Could this be him? How could it be? He was bone dry and looked like he'd been waiting here for hours, sitting on a stool behind a plain white counter.

"Well?" he said.

Lily saw him staring at the bonnet, peppermint stick, and sugar in her arms. "I want to buy these," she said, standing on her tiptoes to place her bounty on the counter.

The man just stared at her until she felt like she had to explain.

"My papa sent me after sugar, but I saw these and I thought—"

"What do you give in exchange?"

"These coins," she said, placing them beside the sugar.

He brushed them onto the floor and rose. Lily found he was not much taller than her, but no less intimidating as a result.

"This is a place of bartering, young one."

"But my papa told me to use the coins."

His roar of laughter sent Lily retreating a few steps.

"Where is this charming *Papa* of yours?"

"At the dock. I'm supposed to bring the sugar back to him."

"Like for like," he said.

"Please, sir, the coins must be enough! My papa said—"

"*Like for like.* For the sweetness of our sugar, you must offer something in return."

Lily looked around for anyone who might help her, but there were just the two of them in the whole vast space. The clerk rounded the counter. At first, he seemed to have a limp, but it was more than that. Worse than that. He moved like a balanced stack of stones trying to keep their shape as they went.

"Since you have nothing to exchange, I'll just have all of that back."

"But the coins!"

The clerk stood still a moment, looking her up and down.

"*Now,*" he said, holding out his right hand.

Before Lily could react, he made a lunging grab, and she screamed. She swiped the goods and fled. There wasn't an exit, just endless rows of shelves with more dolls, clothes, buttons, and baubles. The *Witchhand's* song came from all of them. She looked back and saw the pursuing clerk.

"I gave you the money! Papa said it'd be enough!"

Lily ran harder than ever, but she felt herself going in circles. Her right side hurt. The *Witchhand's* song battered her. But a different melody began to overpower it, and a deep and calm voice sang in her thoughts—

*Left and then left again*
*The exit is before you*
*Despair is what you're feeling now*
*But hope will soon restore you.*

Lily followed the directions and in an eyeblink, she found herself outside but in a maze of alleyways. There was a brick wall behind her back. No door. No tower.

No people.

The tall walls kept her from seeing anything else, even the cliff face that would show the direction of the river. Lily's bottom lip began to tremble.

The clerk's voice sounded from somewhere—from everywhere. "Thief! Shoplifter! I'll find you, girl!"

Lily looked straight up and shouted back, "I gave you Papa's coins!"

The triumph she felt in defending herself gave way to quick terror when the clerk answered: "*Now* I know where you are."

She started running but her toe caught on a cobblestone and sent her onto her hands and knees. The bonnet was now smeared with grime and the wrapper over the sugar almost split open. Dazed, she got up and staggered along, beginning to sob.

She'd never see Mama or Papa again.

The same deep voice called out to her.

*Close your eyes, trust your ears,*
*My song alone can guide you.*
*Safety you will find with me,*
*I alone can hide you.*

The voice was like a rope tied around her waist, pulling her like Bandit and Ruffian pulled the raft. She closed her eyes and surrendered to it, not daring to look again until she felt a pleasant breeze on her cheeks. Lily found herself standing outside a stable, calm, quiet, and solitary. She heard a horse whinny.

Lily peered inside and gasped at what she found.

*Save me from my master's whip*
*Free me from my master's grip*
*Faithful to you shall I be*
*Trust in my sincerity.*

She'd never seen a more beautiful stallion, pure black with intense eyes that blazed with intelligence and pain. Its head was bowed low, tied to a hook in the ground. The tether line wasn't but a few inches long. Fresh red cuts marked the stallion's flanks atop old, puckered gray scars. Flies crawled over the new wounds.

"Who did this to you?" Lily asked as she crept forward.

*Master, master most unkind*
*Hits me even when I mind.*
*Master's rage seeks and finds*
*Master's name is Evan Vines.*

Lily couldn't imagine Mama or Papa whipping an animal for sport. How was such cruelty possible?

Lily set aside the sugar and bonnet and worked to undo the line. The horse clapped its right front hoof at her efforts. She put her small right hand on the horse's right foreleg and patted it.

"I have to help you," she said. "You helped me. I bet that mean man in the store was Evan Vines."

Lily frowned. She couldn't make any headway on the knot.

She wiped away frustrated tears. The horse was counting on her. Then an idea came to her. She reached into her pocket and pulled out the precious peppermint stick. The stallion sniffed at the candy. Lily almost laughed as the horse's nostrils flared, and its eyes grew wide with obvious delight. Lily scratched the horse's ear with her free hand as it started to chew the candy.

"No one's ever been nice to you, have they?"

A voice from behind her said, "And we'll make sure that tradition continues."

# Chapter Twelve

Three men blocked the stable door. Lily saw the store clerk, the Dockmaster, and a third man, younger than the others. He stood as tall as Papa but was much thinner. His hair hadn't a trace of gray, and he didn't have a beard. His blue eyes belonged to a fairy tale prince, but their coldness belonged to a fairy tale monster.

"I think this horse is hurt," she said, trying not to shake.

"Oh, *is* it?"

He now stepped forward with great concern, and Lily thought maybe she'd misjudged him.

"What's this? Candy?"

Lily smiled. "I gave it to him."

"Did you, now?"

He produced a short crop, black as the horse itself and thin as a river reed, with a narrow tongue of stiff leather at the end.

"Nightcamp, you scoundrel!"

Lily screamed when he struck the stallion's ribs. "Stop, please stop!" she cried. She even turned toward the nasty Dockmaster and clerk for help, but both men just stared straight ahead.

The horse bellowed and Lily seized the man's wrist.

"Wormwood," he said, "rid me of this whelp."

The clerk pulled Lily away and held her still. The tall man raised the crop again.

"This beating is *your* fault."

As he turned to deliver the next blow, the Dockmaster bent next to Lily's ear and whispered, "Best to close your eyes."

But she couldn't. It felt too much like abandoning the horse.

"Girl, if you knew this beast's evil heart, you'd whip him yourself!"

A plaintive song burst into her thoughts—

*Not true, not true*

*Every word of it lies*

*Nightcamp is good*

*It shows in my eyes*

Lily fought the clerk's hold, wriggling free just long enough to launch herself against the tall man's leg. She grunted and pulled. He responded with a shocking blasphemy and then a kick that flung her onto her back. In the next instant, he raised the crop at her.

"Now I'll teach you how little girls behave in *my* town."

*"Touch my daughter and no surgeon in America will be able to stitch you back together."*

Papa's voice boomed through the air like a cannon shot. The man stood frozen with the crop above his head. Lily kicked herself away, got to her feet, and ran to Papa. He stood at the stable entrance, his shoulders as wide as the doorway, his hands balled into fists.

"Papa, I'm sorry, I got lost and saw the horse and—"

"Silence your whelp," the Dockmaster said.

"Don't refer to my daughter like that."

The man with the crop said, "In this city, *my* city, you give no orders. Would you like a civics lesson?"

Lily burned with hatred to hear the man threaten Papa. But she knew he wasn't a bit afraid. He could snap that riding crop like a twig.

*Do it, Papa,* she thought. *Show him.*

But his response left her breathless and pale.

"There's no need for threats. I apologize. I didn't realize it was you, Mr. Vines."

"A grave mistake."

"Stand in my shoes, Mr. Vines. I only came here for provisions. Then my daughter takes off on me before I can moor my raft."

"I can attest to that, sir," the Dockmaster said. "The girl is wild."

Lily wiped her eyes. Why was Papa making her sound disobedient? Why did he keep lying?

But Vines's attention had turned to the Dockmaster. "Who are you?"

"This is Mr. Pike," Wormwood said. "I hired him to keep your docks in good order, sir."

"Aye," the Dockmaster said. "I've kept the trash out of Boston Harbor, and I'll keep the trash out of New Vineland, too."

Vines laughed and shook the man's hand. "Good man. Tell me about these two, Pike. Are they *trash*? The girl seems overdue for a thrashing."

Lily saw his grip tighten on the crop. His knuckles had gone white.

"It's her mother's fault, I'm afraid," Papa said. "She's a soft-hearted creature. Makes me spare the rod."

*"Papa!"*

"Be quiet for once, Lily." Papa gave her arm an unexpected jerk. Lily's head became so heavy it may as well have been tied down like the stallion's.

"A problem common to women," Vines said.

"Yes, sir."

"So you stopped in for provisions," Vines said, walking in a slow circle around them. "Why not stay here?"

"I'm a farmer by trade. I've never enjoyed city life."

"A farmer?" Lily heard a hint of suspicion and mockery in his voice. "Plenty of *farmers* have chosen us over their fields."

"Perhaps I will in time."

Mr. Vines stepped right up into Papa's face. Lily tensed but bit back a whimper.

"What's your name?"

*Don't tell him, Papa! Something bad will happen if you do!*

"Hobbs," Papa said.

The clerk stepped forward. "*James* Hobbs?"

Papa looked away.

"What surprises you, Wormwood?" Vines said. "Should I know of this man?"

"He's more than a farmer. Much more, in fact."

Vines raised his eyebrows. "Is that so?"

"I don't know what you're talking about," Papa said.

"Yes, you do," the Dockmaster said. "Mr. Vines, I know for a fact his work is known even in Boston. I even confiscated this from the man's raft because I feared he would try to sell it here on the sly."

"Mouse!" Lily said, amazed to see the little sculpture. She looked to Papa. "I don't understand, Mouse was in my room..."

The Dockmaster showed it to Vines.

"What do I care about something so small?"

"Consider the detail," the clerk said. "Hard to do, especially in—as you say—a small thing."

Vines studied the carving. His lips turned down in a deep frown.

"It seems you're a liar, Mr. Hobbs."

Papa looked hard at the ground. Lily clutched his legs and sobbed. "Please just let us go. I swear we won't be back."

Papa placed his hand atop her head and she fell silent.

The clerk began whispering. Vines flashed a wolfish grin.

"So," he said, pointing to Lily. "The girl's a *thief*."

"That's not true!" Lily cried.

"The evidence is right there on the floor," the clerk said, stooping to retrieve the dirty bonnet and the broken sugarloaf. He presented them to Mr. Vines, whose smile only grew wider.

"Well?"

"Papa gave me coins, and I paid with them. I didn't steal."

Mr. Vines's eyes narrowed as his smile broadened. "We have a different kind of commerce here in New Vineland."

"This is a simple misunderstanding," Papa said. "Lily has been sheltered from the world. The fault lies with me."

The clerk whispered again. Vines nodded.

"Mr. Hobbs, I am in complete agreement with you. The fault *is* yours. Therefore, you shall pay the price."

She saw Papa under the man's crop, saw him starved, saw him marched to the top of the cliff and thrown into the river.

All because of her.

"Please, Mr. Vines," she said, dropping to her knees. "Please don't hurt my papa. I'm sorry I took the sugar and the bonnet. I'm sorry I tried to help the horse. I'll make it up to you. I'll scrub the floors or pull weeds in your garden or—"

Mr. Vines laughed.

His crop made a vicious slash through the air.

"Wormwood has suggested a most interesting arrangement. Would you like to hear the proposal, Mr. Hobbs?"

Papa stood stiff and expressionless. "You've taken away my choices."

"All powerful cities have statues honoring their founder. I have decided to allow a statue of myself to be erected. In pursuit of that, we've acquired a slab of marble some thirty feet tall. I imagine it rising from the middle of the river like a new Colossus, but for now, the block sits on the western side of my tower, awaiting the perfect sculptor. I was making inquiries worldwide, but perhaps the best person for the job is—*you*."

"I assure you, I'm far from the most skilled stonemason in the world."

"As Wormwood pointed out, this little mouse is perfect in every detail. Any cat would attack it in confusion. To save your girl from punishment, you will work on my statue, and you will do so without pay. You begin tomorrow, and you'll work at my beck and call. Do you submit, Mr. Hobbs?"

"A statue like you propose could take months or even years to finish! Would you keep me from my family for that long?"

Vines's smile chilled Lily.

Months? Years? How would she and Mama survive?

"Like for like, Mr. Hobbs. Your daughter's actions warrant a cell block. I've offered you a marble one."

Lily looked up into her Papa's eyes. The dread she found in them was unmistakable. She looked at the horse and part of her wished she'd never answered its song. Better to be trapped forever in the maze of alleyways.

"I agree to your terms," Papa said.

# Chapter Thirteen

## October 1826

"Come on, Pike! It's not like we're climbing straight up the cliff."

Goodman stopped to grin despite his aching legs as he watched the crusty sailor staggering along the trail some fifty yards back.

"This is why I took to the sea early in life," Pike said, wheezing a little as he reached Goodman after a minute. "Travel's much easier when the surface moves under you instead of you moving over it. Give me a moment. Maybe my sails will get a second wind."

They both bent forward with their hands on their thighs, gasping a fatigued duet.

"I swear this trail seems longer than is possible," Pike said. "But it's been straight as far as I can mark."

"I think we're near the top now. It seems to have flattened out. Are you ready?"

Pike's answer turned into a coughing fit. Goodman put an arm about his shoulders and helped him sit.

"I'm not as bad off as I sound," Pike said. "But I better rest a while longer here. Go on ahead."

"Are you sure?"

"If I'm not, just throw my body off the cliff. The river will sweep me out to sea, which is all the burial I need."

"Don't say that!" Goodman said, but Pike just laughed and waved him away.

"I'm sure I'll be back very soon. There can't be much to see, but if I do encounter any strange lights, I'll shout for help."

"Aye, and when you do, I'll be sure not to give it."

Grinning again, Goodman continued his climb. His observation had been incorrect. The trail continued further than he thought. Adventures in the Alps had taught him the concept of false summits, but after encountering three more of them in his route, Goodman stopped and clamped his teeth against a scream.

"I'm going to best you," he said, looking at the path. "You'll run out of land before I run out of determination, I promise you that."

He took a deep breath and launched into a sprint. His legs were leaden and cramping, and the stitch in his side was more like a full tear in his lungs. But he bore down until, at last, the land *did* level out and he found himself on a flat but rocky plateau. Goodman came to a slow, stumbling stop. The top of the cliff was about two hundred yards long and maybe a hundred wide—decent enough space to host a village cricket match.

He stood scanning the area. There wasn't a single detail to catch his interest. *So much for finding a temple to a strange god*, he thought. Goodman stiffened, patting his pockets. They were near dry now.

And empty.

His cherished copy of *Wieland* was lost at sea, so to speak. Goodman frowned and walked toward the western edge to peer down at the river and pay his respects. The sight of New Vineland from high above soon overwhelmed his mourning. The town's docks seemed like shiny brass buttons on the cuff of a suit that was just starting to be sewn. He lifted his gaze past the tower and took in the vast wilderness stretching north, south, and west. Tales of the scale of the North American continent were nothing compared to this mere, fractional glimpse. He was sure one could fit several Englands into the rolling, unpopulated forests beyond New Vineland's boundaries.

A shadow was falling across those trees and then over New Vineland. Goodman looked up to find a large white cloud moving over the sun. He welcomed the shade when the shadow reached him and he turned, intending to hurry to Pike and report the disappointing results.

What he saw stopped him dead. Eight identical tombstones stood in the middle of the rocky plateau. Goodman knew he couldn't have overlooked them. He stared at them as if confronting a pack of hungry wolves, and when he did move, he took cautious steps.

The tombstones were upright with simple, oval tops, smooth, and shared the same gray color of the rocks they seemed to spring from. Darker streaks speckled the surfaces, almost wet in appearance. As Goodman risked coming closer, he reached one trembling hand to touch the first gravestone, certain his fingers would pass through it. As spectral as their sudden and unexpected appearance may have been, the stones were solid. He traced the engraved letters and found them as smooth as etched glass.

*Anna.*

He went to the next one and read it with some disorientation.

*Anna.*

Goodman squinted at the third tombstone.

*Anna.*

"What on Earth?" he said. A graveyard of only people named Anna? Or was it the same person, with a new tombstone added every year in commemoration, something like candles on a birthday cake? Goodman had never heard of such a conceit, but wasn't America about creating one's own traditions?

He frowned. The tombstones possessed no other details, and as he gave them a harder stare a queer feeling of trespass came over him. This place was not meant for his eyes.

"Well," he said to himself with a weary sigh, "I should count myself lucky that my name isn't Anna. It seems a rather unfortunate appellation in this vicinity."

The curtain of shadow began to withdraw as the cloud finished its transit. Goodman found himself standing in the sunlight again. The tombstones vanished, causing him to spring back in astonishment. He stepped forward and waved his hands through the empty space. But it was *not* empty. His fingertips struck an edge and followed the curved form in the air. The tombstones could not be seen in the sunlight and cast no shadow, yet their physicality was beyond question.

"What the devil? Tombstones marked with one name, tombstones that vanish? Did I just lose my senses, or did I never have them in the first place?"

Goodman stayed a few more minutes, maneuvering to make his shadow fall across the tombstones. They did not materialize in his shade.

How could *any* of this be?

# Chapter Fourteen

*October 30, 1826*

*Father,*

*You may think me mad, but I now believe I have come to a most dangerous place, and I must dedicate myself to its ruin. To explain would take a week's worth of writing. I would rather tell you about it in person if the opportunity ever comes. For now, I can only set down my immediate determination. If nothing else, I can read it for myself and remember this moment if my courage falters tomorrow. Know that I do not stand alone. Early in my explorations here, I met a man named Pike, a gentleman of the sea and now of the river, who is just as determined as I to see this business through to the end. You may be heartened to know that I have rediscovered an interest in scripture and faith. Perhaps this devilish place will succeed where your best efforts failed.*

*Pray for me, Father. Call it pride or a loathing of selfishness, but I still cannot find the words to pray for myself.*

*New Vineland may teach me that vocabulary soon enough.*

Goodman blew on the page to dry the ink and rose to leave. Pike should be docking soon, and Goodman was determined to greet him. As he folded the page and put it in the trunk, a sharp knock on the door startled him. *That will be Mr. Watkins again*, he thought. The innkeeper had become ever more aggressive the longer he stayed in New Vineland as a visitor.

"Yes, yes, I know what you're going to say," he said, opening the door.

It was Wormwood the clerk who stood in the doorway.

The little round man entered in his peculiar, scooting gait and shut the door behind him. Goodman backed away and sat down atop the trunk. He'd never seen Wormwood anywhere outside the store, where they had encountered each other, without fail, the handful of times he'd ventured inside. He had yet to make a *barter*.

"We must talk, Mr. Goodman."

"I'm afraid I have an appointment–"

"You have put yourself in grave jeopardy, Mr. Goodman. Very grave jeopardy."

"What do you mean? Why are you here? Where is Mr. Watkins?"

"I have taken care of Mr. Watkins," Wormwood said, moving toward the bed. The mattress sagged under him.

"Taken care of…You make it sound like you murdered him."

"Mr. Goodman, New Vineland was not built for people like yourself."

"British travelers?"

"Most come here because they are called. Invited. But it's natural to expect others to discover us by mistake. New Vineland is open to all who accept its generosity. You're smart enough to guess how that's done."

Goodman didn't even need to consider his answer. "That damn store of yours. The barter system."

"Like for like. A bargain offered, a bargain struck."

"A deal with the Devil!" Goodman shouted.

Wormwood did not flinch at his anger. Goodman stood up.

"I only want answers to my questions. I want an audience with Evan Vines. I must have scoured every inch of town looking for him."

"That is why I've come."

"To take me to him? By all means—"

"I came to advise. Take the bargain—or leave at once. Your presence is becoming disruptive."

"Because I've made discoveries, is that it? Because I've marked how the town border somehow expands a little each day, complete with buildings that couldn't have been erected overnight? Because I know about the gravestones atop the cliff?"

Genuine confusion flashed over Wormwood's expression. To Goodman, it seemed almost thunderous considering how calm and omniscient the man always acted. Maybe this accounted for Wormwood's long silence. For once, he had to think out an answer instead of a rote response.

"There are many mysteries, Mr. Goodman. No one can fathom them all. Most may not be worth any consideration. Remember what I told you before? New Vineland is not a place for questions. *Like for like.* Questions cannot be bartered for answers."

"I won't go, Wormwood. Do what you will, but I won't leave until I have *every* answer."

"If you threaten New Vineland's existence, I won't be able to help you further."

Goodman laughed. "How in the name of *God* do I threaten New Vineland's existence?"

"You do, nonetheless. I say again for your own sake, make the bargain or go. You'll meet a more terrible end if you do neither." Wormwood opened the door. "I urge you again to *go.*"

Goodman stood still in mute astonishment as Wormwood left. He stared at the space Wormwood had just occupied and found it hard to believe the whole exchange happened. He started to open the trunk to get paper and record as much as he remembered while it was fresh, but his rendezvous with Pike demanded his time.

Goodman left the inn, pinching the collar of his coat around his neck as he felt the first burst of brisk air. From the porch, he watched the throng of New Vineland's citizens, always moving, always surging. The sound of their clamor wasn't unlike waves breaking against a rocky shore.

He pushed through them all, shouldering against their unconcerned masses, annoyed but still remembering the courtesies of "Excuse me" and "Pardon me." Goodman began to think of himself as a polite needle darting in and out of ever-coarsening fabric, trailing behind him a solitary thread of sanity.

He reached the docks and walked to the end of the third pier. Pike stood on his boat, which was a bit larger than the last he arrived on and belonged to a mercantile company in Hamilton. Goodman called out and Pike waved him onto the boat. As soon as he was on board, they cast off again and moved down the riverbend before anchoring.

"How's your food supply, Harry?"

"Low."

Pike grinned and opened a crate filled with fruit. "Courtesy of my esteemed employer."

Goodman picked up an apple. Its juices dribbled off his chin as soon as he bit into it. "You're a true lifesaver, Pike."

"We'll see if you find me as fair an inquisitor."

Goodman touched Pike's right shoulder. "You found something related to Anna?"

"Aye, and more," he said. "I only had to question every newspaper printer, priest, and fisherman between Hamilton and Preston Harbor. There was a girl named Anna Freeman. Lived in a fishing community near the Sound. Ten years old when she vanished without a speck of evidence during a storm."

"Recently?"

"Not so much. Around seven years ago. It's thought she got lost and ended up drowning in the river. Her older brother had died that way maybe a year or so earlier, and the girl apparently struggled with the loss. I'm more intrigued by all the other ones though."

Goodman leaned in closer. "Were they all named Anna?"

"Their names were Veronica, Susannah, Andrea—"

"There was not one other Anna?"

"Not in the whole bunch. Try not to look so disappointed, Harry."

"Disappointed isn't the word I'd use. I just hoped we'd have an answer to the mystery."

"We may have stumbled on a different one," Pike said. "Whether or not it's related to what you saw atop the cliff is another matter. The girls who've gone missing came from little villages and towns scattered along the river. New Vineland is almost right in the middle. Most of them went missing in October, often during a storm, but not always. One girl vanished during a harvest festival. Everyone remembered her being there, and then—*poof*. Gone."

"American children seem to disappear more often than their British counterparts."

"That may be, but I wouldn't call one missing girl per year a plague of misfortune. The similarities in age stand out to me. Who knows, maybe they all looked the same, too. Finding that out would be difficult."

Goodman clapped one hand on Pike's shoulder. "I couldn't ask you to do any more. You've indulged me enough as it is. We have a cemetery up there with eight tombstones engraved Anna, but evidence of only one Anna to concern us. As she didn't live or visit New Vineland, what connection could there be?"

Pike shook his head.

"And that's just the problem," Goodman continued. "There isn't one, and yet—I'm *certain* one exists. I just feel it, and I don't think I can let the matter drop."

He saw a trace of trouble in Pike's expression.

"Harry," he said.

"Yes?"

The sailor said nothing for a few seconds. "I want to offer an old man's advice."

"I'm listening."

"Let it go."

"What?"

"Get away from here, like I'm going to do."

They stared at each other as Goodman failed to fight off a chill. His conversation with Wormwood was still too present in his mind and it had him studying Pike's eyes to reassure himself of the humanity there. Pike *wasn't* another Wormwood.

He stared at his feet, considering. Pike might be giving him good advice, but he sounded like Goodman's father right now.

"We can go back to get your personal effects and put them on the boat. I'll take you straight down to Preston Harbor. From there you can go anywhere you want. Louisiana is a good place to start. Or hell, go all the way to South America. Are you listening to me, Harry?"

"I hear you," Goodman said.

"Well?"

"I can't leave. No matter what the risk is, I must stay and figure this place out."

"You left your home to learn about the world, just as I did. New Vineland's not the world. All I'm saying is, don't get so obsessed about one thing that you forget to explore your alternatives."

Goodman nodded and offered a shy smile. "You're right, of course. Look, Pike, I promise to be careful. If I haven't learned anything else about New Vineland by the end of November, I'll surrender. I'll be on the dock when you return and I'll go wherever you're going."

"Is that a promise?"

He held out his hand. Pike took it and pulled him into a hearty embrace.

"I still say you should leave right now, Harry. But that's the problem with you damn Englishmen: you never have the good sense to listen to an American."

# Chapter Fifteen

## June 1830

Bandit and Ruffian didn't sing their pulling song as the return trip began. Their silence made Lily even more miserable and the raft seemed to go very slow, as if the leaden feeling in her chest weighed it down. The silence between her and Papa felt heavy enough to sink the raft. She sat in the middle where the tombstone had been, knees drawn against her chest. Lily didn't question what happened to the stone. She didn't care.

*Papa hates me. He'll never talk to me again.*

She knew that couldn't be true, but as he stood with his back to her, it sure seemed that way. He *must* hate her and would go on hating her every day of their lives. And because he hated her now, Mama would hate her too.

Her foolishness had made Papa into that awful man's slave.

Lily sobbed though she worked hard to keep her crying hidden. The flow of tears seemed as slow as the river as it tickled her face from cheek to chin.

*When I get home, I'll tell Old Ben not to crow tonight no matter what. I hope the Witchhand comes and takes me.*

Then Mama and Papa could start over. They could have another daughter, the one they deserved.

Lily bowed her head and didn't raise it until the end of the trip. She didn't wait for Papa to finish mooring before climbing off and running. She was going to see Fat Jack and tell him what happened. But something was very wrong. Fat Jack sang no songs. The entire farm was quiet. The shock of this dried her tears.

Papa called from the dock, telling her to come back.

She ran to Fat Jack anyway and fell against his shell.

"Oh, it's been such an awful time for all of us since this morning, hasn't it? What happened here?"

*Innocent blood*
*Turns dirt to mud*
*So much sorrow to confess*
*Blood in the dirt*
*Spurt after spurt*
*Red crest attests the rest*

Lily pulled back.

"Red crest?"

She looked in the direction of the hen house and ran to the chicken coop. The hens stood huddled to the side like grieving widows.

A big oak stood between the garden and the house. The chopping block beneath the tree's broad limbs was bloody, as was the old hatchet embedded there. Tail feathers lay on the ground among the fallen leaves. Lily knew those feathers. Old Ben's comb and hackles were red and orange like the sunrise itself, but his tail plumage was the beautiful blue and black of a summer's night.

She watched flies swarming around the blood and thought of the flies on the welts of the stallion. Even now it was probably being beaten harder than ever before just because she'd tried to help it. And here was proof of Old Ben's fate, his reward for trying to help *her*.

*I betrayed him,* Lily thought. *I blamed him and Mama—and Mama took the cleaver and—*

Lily doubled over on the ground atop Old Ben's feathers and blood.

Papa came to stand in front of her.

"I'm so sorry, honey."

His voice was gentle, tender. How she'd have begged for that tone even fifteen minutes ago! Now her eyes narrowed, drenched with the hottest tears of all, and she looked up into his face and said, "I hate you. I hate both of you."

# Chapter Sixteen
## March 1819

Except for when he was forced into a time of stone, Toad had the run of Mother Isobel's long hallways and dim corridors. He jumped from floor to ceiling and crept along the walls in search of his own amusement. Above all, he kept stretching his body the way Mother Isobel told him to whenever she freed him from stone. After the sixth time, Toad was able to stretch his neck halfway across the room. He turned his black eyes up to Mother Isobel and found her regarding him with quiet satisfaction.

His favorite place in what Mother Isobel sometimes called her *workshop* was the stone slab, where he slept and lounged when Mother Isobel left it cleared off. Just now, he perched on the corner of the slab, pouting over its occupant. Mother Isobel had placed a statue there, the sculpture of a man too long for the table. His feet jutted over the edge. The longer Toad stared at the man, the more he resented his place on the slab. He raked his sharp fingernails against the hard marble and hissed until Mother Isobel snapped at him.

"Quiet yourself, son Toad, or the time of stone will silence you."

Toad jumped to the floor and retreated to the line of pedestals on the left. There wasn't much space between the pedestals and each was topped with a stone head.

"Look what Toad can do," he said and began to stretch and weave his body through the narrow spaces. Doing so without knocking one of the heads to the ground was very difficult, but he accomplished it, and his body reformed on the other side. He was sure Mother Isobel would smile at his feat.

"Attend me, Toad."

He brushed a pedestal as he stalked back to the slab, but Toad was quick and caught the bust before it fell.

"Yes, Mother Isobel."

He leapt back onto the edge of the table.

"Precious son of mine. Thou knows so little of thy mother because of the shortness of thy life."

"How old is Toad?"

"Thou were born six months prior," she said.

"Is Toad old?"

"I have carved thee to be timeless," Mother Isobel said. "Age is of no concern. Becoming wise, however, is another matter."

He backflipped in place. "How does Toad get wise?"

"Thy wisdom comes from watching Mother Isobel and obeying her."

His dark, lidless eyes widened. "Toad will be very wise!"

"We will see."

Whenever Mother Isobel worked with stone, she used a black dagger. He'd seen her pull one after another from the folds of her robe whenever she wanted, the way she did now as they stood before the slab. She ran the dagger's tip down the length of the body and then stopped, smiling at Toad. Then he knew she was inviting him to tell her where to begin.

"Feet! Feet!"

Her blade cleaved them off at the ankles and they thudded onto the floor.

"Now the arm!"

"Which arm, Toad?"

"Both arms!"

Mother Isobel stared at him. Toad thought maybe she'd not heard him, so he repeated his suggestion.

She removed the arms. Toad clapped his hands over his lipless mouth, his body shaking as he tried to contain his happiness.

"Will you make him into another Toad, like the last one?"

"Thou would see him with a rounded head?"

Toad nodded.

Her blade moved fast. Bits of stone fell away. Mother Isobel cut and scraped, sawed, and shaped. The statue's long, fine nose fell away, as did the ears. Toad grinned, seeing himself appear where he hadn't been.

When Mother Isobel finished, she stepped back and said, "Is it perfect, Toad?"

"Toad thinks so."

"Are thou certain of its perfection?"

Toad nodded.

Mother Isobel began to sing the song Toad did not understand, but very much liked. She passed the blade just above the statue as she sang, body swaying as she went. Toad jumped off the slab as a gurgling noise came from the statue's new, wide mouth. The legs twitched, and the torso spasmed. Toad hopped up and down next to Mother Isobel as the man's time of stone came to an end. Mother Isobel said he'd been a statue for a century. Toad wondered if that was a long time.

Bright red blood poured off the edge of the slab and onto the stone feet on the floor. Shrieks came from the mouth. Toad tugged on Mother Isobel's robe until she looked down. Once she did, he opened his mouth wide and pretended like he was the one making all the noise. This earned him one of Mother Isobel's thin smiles.

The body rolled off the slab and squirmed along the floor.

"Get up!" Toad said. "Toad says get up!"

His anger grew because the new face looked so much like his own. Why wasn't he obeying himself? Instead, the oval mouth mewled and the round head smashed itself against the stone.

"Mother Isobel, why won't it do what Toad says?"

"Because Toad was not wise."

This answer made him look up and tug on her robe. "Why wasn't Toad wise?"

"Thou first directed me to remove the feet, so I did. Then thou asked the arms be removed, and so they were. Can thou stand without feet? Can thou hold thyself up without arms to pull, hands to grasp? Here is the fruit of foolishness—a wasted gardener."

"What is a garden?"

She knelt and plunged the dagger into the man's neck and kept it there until the body quit moving. When she took the dagger out, Toad found they were no longer in the same place. Toad had never dreamed there was any place outside of Mother Isobel's workshop. The vast blue ribbon overhead made him cringe and scurry around her legs.

"It's going to fall on Toad!"

Mother Isobel kicked him aside and picked up the man's body with one hand. She began dragging it toward the edge of the new land.

Toad hopped along but kept to her back, his baleful eyes never straying too far in their distrust of all that blue.

"Mother Isobel, where is Toad?"

"Toad is in the world."

"What is the *world*, Mother Isobel?"

"Round as thy head, but much vaster and almost as empty.  Come, Toad. Direct thy sight down this precipice."

Toad did and felt a thrill of dizziness that lasted only a moment. The distant ground moved in a steady, pleasing way. How could a floor move? Toad began to ask questions and Mother Isobel seemed pleased by them.

"The world is elemental, son Toad. Air, Fire, Water, and Earth. That is the sky—it is air. Across the way are forests and land—they are earth.

Fire thou hast witnessed many times. Below is the river—it is water. I fashioned thee to be eminent in its domain."

"What is *eminent*, Mother Isobel?"

"It means to be above all else—for a time. Eminence is what all creatures seek and strive to attain, but only stone achieves it. Neither fire nor water harms it. It has no requirement of air. Earth may bury it, but stone knows no grave."

She flung the misshapen body into the air. Toad watched it tumble along the rocks, down and down. He began to hop every time it struck a shelf which sent it spinning and flipping in a different direction. Then came a distant *splash*. Toad had never heard such a beautiful sound. It felt like a song crafted just for him, and he wanted to hear it again. He felt the need to make the same sound with his own body as soon as he could.

"Show wisdom and loyalty, son Toad, and I will make thou eminent among all others in the river below. Toad will become King of the River. See how far it stretches?"

Toad turned his head from left to right and then back again. His eyes became very wide and black. But they narrowed when he lifted his head and saw the tower.

"Mother Isobel, is that where we were? Is that where the altar is, and your statues?"

"No, Toad. But one day, years hence, that will be the seat of *my* eminence. The tower is as much myself as this body who stands before thee. For now, thy father occupies it."

Toad flipped twice and rocked back and forth next to her. "Who is Toad's father?"

"Another who sought eminence and believes the matter accomplished. He is of no importance now, but one day Toad must kill him."

Toad jumped again. "Why must Toad kill Toad's father?"

"Toad will understand when the time comes because Toad will be wise, and when Toad is wise, thou will be King of the River. As thy first birthday approaches, thou must begin acquiring experience so you can serve Mother Isobel best. Thou has already proven a great blessing to me. My Lord has tasked me with great sacrifices and difficult proscriptions. We have kept each other's faith, and through thee, my great Lord has granted me further insight into the song of stone. Flesh to stone and now, at last, stone to flesh. The gift of this knowledge is almost enough to make thy mother forget to eat."

Toad repeated her words to himself. Flesh to stone and stone to flesh. He knew how both felt. The time of stone was awful because he could see through his eyes but not speak or move. Mother Isobel would sit him facing the pedestals and he yearned to stretch and weave his body around them, but his skin would not listen. Just now, his skin was becoming very dry and hot. He thought of the river and knew because it was his kingdom, he would always feel better there.

"Thou will prove thy worth and cleverness by acquiring Mother Isobel her *bread*. She eats it once a year at the hour of thy birth. Her bread must be as fresh as thyself at thy delivery, fresher still if possible, and brought here at the appointed time. I will give thee the needed knowledge. Incline thy head toward the tower and listen."

Toad did.

"Do thou hear the song?"

"Yes, Mother Isobel."

"My Lord used this very tune to bring me to him and to guide my subsequent path across the world until I at least reached this precipice and embraced my portion. My Lord works through bargains and exchanges, and I kept faith with all of them, never wavering until he instructed me to have a child in the fashion he required. My Lord showed me why he chose the manner of thy birth, but thou proved a difficult labor, Toad. Thy original father was supposed to be a fat man of simple venality, but a thin man of loftier ambition interceded and took his place. It is well, and now his greed and vanity serves me and disguises my intent.

"It is the *summoning song* thou hear, and through the tower, its strength will bring me a mighty host of servants. A new country will arise. Thou asked what a garden is, and thou see it before thee. Those small white shapes are flowers of stone, and I will make gardeners to help shape them to my purpose."

"Toad likes the song."

"Thou will learn it and use it to bring thy mother's bread to thee, so in turn, thou may place it into my hands at the appointed hour."

He sprang up higher than he ever dreamed and landed with a lighter impact than he'd ever made. In the space of his jump, Mother Isobel had bared her left breast to the air. Toad bounded against it at once.

"Remember thy mother's milk and keep it holy."

Toad drank. It had been so very long.

"Become wise, and no part of thy flesh will ever suffer the time of stone again."

He pulled his mouth away just long enough to pledge himself to her again. Then he drank as much as she would allow. Her milk was so very cold.

"Then let this next stage of trials begin. I have fed thou, and soon, thou will feed me. Learn the summoning song. Go forth into thy kingdom and learn its uses. Thou will know when the time comes to bring my bread."

Before Toad could answer, Mother Isobel pushed him away and flung him off the side of the cliff. Toad tumbled, helpless at first, the rocks flashing in front of him, replaced by the blue ribbon becoming smaller and the river getting larger. The rush of air pushed and flattened his body. He straightened out just before he plunged into the water and sank straight to the bottom, his webbed feet striking deep into the muddy floor. The water was as cold as Mother Isobel's milk and just as nourishing. He roared, fascinated by the large silver bubbles his shouting made, each as round as his head and so bright, even through the murk.

They rose up and he shook his feet free of the mud and raced ahead of them, breaking the surface in time to hear himself proclaiming up through the water, *"All hail Toad! All hail the King of the River!"*

# Chapter Seventeen

## October 1818

Nightcamp dreamed of galloping across vast stretches of yellow prairie flowers and purple-tipped switchgrass until his hooves trampled a clear path from the ocean to the mountains. He dreamed of unending plains, cool days, and gusting winds at his back. In his dreams, he sprang whole and new from white-crested waves and green seafoam. He came into the world as silver as pure moonlight. The blackness came later, painted across his flanks by deeds done in obedience, so many vile things to avoid imprisonment in stone.

In his dreams, Nightcamp ran backward in time. Faces of man after man, most nameless, more than a hundred in all, flashed past him. Men of all ages, most under thirty and many possessing affable, even charming smiles. If Nightcamp learned anything in the unwanted company of these men, it was the deep divide between a man's smile and his heart.

His running brought him to the moment when the witch stole him from his first master, a farmer who eased any sleepless night with a solitary ride. The man had called him Laughlin, a name that now seemed but a whisper in a cave of whispers, and Nightcamp remembered his weight even now because it was the first he'd ever borne. One moonlit evening, in the middle of another lonesome sojourn, a faint song came upon the air. He heard it coming from up ahead, and his master must have heard it too, for he began to whistle it. As he did, his bearing became stiff and his weight heavier and heavier, until Nightcamp felt as if he had three men on his back and his pace faltered.

A figure stood on the path ahead, and though his master gave no signal to stop, Nightcamp did from the necessity of the burden. An woman came forward. She had a slight stoop, accenting a fall of long, unkempt gray hair, her only modesty. She seized his bridle and grinned. It was a cold night and Nightcamp was used to seeing his breath. The woman's breath was colder than the air and produced no clouds.

She reached up and pulled Nightcamp's master from his back. The man fell and shattered. Nightcamp turned to see three chunks of stone to his right and did not understand. Nor did he understand when the woman cut his saddle away, flung it aside, and lighted upon his back. The iciness of her bare thighs shocked his skin and made him rear, determined to cast her off. But she clung with the tenacity of a burr, clutching and twisting his mane in a bitter grip before driving her feet into his flanks. She was as bare there as she was everywhere else, but her naked heels proved as sharp as daggers.

He heard singsong words in his mind—

*"Take me where I wish to go*
*A place where pretended sisters meet.*
*Thou have felt the wind at thy back,*
*Now feel it under thy feet."*

In that moment, his will was hers. He raced forward without direction, moving over the damp Scottish Lowlands further and further from the village of his master. His two years of life had been spent going back and forth among the same three villages, some six miles between each other on the road that took the same transit as the sun. He'd never gone north as the strange rider compelled him now. The dark unknown exhilarated him with a thrill of danger, as did the woman's praiseful laughter. He felt her marveling at his speed and that only made him strive to go faster for her until he felt his hooves leave the ground. Soon, he galloped over the trees and above mountain passes whose crags, covered in frost, looked tipped in silver.

When she stopped him at last, he found himself in a clearing with several other animals who'd likewise served as mounts. He stood with red deer, highland cows, oxen, and goats. There were thirteen animals and thirteen women. He watched them writhe in a circle, their collective chant turning the tree leaves red like a blush on pale cheeks. Ice spread along the ground and under his hooves. Horrible chills shot up his legs but he refused to take his attention from the dancing women. They moved in a circle, singing a collective song. They began to leap, higher and higher, their landings slower, lighter. At some point, each one jumped and remained suspended in the air, still circling, still singing.

All but the  woman on his back. Mockery rained down from those above as they challenged her to join them in the air. She responded with her own chant, and Nightcamp felt the woman's weight change. She had a sudden heaviness that threatened to buckle his legs. The air changed around her, and some invisible hand seemed to reach up and pluck the women from their floating dominion. They fell one by one but did not land as flesh and bone. Somehow they'd been transformed into stone that broke into pieces on impact. The woman stopped her chant, and in that instant, resumed her sparrow's heft. Nightcamp almost didn't feel her dismount to walk amongst her defeated enemy with much evident satisfaction. Looking up, Nightcamp caught her eye, and heard her voice in his head again.

*Flesh to stone*
*Bone to rock*
*Organs of life*
*Now granite block.*

She directed her chant to the animals. One by one, the cows, oxen, goats, and deer turned to stone. Nightcamp braced himself for his fate, unable to run as she placed her icy palm against his muzzle.

"Fear not, friend stallion. Fast thou are, and more useful as flesh." She placed the palm of her hand between his eyes and pain shot through his head like a musket ball. "I raise thee in intelligence, strength, and life for my service. I will teach thee what thou must know. But mark thee the fate of these false rivals and never let thy gallop outpace thy obedience. Thy name now is Nightcamp, in memory of this gathering. It is Mistress Isobel who owns thee now and forevermore."

She climbed onto his back and seized his mane again, and under her direction, he ran out of the forest under a cold, bleak, and starless sky.

*It is Mistress Isobel who owns thee now and forevermore.*

The strike of a crop made Nightcamp flinch out of his dream and stagger. His new owner, smirking and sour, laughed. Nightcamp was shocked to feel blood. How had the blow cut his skin? The only answer, he realized, was that Mistress Isobel truly had surrendered him into this man's custody and power. Evan Vines could hurt him.

Evan Vines could kill him.

"Lazy beast. With as little as I've given you to do, you shouldn't be tired. Now it's time to make yourself useful. The witch says I'm to ride you from the river's edge straight into the woods until we come to the first sign—whatever the hell that is."

Evan Vines was not the heaviest man Nightcamp ever bore at Isobel's command. Tall but slight of build, he made little impression in the saddle. Nevertheless, the horse decided Vines was the most loathsome and burdensome company he'd ever been forced to keep. He may never know why Mistress Isobel surrendered him into this man's power, but no rationale could excuse such betrayal.

Nightcamp received a spur in his right flank and trotted forward toward the dense tree line.

"I shouldn't have to do any of this. The witch showed me a whole town with the wave of her hand. Why can't she make it happen just like that? Now I must waste my time looking for *signs.*"

Nightcamp tried to tune out Vines's grumbling by remembering the man Vines killed. He was the first man to make a bargain with Mistress Isobel and die before the deal was completed. Nightcamp supposed it mattered little, knowing the fate he'd have met anyway. But why hadn't it befallen Vines yet? What special protection had this odious man earned?

A vicious tug on his bridle brought Nightcamp to a stop.

"That must be it," Vines said.

Nightcamp saw a cairn made from several stones, five feet high. Vines steered him in a circle around it.

"The tower—my tower—will rise on this spot, beast," he said, climbing down from the saddle. He craned his neck up and pointed at the sky. "I'll dwell way up there and look out from the tallest window and everything I see will belong to me. Nothing will stand against me, not some governor, nor any president. New Vineland will grow around the tower and sweep out, and the people will hear about my benevolence and come looking for my protection. Who knew getting power was as easy as placing a baby into an old crone's arms? Do you think others have done the same? Did Alexander the Great and Julius Caesar have some Isobel of their own? Maybe Washington and Jefferson gave her the babies right out of their slave women's wombs!"

Vines was almost skipping around the cairn, and Nightcamp watched the smug fool and dreamed of the day he got his true reward. But dark doubts stole into his thoughts once again. The man's encounter and interaction with Mistress Isobel was already so very different from what Nightcamp knew. What if Evan Vines had earned some sort of favor from the witch?

What if Nightcamp belonged to him for *good?*

*It is Mistress Isobel who owns thee now and forevermore.*

As he watched Vines continue his joyful, private gavotte, Nightcamp's mood blackened further. He was used to being Mistress Isobel's tool but never her bargaining chip. *Please,* he thought, *please let me play a role in this man's death.* He had never trampled anyone under his hooves before, not even considered himself capable of such an act. But time disproved all sentimental notions, and in the end, one's own benevolence quickest of all.

"Now, beast, we will set about clearing the land. All of your power is under my heel. I know you've got strength, but let's put it to a real test. You can thank the witch for this."

Nightcamp stood in place as Vines opened his saddlebag and produced a great length of chain. He chuckled as he brought it over for Nightcamp's inspection. The links were broad and clinked together like shackles as Vines tied one end around the trunk of a massive oak, leaving little slack as he fastened it to the end of Nightcamp's reins.

"Time to see what sort of mettle you have, nag," Vines said. "Bring this tree down. Start New Vineland for me, and try not to tear your mouth apart along the way."

Nightcamp didn't move. He wasn't going to help this man or his vision come true. He thought if Mistress Isobel appeared and threatened to turn him into stone, he'd still disobey and accept the punishment.

But she did not appear, and as Vines flung down the chain and began striking him with the crop, Nightcamp realized the witch understood stone wasn't a punishment for creatures who bear the agonies of the flesh. The lashes opened up his skin again, bringing fresh streaks of blood against his black coat. Nightcamp whinnied and snorted in agony. The eighth blow sent him lunging forward in submission.

The tree must have been hundreds of years old, with roots clutching deep into the earth. Nightcamp's hooves slipped on layers of decaying leaves and then plowed trenches into the underlying dirt. The crop kept biting at him, forcing him to bear down with all his might. A sharp splintering sound disturbed the air. It could have been the crop snapping in half against his haunches, but as he gained a few inches, Nightcamp felt the tree giving way.

Vines quit hitting him, but even if he'd continued the whipping, Nightcamp knew the exhilaration of victory would have numbed the pain. Pride always surged in concert with his power and feeling of achievement, even if the accomplished deed brought him shame. It was the same when he'd pulled the cart across the raging river to bring an innocent soul to a dark fate, all in anticipation of a word of praise and marvel for his work. Yes, it was Mistress Isobel who owned him, and perhaps Mistress Isobel who understood him best.

So he gloried when a final surge brought the tree toppling forward and Evan Vines shouted, "Yes! Yes, beast, yes!" in celebration. Nightcamp looked back to find Vines striking the crop against his thigh and grinning at the fallen oak, though it had come within a few feet of crushing him. Was this courage, or did he now feel such an arrogant mastery over nature that he considered himself invincible?

"That didn't take you long at all," Vines said, deigning to scratch Nightcamp's right ear. The horse shook his head. His blood and spirits were up in triumph. He'd even won over the respect of a man who respected nothing and no one!

"There must be a thousand trees right here alone. But it's early in the morning, and I wager you can have this whole area cleared by nightfall. I'm going to enjoy watching you work, beast. Now get to it! After all, how can you have a town without a town square?"

Nightcamp lowered his head and waited for the next tree to be chosen.

# Chapter Eighteen

*"Thou promised me thy firstborn. Thou promised me my bread straight from the oven."*

*"Won't this child do?"*

*"It is not the bread I was promised."*

*"My wife miscarried! I can't help it...I didn't plan for that...but she's already pregnant again. Three months along now. Won't...won't you accept this little boy instead?"*

*"I fulfilled my pledge to thee, did I not?"*

*"You did. My wife wouldn't start a family until she thought we were prosperous. You made us rich."*

*"Then my bread is due me, underbaked or not."*

*"But she won't deliver for six months! Isobel, this child was born but a month ago. You can see for yourself how...fresh it is."*

This exchange happened in 1760. Nightcamp didn't have a perfect memory of every man he'd watched make a bargain with Mistress Isobel, but some stood out more than others. The man named Morgan Watkins was burned into the horse's memory with all the clarity of a branding iron pressed to hide. Maybe it was the ease with which he put his unborn child up as collateral when all others kidnapped the babies of strangers.

When fate interceded, he was reduced to stealing a neighbor's newborn child. Nightcamp assumed Mistress Isobel, being hungry, would accept it in any case, but he was not surprised at her hardline stance. She was hungry but not *starving*.

*"A bargain is a bargain."*

*"But how...only three months along...how..."*

The man was clutching the stolen baby in the crook of his left arm. Nightcamp watched Mistress Isobel press an obsidian dagger into his right hand and close his fingers around the haft. He shook his arm as if he meant to cast the weapon away, but couldn't relax his grip. He sank to his knees and screamed.

*"I can't cut the baby out of my wife! My God–"*

*"If thy god's power merited even a fraction of its reputation, neither of us would be here now."*

The man was able to drop the dagger and thrust the baby up at her. He renewed his begging, seasoning it with a denunciation of God. He even called her God before his groveling ended. He placed the baby at her feet and stared up into her eyes while his hands made wild sweeping gestures of supplication. Or perhaps not so wild after all, and not so supplicant. Nightcamp noticed a pattern, saw how his fingers spread wide along the ground, and noticed the sweeping was never in the same spot. He was making a feeble attempt to retrieve the dagger. His fingertips found it and curled the handle back into his grip.

The horse looked at Mistress Isobel to see if she noticed. The witch appeared lost in Morgan Watkins' agony, savoring it as a kind of precursor to his unborn infant. What if she truly didn't know what the man was doing? What if Watkins managed to stab her? Could she die? What would her death mean for Nightcamp? He knew he was now a century old. Would he turn to dust in an instant without her magic?

He clapped his right hoof on the ground and snorted. Mistress Isobel still seemed oblivious to the man's hand even as he brought the blade toward her. Nightcamp's fears overwhelmed him, and he charged forward and reared up. The man fell onto his side and scrambled back, dropping the dagger along the way. Isobel cackled as she stooped to retrieve it, touching Nightcamp's face with her icy palms before whirling on the man.

*"Of all my minions, noble stallion, thou alone never fail. Good servant of flesh. Thou, on the other hand, have betrayed our bargain and will become a servant of stone. But I shall carve thee beforehand."*

She fell upon him, slashing with abandon. Nightcamp turned away from the scene, but the screams provided an unwelcome vision. Each cut produced a different kind of shriek, from the short hiss from sliced skin to the gasping cry from mutilated muscle, the throat-parching ululation brought on by a severed tendon, the wet gargle and cough in response to splintering bone. Mistress Isobel continued to work on the man long after he quit making any sound, and then she began her chant. Nightcamp did not turn around until the spell was done, and the stone statue he found was only half the size it'd been as flesh, with a gaping, toothless mouth and a horrific hump on its back. The hands that had offered Mistress Isobel a stolen baby were reduced to three fingers apiece, each shaped into tiny spears of rock. The feet had been whittled into something resembling talons. Nightcamp could not imagine how gruesome the body must have looked before she chanted it into stone. In a way, her magic had sanitized the aftermath.

Mistress Isobel then picked up the baby and said she was hungry. She walked off to eat, leaving Nightcamp to stare at another failed bargainer. He had brought the man to Mistress Isobel, just as he'd brought all of them since he entered her service. But he had no other role in their transaction, which took place through dreams or other means beyond his understanding. Nightcamp always took comfort in knowing both his limited utility in the bargain and the deserving character of the men who agreed to it.

None of the long succession of bargainers who populated Nightcamp's memories were mysteries to him except the last man to strike a pact with Mistress Isobel, the man Evan Vines killed. Nightcamp had not expected this bargainer to occupy any special place in his sentiments when Mistress Isobel came to him at the usual time of year, and at sunrise, saying, *"Once more, I see thee forth with the summoning song in thy bones and heart. Once more, it will guide thee to one whose pulse is in accord with it. This man has struck a bargain with me and knows what he must do. Pay heed to his commands until the time of return comes."*

Nightcamp galloped along the trail down the cliff, following the song as if it were a string. The melody took him across the river and into the dense woods. South he ran, ever south, the summoning song strumming inside him. The land's freshness invigorated him. He wanted to run faster and faster, explore every stream, every cove. He was used to seeing villages and farms every few miles, encountering tedious carts on the roads, the sound of laborers drowning out the song of birds. He'd put leagues behind him now without finding a trace of humanity. How, he wondered, had Mistress Isobel discovered this particular bargainer?

He came to a wheel-rutted road, proving someone must live nearby. The summoning song drew him along as he slowed to a trot, looking for any sign of a dwelling as the day neared sunset. Nightcamp saw nothing but knew from a change of pitch in the summoning song that he was close. The tune led him off the road and through a thicket of trees. There he encountered a crude cabin and a portly, jovial man sitting on a log, skinning a rabbit as he hummed the very tune Nightcamp followed.

The fat man looked to be in his early twenties. He rose as Nightcamp approached and bowed with an awkward reverence that made Nightcamp feel like royalty.

"Are you *her*?"

Nightcamp stood and stared at him. The fat man looked to his left and right and leaned closer.

"I mean, are you her in disguise? I've heard tell witches take the form of animals. I was thinking about that as I skinned each of them rabbits, but I reckon no witch would have put up with that."

He had a boisterous laugh that did not disguise obvious nervousness. This intrigued Nightcamp. Those who made a pact with Mistress Isobel had many qualities in common, and they were all decided men. This one sounded like he couldn't quite believe what he was doing.

The rotund man waddled over to him and ran his hands along Nightcamp's flanks, brushing away foaming sweat with his palms. Then he fetched a pail of water that tasted terrible and stale, but Nightcamp drank deeply anyway as the man started brushing him.

"It's sure a strange thing to realize you're evil," he said. Nightcamp raised his head and glanced back at the man. He looked amused and bashful, a little baffled. "What would my mama say? Well, that don't matter because she's been dead some years now. I'm sure she'd be disappointed. She raised me up in the church after all."

Nightcamp finished drinking and motioned his head toward the road. The prospect of carrying the fat man to the top of the cliff face didn't appeal to him, but it was better than standing here listening to him talk to himself.

"Oh, you want to get going, is that it? Well, not so fast. This witch and I have been talking quite a bit in my dreams. She appreciates I'm a modest man, and she told me she'd send a servant along to help me before I carried out my end of the deal. I've got a field not far from here, full of pumpkins ready to be carted up to Hamilton and sold. They'll fetch me a good price. Didn't she tell you to help me with that first?"

The man motioned for Nightcamp to follow, and he did, cutting through a path that led to a clearing. There he found an old ox cart and a field of pumpkins, each about the size of a cannonball, three or four hundred in all. The man went and picked one, holding it next to his head. "These have been my whole life. Ain't much of a life, I guess. But these are my beauties and my reputation. Merchants are quick to buy up the entire patch once it's available because everyone knows my pumpkins make for the best pies."

He put the pumpkin aside and came to stand next to Nightcamp. They both looked at the patch.

"The problem with pumpkins is they have a long growing season. You wait a long time for your reward. You can't make a living with them. The witch is going to fix it, so I'll have pumpkins year-round, finer than anyone else can grow. And if I choose to cut one open, all I have to do is close my eyes and think of what I need, and that's what I'll find when I dip my hand into the pumpkin guts. Think of a gold watch, and there'll be a gold watch. A bag of doubloons, and there'll be doubloons. But if people are buying my pumpkins every day, I'll never need to do that. I'd rather someone else cut them open for baking pies."

Nightcamp whinnied because he couldn't think of any other sound to make as he tried to comprehend the man's dream. The man sighed and patted the horse's neck.

"I should have asked the witch to send two servants. You to pull the cart, and another to load it. But it's not so terrible a chore, and the evening's cool now. I imagine it will take three or four trips to Hamilton to get the patch cleared and sold. Then I'll settle up with the witch. Already got that part figured out. There's a young couple not far from here, running a little inn. She likes my pumpkins just as much as the folks in Hamilton, and I always give her the best of the bunch. They've a newborn son the witch will like very much."

He took the pumpkin and let it roll down the bed of the wagon, seemed to contemplate the sound it made, and then got to work for the next hour, with no bother over the darkness or the chill. Nightcamp watched the dull orange gourd pile grow in the cart until the man ceased his labor and came to teeter against the horse, his arms wrapped around Nightcamp's neck. Nightcamp started to shy away because of the man's body odor but stopped himself.

"I could eat a horse. But don't worry, you're safe with me," he said, pushing away and giving Nightcamp a playful slap. "I'm tired enough to go to bed and I bet you are too. But if we leave now and ride all through the night, we'd be halfway to Hamilton by sunrise. I'm game to give it a try if you are. It'd sure speed up this business."

Nightcamp knew nothing of Hamilton or its distance, but he bristled at the notion this man thought it'd take a night of riding to reach the halfway mark. Truth be told he *was* tired and hungry, but neither mattered now. This man needed his ignorance corrected and then Nightcamp would bask in his astonishment.

He sauntered over to the cart and positioned himself between its shafts. The man slapped his meaty thigh and said, "I like that spirit, Mr. Horse! Yes, indeed I do!" He set about connecting the traces and securing the straps, then climbed into the driver's seat and flicked the reins.

"I truly hope the load ain't too heavy," he said, and the sincerity of his tone made Nightcamp want to try imitating human laughter. The man's bulk alone was equal to fifty additional pumpkins.

He scraped his right hoof along the ground and surged forward.

The cart budged and rolled back, budged and rolled back. It seemed to have been sitting in the same spot for most of the year. Nightcamp dug in deeper and dislodged the wheels from their stubborn ruts. He heard the driver cheering as he pulled the cart onto the road, his head lifted high. Then he galloped so fast the man shrieked and Nightcamp was determined to turn the cart into a wooden shooting star.

The night became a blue-black blur. His pulse sped from the dark magic Mistress Isobel had poured into his heart. Nightcamp heard only the wind and the man's murmured, fragmented prayers for the first hour of the trip. Then he started laughing and calling on the horse to slow. Nightcamp saw muted lights up ahead from torches and candles and went to a simple walking pace. "My God," the man said. "I can't believe it. Somehow, we're already here...that's Hamilton. Mr. Horse, you just can't be beat!"

Nightcamp pulled the cart into the town square and stopped. The man climbed down and inspected the horse's hooves, scraping out a few embedded stones.

"Such power and beauty," he said. "You're something else. All this and not even a sweat. Your great-great-great-great grandpappy must have been Bucephalus himself."

He pulled the horse forward at the slowest pace. "The marketplace won't open for hours yet. Won't take long to rid ourselves of these pumpkins once it does. But I have a bit of money on me now, and I'm going to spend it on you, Mr. Horse. Let's get you stabled and fed."

The kind gesture astonished Nightcamp and he couldn't believe the man meant it, but he unhitched him from the cart and led him to an inn with a stable. The stableboy showed them to the first available stall, with fresh water and hay waiting. As Nightcamp ate, the man stood grooming him for thirty minutes. Then he said, "I'll just rest here for a moment," and lowered his bulk to the ground. Snoring commenced minutes later.

Nightcamp studied him, so unlike any other who'd ever answered Mistress Isobel's summoning song. Couldn't he be made to understand he had other options?

*He can't understand what he's committed himself to do*, Nightcamp thought. This man was different from the other bargainers. He *had* to be. If he could be shown his mistake, there might be time to avoid his certain doom.

# Chapter Nineteen

Nightcamp thought of the pumpkin grower whenever Evan Vines thrashed him. He remembered how the man had groomed him after they reached Hamilton and how he'd reveled in his success when the market opened. His pumpkins proved as popular as he'd boasted. By late morning they were racing back to his patch for more. Nightcamp ran even faster than before, in part because of the lightened load but more because he found himself wanting to help the man, who didn't even sit in the driver's seat but lay stretched out in the wagon, shouting the horse's praises to the countryside they sped past.

Over the next two days, as they made their trips back and forth from Hamilton, the man began daydreaming out loud. "Wouldn't it be something if we did this trip every day? I'll need to when the patch is growing year-round. What do you think it'd take to get the witch to give you to me? A second baby? I'd be willing to go that far. What do you think, Mr. Horse? Would you like to stay here with me?"

Nightcamp became enchanted by the simplicity of the fantasy and whinnied his response. When they returned from their fourth trip, a little before noon, the man unhitched Nightcamp, fed him, and then brushed him.

"You're the very horse I wanted as a boy. All the ones we ever owned were old, given to my mama by sympathetic people at church. A team of those ancient nags couldn't have pulled a wagonload of pumpkins the way you can."

He laughed, and Nightcamp heard a touch of the old nervousness. He turned his eyes to the man and found him pale, his jowls basted with a heavy glaze of sweat.

"Tonight's the night. You already know that, I reckon."

Nightcamp did.

"I've been thinking about how I'm going to go about it. I don't mean to act like I'm only just now making plans. Truth is, I've thought about it a lot. I've slept on it and seen the options in my dreams. The woman, she'll be no problem. She's strong and young, but I can overpower her. Her husband's a strapping man. I've seen him lift great big sacks of flour like they're empty. No sir, I wouldn't do well in a fight with him. So, I have to make sure there is no fight."

Nightcamp bowed his head.

"The way I see it, the baby's the key to his own kidnapping. If I connive to get ahold of him first, it'll keep the parents fixed in their places. They won't make a move for risk of me hurting their boy. That's how it goes in the dream I have most often. It could be the witch is giving me the dream to show me what to do. Smart of her, if so. Well, it's early yet. I'm going to go inside and sleep a few hours. If I have the same dream, I'll know it's how I'm supposed to go about it."

Nightcamp snorted and whinnied after him but the man did not turn around, leaving him standing there. As the hours passed, the sky darkened, thickening with ominous clouds. By late afternoon, the world was as dim as dusk except when lightning lit everything in purple and white.

The man came out just as the first big drops of rain started. He toted a wicker basket in both hands.

"Sure enough, Mr. Horse, I had the dream again. It wasn't ever stormy though. Do you think the witch called up the weather to help us? It'll be a good excuse when I go to the inn. Now look at this. My mama kept me in this when I was a baby. Can you believe I was ever so little?"

He placed the basket in the cart and stretched a tarp over it. It shouldn't have taken a long time, but Nightcamp watched him smooth it out in the most elaborate way. He was having second thoughts. He didn't want to go through with it. Nightcamp kept telling himself this even as the man came to hitch him to the cart. *It's not too late for him*, Nightcamp thought, all the while knowing it wasn't true. It was too late the moment he answered the summoning song.

Nightcamp nevertheless tried to resist. He pulled back a little and stomped his feet.

"Now what's this, a witch's steed afraid of a storm? Come along, Mr. Horse. Let's get this over and done with."

Nightcamp snorted a sigh and let himself be hitched. The ground was already becoming muddy and difficult to find traction. The wheels slipped in place before catching and moving forward.

He did not hurry to the inn and the man did not try to force his pace. He sat in the driver's seat whistling into the stinging rain. The whistle was a feeble human approximation of the summoning song.

*Not too late*, Nightcamp thought. *Not too late.*

They reached the inn. The man climbed down, soaked through to the bone, his shabby clothes plastered to his fleshy body. He prepared the bassinet and told Nightcamp to be ready, for he would not be long.

Then he went inside.

Nightcamp fixed his stare on the front door. The window next to it showed a bright light. The storm may work against them. There could be many travelers inside. *Yes*, Nightcamp thought. *There'll be too many people. His plan won't work.*

A woman screamed, louder than the thunder. A fearful male voice followed, pleading for his son's safety. The front door flung open as the fat man came running, slapdash and slipping in the mud, but never falling. He struggled to get back into the driver's seat without the use of both hands and still wasn't in it all the way as he shouted for Nightcamp to move.

A man appeared in the doorway, aiming a flintlock pistol and firing. The lead ball struck Nightcamp in the chest and ricocheted off into the mud. Nightcamp shifted to protect the driver as he saw the stranger aiming a second gun. The rain must have already caused it to fail, though, because the man scowled and threw it aside as he came charging toward them. Nightcamp struggled to get traction. The cart's wheels slipped and spun again, and Nightcamp almost tore the shafts and halter away in his next surge of strength. The cart lurched forward, picking up speed. The man made a desperate lunge but missed. Nightcamp looked back to see him picking himself out of the muck and trying to give chase. But he kept slipping, falling further and further behind until he tumbled a final time and just lay defeated in the mud.

"It's done," the driver said. He'd gotten the baby secured in the bassinet and covered. "God help me, but we've done it, Mr. Horse. Take me where I need to go now."

The road was washing out. Nightcamp knew that there could be no excuse, no hindrance. The man was as determined to complete his bargain as any man Nightcamp had ever assisted. But he *wasn't* like them. He didn't understand his own actions—he *couldn't*.

*Somehow, I have to stop this*, Nightcamp thought. *This is a good man. Being kept from fulfilling the pact isn't the same as breaking it.*

The sudden appearance of a tall stranger staggering through the storm came both as a surprise, and an opportunity. Nightcamp stopped even though the driver threatened to whip him. Nightcamp knew the man wasn't capable of such a thing. This was a *good* man.

Then the stranger pulled the fat man from the cart and threatened him.

"Give me the money! You fat men always have a fortune! Give it to me now, along with the cart, and I'll let you live!"

Then the unthinkable happened. Nightcamp lowered his head, mind going blank as he tried to comprehend his failure. He stood still in the darkness and the rain until the usurper climbed up into the seat and ordered him to get going.

He had made a terrible error.

# Chapter Twenty

## March – September 1819

Toad's education went on all day and night as he explored his kingdom and met his subjects. He saw snakes and learned to make his body long and narrow. He floated on his back and looked at the white puffs in the sky. He practiced stretching and shrinking his body and learned to tie his arms and legs in knots. His skin took on the color of what he touched. The sunlight burned him and made his skin feel dry, like the time of stone. The night cooled him like being at the bottom of the river. Above all, he'd learned he lived in a world of taste, and Toad loved the taste of fish and frogs, birds and insects. All flesh was good to Toad.

Mother Isobel had taught him to tell time by the changing face of the moon. Last night, the moon had returned to the way it first looked, and he knew the third time that happened he must return to the cliff with Mother Isobel's bread.

Toad knew he'd learned many things, but he still did not understand the summoning song. This frustrated him because he could make so many *other* sounds from his throat and mouth. What if he couldn't learn the song? How else could he get Mother Isobel her bread?

One day, on his way to visit his favorite subjects, he saw a boy floating in the river further from the shore than most people ventured unless they were on a boat. Toad watched him in silence, several yards behind the boy with just his black eyes above the water. He knew the boy was too old to be Mother Isobel's bread, but he tried the summoning song on him anyway. The gargle he produced was loud enough to draw the boy's attention. He turned and quit splashing about.

*Come to Toad*, Toad thought. *Toad summons you.*

The boy floated in the opposite direction. Toad roared his hatred under the water. Why couldn't he sing the summoning song? Who was this boy to defy the King of the River?

Defiance had to be met with punishment. This was wisdom. Toad imagined tearing the boy in half but then got a better idea. He swam under and past the boy, shrinking and folding himself along the way until he rose downstream as little more than a head with a flap of flesh trailing behind like a tail. He let the very top of his bald head breach the waterline and worked himself against the current. The boy came right at him, and Toad heard him say, "What's that?" before providing his own excited answer: "It must be a turtle!"

A moment later, the boy touched the top of Toad's head. Toad let the petting go on for a few seconds, his jaw unhinging wider and wider with every stroke. The three sawtooth teeth at the front of his mouth were ready.

"Want to come home with me? I've been wanting a pet turtle."

Toad began to shake from holding back his giddiness. With an upward snap of his neck, he brought his teeth to bare and claimed the fingers of the petting hand. The boy bled, shrieked, and thrashed toward the shore, crying for his mother. Shouts came from the shoreline. He'd not even noticed them before, but Toad knew sometimes people gathered near the river for a *picnic*. Toad was not afraid of the grown men who now entered the water, but he decided he'd made his point. He swallowed the fingers and let himself sink before stretching his body into its usual shape. He sped away about a hundred yards upstream and then stopped to watch and listen.

The boy had been dragged to shore. He wasn't talking, but the men who'd rescued him were saying plenty.

*"Must have been a catfish."*

Toad put his hands over his mouth. The finger bones made a tickle inside his stomach.

*"More likely a snapping turtle, I should say. He should have known better than to reach for it."*

They kept going on about all the little creatures that could have been responsible. The idea he could be confused for a turtle or catfish insulted him.

*Toad will show them all who is King of the River!*

There was a boat coming upstream and Toad saw his chance to prove his *eminence.* He shot himself under its hull and swiped at its planks. His claws tore chunks from the wood, gouging holes that let the river surge inside. He heard shouts and cries as the stricken boat rocked. Toad descended further down to watch the chaos as the hull came apart and spilled people into the water, their hands slapping a beat of terror and confusion. No one would think a turtle or catfish had done *this.*

Satisfied, he headed downstream and decided to visit the family of muskrats he'd discovered many days earlier. They would enjoy hearing the story about the boy and the wrecked boat. He knew the location of the family's nest by its scent, and he followed it down the river, mile after mile, skirting rocks, decayed logs, and countless more boats he spared due to eagerness. The nest existed along the bank of a finger of stagnant water on the east side of the river, not too far north of where the river met the great ocean, where Toad still feared to go.

He loved the strong smell of decay in the air and how rafts of mosquito eggs dimpled the stale water in endless honeycomb patterns. He found more of them when he reached the muskrat nest and opened his mouth wide to let the eggs glide down his throat. The larvae would tickle his insides in a few days from now, and when they flew up into his mouth, he'd swat them with his long, flat tongue and savor them a second time.

After eating, he turned his attention back to the muskrats, wading toward the bank which rose a few feet above the waterline. This wall of dirt had many holes but the nest was reached through an opening below the waterline. He plunged his hand into it and began stretching his arm through the long passage that went inland and up to the dry chamber filled with leaves.

"Toad is here," he said, twisting his arm and feeling around for Father and Mother Muskrat and their four babies.

He winced when sharp teeth bit and chewed on the webbing between his fingers. He jerked his hand all the way out and his blood stained the water black. Toad began to swell as he never had before, fueled by a mix of anguish and anger. How could they have forgotten his friendship? How *dare* they forget Toad, the King of the River?

Little purple pores opened across his flesh. Toad had never seen them before. Sound came from them, a low vibration that must have been inside his body. Each pore began to erupt with pieces of song that united across the whole of his body. Toad jumped, recognizing the summoning song. Its melody now surged around him and shot into the water, into the hole. Toad didn't know if he controlled it or how he controlled it if he did. But a moment later, Father Muskrat left the nest and started crawling up Toad's leg.

The song stopped. The pores closed. Father Muskrat continued to climb until it perched on his right shoulder like a dark, slimy parrot. Toad floated on his back and let the muskrat rest on his stomach. Toad grinned, certain he'd never known a greater contentment. Then he sat up and held the muskrat by its tail so that it dangled in front of his eyes.

"Do the babies still look like Toad?"

His first memory of seeing them was very bright and vivid. The muskrat was unlike any other creature in the river. Its odor made him follow it all the way to the submerged hole and he reached his hand in after it, amazed by the series of tunnels. When his hand broke into the main nest, it was attacked by Mother and Father Muskrat as his fingers discovered the wriggling babies. He plucked one up and drew his arm back with both muskrats clinging to him by their clamped teeth. The sight of the pink baby so fascinated Toad that he didn't even feel the pain of the attack and felt no anger toward them once he did.

"You have a good Mother and Father," he told the baby. "The way Mother Isobel is good to Toad. But Toad must kill his father one day. Maybe you do, too."

He came back the next day and pulled out three babies. Mother and Father Muskrat bit his hand with the same ferocity but he ignored the bites and his own black blood. "The King of the River will always care for his people," he said. The muskrats quit biting and Toad knew they were all friends now. It was nice to have subjects who were also friends.

He squatted with the wriggling little forms cupped in his hands and said, "Toad must bring Mother Isobel a baby, but it won't be one of you. Toad wouldn't give you to Mother Isobel even if she told him."

The loudness of his words made him tremble and look at all the trees and then at the sky itself.

"Toad needs to keep quiet," he said, putting the babies back in their nest. He hurried off and stayed away, fearing Mother Isobel had heard and would punish the family for what he said. He hadn't come back until today.

He reached for the babies now but did not find them. Confused, he took Father Muskrat into the woods and sat down at the base of a tree. The summoning song hung around the muskrat like a cloud, making its eyes distant. But how had Toad done it?

"Mother Isobel says Toad is King of the River but only if Toad becomes wise. Toad is learning. The river teaches Toad and today you taught Toad the summoning song. Toad will have to learn it well to bring Mother Isobel her bread."

He told the muskrat about biting off the boy's fingers. He laughed when he finished the story and flung the muskrat into the air, caught it, and brought it to his chest. He did this again and again, higher and higher. The muskrat flipped and writhed, flipped and writhed, until at last, it stopped moving. Toad shifted its weight from palm to palm, cradling its head in the webbing of his fingers. Father Muskrat must have gone to sleep. Toad decided to join him.

When he woke, his skin was becoming dry and itchy. Father Muskrat was still asleep and Toad carried him to the water and sat down like a child in a bathtub. The muskrat floated between his splayed legs, and he went on stroking it from head to tail as its body lolled back and forth. It was becoming stiff. This alarmed Toad and he looked around for any sign of Mother Isobel. He did not hear the chant she used to turn people to stone.

But Father Muskrat seemed to be doing just that.

"Toad will take you back to the babies now."

He dropped Father Muskrat above the hole but the body just floated, unmoving, so Toad shoved it all the way back into the nest. He still didn't feel Mother Muskrat or the babies. Maybe Mother Muskrat was showing them the world.

That night, as he floated downstream on his back, he remembered how the summoning song had come from inside him. The moon's face was changing again, reminding him he had only a short time before he must bring Mother Isobel her bread like a good and obedient son.

*But what if Toad fails? What if Toad can't be wise and learn the song?*

These thoughts seemed to come from outside of his head. Toad realized the moon was shouting the questions down at him. He shook one fist at it and said, "Toad is King of the River!" The moon shouted back, "Toad will fail! Toad will not be wise!"

Toad's rage exploded. He glared at the moon, determined to summon it out of the sky. The moon rained cold doubts and condemnations on him and Toad growled and roared. His body began to break out in purple pores, and the summoning song was gathering around him like a physical thing, and he began to snatch at chunks of the tune and bring them to his mouth and swallow them. He kept eating and swallowing, eating and swallowing, until every meaty note of melody his pores surrendered was locked in his belly. Toad's stomach cramped, but he refused to open his mouth. Something great—*immense*—was happening. It was like thousands of mosquito eggs hatching all at once and flying up his throat. His cheeks bulged until the skin began to crack. He couldn't keep his mouth clenched any longer and his lips broke apart and the song came up out of his stomach like a thick stream.

But he couldn't make it reach the moon, so he aimed the song into the river. Fish of all kinds, fish that never swam together, began to school at his back. The frogs left the banks and swam to him. Water snakes came too.

He worked to close his mouth. At first, this proved impossible, the song was like a solid thing lodged between his teeth. Toad kept trying, though, and the song started to soften and give way. He started swallowing, gulping the song back into his belly. The song settled into the pit of his stomach and died down to a light rumble.

The fish fled him now. The frogs darted back to shore; the snakes slinked off into the murk. Toad watched them go but felt no disappointment. His excited focus had already found a new target. A raft was moving downstream. Three men stood upon it in the moonlight, using long poles to speed their raft along. His liquid black eyes observed their arrogance. Did they not know Toad was King of the River? How dare they trespass!

Yesterday, Toad would have attacked the raft and dismantled it.

But now Toad had wisdom.

He swam towards the raft, making no effort to hide. The men did not see him at first, too lost in talk. Toad tightened his stomach, held it a moment, and then relaxed. As his stomach expanded, the space filled with song and became round with melody. Toad leapt out of the water, flinging himself over the raft.

*"What the hell is that?"*

He came down ahead of it, sending a splash of water into the boatmen's faces. Toad looked up at them, grinning as they staggered and teetered. Their faces were fixed in identical expressions of horror and revulsion. They raised their push poles to attack him.

"All hail Toad, King of the River!" he shouted, then opened his mouth wide. Nothing happened. The summoning song in his stomach stayed there. He grunted and tried to vomit out the melody. He only produced a cough.

The first push pole struck him in the arm, tearing through his skin. Two more lanced him in the shoulder and leg. The men stabbed down at him, their jabs short, quick, and brutal. The sharp points ripped his flesh more and sent pools of dark blood all around the raft.

Toad dove, but one of the poles speared his left leg and held him fast. Toad broke the shaft in half with a swipe of his right hand and twisted free. The summoning song felt like a rock in his stomach.

Another push pole sheared into his side. Toad screamed, and the pureness of his anger relaxed some inner muscle and let the song flow forth. He leapt out of the churning water and perched on the edge of the raft. The men made ready to drive him back into the water.

Toad opened his mouth.

The summoning song struck them, as they dropped their weapons, hands falling docile at their sides. Toad stepped back and the three men stepped forward.

Toad jumped into the water.

Three more splashes followed.

He dove, speeding into the depths with the song flowing back behind him, summoning, summoning. The men followed, their eyes bulging but locked on him in helpless fascination, aware of their drowning, their desperate pleas reduced to bright, silvery bubbles in filthy water. They came out big and slow at first, dwindled to a few pebbles of air, then to nothing. Toad swallowed the song back into his stomach and shot to the surface, aching but thrilled by this night of triumph. The blood kept pouring from his wounds, an inky darkness spreading out downstream along with the empty raft. He watched it fade out of sight before raising his face to the moon to shout, "All hail Toad, King of the Blackblood River!"

# Chapter Twenty-One
## September – October 1819

The moon was just a sliver last night and would be gone this evening. Toad knew it'd be a sliver again tomorrow, and a larger sliver the night after. It would grow fast, and when it was round all the way again, he must bring Mother Isobel her bread.

Toad explored the river, venturing to where it emptied into the great, vast sea. One day he'd gone out into those depths, but right now, the sight of it filled him with dread. He did not even like being near it, but the ports were larger here, and there were more boats with sailors walking along the decks. He needed target practice.

Floating with his eyes above the waterline, he focused on the broad backs of five men who stood on the dock looking out toward the sea. The dock was several feet above the river, giving him a very clear view. His attention shifted among them before choosing the one in the middle. He tightened his stomach to awaken the song and took a breath. As he exhaled, the summoning song rose into his throat and waited there. His tongue curled back and wrapped around it like a physical thing.

He brought his head clear of the water and drew his mouth open wide. Keeping his sights trained on the man in the middle, he stabbed out with his tongue and the summoning song catapulted forward like an extension of it.

Toad knew he'd failed before the melody reached them. He'd meant to shoot an arrow of sound, but he ended up with a blanket that fell over all five men. They responded to it by turning in unison to face him. Toad frowned and gave a single tug of his head. The men jumped into the water. Toad ended the song, and the men regained their senses and began thrashing and yelling in confusion.

Toad submerged and swam upstream, too annoyed to be amused by what he'd made them do. Maybe it would add to the reputation he was making for himself. He enjoyed floating near boats at night and listening to the frightened whispers of sailors as they stood watch.

*"Must have been a freak storm. They were strong swimmers. They could have made it to shore."*

*"But the weather was clear that night."*

*"What else explains it?"*

*"What explains men jumping overboard and not knowing why they did it? What explains a boat just coming apart in the middle of the river like a damn shark attacked it?"*

Toad reveled in their fearful whispers about the shape in the water, a white ghost, a mermaid who sang siren songs. These had become his own kind of bread, and like Mother Isobel, he liked his bread as fresh as possible—like the night he drowned all seven people on a boat and then clung to it as it floated adrift. A second boat moving upstream intercepted it, and Toad heard men scrambling and talking.

*"That's Robbie Jackson's boat. I saw him up in Hamilton last week. He was preparing to bring bags of grain down to Dalton. Those same bags right there. What the hell happened to him and the crew?"*

*"I'm telling you, something around here's strange. There was another boat found floating empty last week. I heard about it from Hartley Kelton."*

Toad memorized the names of people whenever he heard them, wanting to see if casting the summoning song into the air while thinking of a name could bring that particular person to him, despite not knowing who or where they were. No one ever came, but the attempt wasn't fruitless. He found that when he concentrated like that, on a name, the song came out with more purpose and almost with a visible shape, like an arm stretching up from his throat.

He was still fretting over his failure at the dock when he decided to leave the river and come ashore to eat. Toad had decided he wouldn't be a good King of the River if he ate his subjects, and he preferred the taste of land meat anyway. He wouldn't even use the summoning song to lure his prey. Hunting on land pleased him. Squirrels were a particular favorite because their speed and size always promised a fun chase ahead of his meal.

He spotted one in moments and jumped after it, springing into the branches and clawing his way up the narrowing trunk until the top of the tree bent under his weight. The squirrel leapt to the next tree. Toad lashed out with his tongue and almost got it around the bushy tail, but the clever squirrel twisted out of the way and scampered straight down.

The chase went on, scaling the heights of trees and scrambling under brambles and logs. At last, he'd run the squirrel ragged and had it exhausted and defenseless. As he stalked over to it, however, he stopped and cocked his head.

He heard a little girl singing.

Toad crept forward until the song had become very clear and close. He pressed his body against a tree until his skin took on the color of the bark as he watched through a break in the bushes.

The girl had blond hair and a blue dress. Her singing seemed the most beautiful thing in the world, and Toad wondered if she was learning and practicing her own summoning song. Had it snared him without him even realizing it? The thought scared Toad into stumbling back, and he made a loud enough noise to draw the girl's attention. She stopped singing and stared into the trees. Toad wondered if she knew she was staring right at him.

"*Christian?*"

So much hope in a single word.

She came closer.

"Oh Christian, please let it be you. It has to be you. You're not dead, I just know it."

Toad made no sound. He had pressed himself as flat as he could to the tree. If his skin wasn't the color of the bark, he knew she'd see him. She was calling, "Christian? Where are you, Christian?" and moving towards him. If he stayed in place, she'd soon be standing right beside him.

"What's that smell?"

The girl made a face and took a step back.

"Christian, if that's you, I don't care. I'll get used to it."

Toad stretched his limbs up along the trunk until his clawed fingers curled around the lowest branch with clusters of orange and red leaves. He let his arms shrink back to pull his torso upwards, and then he swung all of himself onto his new perch.

"Christian..." The girl stood still another minute, sobbing, and then went back to where she'd been. From his new vantage point, Toad saw her sit down in a little clearing beside a flat piece of rock wedged into the ground. It was strange in shape, beige, and covered in markings. She leaned her head against the stone and began singing again.

*"Christian, I know you're out there,*
*Big brother, not far away,*
*Christian, you'd never leave me,*
*Big brother, come back to stay."*

Toad sensed the power and richness of the melody and realized it must be a summoning song, though he saw no evidence she could project it the way he'd learned to do. He felt a strange pull inside his chest all the same. The longer he listened, the nearer he wanted to be. He moved out along the branch until he was right above her.

A sharp crack came from the tree, and before Toad could jump, the whole branch broke and fell. The girl shrieked but dodged as the limb crashed down with Toad pinned under it. He squirmed, thinking he'd been cut in half, his body bulging on either side of the pinch.

The girl came to stand and sway over him.

*"Christian?"*

She breathed the word, her voice muted by the hands cupped over her mouth. Toad tried to free himself, and as the girl watched, it seemed her fear went away.

"Let me help you!"

She was little, but their combined strength moved the branch enough to let Toad slip free. He leapt into the woods, his only goal being the safety of the river. But he stopped when the girl called out.

"Christian, please don't go! I don't care what you look like now! I just miss you so much! Christian, it's me! It's Anna!"

Toad looked back, knowing full well she could see him by the way her expression changed. She looked so happy and he walked back to her.

"Mommy and Daddy said you died. They even had a tombstone made. Isn't it pretty?"

Toad looked at the flat piece of rock. "What is a tombstone?"

"It's for when someone dies," she said.

"What is *dies*?"

She laughed and sat down, patting the ground.

*She can't hurt Toad*, he thought.

He joined her and then looked at the tombstone. The engravings meant nothing to him.

Christian Freeman

1806-1818

"I knew you weren't dead. You couldn't be. Mommy and Daddy said I had to learn to accept it, but I said you couldn't be dead since no one found you. Where have you been all this time?"

"Toad was in the river," he said.

"They said you'd drowned!"

She touched his shoulder, then pulled her hand back in an instant. She wiped her palm against her dress and her cheeks reddened.

"I don't care," she whispered and flung her arms around Toad. He flinched at first, but as her hold tightened, he found he liked it.

"Toad is sorry he didn't come sooner. Toad didn't know you were here."

She nuzzled against his shoulder. "You're here now and that's what matters. Tell me about the river, Christian. Did you go there to live?"

Toad told her about the muskrats, chasing squirrels, and diving deep. He described all the treasures that lay on the bottom of the river. He liked how her eyes got wider and wider. Even though he did not understand the things she said to him, he wanted to hear her speak. When she laughed, he felt like laughing too.

An idea came to him because he was Toad, King of the River. A brilliant idea. He sprang up high and landed in an exaggerated crumple, so that his body became a blob of flesh with his head sitting atop it, neckless.

The girl screamed and he rushed to get back into his usual shape. "Toad is okay, Anna. Toad just wanted you to laugh."

She calmed down. Then she said, "Do it again, Christian!"

He did, and this time she clapped and laughed.

Toad began to entertain her by contorting his body in every way he could. He stretched himself wide and made a huge arch. He rolled around her as a ball. He stood in front of her and told her to spread her feet wide. Then he slithered his torso along the ground like a snake, moved through the open space, and snapped the rest of him forward. She gasped and turned as he pulled himself back together.

"Christian, we have to tell Mommy and Daddy that you're here."

He shook his head.

"But why? They'll want–"

"Toad can't let them know yet."

The girl nodded in solemn seriousness and Toad went on entertaining her. She kept calling him Christian and the name began to work itself into his mind as he lingered with her another thirty minutes.

"Christoad can't remember your name."

She gave him a playful slap. "You know me, Christian. I'm Anna, your baby sister."

"Anna," he said, repeating it until he knew he wouldn't forget. "Christoad remembers Anna."

Another voice, distant but not *too* far away, called her name. Anna looked over her shoulder and said, "Are you sure you won't come and see Mommy? She wants me to come in."

"Christoad is sure."

She smiled. "I'm going to act sad for Mommy and Daddy so they won't know you're back. I promise to keep the secret. Will you come back tomorrow, Christian? Can we play hide and seek like we used to? Will you tell me more about the river?"

Toad nodded. Then, the most amazing thing happened. She kissed him in the middle of his broad forehead and ran away, saying, "I'm coming, Mommy!" Toad stood stunned by the feeling of her lips. He pressed his left hand over the spot to protect it and kept it there even as he ran back to the river. Once in the water, he swam one-handed. The river mustn't wash away the kiss.

But if it did, maybe he could get a fresh one tomorrow.

# Chapter Twenty-Two

Toad visited Anna every day for the next week and learned many things that increased his wisdom. He loved hide and seek, and because his skin turned the color of whatever he touched, he was very good at it. But Anna was small and knew all the best hiding places.

Sometimes while he watched her search for him, Toad thought about what the moon had looked like the night before. Mother Isobel would require her bread soon and he'd not done any further practice with the summoning song. He swam the river's length sneaking around boats to see if any had a baby on board. He scanned the banks hoping to find more people having picnics. But all the mothers seemed to be gone and their babies were inside houses and he did not know how to find them or how to send the summoning song through closed doors and windows.

*Christoad doesn't have more time to play hide and seek*, Toad thought when the fateful morning came. His agitation sent him all the way down to the sea where he rose and scanned the docks for any sign of a baby. But of course, there were none, just as there weren't any on the boats he checked on his way upstream. What was Toad to do? How would he explain his failure to Mother Isobel tonight?

That question was overwhelming and he sought comfort with Anna once again. He tried to play hide and seek with her, but his mind was distracted, so he could not hide well. Anna must have noticed because she stopped playing and sat by the tombstone. Toad crouched near her and listened. She talked a lot and she kept touching the tombstone as she spoke.

"I never believed you were dead, but I was going to come out here and talk to you every day of my life," she said.

Toad looked at the sky. Big purple clouds had built up overhead and made the world darker than usual. The wind gusted from the north.

"It's cold," Anna said. She looked in the direction of her house as if she wanted to be there. She shivered and Toad put an arm around her. Would he see her again after today? The thought he wouldn't gave him an odd feeling, like something his stomach couldn't digest.

"Christoad is glad he's here," Toad said.

"*Christian*. Your name is Christian."

"Chris...tian."

She hugged him and he kept practicing the name until it came easy to him.

"Thank you," she said.

Rain fell in big droplets, splattering on their skin and the tombstone. Anna's mother called to her. They looked at each other and it was as if they both knew this was their last meeting.

"Please come inside with me this time, Christian. Mommy and Daddy will understand why you look and talk differently. They won't be afraid."

She stood up and grabbed his arm. Her face was too wet to just be from the rain. The sight of it burned inside him and, in an instant, he knew he wanted to see her face forever. Mother Isobel would understand his decision. She would see the wisdom in it.

"Christian has an idea, Anna."

He stood up.

"Christian wants Anna to come with him."

He took her by the arm and started toward the river. He didn't realize he was pulling too hard until Anna screamed.

"Christian, why are you hurting me? Let go of me! Please let go!"

Lightning flashed, followed by immediate thunder. Anna's mommy called louder and closer. Anna shouted back and then begged Toad to let go of her.

"Christian says come with him now!"

He picked her up and bounded through the rain toward the river. Anna screamed the whole way, but Toad was focused on how he'd introduce her to Mother Isobel and explain why he'd brought her to the cliff. He reached the river, dove deep, and sped underwater for several minutes before rising. The storm was raging, the river swift. Anna had fallen asleep and he shifted her into his other arm to make sure not to wake her. Then he submerged again and did not rise until he reached the cliff face.

There was a light blazing from the top and Toad hurried, slinging Anna over his right shoulder before leaping from crag to crag as he made his climb.

"Toad can't wait for you to meet Mother Isobel. You can live with her and Toad and be happy."

He jumped an expanse, misjudged the effort needed with Anna's added weight, and had to dagger his fingernails into the slippery rock to keep from falling. It was scary, but Anna stayed very quiet and brave as he pulled them up to the next shelf of rocks.

Toad reached the top where Mother Isobel stood waiting, her thin gray hair clinging to her cheeks like strings of decaying moss. It had been so long since he saw her that Toad could not believe he'd forgotten her beauty. She stared at him as he approached.

"Where is my bread, son Toad?"

Toad tried to explain everything that had happened, about the muskrat family, the boats, the boy's finger, and how he'd put the summoning song into his belly. Mother Isobel's face somehow became thinner as she listened, but he kept going.

"And this is Anna and Toad is Christian now and—"

A slap to the face knocked him over and left him cowering on his right side with Anna clutched in an awkward embrace.

"What did thou say, son Toad?"

"Toad is Christian now."

Her wrath was unlike anything Toad could imagine. No streak of lightning, no roar of thunder could be fiercer. "False son thou art! Christian? False god for a false son!"

Toad felt the time of stone overtaking his feet and legs. It claimed mastery over all of him in seconds and he was locked in place but still allowed to see, think, hear, and feel. The rain made an awful pounding on his granite head. Mother Isobel ripped Anna from his frozen arms and placed her on the ground before him. She knelt on the other side with her dagger and bent her nose to Anna's neck. She sniffed along the length of Anna's body before pulling back.

"Not so stale as thy age would attest," she said. "And I hunger so."

Toad watched Mother Isobel begin to slice her bread.

# Chapter Twenty-Three
## January – September 1826

Nightcamp heard unceasing motion surrounding him, a swarming movement that echoed down from the darkness overhead. Sometimes it followed him into his dreams, forcing him to gallop away from swarms of a million chasing bees. He could never outrun them, and as they attacked, he whinnied in agony only to wake to the merciless sting of the riding crop.

*"Ah, beast, another day, another beating."*

Was it day? He'd come to calculate the passage of time according to a calendar of thrashings, seven days a week, for the industrious Vines did not honor any Sabbath when it came to inflicting torment on Nightcamp. After the beatings, Vines would stumble back, gasping, sweating, and content. Nightcamp, his head tethered to the floor with no slack, could only track him with one eye as he paced and recovered himself.

He always dressed in the same clothes he wore the night they met, and even in the darkness and with one eye, Nightcamp could see they were becoming ragged, held together less by thread than the fabric's grime. He stank so much he'd ceased to have any recognizable odor at all. His unwashed hair had grown past his shoulders, and the unkempt mess of his beard almost kept pace at his throat. After his breathing slowed, he went through the same pantomime each day of reaching into a pocket that didn't exist and pulling out a watch likewise devoid of substance. He'd shake his head and say, "I must get an assistant, beast. I truly must. While I love my citizens and work hard to make life good for them, New Vineland has become too much for one man to administer. Here it is almost nine in the morning and I'm wasting it with you. Farewell, beast. I'm sure one of the stable hands will remember to feed you."

Then he'd walk off into the darkness.

Nightcamp found focusing on the sounds of the motion helped blunt the pain of the crop and exercised his mind in the tedious waking hours he spent tied and immobilized. His ears twitched, capturing every *click* and *clack*, each *pitter* and *patter*. At first, and for many months afterward—years even—he credited the commotion to the throngs of workmen building New Vineland day and night. But by now those carpenters and masons should have moved far enough away to go unheard. Evan Vines spoke of his thriving city, its expanding borders, and its excellent new construction. Why, then, did the only activity Nightcamp hear come from overhead?

One day—Nightcamp could not even guess the month or year—Evan Vines came in the company of a creature he had trouble recognizing as human. He stood off to the side as Vines inflicted his usual beating but remained within Nightcamp's vision. His presence proved a welcome relief because it gave Nightcamp something new to focus on against the cuts of the crop. He was a man without edges, an eroded figure that reminded Nightcamp of three small boulders stacked atop each other, the way children made snowmen. He was not snow, however, nor was he quite stone. But no one could call him flesh.

As the blows continued, Nightcamp thought he looked like so many of the failed bargainers after Mistress Isobel set about carving them. Every artisan has a recognizable style, and hers did not favor angles or sharp edges. Was there something familiar about the man? Nightcamp thought there might be if only he could lift his head and look at him with both eyes, with a stare not glazed by waves of pain.

The beating did not last as long as usual, however, and when Vines threw the crop down, he took great pains to check the condition of his clothes. They were no better than before, but he said, "What say you, beast? Am I not looking like a prince today? Wormwood, what are your thoughts?"

"More than a prince," the other man said. "A true king."

*Wormwood*, Nightcamp thought, searching his memory for the name.

Vines laughed and let his fingers sweep along the length of his dingy woolen jacket. "I will never wear anything but satin again. And the cut is excellent."

"Most excellent," Wormwood said.

He continued to preen in front of Nightcamp's left eye. He touched his filthy hair and said, "The high and mighty lords of Europe used to wear these for their portraits. It's called a peruke. This is modeled on one worn by Louis XIV. The Sun King, they called him. That's what they'll be calling me all across America before too long. Therefore, why not dress the part, eh beast? Wormwood, bring the saddle."

Nightcamp strained to see the other man shuffle into the darkness. He did return with a saddle, the same one Nightcamp had worn on the morning he bore Evan Vines into his new land. Vines, however, spoke like it was something new.

"Leopard skin," he said, stroking it. "They say George Washington used to ride around New York in a saddle like this after he became President. Good enough for him, good enough for me. *Too* good for the likes of you, beast, but since you're carrying royalty, the indulgence must be allowed. Ready my mount, Wormwood. But first—"

He picked up the crop and delivered five sharp strikes atop Nightcamp's back. Nightcamp felt blood trickle from the cuts as the saddle was settled into place atop the fresh wounds. His back legs came close to buckling.

"Jesus Christ hasn't got anything on you, beast. But that goes for just about everything that ever walked on Earth. The mangiest dog in Philadelphia suffered more than Christ ever did. Any dog's death is about all the world deserves for its redemption. Meanwhile, your death wouldn't redeem a fly's sins after all your black deeds—like hauling babies up cliffs to give to a witch."

Vines tossed the crop aside again as Wormwood finished securing the saddle. He climbed up and then ordered the tether released. Nightcamp lifted his head for the first time in longer than he could estimate. His neck was stiff, the muscles weak. He didn't think he could raise his head until Vines jerked on the reins and snapped his head up and straight.

"March, beast. It's time for the people of New Vineland to see their king as they've never seen him before."

Nightcamp had no clear direction to go in the surrounding darkness so he just trotted straight ahead, his legs cramped and likewise atrophied from his prolonged bondage. He thought he must be the only thing in the world that had ever experienced being turned to stone without suffering the actual transformation. Memories of past glories, recollections of the strength he once possessed compared to the staggering gait of the moment, struck him with the same viciousness as Vines's crop and cut even deeper. As he passed further into the darkness, he realized he did not want to be seen by anyone. The humiliation of his withered and starved body exceeded any physical pain Vines could inflict. He tried to turn around. Vines did not seem to notice. How could either of them see in the strange, pure darkness they passed through?

Suddenly, the darkness was replaced by bright of day. Nightcamp almost reared in reaction to the sunlight, but his hind legs wobbled too much to support him. A sharp tug on his bit told him to stop and wait.

"Magnificent, isn't it, beast? The witch has been just as good as her word. Remember all those acres of trees I had you clear? Look at what's risen in just a few weeks!"

*A few weeks*, Nightcamp thought. He knew that could not be right, no matter how much he might wish it. It was true he'd lost all sense of time now, but he hadn't lost it the moment his head was tied down in the darkness. His torment had lasted *years* rather than weeks. He could not doubt it.

Vines jerked on the reins again and Nightcamp looked from left to right, still struggling with the sunlight. At first, he perceived only splotches of color that obscured the structures, the marketplace, the bustling crowds, and whatever else his rider wanted to boast. But as his vision adjusted, he realized he saw none of these things. They *were* standing on the land he'd cleared, looking down toward the river about half a mile in the distance, but there were no structures, no marketplace, no crowds.

Evan Vines was directing him through a field of statues. Vines talked to all of them. Sometimes he leaned over and put one hand atop a statue and said, "Oh, there's no need to thank me! Your loyalty and your happiness are what I treasure most. I'm glad you've come to New Vineland. Isn't it everything you were promised? Of course, it is. Yes, I must agree with you, sir, for it is *far more* than you were promised and far more than you ever dreamed possible!"

His words and his laughter rang out across the vast field of statues. Nightcamp couldn't begin to calculate how many there were, carved statues of men, women, and children. How had they come to be here? Why did Vines think he was interacting with them? What was Vines seeing and hearing? Nightcamp saw no evidence of a single building. There were no cobblestone streets under his hooves.

Vines pulled on the reins and Nightcamp stopped beside one particular statue of a man. Evan Vines greeted it with a hearty laugh and touched it on the shoulder.

"King Evan! Yes, I do like the sound of that. Bow if you wish, but there's no need for it. This is America, after all, but the gesture is much appreciated."

He pivoted Nightcamp to a statue of a young woman and leaned over to kiss her frozen, outstretched hand.

"I'm *pleased* to hear you like your house. I've decreed that all houses should be built to the exact specifications of the residents."

He made Nightcamp step over to the statue of a boy whose mouth was wide open as if to scream.

"Everything you need, everything you want. Dry your eyes, child, you're under my protection now. There is only happiness in New Vineland!"

Vines spurred Nightcamp forward again. Nightcamp found he was gaining strength the longer he was outside like a flower soaking up the sunlight. His trot stabilized.

"Do you hear them, beast? 'Long live King Evan!' I always thought there was something enormous inside of me, that I had a destiny greater than that of other men. Who would have thought such a thing of a ragged man struggling by the side of the road in a thunderstorm? But, here I am."

Vines's delusion fascinated Nightcamp as his mind began to recover its old alertness. Mistress Isobel had been casting her spell of stone long before Nightcamp knew her, and he could only imagine how many statues she had to her credit. Based on their clothes, these were all contemporary people. How had Mistress Isobel managed to turn so many to stone? What had any of them done to merit such fate? Where had they come from?

Some of these questions were answered the moment Evan Vines grew tired of the adulation of his subjects and turned Nightcamp around the way they'd come. He now saw the one building on the whole plain, a structure as breathtaking as it was sinister. The tower of rock went straight up and seemed to sway and distort in his vision, as if waves of heat warped the air around it. As they closed on it, he saw that the strange throbbing came from the *literal* movement of creatures crawling up and down the length of the tower. They looked like men on their hands and knees making straight vertical climbs and descents with the ease of a baby crawling across a nursery floor. He thought of ants moving about their hill and bees swarming across their hive.

*They're what I've been hearing all this time,* he thought. But there was another sound present, a melody so familiar, so ingrained in him from his long service to Mistress Isobel that he hadn't noticed it at all. The witch's summoning song suffused the tower, surging around it like an almost physical presence, an aura of sound. It seemed to unite the creatures into one chorus, one voice that projected the summoning song out across the sky.

Nightcamp could only marvel at its power even as he considered the dark implications. Mistress Isobel was adept at sending her song across a considerable distance to reach the ears of a single person. In this regard, she was like a fisherman casting a solitary line.

Perhaps she'd discovered the advantages of using a net?

When they got within twenty yards of the tower, the entities moving up and down were close enough for Nightcamp to see in detail. He thought at once of his time in Europe, carrying Mistress Isobel through cold and miserable nights, stopping before ancient cathedrals to peer up at the gargoyles. She spoke of these stone grotesques with great admiration and said they inspired her own carvings.

It was clear she had never forgotten that inspiration.

As they reached the great opening at the base of the tower, with nothing but darkness within, Wormwood stepped into view. His gaze was fixed on Evan Vines with practiced reverence as he dismounted and surrendered the reins.

"My subjects have wearied me. I'm going up to my room to sleep away the afternoon. Take the beast back to the stable and make sure his head is tied down tight."

"Of course, sir," Wormwood said.

Vines entered the tower. Wormwood and Nightcamp watched him disappear into the dark. Then Wormwood turned to him and said, "Do you remember me?"

# Chapter Twenty-Four

"Come now," Wormwood said, his smile as soft and rounded as the rest of him. "Was it so many decades ago when we met in the Bavarian city of–"

*Augsburg*, Nightcamp thought, pacing back a few feet. *1740*. Now that he saw Wormwood straight on and in full, Nightcamp did recognize him despite the changes Mistress Isobel had inflicted.

He'd been a bookkeeper, and at the time, Nightcamp thought him among the most practical of men seeking the witch's bargain. He did not resort to murder or kidnapping to bring Mistress Isobel her bread. He'd solved the problem by going to an orphanage posing as a charitable man. Though his clothes were not the best, he demonstrated his affluence by pointing to his stallion, for only a wealthy man could own such a steed. Even now, Nightcamp remembered the fawning remarks of the priests and nuns as he stood there pretending to be aloof. Wormwood was brought inside and returned not fifteen minutes later with an infant so small and squalling Nightcamp could well believe it was born that very morning.

It was the only successful bargain he'd ever witnessed. Mistress Isobel had her bread, the man his wish. Perhaps fear kept him wishing on the scale he wanted, or perhaps his vision expanded after his first taste of wealth. A year later, he answered Mistress Isobel's summoning song again, and Nightcamp returned to him. Again, he rode to the same orphanage. This time, however, his ploy did not work. The priests remembered Wormwood. It seemed there were now rumors about him, certain suspicions. Where was the child he adopted the year before? Where was he baptized? What was he christened? They looked at Nightcamp and saw evidence of the demonic, for the horse seemed supernatural in its bearing (and this too pleased Nightcamp to hear). Not anticipating this response and out of time, Wormwood rode in stoic silence to Mistress Isobel, perhaps practicing for an eternity in stone.

But not quite an eternity, after all it seemed.

"By now, you've guessed at what's happening here," Wormwood said. "Your eyes see the truth just as *his* eyes see the lies. But even if you were blind, you'd still hear the tower's song and know what it is. The witch summons far and wide. There are more people like me—like *us*—than a less cynical man would imagine. They hear the song. I suppose no one hears it in quite the same way, but they come regardless, and when they arrive, a quick bargain is struck in their minds. Maybe they think they're trading old clothes for new, or a grain of wheat for a loaf of bread. The bargain is struck, and they become hers, part of her ever-expanding garden of statues.

"I can tell you what they're experiencing if you never experienced the time of stone for yourself. Your eyes and ears are granite but you can see and hear with them. Your brain is a calcified block, but you have consciousness. You think you're crying, you're sure you must be, but of course, your stone face bears no trace of wetness. The failure to breathe leaves you lost in a permanent state of suffocation. You never lose the urge to move your arms and legs, and the panic of paralysis never ebbs as you stare at whatever's in front of you and comprehend the glacial pace of time."

Wormwood led Nightcamp back into the tower's stable. He found himself in the same dim room. The hook in the ground waited for him, along with the unmerciful tether that would tie his head down once more. He shuddered to submit himself to it again, though he could not say it was worse than how Wormwood described the time of stone.

Wormwood knelt by the hook, picked up the end of the line, and looked up at Nightcamp.

"For the longest time, I blamed you for my predicament. I fantasized about never answering the song and never meeting you in the first place. Then I fantasized about killing you. I didn't even know if you had a choice in the matter or understood anything that was going on. It seemed that you did."

Wormwood paused, staring at the hook. His dull, almost non-existent shoulders shook. Then he snapped a look back into Nightcamp's eyes.

"*Did you?*"

Nightcamp thought of a hundred lies and denials. Saw himself shaking his head with such ferocity Wormwood would have to believe him and maybe show mercy. Why not lie? Either way, he wasn't responsible for Wormwood's actions, any more than he was responsible for any deed done by Mistress Isobel's bargainers.

*I was only one of her tools*, he thought.

He heard the sound of motion coming from all around him. He raised his gaze up into the darkness of the hollow tower.

*Just a tool.*

Nightcamp lowered his head and snorted out a reluctant breath. Then he nodded. Wormwood winced in response. Nightcamp thought he'd seize the end of the bridle and jerk his head down at once, eager for immediate vengeance. Instead, he dropped the tether and stood up.

"Maybe it's not the mind but the soul that goes on thinking in that prison of rock," he said. "If you spend decades in stone with nothing but your thoughts for company, and you can't accept the reality of your own sins, then you were soulless to begin with. I quit blaming you long ago. I know my sins," he said. "I've spent decades in stone with only my thoughts for company. I know the crime I committed, and the crime I tried to commit. Here I stand, part flesh again, tasked by the witch with special duties because I showed unique competence in my first bargain with her. It seemed salvation to me at first, but now, I find little distinction between salvation and further damnation. But I wish to make one small act of atonement, and here it is. *Go.*"

He pointed into the darkness.

"Leave New Vineland. Run. Escape. With your speed, you'll be far from even the witch's reach before sunset."

Nightcamp moved forward two paces and stopped to consider what Wormwood had said. Just then there seemed a very clear separation between salvation and damnation. Salvation was running from the tower and the stone gardens of the damned and finding the vast plains that existed in his dreams. Damnation was the tether and beatings from Evan Vines. But this was a distinction of the flesh rather than the soul, and if he left this place without trying to thwart it, then his damnation would be more profound than any cut a riding crop could inflict.

*Atonement,* Nightcamp thought. Men who bargained with Mistress Isobel seldom had the word in their vocabulary, but Wormwood had acquired it. He tried to tally all his complicities and couldn't reach a true number. It didn't matter. Their sum was New Vineland, be it real or illusion.

He walked over to the tether hook, stared deep into Wormwood's eyes, and lowered his head.

# Chapter Twenty-Five

## October 1820

The snow came, piling high on top of the cliff. Toad could almost feel the icy crush of its weight as foot after foot packed over him. In those long weeks of white-blue blindness, he learned his memories could be like a river, and he swam there with the muskrat family and then with Anna, teaching her how to hold her breath until she didn't need to surface at all. Moments like this became so real to him, that he had trouble remembering they did not happen. Maybe memories were also like parts of his body, meant to be stretched and reshaped into new forms. Were the new events less real? Toad could not see why they would be, so he focused on stretching even the stretched memories into new occurrences. Anna's skin grew pale, her hair fell away, and her face became as round as his. Hand in hand, they swam south down the length of the river and this time, because he was not alone, he did not fear the sea.

He and Anna were still swimming far from any land or boat when Toad began to see glimpses of the world beyond his dreams. The season had changed and the snow began to melt. He did not feel it warming his body, but he did hear the soft flow of water running off the cliff face to swell the river. The snow seeped away and little things were revealed, like tattered pieces of Anna's blue dress and the decaying remains of her shoes. These were things he'd forgotten and did not want to remember.

There was no trace of Anna herself, but Toad knew this was because she had gone to swim in the ocean with him. So why did he feel she was missing?

He decided it must be because Anna had become a very fast swimmer, and it was easy to play hide and seek in the ocean.

Atop the cliff, the rains came, but most of the time the days were long and sunny. Then, they started growing shorter.

One cloudy morning, two bare feet appeared before him, the skin yellow and callused, the toenails broken and crooked. He heard Mother Isobel say, "Because thou are my son, I offer thee an unearned reprieve. But first, I put to thee one question. Do thou still wish to be Christian?"

Toad did not understand Mother Isobel's hatred for Anna's brother, but his immediate answer sprang to his mind if not his lips.

*No! Toad is Toad and not Christian!*

Mother Isobel laughed and began her chant. Being released from the time of stone must have been a lot like thawing out from snow. His fingers and toes began to flex, his lungs began to fill. When the last trace of hardness disappeared, Toad sprang straight up. He jumped so high he thought he might touch the sun. He landed as a squatting pile of white flesh and smiled at Mother Isobel.

She put her hand atop his head and caressed it.

"Son Toad, my hunger is hard upon me. Will thou bring thy mother her bread again?"

Toad nodded so much that ripples went down his skin.

"Toad will do it right this time and get the freshest bread."

Mother Isobel rewarded him with a pat on the head. "Son Toad, thou have ushered in many discoveries for me. Long have I taken my bread fresh, believing it served me best. Yet my last meal sustained me better than all others. Thou brought bread that looked stale but contained much freshness within. This is the bread I crave again, and I think only son Toad can find it."

They stood on the edge of the cliff and looked across the river. Toad remembered the tower. It looked taller now, and he remembered something else. There were many things he needed to ask Mother Isobel but he couldn't recall them all at once.

"Is it time for Toad to kill his father?"

Mother Isobel clapped her hands together once. "My dutiful, respectful son! That pleasure will come years hence. Attend to the task at hand. Bring Mother Isobel her bread, and if it pleases me, thou shall return to thy kingdom."

"Toad is King of the River!" he shouted, bounding over the side of the cliff. Halfway down, however, he remembered something even more important than killing his father. *Where was Anna outside of his head? Was she with Mother Isobel still? When could he see her?*

By pure instinct, he angled and changed the shape of his body until the wind gusted him hard against the rocks. He launched into a series of springs and jumps that took him back to the top in a few seconds. Mother Isobel was still standing there when he landed at her feet, and she cocked her head when she saw him.

"Son Toad?"

"Toad is ready to get Mother Isobel's bread," he said, "but Toad has another question."

He asked it.

The look on Mother Isobel's face was one he'd never seen before. She did not seem angry with him or wrathful. Nor did she seem amused. He waited in silence for her answer.

"Much wisdom Toad still needs to acquire."

"Anna was helping Toad."

"Anna has helped Toad by helping Mother Isobel," she said.

"Can Toad see Anna?"

"No," Mother Isobel said. "Never again."

Toad listened to this and tried to understand. All he thought about was Anna sitting by the tombstone of Christian. The tombstone was there because she would never see Christian again. He stared at Mother Isobel with his large black eyes until her thin lips turned down in impatience.

"Conditions for thy obedience, have thee?"

"No, Mother Isobel," he said. "But Toad remembers Anna. And Toad...Toad...Toad wants Anna to be remembered."

Toad began to describe Christian's tombstone and what it meant, as he felt sure she'd never encountered such a thing. Her expression was sour at first, but it softened as he went on, and by the end, she stroked his right cheek and no longer looked like she'd just tasted something awful.

"Thy heart is gold and full of faults thou must discover through wisdom. Wisdom, son Toad, is the alchemy that turns gold to lead. So it will be for thee. Make a circle of your arms."

Toad did, locking his webbed fingers together as best he could.

"Mark thou the width of this circle, and gather up rocks into a pile as wide."

Toad moved over the ground on his knees, sweeping his hands to bring the loose rocks toward his chest. The sharper stones cut his rubbery skin and soon the rocks themselves were black and shiny with his blood. Toad ignored this and smiled up at Mother Isobel when he thought his gathering was done.

Mother Isobel extended her hand and began to chant. The rock pile became scorching hot in his embrace but he did not let go. A solid mass began to form. Toad's excitement leapt without bounds when he saw its shape was identical to Christian's except in color. The new tombstone was still black with Toad's own blood.

When the tombstone cooled, Toad let go of it and jumped back. His skin was blistered along his stomach and chest, but he didn't care. The tombstone stood upright without any support and Mother Isobel seemed quite pleased with the result. She pointed her right index finger at the tombstone and slashed the air. Each slash made a corresponding line on the rock.

## ANNA

Toad couldn't read the symbols, but he knew the meaning at once. He found himself under the spell of each line. This was *her* name and therefore Anna herself. He hugged the tombstone the way Anna had hugged Christian's and he went on hugging it until all at once the tombstone disappeared. He looked up to see the clouds had moved, bathing the top of the cliff in sunlight. Toad sprang back.

"Stealth runs through thy veins, son Toad. Thy blood is in the stone, and thy blood flees from sunlight, but the tombstone is there."

Toad thought for a moment, looking at the emptiness. He reached into the space and felt the rock. Mother Isobel was right. The tombstone remained, even though he couldn't see it. In his mind, he heard Anna calling to him and laughing.

*It's hide and seek, Toad! Come and find me!*

"Hide and seek! Toad will find Anna!"

"What?" Mother Isobel said.

But Toad could only hear Anna calling to him. He leapt to the edge of the cliff and surveyed the world, looking up and down the river and at the vast stretches of trees everywhere.

*Come find me, Toad! Hide and seek!*

His whole body shook with joy and he put his palms over his mouth as he laughed. He jumped headlong off the cliff, speeding into the water below. When he landed, the water filled his dry places, smoothing the cracks in his skin and making him feel whole. He touched the bottom, then sprang to the surface and shouted, "All hail Toad, King of the River!"

*You won't find me, Toad! I'm hiding really good this time!*

He submerged and when he saw his first fish, he hungered as never before. Chasing downstream and then up, his mouth open wide, he used his tongue to snag it into his stomach. It was so good he forgot about everything else and went after bass, catfish, and crawdads.

The sky was much darker and the stars were out when he emerged again. He wasn't sure how far upstream he'd swum but there was a gathering of people on the shore. Several bright fires burned and cheerful singing enticed him to move closer.

*Oh where have you been, Billy Boy,*
*Billy Boy?*
*Oh where have you been, charming Billy?*
*I have been to seek a wife,*
*She's the joy of my life,*
*She's a young thing*
*And cannot leave her mother.*

The chorus of laughing and singing voices drew Toad further in. He flattened his body and floated near the shallowest edge; his head propped against the bank. He stretched his neck out and stared, his eyes stung by the firelight. He'd never seen so many people in one place and he knew at once Anna must be hiding among them. Little children chased each other, laughing and squealing. Some older boys and girls sat off to the side, eating and talking. But most of the adults were gathered around the largest fire, and they continued their songs even as the other fires began to die. They sang to thrilling sounds made by two men with instruments tucked under their chins. Toad did not see how anyone could resist the pull of their summoning song.

An old man got up, a little stooped and swaying. Everyone hushed in expectation. He made a half turn, looking at everyone and then out into the water. Toad thought he'd been spotted. The man's eyes were wet and his lips made a small smile. He began to sing in a voice much stronger than his appearance—

*There once was a toad*

*Who went down a long road*
*Talking to anyone who'd listen.*
*"I'm a Prince," said he,*
*And knew they'd all see*
*If only a girl would kiss him.*
*He hopped on a log,*
*But he was only a frog*
*And never a girl did bless him.*
*Now the toad got depressed*
*'Cause he didn't get kissed*
*And returned to the river alone.*
*"I'm a prince!" cried the toad*
*To the moss on the stones,*
*Then floated away on the waters.*
*So listen, you mothers,*
*Take heed, yon fathers,*
*Watch over your lovely young daughters.*
*'Cause the toad, he's still looking*
*Like a prince seeks a princess,*
*For a kiss and more kisses to follow!*

Toad's head moved to the music and the melody overtook him. He sprang up to join them and found himself standing in front of the gathering before he knew what he'd done. The singing stopped. Women clutched their children and, in some cases, stepped in front of them. Toad looked back and forth, confused as to why he'd revealed himself, his black eyes seeking any trace of the merriment present only moments ago.

The old singer, who was closest to Toad and lacked the speed to retreat like everyone else, said, "Who...*what* are you?"

"Anna?" Toad said. "Anna, Toad is here."

The only sound he heard was wood popping and breaking apart in the fire. Then someone screamed. He couldn't tell if it was a man or a woman, an adult or a child. Panic spread across the crowd. Toad called out for Anna again and reached out to touch a girl he thought might be her. It was hard to tell when everyone was running away, and Toad's anger surged.

"Toad wants everyone to stay!"

The summoning song came up from his stomach and struck the crowd all at once. He could almost see the sound shooting forward like a hundred little hands that grabbed onto ankles and wrists, elbows and necks. Once it had hold of a person, it tugged and they all turned back to face him.

Toad hopped up and down. He took one of the dropped instruments but it made a terrible noise for him. He summoned one of the musicians to take it from him.

"Toad wants to hear the music again."

The man began to play and Toad danced among the people, who stood blank and waiting. He circled back to the old singer and said, "Toad wants to hear the song about Toad again."

"Yes," the man said and sang. Toad listened from start to finish and had him sing it thirty more times until his voice was whittled down so much the words were indistinct. Toad's own interest grew just as strained the more he listened and caught the song's mistakes.

"Toad's not a prince. Toad is the King of the River. And Anna *did* kiss Toad, but now she's hiding and Toad knows she's here. Anna? Anna? And Toad was stone, not floating away. Anna?"

It was time to find her. He moved through the paralyzed townspeople, looking around and behind backs, calling out Anna's name as he went. There were many girls Anna's size and hair color but they were not Anna. It was hard to tell with so many different people standing around. As his frustration mounted, Toad used the summoning song to bring all the young girls into a cluster. He then stepped in front of each girl, looked her in the eyes, and said, "Anna?" One girl had a look of disgust bubbling out under her expression despite the fact she couldn't move or talk. Toad remembered the way Anna hugged and kissed him and knew *this* girl would never do that. She would never kiss Toad. She hated Toad. She was just like the girls in the old man's song.

He grabbed her right hand and brought her fingers against his three sharp teeth. Before he bit down, though, he seemed to hear Anna's pleading voice: "*Christian, oh Christian, please don't do it, even if she deserves it.*" Toad let the girl's hand drop back to her side and moved on.

"Anna? Where are you, Anna?"

He came to a girl who made him leap and somersault. She looked so much like Anna he couldn't believe it when Anna's voice didn't come from her mouth. But Anna was very good at hide and seek. She would change her hair and her voice if it kept Toad from finding her, and then she'd spring out at him and laugh. But Toad wasn't fooled.

"*Anna?*"

"Veronica," she said.

Toad repeated the word until he'd shaped the syllables to his liking. "Ver-anna-ka," he said. "Your name is Ver-anna-ka. Toad says say it."

The girl obeyed and Toad leapt in his happiness.

"Toad knew he'd find Anna again! Toad loves hide and seek!"

He roped his arms around Anna and lavished three big kisses on her cheek before he turned and carried her into the river.

# Chapter Twenty-Six

Toad sat off to the side watching Mother Isobel savor her bread until the sky began to brighten. Mother Isobel said little and ignored Toad's questions until she rose at last to deliver a summary judgment.

"Not as sweet as the last, but close. It is a strange matter and a discovery almost as valuable as any new insight into stone. Children elsewhere grow stale from quick experience but in this land, their innocence lasts far longer. Son Toad, thou acquired this bread with impressive haste and it did not disappoint me."

"Toad wants to do good."

"Toad has done very well. Thou have earned your kingdom back and the freedom to enjoy and grow wise in it until the time of hunger comes upon me again. I will return to my sacred work and study with renewed strength."

Toad nuzzled against Mother Isobel's robe and clutched her legs.

"Is there still more son Toad requires?"

Anna's voice told him to remember the tombstone.

Though he couldn't see it, Toad went near Anna's tombstone and started scooping the scattered stones into a second pile. Again, the sharp rocks cut his chest and stomach and his black blood coated the pile.

When he finished his gathering, he smiled and turned his black eyes up at Mother Isobel.

"Thou shall turn this place into a vast graveyard before all is done," she said, laughing. "Speak her name, son Toad."

"Anna," he said.

"Thou are sure of this?"

Toad nodded.

Mother Isobel began the chant. Once again, the rocks grew scorching hot and merged into the shape of a tombstone. She slashed the air with her right forefinger and letters appeared on the flat surface.

## ANNA

"Anna," Toad said, moving his fingers along the engraved letters. He smiled at Mother Isobel as the tombstone faded from view in the growing sunlight. As soon as it was gone, he heard Anna calling to him.

*I'm hiding again, Toad. I'll hide better than ever before. It will take you a very long time to find me this time!*

He turned and ran toward the cliff edge and dove, shouting, "Toad is coming! Toad is coming!" He sliced into the river, touched the bottom, and swam downstream, thinking of Anna. She kept talking to him in his head, teasing him.

*You're getting nearer...no, now you're getting further away. You'll never find me this time, Toad!*

But Anna was wrong. It took Toad only half a day to spot her. She wasn't even trying hard because he found her sitting by the river. Her hair was red but he knew it was Anna as soon as he jumped out of the river, grinning, shouting, "Toad is here! Toad is here!"

Anna screamed because she'd been found. She had a big dog resting next to her and it made a terrible noise and bit Toad's leg. His blood spurted into the dog's mouth and it backed off whimpering, gagging. Toad knew the dog would have bitten Anna too, but he fell on it and killed it while Anna stood screaming for help. Toad said, "Toad's sorry Toad scared you. Toad says be quiet now." He used the summoning song to quiet her.

"You were too easy to find this time, Anna! Next time hide better."

He snaked his arms around Anna's waist and plunged into the water with her. He didn't emerge until they reached the cliff face. Anna was asleep as he took her to the top.

"Mother Isobel? Mother Isobel, Toad is back."

He did not see her anywhere, but in the next instant, he felt her touch on his shoulder. Grinning, he laid Anna out on the ground and shook her.

"Anna knows Mother Isobel. Wake up, Anna. *Toad says wake up.*"

"Why have thou brought this girl here?"

"Mother Isobel knows Anna. Toad wants Mother Isobel to be her friend."

"Thy mother takes her bread only when she must. Take it away now."

He shook Anna again. She did not wake or make a sound and he sat back on his haunches and poked at her in frustration.

"Obey now, son Toad. Remember, I will summon thee when my time of hunger nears."

Mother Isobel turned and vanished. Toad tried to follow but he just walked through more air. He was alone with Anna. She must have been very tired, too tired to do anything but sleep.

But she couldn't sleep well on all those rocks.

"Toad knows where to go."

He slung Anna across his right shoulder and dove into the river. He swam with her along the riverbed, speeding past all the wonders they'd one day share together, like big catfish, the sunken logs, and the round tops of skeletons poking up here and there, smoother than any polished stone. He wasn't sure at first where he meant to go. Then he knew. The muskrat family would love Anna and she'd love them. He imagined them all playing hide and seek together. The muskrats would be very good at the game, but he and Anna would find them together, and then they'd laugh and do it all over again. Every day would go this way and he'd never leave until Mother Isobel called for her bread.

Toad veered off from the main river and moved into the still waters. There were a few mosquito eggs on the surface and he rose to eat them. Before he did, however, Toad realized Anna might never have tasted them for herself. He asked her. When she didn't answer, he forced her mouth open and maneuvered the eggs inside. Toad thought he saw her smile and that made him grin.

"Toad knows you'll like it here. Toad wants you to meet his friends."

They drifted to the riverbank. The muskrat hole was half demolished and almost unrecognizable. Toad let go of Anna and thrust his arm deep inside, stretching and twisting and patting along the way. His fingertips swept across something sharp and he knew he'd found the nest. He grabbed what he could and pulled back.

"See, Anna, this is Toad's friend," he said, turning. Anna had floated several feet away from him and he bounded over to her and pulled her face from the water.

"See Anna, this is Father Muskrat."

The muskrat looked different than before. He saw its bones, and its eyes were dried, sunken little spots. Toad liked the scent it gave off better than ever, and he brought Anna onto the shore, and they all lay on the ground. The falling leaves were orange and gold and red and when they landed on him his skin took on their patterns. This made him laugh. He got up to gather the leaves into large piles. He dove into them and exploded out of them time and again before remembering Anna and the muskrat. Neither wanted to play with him so he positioned them beside each other, scooped up even more leaves, and buried himself with them.

"This will be Toad's kingdom on land," he said in the darkness of the leaves. He liked the tickle they made on his skin. He began to feel tired too and he reached across Anna's body to pet the muskrat. Then he curled himself close to Anna and rested his head next to hers.

"Toad wants Anna to always be with him. King of the River, Queen of the River, and Prince Muskrat."

He snuggled deeper into the leaves; certain he could never know greater happiness and soon fell asleep.

# Chapter Twenty-Seven

## November 1826

Wormwood came every morning with Evan Vines and stood off to the side during Nightcamp's thrashing, saying nothing unless Vines addressed him with a hearty question like, "That was a very good blow, wasn't it, Wormwood?" Then Wormwood would say, "The best I ever saw given" or some other flattery. Despite Vines's emaciated appearance, Nightcamp thought he struck harder than before, and the whippings were becoming a little longer. Once his sadism was sated, Vines always threw the crop aside and walked off into the darkness, saying he'd worked up his appetite and needed breakfast. Wormwood followed him, never lapsing from the role of dedicated servant, but always returning as soon as he could.

When Wormwood came back one particular day, he said, "Hello, old martyr," and untethered him. "*His Majesty* is sound asleep if you'd like to stretch your legs with a run. I know it's been a long while. When you return, I'll have fresh hay and water—and then we must talk."

This comment piqued his interest a considerable degree as he left the tower and stood still a moment, soaking up the sunlight, his black coat even glossier where the blood hadn't dried. This was just the fourth excursion he'd been able to make since his alliance with Wormwood began a few months ago. Each time outside reinforced the bleak and inexorable expansion of the stone gardens. Evan Vines might think New Vineland was only a few months old at this point, but Wormwood had told Nightcamp the truth—it was 1826. He'd surrendered *eight years* of his life to darkness and daily beatings. Despite his anger, Nightcamp told himself not to fret over the wasted time, knowing he'd outlived many generations of horses. He should have become dust so long ago that even another eight years of torment would not balance out the scales of his dark privilege.

He galloped north first, reaching the place he and Wormwood had gone together on his second outing away from the tower.

"I must show you a secret," Wormwood said. "Something you perhaps did not see or understand during your glorified fantasy tour with Evan Vines."

Wormwood had directed him to the very outskirts of the field of statues. There, they beheld a fascinating and sinister activity. Creatures that seemed equal parts stone and flesh roamed among the statues in pairs, choosing one in apparent randomness and toppling it. Then they fell upon their victim, biting and gnawing at its face and extremities. Nightcamp had seen Mistress Isobel work with her carving dagger many times, and these monsters achieved the same dire results with their mouths—and in much shorter order. They were small, no larger than a five-year-old child, with rounded features much like Wormwood himself. It seemed Mistress Isobel had always preferred spheres to boxes, arcs to angles. Nightcamp could tell that when Wormwood watched them, he saw echoes of himself, a reflection of his own fate and transformation. But the carving he'd endured was nothing compared to what Nightcamp found in these wild amalgamations of flesh and stone. Despite their size, they *had* been adults once. Mistress Isobel had cleaved away everything below their kneecaps and shaped their thighs into pegs. Their fingers had been whittled to sharp points of rock. Their mouths were widened, and their jaws seemed mitered into their skulls to maximize the radius of their bites.

"These are her originals, I think," Wormwood had said. "How long the witch has been turning people to stone is anyone's guess. I remember being placed in one of her endless cold corridors where she had her trophies lined up to stare at each other and dwell on our private miseries. True hell was when she came to make a daily selection for a new carving project. A statue would be taken away and returned unrecognizable. Even if the pain couldn't be felt, to know you're being mutilated under her dagger, shaped and reshaped at her pleasure...*for* her pleasure. But it seems her plans were always larger. There may be more people turned to stone here in one day than she would accomplish in years. Now she has new uses for all of us. Some, like me, serve as minders, custodians of the illusion. But these others you see are harvesters—no other term will do. They harvest the statues like fields of wheat. Now watch what happens when they finish."

Nightcamp would never forget his shock as the harvesters pulled back from their work. The statue had been chewed and scratched into one of the gargoyles he'd noticed when Vines brought him back to the tower. Its eyes opened, showing a dim red light inside the sockets. The gargoyle got to its feet and tilted its head back, its mouth open wide as if to gulp the wind. A crude noise came from it at first, almost like a hacking cough. The sound became more refined and recognizable. Nightcamp looked at Wormwood, who nodded in confirmation. The new gargoyle was singing Mistress Isobel's summoning song.

It turned and headed south toward the tower with Wormwood and Nightcamp walking behind it. Neither the gargoyle nor the harvesters paid them any notice. The gargoyle reached the tower and began climbing.

"It won't stop until it reaches the top," Wormwood said, and Nightcamp verified it with his superior vision. The gargoyle and many others like it scaled the tower like bees returning nectar to the hive, and when they reached the apex, they stacked themselves one on top of another like seamless bricks, further stretching a pinnacle that was beginning to exceed the wildest dreams of Babel. The summoning song that infused the tower grew just a little stronger.

"Not just a tower, but a chorus," Wormwood said. "Ever-growing, pushing the summoning song further and further out from the center. Who knows how many ears it reaches now? Who can say how many hearts it possesses? But the proof is here, isn't it?"

*Yes*, Nightcamp thought, surveying the same area again on this new day. *The proof is stronger than ever.*

The harvesters still went about their ceaseless task, and they had more statues to choose from than before. Nightcamp need only to gallop east to the river, as he did now, to see their source. Several boats and rafts were approaching the stone pillars and platform that constituted New Vineland's docks. Much like the tower, the docks were some zooid creature comprised of gargoyles so enmeshed as to appear seamless. Wormwood had assured him no one saw the docks as anything other than a series of wooden piers. Sometimes the arriving boats never reached them in the first place. Anyone wholly under the spell of the summoning song would jump out several feet from the bank and wade to land. It wasn't unusual for a boat's entire complement to abandon ship, never looking back as the current took their empty transport downriver to the waiting sea. Boats that did dock, only to lose their passengers and crews, were destroyed later to clear space for the next arrival.

Nightcamp stopped to watch a group of disembarking people hurry and weave their way through the fields of statues, heading for the tower and the bargain that awaited them inside. He had little sympathy. Whatever awful defect of character allowed them to hear the song in the first place did not deserve to be pitied. But the magnitude and the mechanics of the illusion continued to fascinate him and part of him wished he could experience it through their eyes.

At last, having stretched his legs enough for now, Nightcamp returned to Wormwood and found the water and hay ready. He nourished himself as Wormwood tended to his latest cuts. For the first few minutes Wormwood said nothing as he worked, and Nightcamp felt a heaviness in the air. He looked back at Wormwood and waited.

Wormwood responded with a nervous laugh. "I did promise you information, didn't I?"

The horse whinnied.

"The witch freed me from stone for a specific purpose. I was to be Evan Vines's minder, steering him through the illusion. Illusions can be very fragile things, it seems. Their strength depends on one's imagination and willingness to believe it. In this case, the illusion is centered entirely on Vines, and he sends it out in much the same way the tower sends forth the summoning song. The witch could not have picked a better pole to hoist the flag of her scheme than Vines's own sense of greatness. But even he might stumble out of the fantasy without physical touchstones to anchor him to it. Do you understand?"

Nightcamp nodded.

"You and I *are* those touchstones. I, his assistant and lackey; you, the outlet for his rage. But over time, I've found my responsibilities expanding. It was inevitable people would see the illusion as they passed by and come exploring, even though they didn't hear the witch's summoning song. Killing them would not serve New Vineland's purpose. But if they could be lured into the store and tricked into making a bargain, then they could be added to the tally of the witch's stone servants. All that was required were a few more minders such as myself, physical participants positioned throughout the illusion to cajole and steer them into making the desired decision. I can put forward 100 cases and demonstrate success in 95 of them. In another four of them, the people sensed something was very wrong and left as soon as possible, never looking back. That of course leaves one exception—and as of now there *has* been but one, a man who'll neither bargain nor leave. Instead, he stays and *explores*. Do you understand why this is a problem? How I wish you could talk to me. I know your mind outclasses mine!"

Nightcamp began to walk back and forth. He could see frustration and helplessness building in Wormwood.

*He's right. I can't just stand here and neigh, snort and stomp the ground and call it speech. Mistress Isobel increased my intelligence, but what does it matter if I never use it?*

He stopped to lower his gaze, remembering all of the bargainers who talked to him, including Wormwood himself. New Vineland might not exist if, somehow, he'd managed to *talk back*.

"Oh, it's of no use, I know," Wormwood said. "I shouldn't bring up matters we can't change."

Nightcamp reared and Wormwood fell down in surprise. The horse stood over him and fixed his stare hard into the man's eyes. Wormwood brought a trembling hand to his left temple.

"What is this? What do I hear?"

Nightcamp's thoughts focused on the summoning song. Mistress Isobel had never taught him how to cast it, but the melody was saturated in his bones. He and Wormwood had this in common. Might it be a medium between them as it was between Mistress Isobel and her bargainers?

Wormwood squinted. His lips moved, muttering sounds. Nightcamp heard his own thoughts coming from Wormwood's lips. He rolled up on his stubby, rounded legs, still touching his temple.

"You do understand. Yes. You and I—physical touchstones in a phantasmagoria. But if you add a third physicality, uncontrolled, opposing the illusion, working against it—"

Wormwood winced. Nightcamp saw and even felt his agony and ended the song's connection. Wormwood gasped and hunched forward, recovering himself.

"The man in question is young. English. A wanderer searching for the most elusive thing of all—himself. Such men are primed to hear the summoning song, but he is deaf to it. His heart must be very pure indeed. His first minder was unable to corrupt him and decided it was best to kill him. A wise decision for anyone determined to see New Vineland succeed. But–that's not either of us. Last month, I warned the Englishman to leave or face horrific consequences. Still, he refused."

Nightcamp locked gazes with Wormwood again.

*Bring him here*

*Let us know*

*His state of mind*

*His state of soul*

"I'm not sure he'd come...unless I promised him Evan Vines. But it must be done where there's no possibility of the two of them encountering each other. The British man's aggressive inquiries might destroy the illusion altogether. Perhaps that's just what needs to be done, but what would happen afterward? I'd rather proceed with caution."

Nightcamp agreed.

More than a week passed when he saw Wormwood only in the company of Evan Vines, or in brief solitary visits that afforded no updates. Nightcamp started to believe this Englishman must have left New Vineland after all. Then came the day, many hours following the morning thrashing, when he heard Wormwood approach.

"Just a moment, Mr. Goodman."

The voice that answered sounded young and a little quarrelsome. "Outside the stable? Why would Mr. Vines wish to meet here? This better not be a trick, Wormwood."

"I assure you it isn't. Just a little patience."

Wormwood then appeared from the darkness. "I've brought him," he said, releasing Nightcamp's tether. "His name is Goodman. Vines I know is sleeping, but I think we should make this meeting quick."

Nightcamp snorted.

Wormwood disappeared. Moments later he returned with a tall, thin man who looked puzzled and annoyed in equal parts. But his expression changed the moment he saw Nightcamp's cuts, and he stepped over to him.

"What sort of monster did this? Is there nothing we can do?"

"Evan Vines did this."

"Where is the scoundrel?"

"Not here, I'm afraid."

Nightcamp watched Wormwood retreat a few steps as Goodman loomed over him. "Then what the hell have you brought me here for? You said I could interview Mr. Vines. Instead, all I see is—"

"Mr. Vines's horse. This is Nightcamp, Goodman."

Nightcamp clapped his right hoof on the ground, drawing the Englishman's attention.

"He wishes to interview *you*," Wormwood said.

"Interview? A horse? Damn you for your jokes!"

"I assure you, this is no mere horse," Wormwood said, retreating still further. "He will demonstrate that."

"How? Does he talk?"

"He will—through me."

Goodman laughed and began stalking off into the darkness. Nightcamp ran to block his path and soon had him going backward.

"You lose nothing by hearing us out, Mr. Goodman."

"Nothing but my precious time," Goodman said.

"You've already spent several weeks in New Vineland engaged in fruitless searches. The next few minutes might redeem a lot of misspent hours."

Goodman sighed and nodded.

Their talk lasted much longer than a few minutes and when it was over, Goodman said something Nightcamp did not understand.

"Even Charles Brockden Brown could not write such a story. I don't disbelieve you though, even if you're asking me not to trust my own eyes. You say we're not standing in a stable, yet all I see is a stable. You say the nonexistent stable is part of a nonexistent town, yet I've seen the town, I've walked in its buildings."

"All illusion," Wormwood said.

"But you're not. And the horse is not. And Evan Vines is not."

"True. And here and there walk others, visitors off the river not called by the witch's song—"

"The song I cannot hear."

Nightcamp cocked his head as the Englishman paced about in a circle.

"I've never been able to believe against doubt," Goodman said. "If I were better at it my relationship with my father would be much improved. I still have no proof of God. I *do* have proof of New Vineland's strangeness. So, I'll indulge your story. My interest has shifted to the tombstones on top of the cliff."

"I've already told you we have no knowledge of such things."

"The name Anna means nothing to either of you?"

"Nothing at all."

"Then I must continue seeking the answer. You both act so certain you know just what's going on, but what if you don't? A gap in your understanding might sabotage whatever plans you're drawing against this place and the witch behind it."

Wormwood glanced at Nightcamp. They both looked at Goodman, whose lips turned down a little.

"I see. You *have* no plans. Maybe we should bring my friend Pike into our little cabal. He's a capable man, and he has enough imagination to believe this whole business about illusions—"

"Imagination in this case may not be beneficial," Wormwood said. "It is better you give no hint to anyone. Let Nightcamp decide how your friend can be used best."

Goodman crossed his arms at his chest. "So, in the end, our course of action is to put all of our hopes on a horse?"

Nightcamp sent his thoughts into Wormwood's mind and Wormwood spoke them—

*We seek atonement for our crimes*
*Our lives our forfeit*
*As is our time*
*To end New Vineland is the goal*
*Even if it costs our very souls.*

"Very well," Goodman said, coming forward. "I see your cuts and it makes me think of Christ, though I blush to hear myself say it. I suppose there's a point in all our lives when we talk and hear our father's voices come out."

Nightcamp stood still as Goodman placed his right hand against his wounded flank. His palm was warm, his touch tender.

"I pledge myself to the same cause. Somehow, some way, we'll bring ruin to New Vineland and the witch together. *Even if it costs our very souls.*"

# Chapter Twenty-Eight

## June 1830

*I hate you.*

It was like she'd taken a large rock and thrown it at Papa with all her strength. She knew her words landed harder than any stone. He just bowed his head and walked into the farmhouse. She knew she'd hurt him past the point he could even be mad enough to punish her.

*Papa, Papa, I didn't mean it! I swear I didn't!*

The shout ran through her mind, but another glance at the blood-stained hatchet kept her mouth clamped tight. Mama had done it, but Papa must have known. The whole trip to New Vineland was just to get her away. Mama murdered Old Ben.

*I hate you. I hate both of you.*

She didn't eat that night. How could she? When the meal was set down, Lily became ill and begged to be excused. Papa stopped Mama's scolding, but Lily's anger wasn't blunted. She held onto it throughout the evening and into the night, where it kept her wide awake and glaring at the window.

*If the Witchhand comes, I'm just going to let it in. I hope it gets all of us. We deserve it because of what happened to Old Ben.*

Lily squeezed her eyes shut as she realized what she'd just thought. Silent tears stained her cheeks.

*I was the one who blamed Old Ben. Mama didn't know he was trying to save me.*

Lily began to sink into the depths of her sorrow when the noise at the window shocked her back to the moment.

*Tap. Tap. Tap.*

She held her breath. She didn't even have Mouse to protect her.

*What am I going to do?*

The mere sight of the white palm pressed against the glass dried her eyes in an instant. All thoughts of opening the window to let the *Witchhand* steal her away fell apart against her terror.

The tapping increased, turning into an irresistible rhythm. It was as if the hand were playing piano keys against the window and each little thump made a different sound that combined into a song. Last night, the only command was *open, open, open.* This new melody felt like an invitation to dance.

An invitation to play.

Her fears slipped away despite her best efforts to hold on to them. She hummed the song and slipped out of bed, moving towards the window, stepping in accord with the tune. Vague wishes for Old Ben's crow mingled with hopes that Mama and Papa would come and save her. She put her right hand on the latch.

Before she opened the window, though, she realized the hand was attached to a line of mist that seemed to snake out into the middle of the crops. *Fat Jack,* she thought, and the song's spell broke. The *Witchhand* tapped for her attention, but Lily ignored it and craned her neck to follow the white line. It *did* lead to the crops, almost right where Fat Jack rested.

Was her dear friend in trouble?

*I have to go to him.*

Lily drew a blanket over her nightclothes and crept fast to the bedroom door. Her breath sounded ragged and rattling to her ears, so she determined to hold her breath the entire way to the front door. She slipped out, hurrying on her tiptoes. No sound came from her parents' room. Lily almost felt alone in the farmhouse. The notion chilled Lily, but she pushed past her fear and made it to the front door. She unlocked it, turned the knob, and eased the door open. Why did the door hinges whine louder the slower she went, like a cat's yowling in the middle of the night? She winced, gnashing her teeth, and didn't open the door a hair more than she needed to squeeze through. Then she bounded off the porch only to step on a rock. She grimaced, holding in a groan, wishing she could go back and get her shoes. Doing so without waking Mama and Papa felt like pressing her luck.

She didn't know the hour, but she was sure she'd never been outside this late. The farm she loved so much in the daylight felt strange and mysterious to her. Where were the songs of the animals and plants? Were they still in silent mourning for Old Ben? Where was the monastic chant of the forest? Groans and creaking noises came from the timbers of their home. It sounded like some sort of anger. Mightn't it be? Lily had never once considered it before, but she sheltered in death. How many felled trees made up the walls and the roof? The question couldn't have occurred to her in the daylight. Shaken, she backed away from the house and proceeded with cautious steps toward the crops, where she hoped she'd feel like less of a trespasser.

The *Witchhand* was disappearing into the rows and she pushed through in pursuit. As Fat Jack came into view, Lily stopped and stared. Something had perched atop the pumpkin, a creature whose body was by turns orange and moonlight silver, sagging and stretching along Fat Jack's shell as if it had no bones at all. A whiff of foul odor came from it and she couldn't stop herself from coughing. At the sound, two wide, black eyes appeared in all that white flesh, staring at her. Then the whole of it shot straight up into the sky, not so much jumping all at once but rather launching its torso, which then pulled the legs along for the ride.

The body landed somewhere in the crops, not far away but where she couldn't see. Lily put her right hand to Fat Jack's shell and touched a slippery coat of slime that made her squat and scrape her fingertips against the dirt.

There was movement in the crops. Lily stood up, turning, unable to see anything. But she caught a sniff of the nasty odor again.

"Where are you?"

No answer.

"Who are you?"

Nothing.

"Are you the one who sends the *Witchhand*?"

A stirring to her immediate right jolted her. She saw nothing but the crops.

A sudden voice, deep as a croak, said, "What is a *Witchhand*?"

She couldn't think of an exact answer, so she said, "It taps on my window. Like this."

She imitated the rhythm with her fingers against Fat Jack's shell. This was met with a laugh, boyish despite its roughness, and then the creature revealed itself, spilling at her feet like uncooked dough.

"That's not a *Witchhand*! That's Toad's summoning song."

*Summoning song?* Lily thought. The words were strange but familiar, like something she'd heard before.

"I like songs," she said.

"Toad knows Anna does. Toad's glad to find Anna again."

Lily found herself smiling despite her confusion.

"Toad? Is that your name?"

"Toad is Toad."

"Why did you call me Anna, Toad? Anna is only part of my name, but no one calls me Liliana."

The creature began to gather itself into something recognizable as a body. Lily saw arms and legs, a narrow chest, and a belly as round as his head. Puckered gray streaks marred his skin, reminding Lily of the scabs that formed whenever her arms and legs got cut by brambles and branches. Toad sat on his haunches, knees drawn against his chest, his lidless black eyes fixed on her. She fought off a chill as his mouth wrinkled into a smile, giving her a glimpse of three sharp triangular teeth.

"Toad has missed Anna. Anna hid good this time."

"But I wasn't hiding, Toad. I've been here the whole time."

"Did Anna miss Toad?"

"Yes," she said after a moment's pause. She didn't dare respond otherwise. Who was this Toad? Who did he think *she* was?

"Mama and Papa call me Lily now, Toad."

His mouth looked like it was trying to say her name, but after several failed attempts he said, "Anna."

"You can call me whatever you want. It's okay."

She sat down next to Fat Jack, wishing he was awake to meet her new friend. Toad tapped his hand against the pumpkin's shell and gave something like a smile.

"Toad wants to play hide and seek."

"Is that why you were trying to get me to come out?"

"Toad missed Anna."

"I'm sorry you missed me, Toad. I'm glad you're here. But how did you find me?"

Toad's mouth contorted into a strange, almost black line. He covered it with both hands and his body shook. The noise he made must have been laughter.

"Toad's been watching," he said. "Toad saw you standing by the river."

"When?"

He looked up at the moon and started touching his fingers. The webbing between them fascinated Lily. "One, two, three..."

He touched his fingers again. "One, two, three..."

"One," he finished.

"Seven? Are you counting the moons, Toad?"

*If each moon is a night to him, then that means he saw me on my birthday,* she thought. Mama had excused her from all but a few chores that day, so Lily had spent much of the morning and afternoon by the dock, waving at boatmen as they passed.

And the *Witchhand* came that night.

Toad sprang straight up again, without warning, causing Lily to gasp. She gasped even louder when he came down on top of Fat Jack. His whole body seemed to collapse across Fat Jack's shell, leaving just Toad's head balanced on an egg of flesh that started turning orange. Lily hated herself for being disgusted, but the sight of Toad's form made her stomach churn.

"Toad was going to pull Anna into the water from the raft. Toad almost did it."

"I didn't know that was you," she said. Lily had trouble believing it could be. After everything that happened, yesterday's trip to New Vineland seemed so distant and hazy. But she had some memory of a voice singing to her from the water—

*Under the water, find me there,*
*Weaving delight for you alone.*
*Stone to flesh, and flesh to stone,*
*Venture, venture to my home.*

The voice had been intelligent and angelic, not at all like how Toad sounded now. Was he lying to her?

Then Lily remembered the sense of a hand reaching toward her as she leaned over the edge of the raft. Papa was ordering her back but she was obsessed with looking in the water, reaching toward the hand. She saw it with such clarity now. It *was* Toad's hand—the white skin, the webbed fingers.

Toad leapt high and landed behind Lily, who scrambled to keep her sight upon him. Again, he covered both hands with his mouth and shook and made his laughing sound.

"Anna never saw Toad!"

She laughed. "Because you're so good at hiding. Did you swim with us all the way to New Vineland?"

He gave a vigorous nod and slapped the dirt with his flat hands and feet.

"Toad wanted to summon Anna to him right then."

"Summon," she said, almost to herself.

"Toad is good with the summoning song now. Toad has lots of practice."

"Why is it called the summoning song?"

He sprang again, landed, and rolled back to where he'd been. "Anna's here! Anna's here!"

"But Toad, I'm here because I—"

Lily stopped talking and swallowed, her throat dry. Wasn't she out here because she *wanted* to be? Hadn't she *chosen* to sneak away?

"Once Toad couldn't sing the summoning song at all. Now Toad can see something once and then he can summon it even from the river."

He leaned forward, head turning, black eyes wide. His vision seemed to sweep over the rows until he stopped and grinned, giving her another glimpse of those three sharp teeth. He stared with such intensity Lily had to look for herself. She saw nothing but the crops, quiet in the moonlight.

"What is it, Toad?"

He crouched low, his torso and head near the ground, the rest of him arched high. Lily thought he looked like some obese cat stretching itself after a nap. His cheeks puffed out wider than she thought possible and stayed that way as his mouth opened a fraction at a time. A faint melody seemed to live inside his jaws. Mr. Goodman had given her a seashell once and told her to hold it to her ear and listen to the ocean. The sound building inside Toad's mouth was similar to what she'd heard in the shell. It was a buzz, a rush of wind, but as it grew louder, she recognized the rhythm of the tapping on her window. A beautiful song conjured itself into being. Toad's body jerked forward just an inch. Lily thought it was his tongue that lanced out into the crops. As he held his position, she saw it was the white line of mist, almost solid as it poured out of him. The air around it vibrated and hummed with music. The line ended in the *Witchhand*, just as solid as it felt along the ground, patting the dirt in the beat Lily knew so well.

No other song compared to it in Lily's imagination or memory. In a way, it seemed like the tunes of everything she'd ever heard brought into a joint melody. . Toad sang the song of the trees and the water, the crops, the birds, every insect and flower. And at the spot where the *Witchhand's* fingers tapped, a rabbit came forward, hopping in obedience the whole path to Toad's waiting, physical palm.

"You're better than any rabbit trap Mama and Papa laid out, Toad!"

"Toad's summoning song is so good that Toad can call one bee from its hive."

They sat together petting the rabbit. Then Toad brought it to his mouth.

"Don't!" Lily said. "Oh, please don't eat it, Toad!"

Toad kept going, but at the last moment, he closed his mouth and gave the rabbit a lick and a kiss. Then he put the rabbit down and cupped his hands over his mouth as his body shook. He kicked his legs in obvious pleasure.

Lily laughed too and said, "You shouldn't trick me like that."

She noticed the rabbit still didn't run away.

"Toad," Lily said, "what do you do when you're done?"

"What's *done*?"

"When you don't want whatever you summoned anymore?"

Toad picked up the rabbit and put it in his mouth.

"Toad! How could you?" Lily said, jumping up.

Toad spat the rabbit onto the ground and Lily snatched it up despite the unpleasant and thick slime coating its fur. The rabbit seemed unconcerned.

"Anna can have it. Toad will get another."

Toad went to his previous crouch and stared off into the crops.

"Please don't summon another one, Toad," Lily said. "We can just play with this one."

But she no longer wanted to play with either the rabbit or Toad. Lily looked in the direction of the house, impossible to see in the dark and through the crops. Could she leave if she wanted? She now felt certain she was here of her own free will, but could she resist Toad's summoning song if he *did* use it on her?

"Toad, I need to go back to bed."

"Toad will make us a bed of leaves!"

"Not tonight," she said. "But I want to see you again tomorrow night. You don't have to send the *Witchhand* to tap on the window. I'll come out on my own. We can play hide and seek."

Toad bounded over, turning his right cheek toward her. The motion reminded her of something Papa used to do to tease her whenever she finished visiting him in the workshop. He'd go down on one knee and tilt his cheek upward so she could kiss it.

*No*, she thought. *Toad can't be wanting that.*

Toad puffed out his right cheek, and Lily knew what she had to do.

She was just glad Fat Jack wasn't awake to see it.

# Chapter Twenty-Nine

Lily didn't need Old Ben's crowing to tell her it was dawn. She'd spent the rest of the night awake and staring at the window as she thought of her strange new...friend. Had their meeting actually happened? Could it have all been a dream?

She got out of bed when she heard her parents stirring. Murmurs came from their bedroom but they didn't talk to each other very long before Papa's heavy footfalls sounded in the hallway.

She opened the door in time to catch him moving past her. Her brows knit. Why was Papa dressed in the black suit he sometimes put on when Mr. Goodman came for a Sunday supper?

"*Papa?*"

He stopped and turned. "Are you no longer angry with me?"

Lily blushed, unable to find words as Papa kissed her forehead.

"If anger were the currency of the world, everyone would be a rich miser."

She looked at her feet. "I was just upset about Old Ben."

"You have every right to be."

Lily squeezed her eyes shut against tears and a new surge of rage. Why did Papa have to tell her she should be mad? It just made her want to push him away.

"Precious child," he said, and she realized she'd not defeated the tears after all. His large thumb wiped them away. "Yesterday was terrible for all of us."

She began sobbing. "I thought you hated me too."

"Lily, why would you think that?"

"Because of what happened with Mr. Vines. Papa, I swear I didn't steal anything. I don't understand what happened."

"I know you didn't," he said.

"But you said all those awful things about me—and you didn't speak to me at all on the way back."

Papa clutched her. Until that moment, she never realized how much she needed the fierceness of his hug.

"I can't explain everything, but I never once thought you were lying. As for my silence—I suppose I was a little afraid."

Hearing this made her hug him back with all her might.

"Please don't be scared," she said, her voice so tiny she almost didn't hear it.

"With a daughter as brave as you to protect me? Never. We both have things to do. For you, that means your chores. Obey your mother like you always do. She'll need you to be on your best behavior until I'm back."

"Back from where?"

"New Vineland," Papa said. "Don't you remember?"

"You're leaving *today?*"

He hushed her. "Maybe it's for the best. The sooner I begin, the sooner I'm done."

"At least you'll be home for supper."

The look in Papa's eyes told her she was wrong.

"This could be a very long task, Lily. A statue of the size he wants can take years—"

"Years! But Papa, you can't stay away that long!"

"It's June now. I vow to be done with this business by October, so I can be back to do the bulk of the fall harvest. I can work very fast when I want. But under the agreement I made with Mr. Vines, coming back and forth each day is out of the question. Don't worry, though. Mr. Goodman will come to check on you both. If there's anything that you and your mother need done, he'll be glad to help."

They went to the kitchen. There was a basket on the table covered with a cloth. Lily knew half a loaf of yesterday's bread was there, and Papa tore himself a big chunk and began eating it without any butter.

"This will hold me for now," he said as Mama came down. Lily always liked it when she saw her parents together first thing in the morning. They seemed so happy to see each other as if they'd spent the night apart. And now they would be. Had they ever done so before? Lily couldn't remember a time when all three of them weren't under the same roof at sundown.

"Lily, fetch wood for the fire. Sit, James."

"There's no time, Katherine. I'll be leaving before you can cook anything."

"I can cook very fast if this daughter of ours fetches the wood. *Now,* Lily!"

Lily hurried to obey, scolding herself every step of the way. Why hadn't she already gotten it? It was always the first of her chores and hadn't Papa told her to be extra mindful? She gathered several pieces of wood into her arms, turned, and dropped them on the first step toward the kitchen. Her fingers shook. She bent to get the wood but winced as a nasty splinter pierced her right thumb.

*"Lily! This instant!"*

Mama wasn't using her scolding tone. She was thundering in a way Lily had never heard, and in the next moment, Mama appeared in front of her, glaring.

"What are you doing? Can you not even fetch wood? Is that too hard for you?"

"Mama, please—"

Mama snatched the wood up herself as Lily pleaded her excuses, trying to explain about the splinter. She showed her bleeding thumb. Mama's pitiless, flaring eyes promised great chastisement before she hurried back into the farmhouse. Lily followed and watched Mama shove wood into the stove's belly.

"Katherine," Papa said, his voice soft as he stood over her. "This matter is not Lily's fault."

Mama's eyes closed tight. Her shoulders sagged; her breathing hitched. She dropped the wood and put her face against Papa's chest. Lily heard the rarest, most horrible sound in the world—her mother's sobbing.

"Mama," Lily said, crying too. She tried to hug her mother only to be pushed away. In the next instant, though, Mama had wrapped Lily in her arms and began rocking her.

"My little Lily, I'm sorry I did that. So *very* sorry. Please forgive me, child."

Lily hugged back with all her strength and Papa put his arms around both of them, all three sinking to their knees. Lily wished Mr. Goodman could have been here to lead them in prayer.

"Nothing can break this family as long as we keep faith in each other. We're never alone as long as—"

*Sweetest child*

*Kindest child*

*Nightcamp is here*

*Freed from his tether*

*Away from all fear.*

Lily pulled away from Mama and Papa's embrace and looked toward the door.

"What is it?" Mama said.

"I think someone is outside."

Lily saw her parents exchange grim glances. Papa got them all to their feet. Together they stepped onto the porch and Lily saw the stallion, black as pitch, a creature that looked carved out of coal except for the crisscross of gray scars on its flanks. Now that she saw it outside and unbowed, Lily thought it was the tallest, most powerful horse she'd ever known. Even Ruffian and Bandit, for all their strength, could not compare.

*Nightcamp*, she thought.

"It's saddled," Mama said. "But where is the rider?"

"The saddle is for me, Katherine."

"But the horse couldn't have found its way here from New Vineland on its own."

"I think this is a very special horse," Papa said, leaving the porch. Nightcamp managed to do the impossible in Lily's eyes by making her father seem small as he rubbed the horse's ears. All the while, Lily and Nightcamp looked at each other. A tune grew in her mind, so very much like Toad's summoning song but not identical. No misty hand sprang from the horse's mouth to grab her, but she heard his singsong words flowing into her thoughts.

*Nightcamp's here*
*Remember me*
*Rescuer from misery.*

Lily tried to think back a response, but she found the very song that carried Nightcamp's thoughts to her made it impossible, like putting a paper boat on the river and expecting it to float upstream. Afraid the horse would think she either didn't hear it or didn't remember, Lily also came over and said, "Papa, isn't this Mr. Vines's horse?"

Mama's reaction made Lily wish she'd said nothing at all. Mama fretted over the scars, calling Mr. Vines horrible. When she looked at Papa, it was easy to see she was imagining him facing the same brutality. She hugged Papa and asked him if he was *sure* he had to go.

*Speak now, child,*
*Tell your mother*
*That father's safe*
*She need not worry.*

"It's going to be okay, Mama," Lily said. "Mr. Vines can't hurt Papa. I saw him. He's really small."

Nightcamp snorted at this, and Papa chuckled. Lily joined in and it felt like all three of them were conspiring to make Mama feel good. It began to work. Mama pulled away, wiping her eyes and showing a sheepish smile.

"It's true, Katherine. I'd break the man in half if he swung his crop at me. The only pain Mr. Vines can inflict is keeping me away from the two of you. We must accept that, and it's better if we do so right now. No long goodbyes. I'll get going."

"Without breakfast, James?"

"I'm not very hungry. The bread will tide me over."

"Why can't you ride Ruffian or Bandit?"

"You might need both while I'm away."

"It's just..."

Mama whispered into Papa's ear.

*No trust Mother has*
*In Nightcamp's purity*
*But fear not, child,*
*For Father's security.*

"It's going to be fine, Mama. Nightcamp must be very smart, and I think he likes Mr. Vines even less than we do."

"Nightcamp?" Mama said, turning. "Is that the horse's name? How do you know it?"

"I...I think I heard Mr. Vines say it."

"So strange, but I suppose it fits. Regardless, you're wrong. Though it pains me as a Christian to say it, right now there's no one in the world who could have a greater dislike for Mr. Vines."

Nightcamp snorted again and gave his head a shake. Lily and her parents looked at each other and began laughing despite themselves.

# Chapter Thirty

Lily walked up the road alongside Nightcamp and Papa until they reached the edge of the Hobbs farm. The trip took only fifteen minutes, most of it spent in silence as Lily concentrated on trying to send her thoughts to Nightcamp through the melody. All of her efforts failed. It seemed the path went only one way, and now Nightcamp did not choose to speak to her at all.

Papa stopped and climbed down from the saddle. He knelt on one knee and cupped her face in his hands, smiling.

"My brave daughter."

Lily fought back a surge of tears. How disappointed would Papa be if he knew how little courage she had?

He kissed her forehead and said, "Do you remember when I told you about the Lodge I belonged to? About being a Mason?"

She nodded.

"We talked about ideas of tradition. We talked about women not being allowed to be Masons. Do you recall that, too?"

"I remember, Papa."

"When I return, we will spend as many hours as you wish together in the workshop. If you want to learn more than the few things I've shown you, I will be a patient teacher."

"Do you truly mean it, Papa?"

"More than anything. I may hate my craft by the time I finish that blasted statue. Teaching you will help me recover its meaning. Inside of you is the potential to become a great stonemason. You have the imagination."

Lily threw herself into Papa's embrace.

"It's settled then," he said, standing up. Lily stepped back as he hoisted himself onto Nightcamp's back. "Remember what we talked about. Obey your mother and do your chores."

"I will, Papa!"

"Mr. Goodman will be calling on you and Mama soon."

He waved and looked up the road. As soon as he did, Nightcamp broke into a gallop. Lily gave chase for several futile steps, but the horse vanished behind a bend and soon enough even his thundering hooves were lost to the distance. Papa's absence was real now. The weeks ahead without him in her life loomed as large as that cliff face did over New Vineland, as oppressive and dark as the tower in the center of town.

Lily walked back to the house. The world's songs began to pick away at her cloak of silence, unraveling its threads. The monastic hum of the forest buoyed her spirit. The birds sang in chorus and there were duets between the shrubs and the grass. She closed her eyes as she walked, soaking in the comforting sounds of the familiar. She thought of what Papa said about her potential as a mason. How could she if she heard no song from stone? Would she ever know why those things alone were silent to her?

She returned home determined to set about her chores despite her weariness, expecting Mama's scolding and maybe even welcoming it, for those chastisements were likewise familiar refrains, and hearing them might make her believe everything was well. When Lily entered the kitchen, though, she found Mama sitting at the table, hands clasped, and her head bowed in prayer. Lily stared at her from the doorway. She didn't think Mama knew she was there until she shifted her weight to make the floorboards creak. Then Mama opened one eye and directed a look to her.

"How long have you been standing there?"

"Not long, Mama."

She opened the other eye and lowered her hands. "I suppose I haven't been so deep in prayer since the days after little Adam—"

Lily wrinkled her brow as Mama bit back her words and forced a smile.

"Go and do your outdoor chores first, Lily. I need to be alone."

"I could pray with you, Mama."

"A child who does her chores is already an answered prayer."

Lily nodded and left the house. The barnyard animals went silent as she approached. Old Ben's blood still stained the ground, and her first thought was to kick the loose dirt until the spots were gone. Lily stopped herself just as she drew back her right foot. If only undoing death were so easy. If only removing guilt were as simple. As she stared at the dark blotches, her spirits lowered even further.

*He didn't need to crow at all. The Witchhand wasn't what I thought. Toad's a friend.*

Wasn't he?

Lily fed the chickens, but they turned away from her. She then went to the barn and found the cow singing its familiar, urgent milking song, its rhythm an exact match for the alternating pulls and squeezes she used to empty the udders. She took the clean tin pail from its hook on the wall and squared it into place. Then she pulled the little stool into position.

"At least you don't hate me like the chickens.

The cow's song increased in pitch and speed as she worked. The song had no words, but Lily had heard it so often she'd long ago made up her own lyrics.

*Squirt-Ping Ping-Squirt*

*Keep the milk from hitting dirt*
*Ping-Squirt Squirt-Ping*
*Fresh milk makes the whole morning.*

The cow and its song went dry in unison. Lily took the pail to the farmhouse. Mama was still sitting at the kitchen table, her clasped hands pressed hard to her forehead. Her lips moved and sometimes let loose with angry mutterings. Lily thought God must be listening hard right now.

Without bread baking in the oven, nothing covered the faint stale odor in the air. She knew it was coming off her skin, a lingering whiff of Toad she couldn't scrub off.

Lily retreated to the porch and the cleansing breeze.

*The sunlight's out*
*My shell's getting hot*
*My guts are sure churning*
*Oh don't let me rot!*

"Fat Jack," she whispered, jumping off the porch. She moved through the crops and found her dear friend, big and bright as ever. Toad's stink lingered a little stronger here and Lily patted the pumpkin's shell and said, "You're not rotting, Fat Jack. We had a visitor last night. He's different and a little scary, but I think he's nice."

Fat Jack sang another song complaining about the heat. Lily had never known summer to bother him before. She began fanning him with her hands. Caring for Fat Jack made her forget her troubles.

"Do you feel cooler now?"

He answered with a slight but definite rumble that made her draw back in alarm.

*Fat Jack is fine*
*But the heat is still there*
*Burning inside*
*And not from the air.*

She felt along his waxy shell. He was cool to the touch.

"You're not getting sick, are you? Oh, Fat Jack, everything is wrong now after what happened to Old Ben. He tried to help me and I betrayed him. I didn't *mean* to, but I did."

*There are dancers*
*Who make missteps*
*And blame the musician*
*For their regrets*
*The piper has piped*
*His tune is played*
*Learn to pipe*
*Then pipe away*
*All tunes exist*
*To occasion dances*
*Make better tunes*
*Make better chances.*

"Learn to pipe?" Lily said. "You mean take control, don't you? Like steering a raft instead of leaving it to the currents. I don't know how I can do it, Fat Jack. Maybe when I'm older."

Fat Jack gave no other response and seemed to doze. Maybe he *was* sick. She lingered long enough to sing a song for him and kiss his shell.

"I hope you're awake and feel better when Toad comes tonight. I'm sure he will. I didn't think I'd ever meet someone with fewer friends than me. We must be nice to him!"

Mama called to her from the porch.

"I have to be extra mindful until Papa's back. Oh, I haven't even told you about *that*, have I? Tonight, I promise."

Lily kissed him a final time and bolted for the house. Her feet struck something in the next crop row and she almost tripped. Looking down, she saw it was the rabbit from last night. She bent to touch it and found the body was stiff and cold.

*"Lily Hobbs!"*

Lily gave one final, uncertain glance at the rabbit and ran.

# Chapter Thirty-One
## June 1830

"The stone's twice as heavy as the child it commemorates," Pike said as he and Goodman took it from the wagon and began their awkward walk into the woods. "That Mason of yours. What's his name again?"

"James Hobbs."

"How is it that he hoisted this heavy bastard under his right arm and brought it onto the dock like it was a pillow?"

"He's a strong man."

"Hell, *I'm* a strong man too."

"For your age, Pike," Goodman said, grinning.

"If this weren't a child's tombstone, I'd let you drag it the rest of the way yourself. Then maybe you'd appreciate an old mariner's vigor!"

"I stand rebuked."

They huffed and puffed their way through the cold woods, Pike's griping getting louder and freer with every stumbling step.

"How is it I'm just finding out about this cemetery?"

"It's a personal matter for me. The tombstones at the top of that cliff aren't meant to honor the girls whose names are listed there. Of that, I'm sure."

"So you've made one of your own to do just that?"

"That's right."

"Are you sure you're just *playing* at being a minister, Harry?"

"Sometimes I wonder about that myself."

Pike coughed, struggling a little more with his end of the tombstone. "I can't think of anyone else I'd rather perform my funeral service than—"

"*Stop that,*" Goodman said. "Don't even think about dying."

"Well, it's something you do the closer you get to it."

"You're not close to death, Pike. You have many years ahead of you."

"So I hope."

They went on about a quarter of a mile and then Pike stopped to catch his breath. Goodman, himself winded, was happy to oblige. They both hunched forward, hands on their knees.

"The thing is, Harry, we shouldn't get so busy with honoring dead girls that we forget to protect the living ones."

Goodman's head snapped up. "What?"

"This plan of yours involving the Mason's girl—"

"It's not all my plan, Pike."

"That sweet little girl was terrified yesterday. It made me so sick I almost couldn't stay in character."

"It had to be done," Goodman said, his tone stiff. "Vines had to believe it was all authentic. That means Lily had to believe it too."

*Just as you must believe it's real, my friend*, he thought.

"Oh, that child's fear was *authentic* enough. It gives me some concerns about your Mason."

"I can vouch for his character."

"What about his heart? He must be a cold man to put his daughter in jeopardy the way he did."

"He knew she was in no real danger, not with you and Wormwood secretly guiding her."

"Is that what I was doing? It seemed my job was to scare her out of her wits."

"Wormwood was watching out for her."

"With respect, Harry, I'm not sure you know what you're talking about."

Goodman gritted his teeth and flushed. He lifted his end of the tombstone. "You ready to go?"

Pike hoisted up his portion and they went on in silence until they reached the cemetery. Then Pike let his end drop, staggering a moment as he surveyed the area. He turned wide eyes to Goodman.

"Who cleared these trees? It must have taken weeks."

"James and I did it ourselves."

Pike grunted. "A master Mason and a master woodcutter. Well, Hobbs put his geometry to good use. This is the most perfect circle I've ever seen."

Goodman watched him go over to the tombstones and reflected on the fact that the older sailor had taken his story of the vanishing tombstones at face value. He'd not wanted to see such an impossible thing for himself. As far as Goodman knew, Pike had never made a separate private trip to verify the details. Goodman considered this a pure act of trust and acceptance, but he also thought back on his first meeting with Wormwood and Nightcamp. What had one of them said about imagination not being beneficial? Goodman wasn't sure of that assessment or their reasons for wanting Pike kept ignorant of New Vineland's reality. For all of Wormwood's talk about *physical touchstones* and the importance of never threatening the illusion in Vines's mind, maybe maintaining Pike's ignorance had a simpler reason. It was easier to have the man pretend to be a character in a real town than to explain he was playing a pretend character in a *pretend* town.

As Pike stood there examining the tombstones and muttering to himself, Goodman thrust his hands into his pockets and turned to study the perimeter of the circle. The clearing was Nightcamp's work.

He could not doubt the horse's intelligence now, nor its strength. And though Nightcamp continued claiming no knowledge of the tombstones atop the cliff or their purpose, he'd expressed a desire to help Goodman honor them by creating this secret cemetery.

Pike came over and they got the new tombstone wedged into place, then stood back and bowed their heads.

"Reckon you better say something."

"*What?*"

"It's what ministers do, Harry."

Goodman blinked. No words had been spoken after he and James put the other tombstones into place. The idea of a prayer hadn't even occurred to him. Who were they praying for? How did one pray for a name, the same name repeated over and over, with no face he could attach to it? Deeds spoke louder than words anyway, and the effort to recreate the cemetery and honor whatever person or persons *Anna* represented was the better sermon by far.

But Pike insisted, and Goodman already felt like he'd disappointed his friend enough. He took a deep breath, closed his eyes, and tried to find something black and real in the bright white space of his thoughts. He tried to remember all the times his father led public prayers. There must have been 500 Sunday mornings' worth of memories yet he couldn't recall a scrap of speech. His father had presided over weddings and funerals, with little Harold forced to attend each and every one. Even if he'd been bored and not paying attention, his mind must have retained *something* of those sermons he could use now.

"*Harry?*"

"Lord, watch over the soul of this—Anna."

Goodman bowed his head. His cheeks felt aflame.

*God, You know the truth. A glimpse of it is all I seek. If this cemetery rectifies a tragedy then it is only because You allowed the tragedy to happen. If there are families experiencing grief and terror it's because You are culpable. Why am I here trying to appease an old man's sentiments, an old man who may have as little regard for You as I? There's no church or temple in New Vineland but if there were, it's where You should dwell, illusion for illusion. Maybe there never was an Anna. Maybe Anna is a fevered fantasy. Maybe Your very name is and always was and always should be Anna.*

He opened his eyes and found Pike staring at him, solemn and piteous.

"I'm sorry," Goodman said. "I can't."

"It's okay, Harry. I could tell you were praying in your head. I could see it from how your eyes moved."

"I wouldn't call it a prayer," he said, a little shocked by the venom in his tone.

Pike clapped him on the shoulder. "Maybe it's just as well. I've been at many public gatherings where everyone wished the preacher kept his mouth shut."

His lower lip trembled. "All my life, I've seen the clear signs of evil and not a speck of good."

"Next time, spend a little longer looking in the mirror, Harry. Hell, *good* is in your very name."

"My father's name."

"Like father, like son. Only a good man would have gone to these lengths," he said, gesturing to the tombstones. "This is a deed of kindness."

"That serves no purpose at all if the cemetery it emulates lacks one, too."

Pike grinned. "That only makes what you've done here an act of faith. Try as you might, Harry, you can't escape your own righteousness."

Goodman nodded, unable to speak. The praise made him feel like the happiest of fools and they headed back toward the cart. They spent the first half of the return trip in silence before Pike broke it. He pulled from his pocket the little stone mouse Goodman had given him and held it up for inspection.

"I'll say this, Hobbs *is* a fine stoneworker, regardless of what I may think of him as a father. Those tombstones are of excellent quality. If you saw them gracing any churchyard, you'd think the deceased must have been very wealthy. But detailed sculptures like this mouse are more impressive if you ask me. Vines was convinced, just as you said he'd be."

"He was indeed," Goodman said.

"It's too bad Hobbs isn't very trusting. Here we are on the same side, and he wouldn't say more than a few words after he sent his daughter into the tower. I can't figure him out."

"It proves what I said. Far from being cold, he was worried about Lily even in the face of all assurances. Or maybe he was just making sure to continue the facade, the scared farmer confronted by New Vineland's *cruel* and *oppressive* Dockmaster."

Pike laughed until he coughed, and when they reached the cart he leaned against it, breathing hard for a moment. Goodman started to worry about him, but then Pike chuckled.

"I do play it well, don't I? Ah, if my life had been different, I might be an actor. Imagine me, right now, in London giving a command performance to your brand-new King Willie. Truth be told, I'm not as inexperienced in espionage as you might think."

"Oh?"

"Would you be surprised to know I was in the army in 1814?"

"Not the Navy?"

"I was in Louisiana then and all the adventure was happening on land. Plus, I had a special devotion to General Jackson. We were a ragtag lot but he kept us together. He's not a perfect man. Far from it. But in the thick of combat, you'd follow him to the bitter end. He defended New Orleans when we were overwhelmed. He made us believe we stood a chance. But he couldn't do it without a sneak in the British ranks."

He tapped his chest, grinning.

"You're selling me a dog, Pike."

"I swear it's no lie," he said, holding up his right hand. "It was my first and—until now—only foray into the spying game. I snuck the British invasion plans to General Jackson. After the smoke cleared, we'd stomped your countrymen all the way out of Louisiana."

"It pains me to say so as *King Willie's* loyal subject, but this Jackson sounds like an amazing man. What became of him?"

Pike's eyes widened. He gave Goodman an inexplicable look of incredulity. Goodman just shook his head, at a loss.

"Good God, Harry," Pike said. "He's only the President of the United States!"

# Chapter Thirty-Two

It was eight at night when they docked in New Vineland. Pike began making a pallet on the deck of his boat as Goodman prepared to disembark.

"Are you very tired?"

"Harry, I've never felt more my age."

Goodman nodded. He turned to look at the bright lights in the windows. Every part of New Vineland was aglow and inviting except for the tower, a looming black suggestion against the dark sky. He squinted and peered, shook his head, and scowled.

"What is it?" Pike said.

*It's not right to keep him ignorant,* Goodman thought. *Not anymore. He has as much stake in the plan as the rest of us. He at least deserves to know what the plan is.*

"Do you believe in magic? Real magic, not...card tricks?"

"I suppose anything's possible."

"There was a time in my life when a statement like that would have thrilled me with hope. *Anything's possible.* No limits but our dreams. Now, that very notion fills me with dread. It's terrifying to think that *anything* could be possible. I understand why people strive to seek out limits—to make other people believe in restrictions and bans and regulations."

Pike quit making his bed and sat on the edge of the boat.

"What's going on here, Harry? You've changed since I met you. At first, I was charmed by your adventurousness and imagination. Then I admired your pursuit of justice and determination. Now you pull me into this impersonation scheme, and I have to sicken myself by scaring a little girl half out of her wits?"

"I guess I'm just persuasive."

"You've got leadership qualities, but truth be told I've done more than a few daft things just to escape boredom. I would have gone along even if I thought I was just indulging your madness. But if you're insane it's the most elaborate, dedicated kind of madness I've ever seen. So, I'll ask it again. *What's* going on here?"

Goodman's throat tightened.

"Do you believe in witches?"

"They're why I never married."

"I'm serious, Pike."

"Yes," he said. "I do."

"I'm surprised to hear you say that."

"There's a reason."

"Tell me."

"No," he said. "You're looking for an excuse to be sidetracked. Stick to the point."

Goodman started to speak, couldn't find the words, and reset himself. "What if I told you that almost everything about New Vineland is an illusion? The buildings, the lights, even the people—to an extent. Hell, this very dock."

"I didn't moor the boat to a phantasm, Harry. If it's not real, we'd be drifting downstream."

"I can't explain it all. It hasn't all been explained to me."

"Who did the explaining?"

"You met them today."

Pike cocked his head and leaned forward. "Come again? After Hobbs brought the tombstone off the boat, we waited the twenty minutes you instructed and then set off after her. Right away I could tell he knew more than I did. That chafed me but I didn't break character. When it didn't seem like she was going to enter the store, he stayed hidden and sent me forward to scare her into it. What manner of father would do that?"

"We've been over this before, Pike."

"Then that unpleasant round man, Wormwood, comes and pulls me away, and I get roped into playing a greater game than I imagined. Still, I kept in character. You'd have been proud of me, Harry. Vines didn't even know who I was, but he's an easy man to read. If you know what a man wants to hear, it's an easy enough thing to say it."

Goodman nodded. "Wormwood's one of the *explainers*."

"Then who was the other? It couldn't have been Vines."

"Think back on the story you told me, Pike. You've forgotten something."

He shook his head. "I've mentioned everyone that was there other than the poor horse."

"There you have it."

Pike was silent for a moment.

"I take it back," he said. "You are indeed mad."

"I wish it were that easy."

"Harry—"

"There's an easy way to prove it right now if you're not too tired."

Pike laughed. "I'm more wide awake than ever."

"Then I'll take you to Nightcamp. He may not like it, but he'll have no choice."

"What the hell is a Nightcamp?"

"That," Goodman said, "is the name of the horse."

# Chapter Thirty-Three

*There are no guarantees. But there are promising possibilities.*

James had spoken that sentiment to him at the conclusion of their first meeting, and Goodman repeated them in his mind as he led Pike through the streets of New Vineland. He embraced them as a catechism against Nightcamp's wrath. Was he making a rash decision? Was revealing the truth to Pike a greater risk than he could understand? What if doing so might open up greater opportunities than they'd considered?

No guarantees. Promising possibilities.

"Amazing," Pike said.

"What's that?"

"The sound my feet are making on the cobblestones. Quite the illusion," he said, laughing.

Goodman ignored the mockery and escaped into the happy memory of first encountering the Hobbs family almost three years ago to the day, when he began visiting every little village and solitary homestead farm up and down the entire length of the river, playing his own impersonation game as he sought out the meaning of the tombstones and hoped to prevent any further disappearances.

He was tired and might not have noticed the Hobbs dock at all if a little girl standing on it hadn't shouted and waved her hands.

"Hello! Hello! Hello! It's my seventh birthday!"

He could only grin at the child's exuberance. The bright excitement in her voice lifted away the fatigue of the moment.

"Well," he shouted back, "if it's your birthday, I must pay my respects!"

The girl hopped along the dock as Goodman pushed his raft toward her.

"Papa! Papa! There's a man coming off the river! He's here to tell me happy birthday!"

There was a small structure just up from the dock, and a man came out of it. Even from the river, Goodman realized this was the largest, brawniest person he'd ever seen. He approached the dock as Goodman moored the raft. His hair and beard were coal black except for odd splotches of gray most uncommon in someone his age. Goodman felt sure the man was at most in his early thirties, no more than a handful of years older than Goodman himself.

"Welcome," the man said, reaching out. Goodman found his hand engulfed. The stranger may have intended to help him onto the dock, but Goodman felt hoisted into the air. As soon as his feet touched the planks, the little girl hugged his right leg and repeated it was her birthday.

"Lily!" the man said.

Goodman grinned. "There's no use for a robber trying his luck here. First, the child sounds an alarm better than any watchdog, and then, she detains you faster than any constable."

The girl tried to pronounce constable, settled for *consable*, and asked him what it meant.

"Someone who arrests criminals," Goodman said.

"What's a criminal?"

Goodman and the girl's father exchanged looks and started laughing. Having read more than his share of stories about bandits when he was her age, he could only marvel at her innocence. Introductions were made and the three of them started up the path toward the farmhouse. Lily ran ahead to tell her mother, who came out to meet them. Katherine Hobbs was a striking woman and cordial, but her hands worried themselves under a kitchen towel. Goodman did not sense the same overt friendliness from this couple that he'd encountered without fail among all the others he stopped to visit. Even those who'd lost fathers and grandfathers fighting the British took no offense at his accent. Any whiff of distrust that might exist evaporated when he announced he was a traveling pastor–just as it seemed to do with Katherine.

"You'll stay for supper, Reverend Goodman? We have more than enough."

"I would be honored."

She motioned them into the house. Before he could enter, though, Lily said, "Papa, I want to show him the animals."

"I'm sure Mr. Goodman has seen chickens before."

"No, Mama, I mean Adam and the others. *Please*?"

She made the plea to Goodman rather than her mother, even tugging on his arm.

"Why yes," he said. "I'm very eager to meet Adam. Is he a cow?"

"He's a rabbit!"

"Oh, a rabbit. I'm very fond of them."

They went around the side of the farmhouse and Goodman found a wonderful and perplexing menagerie of animal statues on the ground, each rendered in such detail they seemed almost alive. There were rabbits, squirrels, mice, raccoons, and even a fox, all living in stone harmony like a depiction of Noah's Ark. Lily sat down next to the rabbit and began to stroke its ears as she explained that her papa made the animals and they were her friends.

"But then Jack came along, and I can talk to him and he talks back. These don't talk back."

"I see," Goodman said, sitting down next to her.

"Jack was small, but he keeps getting bigger."

"Is he your dog?"

Lily shook her head and giggled.

"Your cat?"

She put her hands over her mouth like she was trying to stifle the world's loudest laugh.

"Hmm," he said, warmed by her mirth. He tapped his chin. "Is it that cloud up there?"

Now the girl could no longer hold back and said, "Jack's a pumpkin! He sings and if he gets any bigger, he's going to be Fat Jack."

James Hobbs came around from the side. "Lily, go to the kitchen and help your mother."

The child stood up. "Do you like them?"

"I think they're the nicest animals I've ever seen."

"Then you're going to love Jack! Papa, I'm going to show—"

"You're going to help your mother like I told you. It's your birthday dinner after all."

"Maybe after supper, you can show me your friend," Goodman said.

The child kicked at the dirt a little bit and stalked off in reluctant, temporary defeat. The men watched her leave and then stared at each other. James crouched, picked up one of the figurines and stared at it lengthening silence.

"You're a lucky man, Mr. Hobbs. She's a lovely child."

"I am and she is. Please call me James, though."

"If you'll call me Harold."

"Very well."

Silence fell between them. Goodman looked everywhere, pretending to be enraptured by the trees the way he supposed a man of God should be. Then he pointed at the stone replicas. "These little statues are incredible. Lily says you made them. Is that true?"

James ran a hand through his hair as he said, "Yes, that's—" He stopped, studying his hand. Then he gave his head a firm dusting off and the gray splotches flew off him as dust, leaving his hair and beard black.

"Masonry makes a man old before his time," Goodman said.

"I'm afraid you caught me at play. Yes, I made the animals. Masonry is a passion of mine. Maybe too much of a passion."

"The quality of your work is astounding."

"Lily has never had other children to play with and tends to create her own friends. She's an imaginative child. I made the animals to help her exercise that imagination."

Goodman picked up a stone owl. Despite its heft, its size and detail were so identical to a real one you'd be forgiven for thinking it might fly away. "You call your artistry play? I have to think many wealthy people in the world would hand over a fortune for your pieces."

"I've no interest in fortune. The simple farming life with my family is all I want."

*He must be lying*, Goodman thought, though he couldn't explain his certainty. Maybe it was too difficult to conceive how anyone with such evident skill and talent considered its practice a passing fancy.

They fell into what Goodman interpreted as an easy conversation almost identical to the polite small talk everyone along the river used with him. He'd come to appreciate its universal patterns, as stylized as any dance. It always began with a casual look at the sky and a nod, followed by a comment on the weather. At this point, Goodman knew he was supposed to look up as well and affirm whatever observation had been made—*Not as hot this week* or *Been breezy these last few days*. Over time, the conversation turned to personal matters, all the more so since they believed they were talking to a man of God. He'd say, "I'm a pastor in search of a flock along this river Jordan," and some laughed and told him he'd mistaken his geography. More often than not, he found people desiring to hear more. The larger towns had churches, but many of the villages and communes did not. On some isolated farms the head of the household served as minister. Whatever their situation might be, it was clear to Goodman they yearned for someone like his father.

*"Who are you really and what do you really want?"*

# Chapter Thirty-Four

They reached the stable. Nightcamp was there, almost impossible to see in the murky space, but the horse was awake.

"God," Pike said. "This poor old horse has seen enough abuse for a herd. There was a moment yesterday when I thought your stonemason was going to lose his composure and kill Evan Vines. Maybe we should have let him."

*"A grave mistake."*

Goodman squinted to his left, but Wormwood came toward him from the right. He went rigid when he saw the look of scowling disapproval.

"I remember you," Pike said. "I don't like you any more than I did before."

Goodman held up his hands and stepped between them.

"I know I've brought my friend here over your objections, but I believe he can help us. He's *already* helped us. Without his efforts, Vines wouldn't have been fooled."

"He accomplished this feat *without* knowing anything at all."

"Well, I know some things now. Harry tells me I'm standing in a figment of my imagination."

Goodman found Wormwood glowering at him and raised his hands. "I brought Pike here because we have to think of all the possibilities."

Wormwood started to speak but stopped, his body twitching. He then put his hand to his temple. Nightcamp gave the slightest snort and then Wormwood opened his mouth again.

*"Allies are a proven need*
*Critical to our goal.*
*I've seen this man*
*I know his deeds*
*They reflect a worthy soul."*

As Goodman listened to Wormwood, he noticed Pike was looking at Nightcamp. He knelt next to the horse and untied the tether.

"My God," Pike said. "That was you talking, wasn't it? Somehow, that was *you*."

"It's just like I told you," Goodman said.

Wormwood moved between them.

"That may be, Harry," Pike said, grinning as he looked between Wormwood and Nightcamp. "But it looks like the *horse* wants to do the talking now."

And so it was. Goodman retreated to a corner and sat on the ground, listening to Nightcamp and Pike converse through the medium of Wormwood. He soon found himself a forgotten party, but Goodman did not mind. In fact, he now felt the day's fatigue flooding over him and yawned.

"Never mind me," he said. "I may just nap."

No one acknowledged him. Pike listened to Wormwood and stroked Nightcamp's ears. This made Goodman smile. Bringing Pike here was the best decision.

*You were right, James. No guarantees, but promising possibilities.*

He fell asleep.

# Chapter Thirty-Five
## June 1827

*"Who are you really and what do you really want?"*

Goodman knew he'd flinched at the sudden change in James's demeanor. He couldn't hide it, so he thought it best to ignore it.

"It's as I said, James. I'm a minister in search of a flock. Nothing more."

He put the animal sculpture down. "Spreading God's word from town to town, is that it?"

"It is."

He did his best to keep meeting James's critical stare as his right hand fished a Bible from his leather satchel. He held it up only to have James snatch it out of his grip and flip through it.

"Has this ever been opened?"

Without another word, James tossed it on the ground. Goodman stared down at it and felt frigid in his bones, shocked into paralysis. He might as well have been one of the stone animals. Several moments passed before James picked the Bible up himself and dusted it off.

"I'd think a man of God would be a little more offended."

"I was just surprised."

"What's your favorite scripture?"

"Psalm 46:1," Goodman said, knowing it was his father's personal choice. But in the tension of the moment, he couldn't remember a word of it.

James found the verse, read it to himself, and grunted. Then he closed the book and said, "Why did you come to my dock?"

"I saw it from the river."

"Do you stop at every dock you float past?"

"Lily called out to me. You must have heard her. If I've done something to give offense, I'll leave right now. If the meal is as cold as this interview, I doubt I'll enjoy it much anyway."

Goodman started to rise only to be pulled down with gentle but implacable force.

"I'll know what you're really after before I let you go."

"Why do you think I'm lying to you, James?"

"Let's just say that past experiences have taught me to be a protective father."

Goodman went rigid. He stared into James's eyes and saw an awareness he'd not seen in anyone else.

"Very well," he said. "I'm a man who's heard stories. Horrible stories. And I'm trying to figure out what's behind them."

"What stories might those be?"

"The lost girls. All older than Lily, but only by a few years. It seems one disappears every year."

"This would be a fortunate land if only one child were lost per year."

"I think you know I'm referring to something different, James. Disappearances that don't seem to be whims of chance."

He spoke all the names he knew from both Pike's investigations and his own. *Anna, Veronica, Bethany.* James stared off into space as Goodman completed the list.

"Horrible," James said.

"Do you know of the town called New Vineland?"

"Of course."

"Have you ever been there?"

"Once."

"You weren't enchanted by all it has to offer?'

"All cities are the same to me," he said. "My wife and I are reclusive by nature. We steer clear of people for the most part. I have my family and my farm—that's all I need or want."

"I've had people tell me their own little villages have been abandoned," Goodman said. "They've shown me empty houses where their neighbors went on a trip to New Vineland and never came back."

"People move all the time, Harold. They all have their reasons."

Goodman laughed. "You're pretending to be a rationalist the way I'm pretending to be a preacher."

"I hope I'm better at keeping up appearances."

"I've witnessed aspects of New Vineland that make reason useless!"

He leaned in and told James about the top of the cliff face, about the tombstones that revealed themselves only under the shadow of a cloud. As he finished, he regretted his outburst, certain he'd lost whatever hard-won interest he had from James. But if anything, James's expression showed fascination.

"There's no rock in the world that has properties like that," he said.

"These tombstones do. You can go up there anytime and verify it for yourself. Be careful if you go on a sunny day, though. You might accidentally stub your toe."

James grunted. "They really only repeat the same name—Anna?"

"Does it mean anything to you?"

"Nothing at all."

"Up and down the river, there seems to be at least one girl who's vanished every year since New Vineland was founded and an equal number of tombstones on the top of that cliff. The girl who disappeared *first* was called Anna. There has to be a connection. If I can find it, maybe we can prevent that abominable cemetery from growing."

James took a labored breath. "A man pulled into my dock two weeks ago. He was searching for his daughter. I suppose he hoped the girl had run away from home. I didn't dare tell him I suspected she was dead."

Goodman stood up. "What leads you to think she is? As you said, children *do* disappear from time to time."

"Because he wasn't the first man to come off the river looking for his missing daughter over the last few years."

"I understand your suspicion of strangers now."

James also got to his feet. "When was the last time you counted the tombstones?"

"My current trip has kept me away from New Vineland for almost a month."

"Then spend the night, Harold. Tomorrow we'll go there together and see if a ninth Anna has been added."

"Finding where the current tombstones are is not a problem, but it's a big space. Trying to feel for a new one could be a long and tedious process—a wasted trip if the clouds aren't just right."

James pointed out and up and Goodman turned to look north. Many fat white-gray clouds stood tall in the distance.

"You're right, Harold. There are no guarantees. But there are promising possibilities."

# Chapter Thirty-Six

They set out the next day in Goodman's raft, with two horses on a tether line pulling them upstream while he and James worked the push poles. Before they set off, Lily and Katherine came to the dock and Katherine handed James a leather shoulder bag. Lily announced she was coming with them but her mother had other ideas. After hearing her enumerate the girl's list of daily chores, Goodman understood why Lily wanted to be on the raft.

"Thank you," he said once they were far enough away to avoid being overheard.

"For what, Harold?"

"For trusting me. Or at the very least, being willing to entertain my story. Many men would not."

He looked overhead. The sun was bright, but yesterday's distant clouds had gathered close and low. They were moving, too. The sunlight winked on them multiple times during the trip, adding to Goodman's anticipation.

No, he told himself, most men would not be trusting or caring enough to humor a total stranger with an absurd story. Why was he really coming?

They spoke little for the duration of the journey. As soon as the cliff face came into view, James whistled at the horses and they stopped.

"What's wrong?" Goodman said.

"We're going to cross here," James said, bending to untie the tether line.

"The river is narrower near New Vineland."

"But isn't it better to cross where there are far fewer eyes watching us?"

Goodman blushed. "You're right, of course. But what about your horses?"

"I don't know how it is in England, but *American* horses can take are of themselves. They'll wait for us."

He freed the line and Goodman felt the immediate force of the river pushing them back. James took up his push pole and moved to the front. They fought the current together, though James seemed to have enough solitary strength to do it all himself. Goodman doubled his efforts but still felt like a child who only thinks he's helping an adult do some Herculean task.

When they got to within ten feet of the shore, James jumped into the water, grabbed the raft, and pulled it onto the bank. The force knocked Goodman over before he even knew what had happened and he sat in the middle of the raft looking up at James and his extended hand.

"Glad I was able to help," he said, getting up on his own.

"Grab the shoulder bag, please."

Goodman did and they stepped onto the rocky shoreline.

"There's a trailhead over there."

"How long is it?"

"That's a very good question."

He shrugged off James's puzzled look. They started walking and were on the trail for about an hour when James stopped and reached into the bag, producing a stack of cookies wrapped in cheesecloth.

"Katherine is too Christian to admit to any superstitions, but she always bakes special biscuits for me whenever I take a trip that worries her."

"She knows where we're going?"

"She thinks we're going to New Vineland, which is worrisome enough in her mind. Not that I told her this, and not that she asked. Katherine knows that if she asked, I would tell her. She also knows that if I didn't already tell her then I prefer she not ask."

"You've an unspoken trust between each other."

"That's a way of putting it."

Goodman took a biscuit when offered and had no trouble admitting it was among the best he'd ever tasted, buttery, honey-sweet, and moist. He had another.

"A delicious wish for good luck if ever one existed," he said.

"Baking is her passion the way stonework is mine."

They set off on the trail again.

"You seem to have the ideal life," Goodman said. "A tranquil farm, a wonderful wife and daughter, and leisure time in your workshop. Fresh milk, eggs, and bread every morning. Wordsworth would do well to dwell with you."

James grunted. "I prefer Byron when I bother with poetry at all."

"Byron's something of an idol of mine, you know."

"Of course he is, considering your name. You're literally *Childe Harold.*"

Goodman chuckled and slapped James on the back. The familiarity of the act shocked him just a little. Perhaps Pike's mannerisms were rubbing off on him. But James either didn't notice or didn't care and they continued their trek, their talk easy and baited with fragments of poetry.

"You have a good memory for verse," Goodman said. "And you've read more of it than you let on."

"I sometimes read poetry to Lily at night. There's nothing she won't absorb. Katherine frets over her curiosity when Lily asks about life outside of the farm."

"You've never taken her elsewhere?"

James's answer surprised him with its sudden terseness. "She's safer where she is."

After this exchange, there was not much talk and Goodman wondered if he'd somehow given offense. He could not imagine how he'd done so, but he settled into the glum reality of the silence as they continued their trek. The path was no less infuriating than all the other times he'd climbed it, offering false summits, winding when it should have been straight, lengthening when it should have run out of distance much sooner. But James must have seen something Goodman couldn't. He broke into a run. Goodman called after him and then started running too, but matching James's speed was futile after a few minutes. He stopped, doubled over from a pain in his right side. When he looked up again, James was out of sight.

He staggered on as best he could but didn't see James again until the path at last showed mercy and took him to the top. It was only at this point he even thought to notice the light. The sun was blocked by a massive, slow-moving gray cloud. The tombstones were visible and James knelt before them.

There was a ninth.

James was weeping. Was he thinking of the father who stopped at his dock? Was he imagining how he'd feel if Lily were the one who'd vanished? Goodman found neither possibility wholly adequate and came closer.

"Lily wasn't always an only child, was she?"

"No."

Goodman came around to stand on James's right. "*Whose* tombstone were you hoping to find up here?"

"It doesn't matter."

"James, whatever you know, *please* tell me."

As they went on staring at the tombstones, sunlight swept toward them from west to east as the cloud coverage ended. The tombstones vanished like obliterated shadows. James put his hand on the spot. He stood up, keeping his fingers anchored, and went around the back of the tombstone. Then he gripped the invisible edges tight.

"What are you doing?"

James pulled up, his impressive muscles straining. After several fruitless attempts, he fell back, gasping.

"Feels like it's wedged into the core of the earth."

"You're trying to take it?"

"Back to my workshop," James said. "But I suppose it's impossible."

He started toward the path. Goodman watched him for a moment.

"What was Lily's older sister's name?"

James froze. He did not turn around. "It was a brother."

"Then what was *his* name?"

James cast a baleful glance at him over his right shoulder. "You're a stubborn bastard, aren't you?"

"My best or worst trait, depending upon who you ask."

"When we get back to the farm, I'll show you what I came here hoping to find."

# Chapter Thirty-Seven

When they returned to the farm dock, James put a finger to his lips and they disembarked in total silence. There was no sign of Lily anywhere. Goodman wondered how many of the chores the girl had completed in the few hours they'd been away.

He followed James into the woods at the back of the farmhouse. They continued to move with exaggerated care as if the sound of crunching leaves might send Lily chasing after them. It was clear James intended to show him something Lily did not know existed. The further into the woods they went, the more Goodman's discomfort rose.

Though his imagination conjured skeletons, what Goodman found was a little clearing where a stand of trees had been cut to stumps of identical height, level with his kneecaps. The stumps served as natural plinths for a series of marble busts. As they got closer, Goodman saw the first bust was of a baby. The details were just as precise and lifelike as Lily's collection of stone animals. One could imagine the mouth wailing for mother's milk at any moment. As Goodman took in the total effect of the bust, he was certain he'd never seen anything like it anywhere in the world.

He looked to James, prepared to ask the obvious question. When he found James standing with his head bowed and eyes closed, Goodman knew the question could wait. He went from bust to bust. The infant became a toddler, a bright-eyed boy with an honest face and mischievous smile. The toddler aged. The face became fuller, the hair longer. Without question, it was the same child, the changing features from year to year rendered with more accuracy than even a master artist's study. Goodman turned and counted the busts. There were eight sculptures but nine stumps, and the latest showed traces of fresh sap.

"I know you've noticed," James said. "No reason not to say it."

"The number of stumps and the number of tombstones seem to match."

James went to the first bust. "This was my son. Adam."

"Beautiful boy."

"Sometimes, I wonder if we were arrogant. God made and named Adam, after all. Katherine and I saw a new start in his birth. She was running her uncle's inn and I was content to help her. Then..."

Goodman touched James's shoulder but he flinched away.

"*Then* the devil came through the door on a stormy night, and I couldn't stop him. Adam was but a few months old when he was taken."

"When was this?"

"Eight years ago. When you talked about the tombstones and the name Anna, I suppose part of me kept hearing *Adam*. Every year, I sculpt a new bust of him as I imagine he'd look like now."

"Does Katherine know?"

"I'd never inflict such pain on her."

"It wouldn't necessarily be pain."

"It could be nothing else. She still feels the loss even more than I do. Sometimes I come out here and talk to the busts and suffer the brutality of their silence. The worst hell is to have a child dead in your mind but alive in your heart. Sometimes when I'm lost in a new bust of him, I feel like I'm somehow communicating with him. That he's somewhere in the world and I'm getting a glimpse of his true face."

"Maybe you are."

"No, Harold. This is a shrine to a ghost. I didn't think we'd have another child. We wouldn't have if we'd stayed at the inn. We didn't move far but this land felt a thousand years removed from the past. Neither of us will forget Adam, but Katherine decided she wanted to try soon again."

"Lily knows nothing about her brother?"

"We struggled with how and when to tell her. We've come to realize there'll never be a right time."

"But surely a time, whether it's right or not!"

"Maybe she already knows without really knowing. Lily is a strange child. She talks to our animals and has me half-convinced they're talking back. I've caught myself wishing such moments were Adam's spirit trying to communicate."

"James, I don't wish to be indelicate, but I need to ask. You must have gotten a look at the man who took Adam."

"Just a brief one."

"Do you remember any details? This man could also be responsible for the other girls."

"I think there must be a connection, but not because of the man."

"Then what?"

"After he ran out the door, I got my pistols and followed. It was very dark. A terrible storm. The man was putting Adam into a cart. I decided to shoot the horse. It was black, difficult to see, but so large. I thought I couldn't miss it. But I must have because the horse wasn't hurt. The rain caused my second gun to misfire and the cart pulled away. I chased it as best I could but I kept slipping in the mud and falling further and further behind. That was the end of it. In the morning, though, I chanced to find the lead ball on the ground right between the deep imprint of the horse's front hooves. A reasonable man would think the bullet must have struck part of the cart. But I'm sure I hit the horse. I started thinking about animals made of stone, how invincible they'd be."

*Nightcamp*, Goodman thought. James's description left no doubt. Nightcamp had talked about seeking atonement, but until now Goodman had no inkling about the magnitude of his crimes.

*Do I now?*

He realized James was waiting for him to speak.

"I agree, there must be a connection. Let's help each other find it—for the sake of all those girls and for Adam."

They shook hands.

"Masons have many credos, Harold, but my Lodge followed only one. *Magna est veritas et praevalebit*. That means 'The truth is great'—"

"— 'And will prevail.'"

*But not without our help*, Goodman thought.

# Chapter Thirty-Eight
## July 1830

*"It's a beautiful bay mare, Harry, no doubt about it. But after a ride on Nightcamp, I'm afraid I'm spoiled for any other horse."*

Goodman thought about Pike's boast as he made his early morning ride toward the Hobbs farm. Yes, the horse *was* a beautiful bay mare, a charitable gift from a farm family further south of the Hobbs homestead. He had to admit he preferred horse travel to the river, and he'd shown off the horse to Pike expecting some good-natured mockery from the sailor.

*"You rode Nightcamp? When?"*

*"Three weeks ago. We rode on the night of Independence Day, though I know that holiday is hateful to you British."*

*"My God, where did you go? Why?"*

*"I can't tell you. But I've come up with a doozy of a scheme in case the statue fails. I'm afraid I'll have to leave New Vineland soon."*

*"Come off it, Pike! I revealed everything to you."*

*"After a while."*

*"Damn you."*

*"Why Harry, if I didn't know better, I'd think you're jealous of my friendship with Nightcamp."*

Maybe he was. Here Pike was, hinting at a clandestine mission with Nightcamp; and Goodman had only introduced them to each other two weeks before *that*. Had a month really pass since that night? How could it be *just* a month? He felt like a man torn between two very different perceptions of time, and the source of his confusion was the statue's progress. The obligations of his disguise as a traveling pastor kept him from staying in New Vineland to watch James at work. But when he managed to return every few days, the changes were apparent. What had been a thirty-foot block of stone four weeks ago now showed recognizable facial features, and suggestions of arms and hands. The remarkable advancements came so fast it was impossible to think a whole month had passed, yet by all rights a single sculptor should have taken half a year to match James's achievement.

But how had he accomplished it?

*"It's a startling thing to watch him work, Harry. Evan Vines stands on this platform to the left and holds the same pompous pose for hours on end. He could save himself the trouble. Once Hobbs starts work, I don't think he ever bothers to look up. He's got it in his head and knows just what he wants. I tell you, sometimes he doesn't even seem to be sculpting the rock. More like...communing with it. It never seems like he's doing that much work. A chisel here and there. But then you see the difference the next day, and you scratch your head."*

Pike's description had troubled Goodman. In the past, whenever James spoke of his obsession with stone, he sounded like a man describing an opium addiction. *"I forget everything. Time means nothing. Food and water are pointless. Even family—"* and here James choked up like a man realizing the depths of his damnation. Goodman always believed James was being dramatic when he went on like this. The notion he could forget about Katherine and Lily seemed ridiculous. But since he started work on the statue, had he mentioned them at all? Did they concern him in the slightest?

*Of course, he does. James can surrender to his compulsions because he knows I'm looking out for his family. He'll never forget them.*

When he arrived at the Hobbs farm, he found Katherine hard at work in the kitchen. She offered him the briefest of smiles.

"Is James well?"

"He is."

She nodded and turned her back to him, as she had every other time he'd visited in James's absence.

"He's doing the Lord's work," Goodman said. "You have to understand that."

"I haven't been asked to understand anything. Just to accept it. I've done so because I trust my husband, but you'll never know how I feel about being kept ignorant of everything that's happening."

"I promise you it's for the best. James thinks of nothing but you and Lily."

He saw her back stiffen. "The tomatoes are ready to be harvested."

Goodman frowned and nodded. "I better see to it then. Anything to help."

He took a basket and went into the crop fields. He found Lily sitting next to that strange, impossible giant pumpkin. There was a faint but lingering stink in the air, like rotting fish. He'd noted it before and wondered if the pumpkin might be rotting from within.

"Mr. Goodman, Fat Jack was just singing about you!" the girl said, running to hug his leg.

He smiled. "And how did the song go?"

She laughed. "It's a secret!"

"I see. Well, I'm here to help with the farm. Your father told me to tell you that he misses you very much and he'll see you soon."

"When?"

"That's still very hard to say. But at least I'm here, right?"

Lily walked back to the pumpkin and Goodman cast a baleful glance at the sky.

*I'm unwanted and useless everywhere. My friends are making plans behind my back and not telling me things I deserve to know. Oh, Katherine, believe me, I quite comprehend how you feel. But you have a trust I don't have. As soon as I'm finished here, I'm going to ride back to New Vineland and demand Pike and Nightcamp tell me what else they're scheming.*

# Chapter Thirty-Nine

## October 1830

Lily wiped the icy dew from Fat Jack's shell and smoothed the blanket over him as best she could, though it covered less than half of the pumpkin's massive body. She shivered and wished she'd brought a second blanket for herself and a third for Toad, though he never seemed bothered by temperature. Since their first meeting in June, the hottest summer nights never troubled him, and he seemed to welcome the mosquitos that swarmed over his white body. There were no insects to trouble them now. It was almost becoming too cold for her to stay out at night. Could she maybe sneak Toad into the house? Her imagination offered so many possibilities, but reality crushed them every night they met.

"There," she said. "Fat Jack might be a little more awake if he's warm."

Toad sprang atop the pumpkin and squatted there, puffing his cheeks wide and turning his head left and right.

"Guess what Toad's doing."

"You're an owl in a tree."

Toad put his hands over his wide mouth and his body shook.

"You're pretending to be a lighthouse?"

"No. Anna won't ever guess."

The lower half of his body expanded across Fat Jack, almost as if his flesh were melting and running. It began to take on the pumpkin's orange color.

"Don't worry, big egg. Toad keeps you warm."

"You're a hen!"

Toad shook again. All at once, his flesh drew up and he sprang to the ground and danced around Lily. She started to clap before she remembered it was the middle of the night. After four months of meeting Toad in the crop rows every night, Lily now realized Mama was a deep sleeper, but she didn't dare put her faith in that as Toad began hollering about getting Fat Jack to hatch. She put her finger to her lips. He went silent and sank into himself until his round head floated atop a puddle of skin.

"Now don't pout, Toad. I can't stay out here if Mama wakes up. Hopefully, she goes on sleeping just like Fat Jack does," she said, rubbing the pumpkin with the blanket. "I do wish he'd wake, though. You'd like his songs."

Toad's flesh rose into its usual shape. "Maybe Toad can summon him."

"But Fat Jack is right here, Toad."

"Toad's summoning song will wake him."

"I don't know if that's a good idea."

"Anna never likes Toad's ideas."

He collapsed back into a fleshy puddle.

Lily sighed and sat down. She was very cold and wanted to be inside. More than anything, she wanted Papa home. In a strange way, Toad's company was almost a replacement for Papa. At the very least, his strangeness had blunted the loneliness she felt over Papa's absence throughout August. But once September came and the air began to cool, Lily found Toad's visits weren't enough. Why couldn't Papa come just once? Mr. Goodman came every other week, always assuring her of Papa's progress. *"He finished the face now and it's a glory to behold."* *"When I saw your father the last time, he was hard at work on the right leg. From the foot to the knee is taller than your house."* Lily cherished every scrap she heard and often daydreamed about watching Papa work on such a large block. But every time she thought Papa must be close to finishing, Mr. Goodman gave the saddest shake of the head.

"Why is Anna quiet?"

She frowned, unable to count how many times she'd spent the whole night getting him to call her "Lily." But the next night she was Anna again, always and forever Anna.

"I'm missing my papa, Toad."

"Where is he? Toad can summon him for you!"

"I don't think even you could reach him from here. Papa's in New Vineland."

Toad jumped up and landed on the other side of her, pushing his face too close to hers. It startled Lily, but his earnestness also made her giggle. "Toad knows New Vineland. Toad's papa is there."

"*Your* papa?"

Toad nodded.

"Is your Mama there, too?"

"Mother Isobel watches over Toad."

"Your mama's name is Isobel? Mine's Katherine."

Toad's long tongue swiped across his face before slurping back into his mouth.

"Katheranna," he said. "Mother Isobel says Toad will kill his papa when the time comes."

Lily gasped. "Your mama wants you to kill your papa?"

"Mother Isobel told Toad."

"But why? Don't they love each other?"

"Love?"

Lily got up. "Don't you know what that is?"

Toad shook his head.

"But you must, Toad. You're so nice."

Toad's black eyes stared out from his round white face.

"Love is like the summoning song," she said. "Except I think it's when two people sing it at each other at the same time."

"Will Anna sing her summoning song at Toad?"

"I don't know how."

"Toad will have Mother Isobel teach Anna. Then when she hides next time, she'll know when Toad goes seeking."

"Why would I hide?"

"Anna always hides, and then Toad finds."

"But I keep telling you, I haven't been hiding. I've been here all this time."

"What's all this time?"

"Since I was born. I've been here for ten years, Toad."

Lily didn't see any trace of comprehension in the dark pools of his eyes. But his white skin flashed bright red and she took this as a warning.

"And you found me, Toad! You're so clever, the way you found me."

"Toad always finds Anna."

His color faded back to imitation moonlight. He stretched himself out longer than Lily could believe. Everything below his waist flattened and snaked its way out of the crops and toward the river.

"Toad heard Mother Isobel's song calling him. Is Anna ready to hide again?"

"You want to play hide and seek right now?"

His arms wrapped around her like a tight piece of rope. She screamed and Toad turned and began taking her toward the river. Lily cried out again and again toward the house and the pumpkin. Her thoughts blared in panic.

*Fat Jack, help me! Please help me, Fat Jack!*

A rumble came from the ground, strong enough to trip Toad. As he let go of her, Lily ran back to the pumpkin and tried to get on top of it. Fat Jack's shell had somehow become hot, almost scalding, and Lily fell back wringing the pain from her palms. Steam misted the air around the pumpkin.

"Jack?" Lily said, her voice trembling. "Fat Jack, can you hear me?"

Whatever life had animated inside Fat Jack died away at once. He didn't speak. The rumbling ceased and the shell began to cool. Toad meanwhile hopped around the pumpkin, touching it and drawing back, like someone poking and goading an idle bear. Lily turned and rushed toward the house, running her hardest through the crops. Sharp, stiff leaves and stems scraped her face, arms, and legs. She ignored the pain, convinced Toad's arms were wrapping around her wrists and ankles. But he wasn't there. She was going to make it inside.

As she gained the porch, Toad sprang upon her, shouting, "Anna, Anna, Anna! Toad always finds Anna!" Lily fell forward, pushing through the door and landing across the threshold with Toad on her back. He was jumping on her, pummeling her with his bulk. She struggled to breathe against his crushing weight as Toad went on hollering, "Anna, Anna, Anna!"

Too many things happened all at once. She heard Mama screaming from the stairs. Then a new, overpowering sound came from outside the house. Thuds, scrapes, bangs, scratches, and many more noises told her something—many things—were rushing onto the porch, onto Toad.

Toad shrieked.

He crashed through the house, giving Lily a chance to roll onto her back and wheeze. Mama rushed down to protect her, one hand cupping Lily's head to her breast. Her other hand held Papa's gun.

"Lily, what's happening?"

She couldn't answer. Toad rolled and flopped about the floor; his body swarmed by animals that must have come out of the forest to attack Toad. That's what Lily kept telling herself even as she realized the impossible truth.

They were Papa's stone animals.

They'd come alive.

Sculpted rabbits, raccoons, and foxes worked to pin his arms and legs. Rock mice and rats scurried across his body, biting as they went. A crow Papa had made from a chunk of obsidian pecked at Toad's eyes as Toad stretched his neck and twisted about to dodge the menacing stone beak. He opened his mouth, showing those three sharp triangles of teeth, and lashed his head forward to bite off the crow's head. A shriek of pure agony followed as two teeth broke on the rock. Blood as black as ink, blacker than the crow itself, flowed from his mouth and from the smaller cuts across his body.

Toad stumbled past them, flailing. Somehow he found the door and fell outside.

"Anna! Toad needs help, Anna! Toad needs Anna!"

Lily pulled against Mama's restraining hand.

"That's Toad, Mama! I know him."

Mama's expression was blank. Her lips moved and Lily thought she was trying to say a prayer. But when the words came out, she heard: *James, you promised...James, what have you done?*

Toad went on flailing and rolling, throwing some of the statues off him while others clung tight with their stone teeth and claws. His mouth was open, and the wispy hand of the summoning song went from animal to animal in a desperate frenzy. Papa's sculptures did not answer the call. Instead, they pressed their attack, flipping Toad onto his belly. He now looked like a little boy being buried under a pile of rocks.

"Mama, please let go! Toad will die if I don't help him! I have to save Toad."

"James," Mama whispered. "James, you promised me!"

Lily couldn't believe she could ever do this, but she had no choice and bit down on Mama's arm. Mama cried out, released her and Lily crawled forward. Toad wasn't moving much now. The crow had perched atop the back of his round head, its merciless stone beak stabbing into his skin over and over, puncturing him like a leather needle punch. Lily grabbed the bird and it went lifeless in her grip. She threw it aside and began swiping the animals off with her forearms.

"Lily, get away from it!" Mama shouted from the doorway.

But Lily went on knocking the animals off Toad, giving him a chance to get up. He limped and stumbled toward the river with Lily, Mama, and more stone animals following. Other statues still clung to him and when he reached the dock, he tore most of them from his legs and chest and threw them into the water. The last sculpture still hanging on to him was the owl that had become Lily's favorite the moment Papa revealed it. Toad's body was covered in so much blood he almost seemed invisible to Lily, but she saw him rip the owl off his shoulder, its talons tearing up a chunk of blubbery flesh along the way. Toad raised the owl high and pitched it into the water, screaming, "Fly from the water! Toad dares you to fly!" The rock owl flapped its heavy wings even as it sank out of sight.

"Toad is King of the River!"

"Toad, please listen to me," Lily said as Mama came up behind her, aiming Papa's pistol at Toad's head.

"Get behind me now, child."

Toad crouched. Lily thought he was going to lunge. But he stayed still. Was he too hurt? Was he afraid? He seemed fascinated by Mama's face, his black eyes wider and rounder than ever. Mama was likewise fixated on Toad. The hand holding the gun shook but she didn't lower her aim.

"Lily," Mama said.

"Anna," Toad said.

Lily looked between them.

"Do as I say. Get behind me."

"Anna's going with Toad now."

Lily stepped closer to Mama. "I'm sorry, Toad. I need to stay here."

"Toad is taking Anna."

Toad leapt. Mama fired the gun and Lily heard a shocking, sickening splat from Toad's body, followed by a fresh shriek. But he didn't stop. His arms wrapped around her waist again and lifted her into the air.

The last thing Lily saw and heard was Mama running toward her, crying, "No! No!" Toad sprang and flipped. The sky became ground, the ground became sky.

Then Lily's world turned into freezing water.

# Chapter Forty

Lily woke to the feeling of ants crawling on her. Her arms, legs, and face were covered in little prickly sensations that jolted her to her feet as she slapped and scratched at her body. She stood breathless and confused in the morning light, leaves stuck to her hair and clothes. Her feet were lost in a pile of them that went up to her knees. She saw the imprint of where she'd been sleeping and realized she must have been buried under the leaves.

"Toad?"

Her voice sounded small, lonesome, and scared as she looked around and tried to make sense of her location. She walked over to the shoreline of a little finger of water just off from the river. The water did not smell good at all. How far away from home was she? Where was Mama? For all her questions, Lily felt little panic. This place, though unknown, was not strange. How could it be, thanks to the familiar song of the trees? She took a deep breath and headed into the forest.

"Where are you, Toad?"

The river had washed his blood from her skin and clothing. She saw no trace of blood on the ground. Could he have returned to the water? Were the leaves meant to hide her from danger while he was away?

*What if he's not coming back? What if he's dead?*

She tried not to think about it, but how could she not remember the way he'd been hurt? Mama had shot him, and Papa's animals...Lily felt dizzy. So much of what happened felt like a crazed dream. The rock animals couldn't have come to life. Why would they? *How* could they?

Lily's stomach rumbled. She wished she could eat every question going through her mind. She might never go hungry again.

"Toad?"

She heard something a little further into the woods. The sound wasn't unlike the snoring Papa did for about ten minutes after he fell asleep. Lily crept toward the source of the sound, careful about the noise of dead leaves and brittle sticks under her footfalls. She ducked to look through a screen of bushes and weeds and put both hands over her mouth to cork the cry building in her throat.

Toad was sprawled across a heavy chair that was broken in places and might have been dredged from the river. The left armrest was gone but the lower half of Toad's body was draped over the right armrest and his legs trailed along the ground like two thin lines of spilled flour. His torso was folded in on itself like a stack of towels and his head somehow rested atop it all like a disconnected plate. His eyes appeared to have sunk deep into his flesh. The cuts on his skin formed black scabs that seemed to be fading.

Around the chair, Lily found a collection of objects that seemed arranged rather than scattered. Most of them were the remains of long-dead animals and various pieces of bone. There were skulls of dogs and cats and one that looked like a person, though Lily had only seen such a thing in drawings. Toad had also collected pieces of driftwood, broken push poles, and what might have been planks from the side of a boat. There were shells and little crawdad claws and marbles and any number of stones polished smooth by the river. She would not have given most of what she saw a second thought, but encountering them together in this place gave the collection a somber air. They must have been very important to him and she wanted Toad to tell her their stories.

Two final things caught her attention. There was a stack of blue and yellow butterfly wings impaled on a long stick and the broken husks of cocoons scattered about on the ground. The wings were in tatters and faded in color, but there must have been hundreds of them. Lily couldn't conceive why Toad had collected them. The second object was just as mysterious. She picked up the sad remains of a leatherbound book. Cracked and deteriorating, the back cover was gone but the front piece remained and the stamped letters were legible. *Wieland. Charles Brockden Brown.* She opened the book and found the pages brittle and damaged, the text faded to suggestions of words.

Could Toad read? Lily couldn't imagine it. Did he *want* to read? Mama and Papa had taught her, but even now she still loved being read to, especially by Papa. She looked at Toad and knew no one had ever read to him. How terrible it must be, she told herself, to only know stories you had to make up for yourself.

She felt compelled to touch his head, taking pains to be delicate. After all the nights she'd spent with him, Lily knew so very little about him, and many of the things he said could not be understood. Did he really have a papa in New Vineland? And why did his mama want Toad to kill him? Was anything he said true? He looked so much like a frog, but over time she'd started seeing him as a boy pretending to be a frog. Or perhaps a frog trying to impersonate a boy.

Lily considered the moldering book in her left hand.

"Would you like me to tell you a story, Toad?"

Papa and Mama had very different notions of what she should hear. Mama read the Bible to her, and some of it she enjoyed, like when David beat Goliath. Papa's tales were better, full of myths and monsters. Sometimes he read them from a book and sometimes he spoke them from some page inside his head. Lily liked these stories best. They just felt truer.

One in particular she knew by heart. The words came to her as she sat by Toad's chair and looked at the trees.

"Once upon a time," she said, "there was a nasty little girl who just happened to be the daughter of a king. She had always gotten everything she wanted and was very spoiled. Some days it seemed like she wanted everything in the world. One thing she'd never asked for, however, was a frog. She hated frogs because she was afraid if she touched one it would give her warts. No prince would be in love with her if she had warts!"

She smiled, remembering the face Papa made whenever he said *wart*.

"One day, the princess went to look out the window of her castle, when she saw a frog on the windowsill. The room was very high up, so high even the trees seemed small, so she was confused about how the frog had gotten there."

*"Toad knows how he got there. He did what Toad would do and jumped!"*

Toad spoke so fast that Lily couldn't comprehend he was really awake before he gathered himself and jumped from the chair. She looked up and didn't see him at all. She stood.

"Toad?"

His voice came from the treetops. "Can Anna find Toad?"

"I can't," she said, turning. "You're so good at hiding, Toad! Where are you?"

"Here," he said, and she spun toward a tree on her right.

"No, Toad's really *here*."

"Now Toad's *here*."

His words came from so many directions it didn't seem possible. He must have been jumping from branch to branch faster than she could see. His playful delight in showing off made her very happy. Toad was *fine*.

"Okay, okay. Come down, Toad! I want to see you!"

She heard a thud behind her. Toad had dropped into his chair and lounged there, his bright black eyes smiling just as much as his mouth, which showed a glimpse of his broken teeth.

"All hail Toad, King of the River!"

Lily gave a little bow because in the stories Papa read to her everyone bowed before kings and queens.

"Is that your throne, King Toad?"

"Throne?"

He said the word like he'd never heard it before. Then he got up and stood over his prizes.

"This is Muskrat," he said, holding up a little skeleton. "Muskrat was Toad's first friend, so Toad wants him to stay here always. And this is stone, and this is bone, and this is Anna."

Lily swallowed. He was holding up the human skull.

"But Toad," she said. "I'm Anna."

Toad held the skull out to her. She was afraid to touch it and so she pointed out the butterfly wings.

"Why did you do that, Toad?"

"Toad hates when the worms become leaves."

"They're called butterflies," she said. "Don't you think they're beautiful? I like to look at cocoons and wait for them to open—"

"Toad knows cocoons. He likes their taste."

"Oh. But here's one you didn't eat," she said, spying a whole one on the ground. She doubted anything was alive inside it.

"Toad likes it when they're fuzzy worms. Toad hates it when they're leaves. Toad hates when things change."

"I think the change is wonderful. Cocoons should be protected and cherished and—"

He took the cocoon and put it in his mouth. Then he brushed past her and returned to his chair.

"Toad wants Anna to stay this time and not hide again. Toad is tired of hide and seek."

"That's very nice of you, Toad. But I have a home."

"Toad doesn't like it there."

"My mama will be worried about me. She won't understand what happened, but she'll want to meet you. Can't we go back?"

Toad sulked, his body seeming to melt across the chair and down the sides.

"*Please* Toad," Lily said, taking a step toward him. "Without Papa there, Mama will be lonely and she'll need help with the chores. Who'll look after Fat Jack if I'm not there? I can come back anytime. I promise I will. Or maybe you can stay with us."

Toad drew his legs up against his chest so tight it all became one flesh. His black eyes stared straight ahead.

"Toad? Are you okay?"

"Anna's mama tried to hurt Toad."

"She didn't mean to," Lily said, her throat going dry. "She was just trying to protect me."

"Toad knows he knows her."

"What?"

"Toad knows it here."

"In your heart?"

"Toad knows her."

Lily bit her lip. Toad's stare deepened. She didn't know what he was seeing but felt certain it wasn't the trees.

"You said you'd watched me from the river," she said. "Maybe you saw Mama with me too."

"No. Toad knows her."

She looked at the book, then at the rest of the collection, and then back to Toad. He sat as motionless as stone, and no matter how hard she tried, she couldn't get him to speak again.

"Would you like to hear another story, Toad?"

He stared ahead in deepening silence.

Lily sighed, sat, and began telling a tale about a little girl lost in the woods.

234

# BONE

# Chapter Forty-One

## July 1830

*It has been too long, friend stallion.*

The words came as if carried on a cold wind just as Wormwood untethered him for the night. Nightcamp remained in place, a rare instance of being too scared to move. Wormwood must have noticed because he backed off a step.

*Long hast thou suffered, but suffering feeds and strengthens the spirit. Accept this from one who knows.*

Nightcamp worked to make his thoughts go blank despite a bevy of questions and concerns. Part of him wondered if Mistress Isobel's voice was some remnant from a dream the untethering had disrupted. He felt less hopeful of that now. The summoning song, so persistent and pervasive all around him, was just a touch stronger and more focused as if aimed at him. It had been so long since she contacted him that he'd forgotten how her presence in his mind felt, each word sharp and cold like the tip of an icy dagger. He looked at Wormwood, who intuited not to speak. He even seemed to be holding his breath for fear of making any sound at all.

*The hour of thy tedious enslavement draws to its close. I will send forth my own son to destroy your tormentor. Then we will ride together at the head of a mighty host and put the wisdom of stone into the hearts of all mankind. Thy bearing shall cast fear and admiration even beyond the lengths of my great tower's shadow.*

A vicious thrill shot through him as scene after scene of triumph played out in his mind's eye. Nightcamp knew this was not his imagination at work. The images were shown to him by Mistress Isobel, a taste of the greater rewards to come.

*Soon.*

The stronger sense of the summoning song faded away. When it was gone, Nightcamp allowed himself a bit of movement. His hind legs almost buckled causing Wormwood to touch him.

"Was it the witch?"

Nightcamp whinnied.

"After all this time? Do you think she knows what we're doing?"

*All is not well*

*But the plan seems intact.*

*Questions I have,*

*Information we lack.*

Nightcamp and Wormwood left the tower and walked around to the western side, where James Hobbs labored—though Nightcamp felt *labor* was not the right word for the man's dedication.

Compulsion might be the better term.

The block had been placed on the western side because the tower itself was the only structure that could hide it from any eyes gazing down from the cliff to the east. Nightcamp remembered the mason's reaction when he saw his 30-foot medium for the first time. James Hobbs had whistled and said, "I can see I have my work cut out for me." He'd sounded neither intimidated nor tentative. If anything, Nightcamp thought his tone better suited a starving man being seated at a banquet.

Now it was the evening of this land's so-called Independence Day, and Hobbs worked alone before the block, which was surrounded by ladders and three levels of wooden scaffolding. Wormwood had described the daily ruse the mason affected while Vine spent hours holding a majestic pose that could only be kept in his own imagination. His body was more withered and broken than ever, stooped, unwashed, wizened. For all of James Hobbs's uncanny abilities, he could not see past the illusion of New Vineland any more than Goodman or Pike. His sculpture reflected the magnificent figure Evan Vines projected in his mind.

In the morning and afternoon, Hobbs employed all the traditional tools of his trade, and the results were a tedious, painstaking process that suggested the statue might be completed in two years. Once Vines was asleep, however, the mason put aside the quaint hammer and chisel and began his true sculpting; a swift and beautiful artistry that conquered the stone slab at a breathtaking rate, conjuring the figure of Evan Vines from deep within the slab the way water might be drawn up a siphon. He moved along the block, both palms flat to it, his right ear pressed as if listening for a heartbeat. He seemed to hear it, and he moved along like someone following the path of a pulse. As he walked, he broke into a singsong chant—

*Bikoyas stona*
*Stona ne kwes*
*Bikkoyas stona kwano*
*Stona petnos*
*Stona dantos*

Was this magic? Was it something else? Nightcamp could not guess. Sometimes Hobbs's voice struggled to qualify as a whisper. At other times, he shouted the words at such a volume that Wormwood worried he might wake Evan Vines. The language was unknown to Nightcamp and not at all like the songs he'd ever heard Mistress Isobel sing. Nor did the great slab respond to Hobbs in a way Nightcamp could understand. As he sang and his hands moved, fissures appeared across the face of the rock. Pieces fell away in precise chips, further bringing the image of Evan Vines to the fore. At times, Hobbs seemed in contact with an entity locked deep inside the block, coaxing it to the surface. So far, he brought forth the statue's arms and legs and an identifiable outline of the face. The details became finer with every sunrise.

"His progress is remarkable," Wormwood said. "This man's gift is allowing your scheme to take root faster than I would have thought possible. It gives me hope."

*As fast as we're moving*
*It may be too slow*
*The endgame is looming*
*That much we can know.*

Wormwood flinched at this. "What did the witch say to you?"

*She claims that her son*
*Will kill Evan Vines*
*Then she'll marshal her servants*
*To the doom of mankind.*

"Son?"

Nightcamp snorted his confusion.

"Some *other* monstrosity she mothered out of rock, I suppose. How much time do we have?"

He shook his head and Wormwood's anxiety became palpable.

"Then we must tell Hobbs. Somehow he has to go faster. Even if we don't have precise information, if the witch is contacting you now then it must mean she plans to move soon."

*Her sense of time*
*Is different from ours*
*Years her minutes,*
*Centuries her hours.*

Wormwood nodded, letting out a sigh. "Yes, of course you're right—as we both well know. But the situation is intolerable. She could strike in the next hour or the next decade. Isn't it prudent to assume more immediate action?"

Nightcamp agreed.

*A second plan we must enact*
*To safeguard the main attack.*
*Find me Pike, we must now accept*
*The idea that we did reject.*

Wormwood frowned. "We rejected it for good reason. But what other option is there? I'll see if Pike can be located."

Nightcamp returned to the tower, thinking of the night Goodman brought Pike to him. He'd liked the man at once, sensing he was the sort who preferred the company of animals to humanity; and though Nightcamp required Wormwood's mediation to speak to him in a direct way, in short order they had grasped each other's thoughts without assistance.

When they finished their initial interview, about an hour later, Pike had sat back and said, "Well, I'll be damned, Harry. Everything you said was true."

They both looked at Goodman, who'd fallen asleep. Pike then stroked Nightcamp's neck and said, "That's babes for you. They need their rest, don't they, fellow old timer?"

Nightcamp snorted.

"He likes you," Wormwood said.

"I like him. There are men who talk to their horses like they were people. Tell them their sorrows, their loneliness. Some people call that pathetic, but to me, it always seemed the wisest choice of company."

"None of us measure up to him," Wormwood said.

Nightcamp had caught himself raising his head high and forced it down in humility. As Wormwood went on, though, the humble pose became hard to hold. Then Wormwood made the critical comment.

"He's our general. Without him, we'd have no plan to destroy New Vineland."

"A regular four-legged Napoleon," Pike said. "I may have been in the dark until now, but Harry's been hinting at a greater purpose for some time. It seemed like it was just the two of us against New Vineland, and I thought we should seek help."

"Help?" Wormwood said. "From whom?"

"The same man I was suggesting to Harry. Andrew Jackson."

The name meant nothing to Nightcamp. Wormwood also appeared at a loss.

"The three of you aren't much up on politics, I take it. Jackson is the President of the United States. He's not a man to ignore a threat once he's aware of it and he commands the army—which we're going to need sooner or later. I'm thinking *sooner*."

Nightcamp had shared Wormwood's immediate dismissiveness.

"Have you not understood what we've told you? No army can hurt this place. The buildings you see do not exist. The people are no longer flesh and blood."

"The tower's real, isn't it?"

"Yes."

"It's made of stone, isn't it?"

"Yes."

"Well, Wormwood, I haven't seen a stone structure yet that can outlast massed cannon fire."

"The artillerymen wouldn't manage a single barrage. The witch's servants would swarm and slaughter them. What good could rifle fire or bayonets do against rock?"

That had been the end of it as far as Nightcamp was concerned. He respected and admired Pike's passion, but the man's hopeful imagination had exceeded all reason.

*And now we're rushing to embrace it after all,* Nightcamp thought.

# Chapter Forty-Two

Wormwood returned with Pike, who came straight to Nightcamp, beaming and animated, his excitement taking a decade off his appearance.

"You're making the right decision!"

Wormwood tried to caution him, but Pike wasn't listening.

"Andrew Jackson discounts nothing, especially if the warning comes from me. This isn't that Massachusetts bastard Adams we're dealing with now. I can just imagine trying to convince old John Quincy to marshal the army against a witch. But Jackson's dealt with one before."

Nightcamp cocked his head. Wormwood squinted. Pike looked between them, grinning.

"That got your attention, didn't it? You didn't give me a chance to tell you about it before you shut me down. The President is from Tennessee, and after the war in Louisiana, he returned to his home state. Some of us loyal soldiers went with him. Along the way, we heard about a man named John Bell, whose family was said to be bedeviled by a witch. Jackson determined to see it for himself."

"And?"

"I wouldn't call the result a climactic battle. We heard a voice mocking us, and some force played havoc with our horses. We could do nothing against it and left the next day in failure."

"The witch we're facing now does not play pranks, Pike."

"President Jackson's *not* a man to forget a failure. If I were to tell him the Bell Witch was at work here, he'd have troops marching by morning. That's probably just what needs to happen too, I wager, if you're reconsidering my plan now."

Nightcamp noticed Wormwood looking toward him for advice on what to divulge, and he gave a nod of permission.

"It seems the situation has changed."

Pike turned to Nightcamp. "Whether it has or not, a truly great general doesn't leave himself without options. I don't question your decision to put it all on Hobbs and his statue. Maybe in the end the battle has to be stone versus stone. That doesn't make bone and muscle worthless. Even having them as a diversion is better than nothing, and believe me, Jackson will find a way to make himself a little more valuable than mere fodder."

"We're in agreement," Wormwood said. "Are you prepared to leave now?"

"I am. If I ride hard, I can be in Washington in four days."

Nightcamp snorted. Wormwood likewise laughed.

"What's so funny?"

"It's just that you've never been on a horse like Nightcamp before," Wormwood said as he prepared the saddle. Nightcamp liked how wide Pike's eyes became.

"You're taking me yourself?"

They went outside again and Pike hoisted himself up. Nightcamp felt him settle in and take hold of the bridle.

"Careful now. I was never a great rider. Always more comfortable in a boat—*whoa!*"

Nightcamp sped forward, streaking into the night, enlivened by the cold air. If the rushing wind bothered Pike, he showed no signs of it. Far from seeming uneasy in the saddle, he whooped and hollered, his glee most boyish and wonderful to Nightcamp's hearing.

"Incredible!" he shouted into Nightcamp's right ear. "I feel like a man who's been on a river barge his whole life experiencing a clipper ship at full sail! Every star looks like a comet!"

Nightcamp galloped harder than ever, thundering over roads, skating across creeks and ponds like some flat piece of onyx skipped by a titan. Pike's weight was perfect on his back, a complement, an extension of himself rather than a burden. For a time, he let himself forget about any mission, any sense of urgency. He ran with more freedom than he ever found in a dream, powered by two jubilant hearts.

They reached the Capitol at midnight. The Executive Mansion was a testament to the magnificence of stone, Grecian, white and hard. Even the candlelight in the many windows offered no hint of softness. The sentinels standing on either side of the entrance seemed to flinch out of a standing sleep as Nightcamp stopped. Pike got down, stumbling a little, calling out to the startled guards. For a moment, Nightcamp thought they were going to shoot him on sight.

There was an argument. The guards must have thought Pike a crazy man, or some Independence Day reveler who'd celebrated to excess in a tavern. The commotion stirred life inside the house. One of the candles left the upstairs window. Mere minutes later, the front door opened. The man standing there could only be the President, regardless of the late hour. He stood tall and pale, ramrod straight. Nightcamp sensed his stern bearing, his coldness. Pike told him the man's nickname was Old Hickory, but Nightcamp found nothing arboreal about the man. He too was stone.

He dismissed the guards with a wave and gripped Pike by his forearms.

"By God, Pike, it's been too long! How is it you're here? Why?"

"That, sir, is a matter of urgent discussion. Is there a place where the three of us can talk in private?"

"*Three?*"

Pike rubbed Nightcamp's muzzle.

Nightcamp saw Jackson's eyes gleam dark with intrigue. The man seemed to share a certain sentiment with Mistress Isobel, a willingness to take pleasure when and where they could find it, even if from the mouth of a madman.

"Very well, Pike," he said. "May I suggest the Presidential stable?"

# Chapter Forty-Three

President Jackson wasn't quite as credulous as Pike claimed he'd be.

"I could almost believe you based on the horse alone. At the Hermitage, I have many prized thoroughbreds, but none compare to this. A creature of pure, indomitable will, aren't you?" he said, stepping close to look into Nightcamp's right eye. His gaze was practiced and observant. Even Mistress Isobel's stare did not feel as penetrating.

"Yes, pure will," he continued, stepping back. "Magnificent. Washington would have traded Nelson and Blueskin together to acquire him. A *witch's* steed."

"Mr. President, everything I've said about New Vineland is true."

Jackson waved his hand. "Pike, Pike, the place is not unknown to me or the government. Congressmen have been receiving letters about the place for years now—concerned fathers upset over the disappearance of a wayward son, towns left half-abandoned because New Vineland's delights lured them away. I wish Calhoun and most of my cabinet would take a trip to the place, along with their bitch wives. I might get a bit of peace if they vanished forever."

"This is no time for jokes!"

"Who's joking, Pike? New Vineland has been investigated by at least one congressional committee. They've gone there and found nothing amiss."

"Then they fell for the illusion. It's lucky they weren't trapped by it themselves. There are also certain people scattered throughout the town, special servants of the witch called minders who make sure the facade is maintained. The committee members must have been intercepted."

Jackson laughed. Nightcamp could see Pike was fuming and more than a little hurt by his friend's disbelief. Jackson must have seen it too, and though he gave little evidence of caring for anyone's feelings, he seemed to have a true affection for the sailor.

"What would happen if they hadn't been intercepted?"

"If they'd gone into the tower and made the bargain I told you about, they'd become stone statues."

Jackson shook his head.

"Mr. President—*Andrew*—you have to trust what I'm saying. Remember our run-in with the Bell Witch? There was a time when you believed in such things."

"There was a time when I wasn't President of the United States, too."

Pike scowled and turned to Nightcamp. "Come on. There's nothing for us here. We'll have to go it alone and hope your original plan is enough."

"Ah," Jackson said. "The horse's plan to have a mason sculpt a massive stone statue that he can bring to life?"

Nightcamp whinnied and tapped his right hoof against the floor. Jackson cocked his head.

"What does the infernal creature say, Pike?"

"I don't know. His interpreter isn't here. But he's probably calling me a damn fool."

Nightcamp was ready to have Pike climb into the saddle, but the man stopped. He scratched Nightcamp's ear and pivoted back to Jackson.

"Do you not believe *anything* I've told you? Or is it that you can chew on the individual bits and pieces but can't swallow the whole?"

Jackson's lips became a thin line. "What gambit are you trying now, Pike?"

"For the sake of humoring me, I only ask for one thing. If I can prove one element of my story is true now, will you make a leap of faith on the rest of it?"

"Perhaps."

"Damn perhapses! You say you admire Nightcamp. I'm asking you to take a ride on him. That's the surest way I know to prove his speed."

Nightcamp snorted in surprise at the offer. He snorted again when Jackson responded with a brief clap of approval.

"Oh, that's very good, Pike. And very tempting. But if he is as you say, I'd be surrendering myself to your power. The witch's steed could kidnap me all the way to New Vineland or to anywhere else it liked, and I'd be helpless."

Nightcamp lowered his head in respect for the man's reasoning and a begrudging approval of his suspicious nature. Too much suspicion brought paralysis but the right amount brought wisdom. And Jackson did not at all seem like a paralytic.

"You have to meet us halfway," Pike said.

"Do I?"

Nightcamp looked between Jackson and Pike as the two men engaged in a stare-down. He could already tell Pike wasn't going to win, and that proved correct. Pike sighed and turned back to Nightcamp again, putting his foot in the stirrup.

"I never dreamed seeking the aid of Andrew Jackson would be a wasted effort."

As Pike started to hoist himself across Nightcamp's back, Jackson reached out and touched his shoulder.

"I have a proposal."

It was almost painful for Nightcamp to hear, the way all the hope flooded back into Pike's voice at this mere morsel of new possibility. "*Yes?*"

"I do require proof, Pike, but I won't submit myself to any test. I will, however, send another."

"What do you have in mind, Mr. President?"

"I want you to stay here with me, Pike. I could use an old confidant at my side here in the Capitol, even a crazy one."

Jackson silenced Pike with a raised hand when he began to protest.

"The horse," he continued, "will take my servant Charles back to New Vineland. He will stay there for one week, and then you will bring him back to me. I will hear what he has to say."

"Don't you see that won't matter? All he'll report on is the illusion. The only proof would be if he took the bargain—"

"Then I'll see to it he does."

Silence fell over the three of them. Pike looked old and pale.

"You'd be sacrificing him," he said in a dead tone.

"Sacrifices are made all the time."

"It's not the same thing, and you know it."

"Those are my terms," Jackson said. "Charles can be ready by the morning. I'll leave you and your conspirator alone to decide."

As Jackson turned to go, Pike said, "You're not the person I thought you were, Mr. President."

"Perhaps not," Jackson said. "Nevertheless, I'm the person you need."

# Chapter Forty-Four

As Nightcamp returned to New Vineland, he told himself he was just missing Pike. He didn't know if all horses were the same when it came to remembering those they'd borne upon their backs, but Nightcamp's memories were based more on how their weight felt rather than any voice, face, or name. Most details of his first owner were lost to him except an echo of his heft. So it was with all subsequent riders, from Mistress Isobel's sparrow weight all the way to the sharp angles of Evan Vines's figure. Some bodies felt better than others. Felt *right*. The sensation had nothing to do with mere matters of pounds.

The man in the saddle now, Charles, was about the same height and weight as Pike, yet his heaviness and discomfort were palpable. He said nothing during the whole return trip to New Vineland until they got within sight of the town, and then Nightcamp heard him gasp. "I didn't think a place like this could exist. Sakes alive, look at that tower. That's where Master said I was to go. At least it's impossible to miss."

The man's weight got heavier the more he talked. He had a light-hearted tone, but Nightcamp heard the underlying nervousness, the fear. The further along they went, the more Nightcamp felt the queer sense he somehow carried himself upon his back, a twin in human form.

*Sacrifices are made all the time.*

Such an easy sentiment to express when calling upon others to make it for you. Nightcamp thought of the countless times he'd carried men to their doom. Changes in roads, lands, and places didn't matter: it was always the same trip, the same destination. How strange and different the burden seemed now. Nightcamp wanted to credit a transformation in himself, won through guilt and suffering, unrecognizable to others. In the end, though, the distinction rested with the character of the man on his back. He was the first person to sit atop Nightcamp's back through no fault of his own, the only rider to never choose the journey.

They arrived a little before sunrise, a few hours later than they could have had Nightcamp run anywhere close to maximum speed. He did not go straight to the tower as he supposed he should have. Instead, he took Charles to the docks. A flotilla of boats was arriving from both directions, filled with people who answered the summoning song. Nightcamp snorted and Charles climbed down with evident confusion, looking toward the tower. Nightcamp studied him, desperate for any evidence the man heard the song as well.

*Please hear it,* he thought. *You must.*

But Jackson's slave stood shaking his head at the people rushing by. "They sure are all in a rush to get into that tower. Master Andrew's given me some strange orders in my time, but this one's the strangest. Almost as strange as you are, I guess," he said, putting a hand on Nightcamp's neck. He whistled and Nightcamp felt his fingers touch the scars on his flanks.

"Someone's been mighty mean to you, haven't they? I know all about it. Take a look."

Nightcamp was seldom astounded, but what Charles did next managed it. The slave pulled his shirt over his head and showed the marks on his back. He turned to Nightcamp and gave a grim little nod of understanding.

"Master Andrew never beat a horse, though," he said. "At least I never seen him do it. He favors them over us when it comes to value."

A trembling went up Nightcamp's legs. He sent his thoughts out toward Wormwood in an urgent call, though he stopped short of explaining the matter. Charles put his shirt on and started toward the tower. Nightcamp walked beside him, trying to think of any alternative. With so many statues to choose from, couldn't they find one that looked close enough to the slave to fool Jackson? But what would happen if the *deception* didn't fool him? He'd demand Charles be brought to him at once, with no chance of moving forward with Pike's plan.

*Sacrifices are made all the time.*

Wormwood intercepted them. Nightcamp saw his confusion.

"Master Andrew told me to go into the tower and ask for something," Charles said. "He didn't say what, though."

"You're one of Jackson's slaves?"

"Yes, sir."

Nightcamp was about to surrender and reveal the details to Wormwood, but he found he didn't have to.

Wormwood had guessed.

"I'll take it from here," he said, leading Charles away. Nightcamp forced himself to follow, but he just couldn't make his pace keep up. He went on listening as he fell further and further behind.

"Inside the tower, you'll find your heart's desire," Wormwood said. "You need only give something of yourself in exchange for it."

"But I don't have nothing. I'm property my own self."

"An unimportant matter inside the tower, my friend."

Nightcamp stopped altogether and hung his head. Wormwood went on talking, his tone convincing, his words promising. He must have given the same talk hundreds of times before to those who chanced upon New Vineland and needed *minding*. He must have been long past addressing any qualms.

Or perhaps he shared Jackson's sentiment.

*Sacrifices are made all the time.*

Nightcamp waited until they were gone and then he entered the tower as well. He would never understand the dimensions of its darkness and the forces that guided people once they were inside it. He felt no presence except himself and saw nothing but the hook on the floor. He could not tether himself, but he waited over it with his head bowed anyway and stayed that way for hours until Wormwood arrived just ahead of Evan Vines. He said nothing as he removed the saddle and then tied him down. He stepped back as Vines shambled into the room as broken as ever, almost feeble in voice when he asked for the crop.

The first strike was not so solid, but he gained strength as he went. The crop struck Nightcamp over and over until he was snorting short, agonized breaths. Nightcamp thought of Charles's back. Where was the man now? Was the deed done? Might he somehow even be glad for a stone existence, his body invulnerable to the whip? Anger shot through Nightcamp. How far he'd sunk to let himself clutch at such justifications! Vines was about to toss the crop aside when Nightcamp kicked back with his right leg and then his left. He bellowed in defiance.

"What's *this*?" Evan Vines said, his voice sounding decades younger. "Have you been keeping this spirit hidden from me? Have you been mocking me with fake submission? Oh, beast, now I'll make you pay!"

"But sir, you're due to pose—"

"Forget the statue for now! It can wait in the face of this pleasure."

The crop fell upon Nightcamp's body everywhere like a swarm of angry bees. Wild fantasies of transfiguration ran through his mind as the lashings drove him to the edge of madness. He saw himself as a piano whose every key was a different kind of pain, and Evan Vines sat playing every possible note, working the screams from deep within the well of his being. By the end, as blood dripped from cuts on both flanks, he thought he was crying out in a human voice. *No no no no no!* After all he'd done, after what he'd allowed to happen, only the most profound beating could wring humanity into him rather than out, and when Vines at last cast the crop away in sweaty exhaustion, Nightcamp thought of Charles, saw himself as Charles, and wished he could be even more flesh than he was for the sake of Charles—flesh to be cut all the way down to the bone of truth.

Vines left without a word. He did not even call for Wormwood to attend him, and as soon as he vanished, Wormwood came to Nightcamp with his hands out but not touching, as if he had no clue where to begin.

"What are you trying to prove?" he said. If his words were reproachful, his tone nevertheless was soft and anxious. "Did that make you feel better? What's done is done. Blame me. Blame Jackson. He needed proof. I suspected as much despite everything Pike was saying. There are men who are born belonging in fairy tales, impractical dreamers from the start. This is Pike. Goodman too. There are men who are born belonging in encyclopedias and old esoteric texts, like our Masonic friend. Then there are men like myself, and Jackson, men born belonging in a ledger book. Some men are born as high numbers, and the rest of us strive to become such. Regardless, our calculating souls are the same."

He left and returned with balm. Nightcamp writhed as it was applied to his cuts.

"I've secured Charles's statue to keep it safe from the harvesters. At sundown, when I know Vines is asleep, I'll have it loaded into a cart. Jackson will be eager to get the proof he needs, and we're in no position to delay any longer than we must. I only hope you'll be able to run tonight. This beating is going to challenge your quick ability to heal."

Nightcamp snorted. Wormwood went on applying the ointment until it was gone. Then he came to stand before Nightcamp, laying both hands on his muzzle.

"I best get back to attending Evan Vines, though I suspect he's lost in his posing. He's the rare breed of man equal parts fairy tale and ledger book. I'll come back when I can to give you food and water. Rest as best you can until then, my friend."

He turned to go. Nightcamp opened his thoughts to him.

*In what book*
*If you had to guess*
*Was Nightcamp born—*
*What suits him best?*

Wormwood turned back to him and offered a sympathetic smile.

"The answer is impossible," he said. "You see, you're writing it even now."

# Chapter Forty-Five

Nightcamp fought off memories of the last time he'd been hitched to a wagon as Wormwood finished securing him into the traces. The statue of Charles lay on its back in the bed, and though Nightcamp could not see behind him, he was glad a tarp covered it.

"Run well, but be careful of the cart."

He started forward. The wheels moved well enough, without any wobble or instability. Wormwood's point was well-taken, though, and he dared not proceed to the Capitol at more than a quarter of his top speed. Though this far outpaced other horses, Nightcamp found the adopted trot frustrating, as if he'd been asked to gallop down the middle of a river of molasses. After two hours, however, he risked picking up speed. He and Pike would already be meeting with Jackson by now if it had been just the two of them, like last night.

When he at last stopped the cart before Jackson's mansion, the posted sentries did not so much as look at each other despite how odd the appearance of a driverless cart must have been. Nightcamp did not have to wait long before the door opened and Pike ran out to greet him, his initial enthusiasm blunted by the object under the tarp.

"It's done, then," he said. "Of course, it's done. Damn Jackson for this. I hope you can forgive me for putting you through the task. I've been wrestling with it ever since you and the slave left. It could never be the right decision, but we had to take it. Jackson forced us."

Nightcamp found listening to Pike painful and too much an echo of his own past thoughts. They started toward the stable where Jackson came to meet them with several more slaves. He stood by, ordering the tarp removed, and the statue placed on the ground.

The other slaves, not understanding, gave a collective murmur of awe when they saw the statue of Charles. They spoke of how Master Andrew had showed favor to Charles. Jackson did not disabuse them of the notion before ordering them to leave. Once they were gone, he circled his transformed servant like a curator looking for flaws in a potential acquisition. This inspection took several minutes with no sound from Jackson beyond the occasional grunt.

"Now do you believe me?" Pike said.

Jackson drew himself to his full height. He stood about five inches taller than Pike.

"How do we change him back?"

"You *don't*," Pike said. Nightcamp thought he went out of his way to sound cold.

"Then this witch of yours has cost me a valuable servant."

"Mr. President, if you'd accepted my word in the first place—"

"Watch yourself, Pike. Regardless of our friendship, *watch yourself.*"

"I won't. Not anymore. You blame the witch, but you had a hand in it. Call me impudent if you want. Have me jailed or drummed out of the country if you want. It won't matter. There won't be a country before too long."

"I fail to see how statues can hurt us."

"You're standing around like a statue yourself! Haven't you been listening? It's that damn tower that's going to be calling to all four corners of the continent before too long. It's what happens to the statues later. Congratulations, Andrew—seventh and *last* President of the United States."

Nightcamp expected a burst of rage from Jackson. He thought the President might even strike Pike. Anger simmered behind his eyes, that much was obvious, but Jackson had more emotional control than Nightcamp credited him. His gaze fell back upon the statue of Charles. Nightcamp allowed himself a full look at it. The slave's lips showed a slight smile like he approved of his fate. Nightcamp scolded himself for the thought.

"Not last, I think," he said. "Not if we act fast."

"Damnit, Andrew, that's what I've been—"

Jackson held up a silencing hand. "I'll meet with Secretary of War Eaton in the morning."

"And tell him *what*?"

"About the city of New Vineland and the nest of insurrectionists that I've discovered there, a growing tumor in the nation's body."

"Will he believe that about a city that still can't be found on any map?"

Jackson smiled. "Whatever story I tell matters very little. Eaton is my man, much more so than the vipers who call themselves my cabinet—men ruled by the petty jealousies of their wives. I tell you, Pike, I'll be most glad for combat again. It will be nice to get away from scandals and petticoats, back into the saddle and war's fresh air."

"When can you attack?"

"I can have 4,000 men and 200 cannons positioned to attack New Vineland by October."

"October! My God, man, I thought I'd gotten through to you. We need you *now*."

"Much of the army is engaged on the frontier. It will take time to move them east. In the meanwhile, there will be a call up of militia reinforcements."

"It just all feels like dripping molasses, Andrew, when we need a waterfall."

"All wars would be started and finished in an eye blink if logistics weren't an issue."

Pike grumbled but admitted it was so.

"We'll be there," Jackson said. "And when I arrive, it will be like back in the days leading up to New Orleans. Do you recall the vow I made about the British? *By the eternal, they shall not sleep on our soil.* I make the same pledge again now. I'm coming for the witch, and I'll turn that town into a fire that sends her ashes straight to God for Judgement."

Jackson left, as straight and stern as ever in his bearing. Nightcamp thought the man energized by his own violent promise and he did not question one word of his commitment.

His doubts lay elsewhere.

He and Pike returned to the road.

"October," Pike said. "It's so damned far away, isn't it?"

Nightcamp shook his head. Having lived as long as he had, months into the future felt as soon as tomorrow.

He needed no reminder that Mistress Isobel had lived far, far longer.

# Chapter Forty-Six

## August 1830

Nightcamp was still thinking of Pike and missing his company after Jackson summoned him back to the White House to act as his aide-de-camp. The soldiers were completing their assembly and would be ready to march by the second week of September, with the attack planned for late October.

*"It's happening. Back in July, I had my worries, but now that we're a little bit closer, I don't feel as worried. Do you? As long as James can keep up his end of the deal and has that blasted statue ready. I just hope it can do what he says it will. But if it doesn't, our boys can take up the slack."*

*I just hope it can do what he says it will.*

Nightcamp stood very still in the dark, allowing a nightmare vision to play itself out in his mind. He saw himself making a desperate run toward a vast plain. The towering statue of Evan Vines pursued him, each stride spreading fissures into the ground beneath his hooves, making him tumble. Evan Vines's voice boomed across the horizon, but the words belonged to Mistress Isobel.

*"All thy scheming came to nothing, beast! Thou did my bidding all this time and mistook it for thy own cleverness!"*

The statue raised its massive stone foot until the shadow fell upon him. Then—

Nightcamp willed the vision away as Wormwood came to untie him.

"You are tense, my friend," he said, stroking Nightcamp's muzzle. "Your eyes were seeing something besides the dark, I think. Was it some vision from the witch?"

*From Mistress Isobel, perhaps,*
*Or my tormented mind*
*Obsessing over danger,*
*Obsessing over time.*

"What I've come to tell you may or may not ease that torment. Hobbs has snapped out of his trance. I think he willed himself out of it. He asks us to come to him."

They went out to the western side of the tower, where two months of the mason's work showed results closer resembling a year. Evan Vines's loomed overhead in its cage of scaffolding, and Nightcamp's vision threatened to reassert itself before he forced it away for good. The statue stood on wide legs and seemed finished from the knees up. Its arms were akimbo. The left hand remained unformed, but the right hand was so realized its fingertips might leave prints. The torso was broader and rather more muscled than Vines himself, the chest almost Herculean beneath the intricacies of the statue's sculpted frock coat. The head was complete in every way and belonged to the noble hero of some little girl's storybook.

Hobbs stood leaning against the statue's unformed feet. His eyes were closed, and once again he gave the uncanny impression of someone listening to voices within the stone. His strange trance state had been impossible to breach whenever Nightcamp visited in the past, but now he opened his eyes at the sound of the horse's hooves and came running to them.

"What is the date? What is the year?"

The man's anxiety was no less startling than his appearance now that Nightcamp could give him a direct look. The mason's beard and hair were long and unkempt, and the hint of gauntness in his cheeks resembled some ascetic who'd sworn off food in order to achieve enlightenment. It was not unlike how Evan Vines must have looked in the early months of New Vineland's existence.

"I said tell me the date!"

"August 20, 1830," Wormwood said. "You've been working since—"

"June—June—it was June when I came."

"Yes."

The Mason squeezed his eyes shut and cocked his head. "June 10th, I think it was. My wife—my child—"

"Both are safe," Wormwood said. "Harold visits them. All is going just as we planned."

The stonemason sank to his knees and looked up at the statue. His whole body trembled. "I'd forgotten them. I'd forgotten everything! *This* became my world."

He wept a burst of bitter tears that nevertheless put Nightcamp at ease for the first time since work on the statue began, when he pondered the dark possibilities that the mason could be too much like Mistress Isobel for comfort.

But Isobel would never cry.

"The stone is calling to me again," he said. "I can't resist much longer."

Wormwood crouched beside him. "Resist? Are you in danger?"

"No," Hobbs said. "The stone is our ally. But like any ally, it has its demands."

Though the question was directed at the mason, Wormwood stood and spoke straight at Nightcamp.

"*What* demands?"

"My time—my communion. I'm losing Lily."

"I tell you, the child is—"

"I'm losing the memory of her face and I can't help it."

Hobbs placed both hands against the stone. A sound came from deep within the statue, unlike anything Nightcamp ever heard. Not a rumble, not a pulse, not a friction. A murmur of life. Then the statue's right hand moved. Wormwood staggered back behind Nightcamp, whispering a blasphemy. The statue shook off the array of scaffolds and ladders, sending them into a crashing heap that left Hobbs unfazed. The statue placed its right hand next to him, palm up, and the mason stepped into it. When he turned to face them, Nightcamp saw his eyes glowing with bright cataracts of white light.

As the hand lifted him toward the statue's head, he called out, "Our great work continues!"

"Startling," Wormwood whispered. "But *magnificent*."

Yes, it was, Nightcamp told himself. But he returned to the tower pursued by memories of his vision and chased by hope and doubt in equal measure.

# Chapter Forty-Seven

## September 1830

In the third week of September, Pike made an unexpected and anxious return to New Vineland. Wormwood brought him to Nightcamp, who felt the man's weight slump against him as Pike hugged the horse's neck.

"I should have listened to you both. All the work we did to convince Jackson, but you were both right all along."

"What's happened? Wormwood said.

Pike stepped back and all but fell to his knees in front of Nightcamp.

"I made a horrible mistake."

"*Tell us.*"

"I'm such a fool!"

Wormwood and Nightcamp exchanged glances. Wormwood's expression showed equal parts annoyance and alarm. Nightcamp bridged their minds and sent his thoughts through Wormwood's mouth.

*Mistakes get made*
*And can be corrected*
*Tell us the error*
*That you've detected.*

Pike answered with a rueful laugh. "It's just the stupidity you both tried to warn me about all along. We've got the lads on the move. That isn't the problem."

"Answer straight," Wormwood said. "Time is wasting."

"Jackson has me riding up front with him most of the way, but that's never where I like being. So when I could, I'd sneak back and talk to the lads. They're good boys, all of them, but they don't know what they're getting themselves into. What *I* got them into. I told the President it wouldn't do to keep them ignorant and he told me to mind my tongue—just about the last thing in the world I'm good at. I got the company commanders gathered and laid out the facts. They laughed at me! Soon word spread about the lunatic sailor talking about gargoyles and witches. Jackson's furious with me. I didn't tell him I was leaving camp, but I doubt he'd want me back anyway."

Nightcamp pulled his thoughts back into his own mind, leaving Wormwood looking vacant for a moment. He blinked and said, "How long have you been riding?"

"A full week. The army's making less than ten miles a day. The supply train is long, and the larger cannons don't move well even on flat terrain."

Nightcamp turned his head to think.

"I know it's war. Soldiers die. But Andrew isn't allowing those boys to know what they're up against."

Nightcamp sent his thoughts to Wormwood, already predicting the reaction.

"That's madness."

"What?" Pike said.

"Nightcamp proposes a live demonstration of the threat."

"But how?"

"He would have us capture one of the gargoyles, bind it, and then bring it to the army so they can see the truth."

Pike's eyes widened. "That could very well be just the trick we need."

"Or the act that sends the whole army running back the way it came," Wormwood said. "There's wisdom in Jackson's decision."

"There's no *wisdom* in keeping a soldier from knowing what he's up against!"

"The army is a contingency plan. A distraction. That's all it ever was."

"All those young men's lives—a distraction? You callous bastard!"

"Only the statue matters, and we've now seen that Hobbs can make good on his promise. Besides, we don't know the limits of the illusion. Remember, Pike, if the illusion still holds even a hundred miles from New Vineland, the gargoyle will seem like any poor wretch in the soldiers' eyes. How would you convince them otherwise?"

Nightcamp clapped his right front hoof against the ground and Wormwood went silent. Then Nightcamp directed his instructions to Wormwood, who in turn fetched the saddle. Pike clapped his hands.

"He's sided with me, hasn't he? That burns you up, doesn't it, Wormwood?"

"The destruction of New Vineland and the witch are all that matter to me. I maintain this is a mistake. We don't even know what communication the witch has with these gargoyles. If they're nothing but mindless servants, the abduction of one might not matter. What if they're not mindless? What if she sees through them, hears through them, even feels through them in some way? We risk sabotaging our master plan to support a backup tactic of questionable worth."

Pike took the saddle out of Wormwood's hands. "I trust his judgment over yours. Go back and play nursemaid to Evan Vines. Nightcamp and I have work to do."

# Chapter Forty-Eight

Nightcamp and Pike stood in the northern field of statues with Pike holding three lengths of rope.

"I should apologize to Wormwood. I let myself get too worked up. Are you sure he isn't right? You're not just humoring me, are you?"

Nightcamp whinnied. In front of him, two harvesters knocked down another statue and swarmed over it.

"If we're going through with this, all I ask is you don't pick a child. Like that boy over there. Or at least it looks like a boy to me. Damn it all, what if Wormwood really is right? If the soldiers just see a human being, then we'll just be digging ourselves a deeper hole."

The harvesters chewed away at the statue's fingers, leaving jagged claws.

Pike dropped one of the ropes and bent to pick it up. His hands had developed a tremor.

"Just not a child. It can't be a child."

The harvesters bit the statue's face, eating away at the nose, and the ears. Their teeth sheared and reshaped the stone ahead of their polishing tongues. The gargoyle was almost complete. Soon it would rise, reshaped and alive. It was on the slighter side compared to most—a perfect target.

Nightcamp whinnied and motioned with his head.

"Which one? That woman there?"

The two harvesters backed away. The disfigured statue lay still a moment longer.

Then it opened its eyes.

Nightcamp sidestepped a few paces and Pike tried to understand. "This man? Or this one? There are so many people here."

The harvesters moved on to another statue as the new gargoyle sat up. Nightcamp made a gesturing nod.

But Pike moved past it and spun around. "Nightcamp? Where did you go?"

The gargoyle got to its feet and walked right past Pike, continued looking to his left and right. Nightcamp could only imagine the crowd he saw, masses of people moving to and fro on non-existent streets. It must have overwhelmed his eyes.

The gargoyle started toward the tower and Nightcamp followed, snorting all the way. Pike started to follow but ended up further away. He dropped the ropes and raised his hands in hopeless confusion.

"How the hell did I end up in this alley?"

He was only twenty feet away, but Nightcamp knew he'd have to lead both Pike's mind and body out of the illusion. He prepared to cast the summoning song.

"No," Wormwood said, coming up to him. "Keep track of our quarry. I'll attend Pike."

Nightcamp trotted toward the tower as Wormwood walked up to Pike and turned him around.

"How did I get clear on the other side of town?"

"There *is* no town, Pike. Will you never accept this?"

"I suppose not."

"For those who do not hear the summoning song, the witch's illusion is designed to add layers of confusion that wear away a person's willpower. This makes them more likely to accept the bargain when they find their way into the tower."

Pike clapped a hand on Wormwood's shoulder and offered his apology.

"If we have flaring tempers, it just proves we're on the human side of this fight. Now let us hurry. Nightcamp has chosen a gargoyle to take."

"I know, but my damn eyes can't see it."

"I will help you."

The gargoyle was almost at the base of the tower and getting ready to climb. Nightcamp could delay no further. He reared and came down on the gargoyle, knocking it flat on its back. He kept it pinned, but the gargoyle showed tremendous strength against his hooves. It made a growling noise like a bag of marbles rubbing together, louder and louder, and Nightcamp snapped a look at the tower for any sign of a response.

None came.

It seemed Mistress Isobel's stone servants were not akin to a living hive that swarmed over the distress of a single bee. They were closer to an elaborate tapestry on the loom of her magic.

And a tapestry could miss the removal of a single thread.

With renewed confidence, Nightcamp directed Wormwood and Pike in binding the creature tight before loading him into the back of a cart. After Wormwood hitched Nightcamp between the traces, Pike started to climb into the driver's seat.

"I'm afraid that won't do," Wormwood said. "You must also ride in the back of the cart."

"To keep the thing from escaping?"

"No, Pike. Your eyes are the proving ground. If the gargoyle still looks human to you when you're approaching the army camp, tell Nightcamp to turn around. It will mean the illusion continues to hold and our mission is pointless. Do you understand?"

"Better than ever."

Wormwood went to stand in front of Nightcamp.

"This is dangerous work, my friend. You can't possibly be back by morning. If Vines finds you missing, I'm not sure what the consequences will be. I've been preparing for such an eventuality, however, and I think I can keep him sedated a full day."

*Your bravery exceeds—*

Wormwood raised a cautioning right hand. "It does *not* exceed my crimes. Go now and go safe."

Nightcamp shot forward.

# Chapter Forty-Nine

By dawn of the next day, with New Vineland more than seventy miles behind them, Pike shouted out an unfortunate update.

The gargoyle's appearance had not changed.

There has to be a limit to Mistress Isobel's illusion, Nightcamp told himself. Her reach had never extended so far before. But another hour's run passed, and then another, and Pike's report did not change.

By noon, Nightcamp realized a grave reality.

They happened upon five men walking along the side of the road in army uniforms. As they were still hours away from the army's main encampment, Pike assumed the soldiers belonged to an advance scouting party and hailed them. They did not respond. Nightcamp recognized their vacant expressions. He'd seen it often from those who pulled into New Vineland's docks.

Pike muttered a curse that told Nightcamp he understood the implications too.

"They've mutinied," he said. "Those lads must be hearing that song Wormwood's always going on about. It's gotten into their heads even this far away, hasn't it? Is there no way to counteract it? Every good sailor knows the story of Odysseus and the siren song. Maybe put beeswax in everyone's ears?"

Nightcamp shook his head, snorted, and picked up his pace again, though a mouse-like fear now nibbled at his strength. The road ahead was sunny and clear, but he felt like he was riding in the shadow of Mistress Isobel's tower. He sped along in silence another hour, and then Pike's sudden cry startled him into stopping.

"I see it! The man's gone, and all I see is—"

The fearful tone of his voice lightened and became one of delight.

"—a *monster*. Now that I see it, I can't believe I never could. But if I'm seeing it now, then that means the soldiers will see it too!"

He begged Nightcamp to hurry onward, but Nightcamp needed no encouragement. This bit of hope renewed his strength and he resumed pulling at full speed. By 1 PM, they reached the army's vanguard. The sentries laughed when they recognized Pike.

"It's the President's mad deserter friend. Find any monsters lately, old man?"

Then they heard the gargoyle's snarling. Nightcamp found their changing expressions most satisfying.

# Chapter Fifty

They were escorted to the main camp, where Nightcamp saw
hundreds of tents extending off in the distance. One more immediate
tent was larger than the rest, and a man came out of it to meet them
as Nightcamp came to a stop just outside.

"Captain Lee," Pike said. "Where is the President?"

"Dealing with deserters, Pike. You're just in time to join them—"

Several rifle shots sounded from somewhere in the woods. The
captain offered a grim smile.

"—Or maybe not. The President felt a few executions might
dissuade any more soldiers from abandoning their post."

"We have to tell Jackson to stop! If any man wanders off, it's not
their fault."

"More *witch* nonsense from you, Pike?"

"See the evidence for yourself!"

Nightcamp craned his neck back to watch Pike lead a gathering
of men to the cart. The gargoyle once again growled and thrashed
against its bindings.

*"What in hell?"*

"Not hell, Captain Lee. New Vineland. This is the face of your enemy. Everything I've told you is true."

The soldiers began gathering until a ring several men deep surrounded the cart. Nightcamp would have thought it impossible for anyone to cut through the crowd, but the troops parted for Jackson as the Red Sea did for Moses. He stepped straight up to Nightcamp and gave a wolfish, appraising smile. Nightcamp could not decipher the man's thoughts, but his sternness was on clear display, his skin tinted with the grime of dust and sweat.

"What is this disorder?"

Captain Lee snapped a smart salute and said, "Pike has returned, Mr. President."

"So I see."

"He's brought back...something."

"So he has."

Nightcamp again craned his neck to watch Jackson push Pike aside and look into the cart. He stood staring at the enraged gargoyle and his expression never changed.

"I had to show them, Mr. President. Them and you."

Jackson grunted and returned to the front of the cart. He put his hand on Nightcamp's muzzle.

"Very well, Pike," he said. "*Show us.*"

The gargoyle was taken from the cart and carried over to a stout oak tree. Its furious writhing threatened to break the heavy ropes and shake off the two men who worked to keep it pinned against the trunk. Pike stood a few feet away, lecturing the attentive crowd about the truths of New Vineland. Nightcamp, still locked in the cart's traces, found himself alone with Andrew Jackson.

*"What you must understand is all the people of New Vineland are like this. They'll look like you and me, even the children. But it's a disguise."*

Jackson stroked Nightcamp's mane. "Pike is one of the few men I've ever met whose stubbornness equals my own. When two men meet their match, they either become mortal enemies or blood brothers."

*"As you can see, its body is stone, solid all the way through. So in the thick of the battle, don't even bother with a bayonet at close quarters."*

Jackson moved close to Nightcamp's right ear.

"You can't lead a nation without understanding the impulses of people. I knew I couldn't reveal the truth without damaging my own credibility. I also knew Pike couldn't stand to keep the men ignorant. He may think he acted on his own, but my measured inaction guided him. Do you understand me?"

Nightcamp answered with a soft whinny.

At the tree, Pike now had a line of soldiers aiming their guns at the gargoyle's face.

*"Make ready!"*

"That's good," Jackson said, bending to unhitch Nightcamp from the cart. "This witch of yours may be cunning, but she's an amateur compared to me."

*"Aim!"*

"Pike stays with me. Return to New Vineland now. If you have any other allies there, tell them this army will be in position to attack New Vineland in exactly two weeks from today. At the midnight hour, the cannons will fire, and the witch will suffer a bloody fall harvest."

*"Fire!"*

# WATER

# Chapter Fifty-One

## October 1830

As the farmhouse came into view, Goodman felt something was very wrong. It was almost nine in the morning, yet no smoke came from the chimney. The air was crisp, and his breath fogged out in front of him and his horse.

He was approaching the farmhouse from the southern road, having been obligated to venture further down the river than he wanted in order to minister to another farmer and his extended family. With his mind on New Vineland and all of their plans nearing their conclusion, Goodman found himself giving a short but powerful homily on the triumph of good over evil. Not, perhaps, what the farmer expected, but welcome all the same. His heart was swelled all last night and this morning with the certainty nothing could be wrong.

Yet there was no smoke coming from the chimney.

*Katherine and Lily should have been up for a few hours by now*, he thought. *And they had plenty of firewood.*

He urged the horse onward, wishing it had Nightcamp's blazing speed. The horse ran well but it still took another fifteen minutes to reach the front door. Goodman almost fell out of the saddle in his rush to dismount. The front door stood wide open and appeared battered. Strange gouges and stains marked the porch planks. Several of James's stone animals were scattered about the ground.

"Katherine? Lily?"

He searched the farmhouse, dread darkening his thoughts with each empty room. Goodman kept calling their names, wondering if they might be injured, or perhaps hiding in fear. He came to the kitchen and confirmed the stove had not been lit. There wasn't even wood in the furnace.

*Something terrible has happened.*

He went outside and noticed patterns in the dirt, a mix of human footprints and strange impressions and smears. He broke into a run toward the river and saw Katherine sitting at the dock. He shouted to her in vain.

"Good God, what's wrong with you?" he said upon reaching her. More stone animals littered the dock. Katherine even cradled a sculpted opossum, stroking it, her gaze glassy.

Goodman noticed a gun at her feet.

"Katherine?"

Her vacant eyes were fixed on the river. Goodman started to shake her, then let go, working to calm himself.

In a soft voice, he said, "Where is Lily? Has there been some sort of accident?"

A small sob and sniffle proved she wasn't catatonic. A minute passed with no other answer. Goodman looked to the river with fresh fear.

What if Lily had drowned?

*"He promised me."*

Her voice was as gentle as the sound of the water and the words almost flowed away before he heard them.

"Who promised you what?"

"He promised."

Her tone became more bitter.

"Help me to understand," Goodman said.

Her eyes regained a little focus. She looked at him with a mix of anguish and disdain. "Everyone who knew."

"Knew what?"

She held up the stone opossum. "It quit moving when Lily left."

"Katherine—"

"Don't pretend not to know. James never quit experimenting with stone. In my heart, I knew he wouldn't even if he did make a vow. A woman overlooks so many faults in a man she loves, but I should not have let myself be blind to his real passion."

"I assure you James loves you very much."

"Oh yes," she said with a rueful laugh. "I remember how he once expressed it. Six months into our courtship, he presented me with the figurine of an angel, carved from quartz, so it was by turns white and clear. It was made to fit my palm, and how I marveled at it when he placed it there. Then he placed his palm over mine. Smiling, he closed his eyes, and he said something, words I couldn't make out. There was a flutter against my skin. He took his hand away and the figurine stood up in my palm. The little angel's wings moved."

"How beautiful and strange," Goodman said.

"You may think so, but I threw it down as unnatural and ungodly. I accused him of so many things. Black magic. Devil worship. Atheism. He protested but I didn't care. I told him he must never pursue such devilry again. I told him he had a choice to make. He left. A day passed. Then another. Then a third. I cried because I knew my faith had cost me a wonderful man. But I also knew my faith was right, and James was walking a horrible path."

Goodman bowed his head. "It's clear he chose you."

"Yes, on the fourth day, he returned and pledged to never again create a thing that moves except for whatever children God sees fit to give us. Did I really believe this? No, but in my desire for him, I ignored the doubt. Now I can't help thinking God is punishing us for his transgressions."

Goodman flinched.

"Whatever's happened, I don't think James is to blame."

Her eyes took on a touch of petulance. "You know about Adam. James never said he told you, but I knew."

"Yes."

"The night the stranger took Adam away, I sat alone in the dark trying to pray. But all I thought about was that quartz angel and how it moved, and the words my husband spoke to make it happen. It was like James had stolen a soul and put it into the rock, and now God was taking Adam's soul in return."

"If God works that way, then God's not worth worshipping!"

"It doesn't matter what we say or hope. I used to hope Adam wasn't dead. I never felt he was. Now...after what I'm sure I saw...maybe it'd be better if he had died."

Goodman scowled despite himself. "I can't follow a word you're saying now. You're speaking nonsense."

Katherine threw the stone opossum into the river. It made a muted, inglorious *thunk* and sank.

"These sculptures were supposed to keep Lily amused, or so James said. Part of me knew he was lying about that too. I didn't know what they'd do, only that they'd somehow protect Lily from danger. After losing Adam, we became overprotective. I'm not sure she saw the outside of the house until she was four. James said we couldn't let our fears turn Lily's whole childhood into a prison, but the animals prove how afraid he was."

"What happened here last night?"

"Something came. Horrible, a monster, yet...you can't understand, Harold. Only a mother could. Mothers always know their sons. Adam was here last night."

Goodman stared at her without trying to hide his intentions. He sought signs of madness in Katherine's eyes.

"I'd know him anywhere. I'd know him no matter the circumstance. Adam came here. He came for Lily. The statues attacked him. God help me, I even shot at him—my own son."

"Katherine—"

"I recognized him. I knew who he was. And I think he recognized me too. I can only pray he did because he took Lily with him."

"Took her *where*?"

She pointed to the river.

# Chapter Fifty-Two

Less than an hour later, they departed the dock on a raft, standing side-by-side with Goodman working the push pole and Katherine staring down the river like she knew just where to go. Goodman didn't dare question either her certainty or her decision to gather the remaining stone animals into the middle of the raft.

"Where are we going?"

"I'll know when we get there. I had a feeling when I looked into that creature's eyes. Now I know I've sensed him before, the day James and Lily set off for New Vineland. I was in the kitchen and suddenly it felt like Adam was close. My heart was so light like he'd just been away on a long trip. I ran to the dock certain I'd see him there, a fine twelve-year-old boy with a bright smile for his mother. There was nothing there, of course. Just Lily and James about to depart, and the river itself. But he *was* there."

Goodman worked the push pole. He felt Katherine's stare like a knife's tip pressed to the nape of his neck.

"You don't believe me, do you?" she said.

"My days of incredulity are long behind me."

"No matter what he looks like now, no matter what's been done to him, he has a soul. *That's* what I'm feeling between us, and that's how I'll find him and Lily again."

Goodman glanced back to see Katherine picking up one of the animals. She caught him looking.

"You knew about these, didn't you?"

"Lily showed them to me many times."

"I didn't ask if you know *of* them."

Katherine's face seemed so stony he doubted even James could chisel mirth there.

"Why do you think James would tell me something he wouldn't tell his own wife?"

"Men are a cult of secrets."

"I've got precious few at this point."

"But *some*."

Goodman quit working the pole a moment and took a deep breath before giving a reluctant nod. "He showed me how he could bring stone to life—for lack of a better term. But he only showed me out of necessity."

"What is my husband doing in New Vineland, Harold?"

"Just what you've been told."

Katherine scowled. "I've been such a fool. James told me Lily was falsely accused of theft and he was forced to carve the statue to save her."

"That's what happened."

"Maybe on the surface," she said. "But everything that happened can't be coincidental. Do you think so little of me to deny this?"

Her stare was withering, and Goodman found he couldn't hold her gaze. She was right. At this point, how *dare* he keep up veils she was already penetrating? "The reason is the destruction of New Vineland."

"How does my husband and his statue accomplish *that?*"

"James is building an enemy within New Vineland's heart. The colossus he makes will be turned against the city. But for that to happen,

Evan Vines had to be convinced it was both his own idea and an inflicted punishment on James. We...we used Lily to help with the ruse. She had no knowledge of it."

Goodman dared risk a look at Katherine's face and found a rage so icy it compelled him to shout out, "She was never in danger! Please believe me—"

"How *dare* you?"

"She had to be convincing in order to fool Vines. We showed him one of James's little animal carvings to convince him of his skill as a mason, and he fell into our trap."

"Bastards." Her voice was little more than a whisper, but the curse rang in his ears like cannon fire.

"Please try to understand, Katherine! We had to take desperate measures. New Vineland is a place of evil."

"You can't destroy evil with evil, Harold."

"If there was ever an example of a man doing the Lord's work, it's James. He's miserable being away from the two of you."

"Many things that seem Godly are Satan in disguise. As soon as I have my children back, I'll go to New Vineland, find James, and judge for myself."

"What if *Adam* doesn't want to come? What happens if he attacks you?"

Katherine nodded toward the stone animals. "Then his father will just have to have another word with him."

# Chapter Fifty-Three

"There," she said some thirty minutes later, pointing to a place along the east bank. Goodman squinted at what appeared to be a calm inlet branching further inland and began pushing the raft across and against the stream. His back and shoulders ached but he fought through the pain when he heard the frantic splashing behind him and saw Katherine had gotten to her knees and was using her hands in a pathetic attempt at paddling.

"I feel him so strongly now, Harold. Adam *is* down that way."

Goodman gritted his teeth, stabbing the raft pole again and again into the water. They'd reached a place of total isolation. If they were attacked and overwhelmed, where could they shelter? Who would help them?

The statues were stirring.

Their movements had an eerie fluidity, not at all like flesh and muscle but also nothing of the scrape and grind expected from rock. "Katherine!" he shouted, starting to push the raft back.

"What are you doing?"

"If the animals are active, then going into the inlet is dangerous."

"Get me there or I'll swim the rest of the way!" She yanked on the push pole as the raft began drifting with the current. They would be past the inlet in less than a minute.

"But the statues—"

"Adam won't hurt me."

She almost wrestled the pole from Goodman's grip. Her urgency shook and shamed him. *Well*, he thought, *we've come this far. No turning back now. Finish crossing your Rubicon.*

He took the pole and made a furious assault against the current, throwing the last of his strength into the act. The raft surged against the current and powered through into the still and stagnant pool of the inlet. Goodman collapsed on his hands and knees in a coughing fit as the raft's momentum kept it heading toward the shore. The stone animals gathered on the edge of the raft, their black eyes trained on the land and a thick and dreary wall of trees.

*If there ever were a Grendel, here's his abode.*

"You're still *sure*, Katherine?"

She touched her chest. "I'm sure."

Goodman pushed himself up and regarded the animals. They were more animated than ever.

"I wish James might have sculpted a few wolves or lions to go with all the squirrels and rabbits."

The raft came to an abrupt halt atop a thick, muddy sediment about four feet from land. The animals leapt into the water and began thrashing and fording their way to shore.

"Astonishing," Goodman said.

Katherine jumped from the raft and moved ahead of them. As the statues began to regroup, she stood in front and said, "No. Stop now."

From the raft, Goodman said, "They won't listen to you."

But they very much did obey her. Did she know they would? Had she made this discovery last night? Or was it more intuition, more feeling? Goodman left the raft and came to stand beside her.

"Follow us," Katherine said, "but no more than that."

The statues formed into something like ranks at her feet.

"Better than the King's regulars," Goodman said.

Katherine grunted at this remark. "God forgive me for not having the courage to face the task at hand without having these monstrosities at my back. My children are that way, Harold."

They proceeded with little attempt at stealth. Between their own footfalls and the movement of the statues, the incessant crunching of dry, dead leaves left Goodman wincing. The playful sounds further ahead were louder by far, though, and their approach went unnoticed.

*"Does Anna see Toad now?"*

*"I don't see you, Toad."*

*"Now does Anna see Toad?"*

*"No. You're so good at hiding!"*

Lily's voice was recognizable right away, but the other spoke in a deep and sickly tone so at odds with the frolicsome nature of the words. It was like a child talking through a dying old man's mouth. Goodman thought of the ogres and trolls that populated every fairy tale, hideous monsters whose greatest desire was to eat girls like Lily.

"Can that truly be your son's voice?"

Katherine had her eyes shut and hands clasped at her chest. She might have been listening to Mozart.

"Adam," she said, moving forward. Goodman grabbed her elbow.

"Let me go first—just in case."

She brushed him off and ordered the statues to stay in place. Goodman stood rooted too, ashamed of his leaden feet compared to Katherine's brave pace. She'd moved ahead some thirty yards when Lily shouted, "Mama!"

Goodman grinned when Lily rushed into Katherine's arms. Then he noticed a hideous form dangling from a tree branch above their heads. The body was almost the same color as the tree, and it reminded him of a blob of melted wax that was running and cooling at the same time.

Its head draped further and further down as if attached to a python's body, and the more it descended the whiter its skin became. The head was as round and smooth as a globe, with no visible mouth and two liquid-black eyes.

Fear stole all the air from him. Here was some horror even Charles Brockden Brown never conceived. He tried to sound the alarm as the monster's head grew closer, like a spider about to fall upon its prey. He pointed with more urgency, gesturing, stabbing the air with his finger. The more he tried to shout, the more his mouth refused him.

The creature revealed its mouth, a dark opening with broken teeth. It got wider and wider, unhinging like a viper's.

*It's going to swallow them whole if I don't—if I don't—*

He lunged just before the creature said, "Here's Toad!" and dropped. Goodman pushed Katherine and Lily aside and the full weight of the monster's body landed on him. It felt like being buried under a thousand pounds of wet sand. He gasped for breath in the folds of blubbery white flesh that reeked of stale river water and decay.

*"Toad! Toad, get off of Mr. Goodman!"*

*"Adam, listen to me. Listen to your mama."*

*"Toad—"*

*"Adam—"*

The crushing weight sprang away from him with the same abruptness as it landed. Goodman rolled onto his back, wheezing, trying to see through explosions of colored blotches.

Lily knelt beside him, helping him sit up. "Thank you, Mr. Goodman. I wasn't sure how I was ever going to get back to Mama."

"Safe...statues...escape..."

Lily patted his hand, making him feel like a foolish little boy being comforted by an adult woman. He began to catch his breath and they got up together. Katherine and the creature stood a few feet apart, regarding each other. Katherine's head was tilted a little to the right, and her lips had the sweetest smile.

"What is it?" Goodman said.

"That's Toad," Lily said. "That's my brother."

"Did *he* tell you that?"

"He recognized Mama. We've been talking and playing hide and seek. Toad talks best when he's playing."

"That thing could be lying."

"But look at Mama. She knows!"

"She *believes.*"

Katherine spread her arms wide and Toad slinked into her embrace. Her hug looked like someone grappling with an oversized slug. Goodman looked away in revulsion and noticed an area to his right where a crude, half-broken chair was surrounded by an assortment of things that reminded him of a pack rat's nest. He went closer to investigate the refuse and made a chilling discovery.

*Bones*, he thought. *Those are bones.*

How he wished the stone animals might become a little defiant and move in closer, just so the creature knew they weren't defenseless. Katherine and the monstrosity had settled to the ground. She was holding its hand and talking in a voice too soft for Goodman to hear. It responded with gibberish—

*"Toad isn't Toad? Toad is Adam and not Christian but Toadam is Anna's brother but not Christian like Anna said."*

Goodman looked back at the bones, which included a few skulls. It was easy to imagine the fiend adding three more to the collection.

He had to arm himself.

He picked up a piece of bone that might have been some poor man's forearm. It was the closest thing he could come to a dagger.

But the grotesque collection consisted of far more than bones. There were coins, silverware, cups, river rock, scraps of wood, and pieces of moldy fabric scattered everywhere. Then he saw the book and it stopped him cold. He stood stupefied by the unexpected familiarity and knelt to retrieve it. *Wieland* was damaged beyond belief and started to crumble in his hands.

*Here? But how? How in the world, after all this time?*

Understanding flashed through him and he turned, shouting, "You attacked my raft!"

"Harold—"

"Four years ago," he said. "Not long after I came to New Vineland. I wanted to see what was on top of the cliff. Halfway across my boat was destroyed. I lost this book when I swam to shore. Yet *here* it is."

The creature broke free of Katherine.

"Toadam is King of the River! Give Toadam back his prize!"

"This book is mine."

The creature swiped at him with its long arm. Goodman only just dodged its jagged fingernails as Katherine and Lily cried out.

"Why did you attack me?"

"Toadam protects Mother Isobel."

"Isobel! The witch that's behind Evan Vines and his damned town!"

"Mother Isobel looks after Toadam—"

"—You're responsible for the deaths of those girls—"

"—Mother Isobel—"

"—You're responsible for that cemetery—"

"—So Toadam won't know the time of stone again—"

"—I know all of their names. Anna, Veronica, Bethany—"

"—*Anna, Anna, Anna, Anna!* —"

The creature's voice thundered over everything else and rang through the forest. Goodman retreated in the face of the monster's rage. But even in his fear, all he could think about was the repeated name. *Anna.* His pulse went wild to realize he was arriving at the center of the maze he'd stumbled into so long ago.

Lily jumped between them.

"It's okay, Toad! Mr. Goodman didn't mean to upset you!"

"Listen to me, Adam," Katherine said. "Listen to your mama, who's missed you all these long years."

The creature's head swiveled back as if it had no spinal column at all.

"Mother Isobel named Toad Toad but Toad's name is Toadam."

"I named you Adam.

*"Toadam."*

The creature arched its back and little tongues of fog came from its open mouth, snaking out in all directions. Each tendril formed tiny hands that began to grope through the trees, wrapping onto the silent, watchful birds. Moments later, sparrows soared toward him, becoming a suicidal flock that flew straight into his waiting mouth. The creature gulped and gulped and his white belly grew round.

Goodman shuddered, astounded and sickened. The creature's belly shook from within and he slapped it until the movement stopped. Then it smiled in obvious contentment.

"Kill it," Goodman said. "Katherine, have the statues attack now!"

But Katherine seemed blind. "Adam, my precious Adam, please be at peace."

"Toad is Toad."

"No, you're *Adam*. My very own Adam."

"Toad...Toadam...Toad..."

The monster shrank back, shrieked, and shot its arms out like ropes that wrapped around Katherine and Lily's waists. Before Goodman could react, it lifted them off the ground and sprang toward the river. Goodman gave chase, following Lily and Katherine's cries. By the time he reached the edge of the pool, however, the monster had carried them into the river.

Then took them under.

*Dear God.*

He looked at the decaying remains of *Wieland* and thought he knew just where the creature was going.

# Chapter Fifty-Four

Toad's breakneck speed terrified and thrilled Lily by turns, leaving her fighting to hold her breath even as she wanted to shout her joy. The river's song, which she'd heard ever since she could remember, was different now, charged with Toad's speed against the current. The song pummeled her, driving its melody into every pore. The water urged her to open her mouth and let its music flood into her being. She surrendered, but the rapture she expected became terror and panic as she began to choke.

Then she could breathe again.

Her thoughts began to wander outside of herself. How had she never understood the river's song was a chorus, not the work of a single voice as she'd always perceived it? Every creature contributed to it. The river sang in memory of every raindrop that ever swelled it, and experiencing its song as she did now was the same as spending your whole life with your back to the wind before turning your face to it just once. It took your breath away even as it filled your lungs in a fuller, fresher way than you could ever imagine.

And her lungs *were* full and didn't ache for air. The river's song sustained her. The water inside her mouth hummed against her teeth and tickled her cheeks like a fuzzy, stingless honeybee. The melody wasn't just keeping her alive. It was inviting her to add to it, to shape it.

To use it.

Lily imagined the melody as a solid thing, a rock she held in her mouth. She thought of how Papa chiseled and reshaped stone. The song was her rock and her tongue was the chisel.

She looked for Mama as Toad streaked along.

Mama's eyes were closed.

"Adam," she said, her voice coming out in clear silver bubbles of words and music. "Mama needs to breathe."

Toad launched up. He broke the surface and Lily touched Mama's cheek. It was cold and lifeless.

Lily began to sing.

*Mama, Mama, come back to us*
*Your darling children implore you*
*The song of water fills your lungs*
*The river's song restores you.*

As she sang, Lily imagined the song flowing through Mama's body like a river over parched land, bringing life. The image and the song joined together. Her entire being vibrated with melody and power. She thought of the water nourishing Mama like a wilted flower being coaxed back into bloom.

Mama coughed and opened her eyes.

Lily stared in disbelief and awe.

*Did I do that?* How *did I do that?*

She didn't think she could do it again if she tried. The hum of the river was already leaving her. She found her fingers curling in a vain attempt to hold onto it.

"Adam, Lily," Mama said. Her voice was strained and weak, but she had strength enough to reach for them both. They floated in the middle of the river, holding each other.

Lily saw the cliff face not far in the distance.

"Are you taking us there, Adam?"

"Mother Isobel will tell Toadam the truth. Mother Isobel looks after Toadam."

Just then a tremendous cracking sound came from the cliff. A piece broke apart and started to fall. Then it veered straight for them.

Toad took them under in a flash, diving deep. The rock slammed into the spot they'd just occupied. The river's song shattered like glass, and the beautiful and unified chorus turned into a chaos of broken voices. Another rock, even larger than the first, plunged into the water right overhead. Once again Toad sped them out of the way in time and surged to the surface, springing far from the river and landing some fifty yards up onto the shore.

"Mother Isobel is angry with Toad."

"But you haven't done anything wrong!" Lily said. "Oh Adam, let's just get away from here. Mama and I can look after you. And Papa too."

"Toad forgot Mother Isobel. Toad left her hungry. Toad will suffer the time of stone."

Despite anything Lily or Mama said, Toad rose and started up a nearby path, not jumping or striding but moving in a resigned march.

"Mama, what are we going to do?"

Mama's silence scared Lily more than any plunging boulder.

Mama didn't know.

"I'm going to follow him."

"*No!*"

Lily retreated a few steps as Mama rose. She seemed taller somehow as she glared at the top of the cliff.

"We'll go together. Whoever's up there took Adam from us. Deuteronomy tells us that vengeance and recompense are reserved to the Lord. I pray he finds us worthy tools for delivering both."

# Chapter Fifty-Five

They heard Toad's pleading as they neared the top.

*"Toad went to find Anna again and bring her, but Toad was tired of hide and seek and—"*

*"Silence, son Toad. Thy trespasses are considerable."*

*"Toad wants Mother Isobel to tell him if Toad is Toad."*

Mama raised a cautioning hand and they stopped. Toad went on trying to explain himself, his thick, creaking voice reduced to whimpers. The second voice belonged to a woman, but Lily had never heard someone speak with less warmth or tenderness. Every syllable lingered in the air, pointed and menacing, the language of icicles.

Mama said, "Lily, I want you to stay here."

"But you said we'd go together!"

"Hush, child. We have gone together. We *are* together. But wait now. This is a mother's task alone now."

Lily forced herself to obey and watched Mama square her shoulders and disappear around the final bend. She strained forward, hands clasped under her chin, and listened.

*"Adam, your mother is here. Your* true *mother. I've come to take you from this witch and the Devil she worships."*

She'd never heard Mama speak with such firmness, such courage. There wasn't a trace of fear in her voice and she felt ashamed of her own trembling. Being an adult, a woman, and a mother meant facing any danger with a brave face. She was sure Mother Isobel would flee. Mama would melt all of her ice and send her dripping down into the river. The longer Mother Isobel kept silent; the surer Lily became. Mama had already defeated her just by standing tall and proud.

Lily just knew it.

*"Thou were naught but the vessel and the birth canal. Woman, I shall correct thy ignorance."*

Mother Isobel didn't sound frightened at all. She was mocking Mama. How could that be? *Why* wasn't she afraid of her? Didn't she know Mama's strength?

Lily took two steps forward, wringing her hands.

If Mother Isobel wasn't afraid of Mama, then she wasn't afraid of anything. Was she so powerful? What could she do?

*I have to help her.*

Lily sprinted up the last bit of path and found Mama facing off against the dark figure of a very old woman who perched on the sheer edge of the cliff. Toad was crouched on all fours between them, his body a ghostly, pathetic blob, his black eyes swiveling back and forth from woman to woman.

"Witch, he is my son."

"He became my flesh the moment I carved him."

Mama began to pray. Lily looked up, expecting an army of angels. Clouds moved overhead but the blue sky was impassive.

The old woman stepped forward. She seemed so slight and brittle, like the petals of a dead flower. She cocked her head and listened to Mama's prayer.

"Woman, thy god is but two sticks bound with twine. Mine is a Lord of stone, and I am the rock of his faith. Thou have corrupted son Toad into misfortune."

"Toad wants to be good—"

"Son Toad must know a long penance for his treachery. The time has drawn near at last for the death of thy father. Because of thy misdeeds this day, I will pass the honor to a truer servant."

"Toad will kill him now, Mother Isobel!"

"No, Adam!" Mama said, ceasing her prayers. "Your father is a good man. You must not harm him."

Mama put herself between Adam and the witch, bringing cold anger into the old woman's expression. She raised her left hand and sang a few phrases Lily couldn't understand. Mama froze in place. Her skin, her hair, even her clothes became ashen.

"No, Mother Isobel! No time of stone for Mama, no time of stone!"

Lily was breathless, almost swooning. She wiped the tears from her eyes before straightening her back like Mama had.

She came forward.

"Please don't hurt my Mama or brother."

The witch's colorless eyes gazed upon her with something like fascination.

"Thou are a different sort."

"I don't understand."

The old woman sniffed at her and paced around her in a tight circle.

"Thou are a child who hears the world's songs."

"Since I was very little. Before I knew what a song even was."

"Son Toad, is this the girl you were bringing me?"

Toad hopped between them and said, "Mother Isobel knows Anna."

She held out her hand and Toad came to place the globe of his head under her palm. Lily watched her bony fingers pet and stroke him.

"Can Toad gather rocks for the tombstone so Anna can hide again?"

The witch ignored Toad. Lily found herself the entire focus of her attention.

"Which of the world's songs pleases thee most, child?"

"Fat Jack," she said, then noticed her confused reaction. So Lily changed her answer and said, "Before it was the trees, but now it's the river."

"Water is a powerful blade. Do thou carve?"

She startled Lily by producing a knife from the folds of her robe. It had the blackest blade Lily had ever seen.

The witch placed the tip against Toad's head and repeated the question.

"Mama and Papa don't let me play with knives."

Mother Isobel laughed as if she'd just heard the best joke. Lily stole a glance at Mama, hoping for some sign of movement. The witch noticed.

"Stone she is now. Flesh she can return."

"Would you please? I'd give anything."

Mother Isobel stood in front of Mama, caressing her stone body with the knife. Lily held her breath.

"Carving begins in the mind, child. All the world's melodies are carving songs. Each song invites us to carve and put the mind's delight in the palm of the hand. Does the song of trees not call thee to reshape their wood?"

"Not the trees, but sometimes the clouds," she said.

"Clouds belong to the water's song."

"Sometimes if I lay on my back and think, the clouds will change their shape for me."

"Show me proof."

Lily frowned; certain she'd fail. But what choice did she have? She pointed to the largest cloud, almost stationary over New Vineland. She closed her eyes and concentrated.

The song of the river rose to her. She felt it enveloping her as if she were neck-deep in the water. She swayed like gentle waves lapping the shore.

She began to hum.

*All the world's melodies are carving songs.* Lily had never considered such a thing before. The notion offended her. She couldn't imagine taking a knife to anything that sang to her.

*But the river carves everything. It cuts through land and wood and its own shape is determined by the space it makes for itself.*

She opened her mouth and the river's song came forth, tremulous, beautiful. She didn't know what the words were, or if they were words at all. She sang at the cloud with a clear image in mind for its billowy white mass. She saw a pirate ship with three masts and a deck lined with cannons. The cloud began to swirl and change. Winds came to scoop at the cloud like delicate chisels. Lily's pulse quickened in triumph. Mother Isobel was right: carving began in the mind.

*I call you forth*
*To change your shape*
*Sail and mast*
*A pirate ship*
*The sky your sea*
*The sea your sky*
*Change your form*
*To please my eye*

The cloud became the exact ship she saw in her mind, and it sailed toward them and the overhead sun.

Toad jumped around and said, "Anna never told Toad she could carve."

Lily smiled despite herself. "I didn't know I could." She turned to Mother Isobel, expecting to see approval, perhaps even an impressed look. The old woman showed nothing but sourness.

"Clouds are a poor and paltry medium for thy powers," she said. "Thy heart cries out for stone."

"But rock has no song," Lily said.

"Thou are deaf to stone?"

Lily nodded.

Mother Isobel looked to Mama's statue. "I might teach thee to hear it."

"Will...will that take long?"

The woman contorted so much in her laughter that Lily wondered how she didn't fall over.

"Please let my mama go, and I'll stay here and learn. Toad can take Mama back to the farm and—"

"Child, how can thou learn to carve without a practice stone?"

Lily scanned the ground. All she saw were bits of gravel and small stones. Even Papa couldn't do anything with them. When she looked up again, she found Mother Isobel standing in front of Mama, dagger in hand.

"As Toad is my son, so thou become my daughter. Thou can afford to lose this false mother."

"Please don't hurt Mama!"

Shadow fell over them. The cloud was beginning to lose the shape Lily gave it, but the remains of the ship had sailed over the sun. How Lily wished she could conjure its cannons to fire and destroy Mother Isobel.

"Thou still refuse my offer?"

"Yes!"

"You would prefer her as flesh?"

Lily got on her knees despite the pain from the rocky soil. "Please change her back."

She shivered in her fear. Toad jumped over to her and put his arms around her. "Toad always keeps Anna warm." His body blocked Lily from seeing what happened next. She heard the old woman's singsong chant again, followed by Mama saying, "Lily? Lily, child, run away! Run—"

"Flesh carves as readily as stone," Mother Isobel said, and Mama shrieked.

Lily fought off Toad's embrace and got up to see Mama crumpled on the ground, the dagger lodged in her stomach. Her blood seeped out around her. Lily collapsed beside her, hugging her, sobbing. She flashed a hateful stare at the old woman and said, "Why are you doing this?"

"You need a lesson in the value of stone."

"What lesson? Oh Mama…Toad, help us…Please help Mama. She's your mama, too!"

"Thou can still save this false mother."

*"How?"*

"The blood is the life, is that not so? Trees have their sap, and the soil its hidden geysers. What on this earth does not bleed?"

"Rock," Lily said.

"Then beg me."

Lily brushed the hair from Mama's face. Her eyes didn't seem to fix on anything and her cheeks were white. The only color anywhere was the wet red patch expanding around the knife's hilt.

She knelt again. Her heart had never known such hate or desperation. *"Please!"* Mother Isobel loomed before her, her face a mask of evil satisfaction. Despite her anger, Lily felt relief when she heard the old woman chant again. If Mama was returned to stone now, she might still be saved. Papa would know what to do. She listened to the chant, trying to comprehend it. Toad had begun to mutter to himself, though, and his voice was louder.

"Anna. Toad misses Anna. Toad is Christian and…Toadam…and Toadam misses…misses…Mama…"

"There," Mother Isobel said. "A fine block of stone for thy apprenticeship. In time, thou will become adept and help me in the great work to come. Across the river rises the new world promised by my Lord, and together we will carve it in his image—"

The tombstone seemed to come out of nowhere. It struck the old woman in the back and knocked her flat on her face. Lily turned to see Toad ripping the next tombstone out of the ground. He took it and jumped, bringing it down on her back. Until now, Lily didn't think Mother Isobel was capable of feeling pain. But she shrieked under the force of the attack and staggered up as Toad jumped back to fetch another tombstone. Lily didn't understand what they were or where they'd come from, but she rushed to help him. Toad tore the third tombstone free and flung it at the witch, who only just dodged the heavy stone.

"Ungrateful son," she said, pulling her dagger from Mama's statue. She held the black blade up in front of her face. "Carved Toad as a babe I did and made thee beautiful."

"Toadam! Toadam is Toadam, not Toad!"

He tore the fourth tombstone up and threw it. This time Mother Isobel proved more spry and sidestepped with ease.

"A thousand years in stone will not repay thy betrayal, but I will consider it a fair beginning."

She began her chant. Lily grabbed Toad's right arm, urging him to flee before the spell could seize him. He wrapped his arms around her and sprang off the cliff with a tremendous jump. He grunted and flinched in the middle of his suspension, then went silent as they plummeted. Lily heard the old woman screaming overhead. Rocks of all sizes launched themselves from the cliff face, but Toad twisted his body away from the large pieces and used his back to protect Lily from the sharp grapeshot pellets of small rocks. Drops of his black blood trailed into the air behind them as the river grew near. Lily gritted her teeth as she stared straight into the water, but at the last moment, Toad managed a final flip that made sure he bore the entire brunt of the impact.

The river swallowed them.

# MIND

# Chapter Fifty-Six

## October 1830

Toad struggled ashore with Anna pulling on his arms and begging him to keep going. He tried to crawl but then his arms buckled, reducing him to a forward squirm as he coughed and wheezed.

"Toad is tired," he said and collapsed face down in the dirt. An icy chill spread through him. He felt a stiffness spreading from a spot in the middle of his back. It felt like the time of stone overcoming him and he mustered the strength to probe the spot with both hands. His fingers found the handle of Mother Isobel's dagger. Anna's hands covered his own, bringing warmth.

"She must have thrown it at you just before we went off the cliff. Let me try to take it out."

Moments later, a searing pain shot through Toad's body, making him thrash and howl. Anna jumped back, crying.

"It won't come out! Oh Toad, I don't know how to help you."

"Toad knows what to do."

Toad bunched his shoulders, causing a ripple along the folds of his flesh. He repeated the motion, and the ripples became waves of flesh surging around and over the hilt, swallowing the blade deeper into him.

Anna gasped. "Where did it go?"

"Toad makes Mother Isobel's blade play hide and seek," he said, feeling the handle sink under his skin. The hard work over, he rolled over and brought his legs up against his trunk and contorted several times, each motion driving the dagger even further into his body. At last, the blade pierced his stomach and fell into the pit of his belly. There was a searing jolt of pain but Toad knew his stomach had bested many sharp things, broken glass and splintered timber, the tips of push poles, and jagged shards of bone. Mother Isobel's dagger could not harm him there.

"Are you...are you okay?"

"Yes, Anna. Toad is okay."

Toad thought he might sleep and rolled over again. Anna knelt and put her palms along his skin. She started picking at his flesh and it tickled him.

"What is Anna doing?"

"You've got pieces of rock stuck in your skin. You kept them from hitting me, Toad."

"Toad will always save Anna."

They fell silent for a few minutes.

"Toad, call me Lily. That's my real name. *Lily.* And your real name is Adam."

"Toadam–"

"Not Toad and Adam. Just Adam. That's what Mama and Papa named you."

"Mother Isobel named Toad—"

"That old woman stole you. My mama is your mama. We're brother and sister. You're Adam and I'm Lily."

"Anna—"

"*Lily.* And you're Adam. Try saying it just once."

"Toad—"

"*Adam.*"

He felt her hand resting flat against his back, offering warmth against the remaining chill. Brother and sister. Anna and Christian. That meant brothers and sisters stayed together. They protected each other, and if one was gone, the other kept watch and waited. Anna and Christian. Brother and sister.

Toad and Anna.

Toad and...Lily—

Toadam and Anna—

Toadam—

*"Adam and Lily."*

She clapped and cheered. Toad repeated the new names just to get her to clap again. More than ever, Toad was glad he was Adam. But if he'd always been Adam, why did Mother Isobel call him Toad? Who was she? Who was Mama?

He rose, wincing a little from the pain in his stomach. Hunched forward, he stumbled back to the river with Lily following. At the bank, he dropped to his knees and stared at his reflection.

"Adam." The name still didn't quite fit in his mouth or mind. But he could make it fit the way he'd made the dagger enter his belly. He just needed to keep working the word deeper into him.

"Adam, Adam, Adam, Adam."

Lily laughed, hugging his shoulders. Her face joined his in the water, brown eyes, and black eyes staring back at themselves. The water rippled from her tears and their reflections scrambled into each other. In the merger, he saw a different version of himself, a new face.

"Yes, you're Adam, my brother Adam, and I'm your sister Lily. From now on we'll always be together even if we're apart. We just have to find Papa. I know he's in New Vineland, but I don't know where. I don't think we're far away from it. We have to tell him about you and what happened to Mama. He'll know what to do."

He turned from the riverbank, tried to stand, and felt a hurt that brought him back to his knees.

"Adam needs to sleep."

"Will you be safe here while I go to find Papa?"

He shifted, and though he felt another internal stab from the tip of the dagger, he made no sound. He crawled back to where he'd been.

"Adam thinks so."

"I know what I can do. It's what you did for me when I was tired."

He smiled as Lily ran here and there collecting fallen leaves and piling them on top of him. He began to feel warm and content. Lily went on hiding him under leaves until only his head remained uncovered.

"Remember what I said, Adam. We're brother and sister. From now on, we're always together, no matter what."

"Adam remembers."

She kissed his head.

"Papa's going to give you a great big hug when he sees you again. Just rest now. I'll be back as soon as I can."

# Chapter Fifty-Seven

Toad was swimming with the muskrat family in the quiet pool away from the river. It was very hot. Even the water felt warm. He stopped to float on his back, and the muskrat and five children climbed atop his white belly, dried themselves, and chattered. Father Muskrat looked at him and said—

*"You! By God, it took me over a day to track you, but I didn't give up. Where are Katherine and Lily? Tell me now!"*

He recognized the voice in a vague way, though he'd never heard the muskrat speak. He reached to pet the top of its head. The children were clamoring for him to float under the tree where the caterpillars had spun their cocoons. Hundreds of them were hanging from the branches like strange, special leaves. Looking at them made Toad feel hungry.

Father Muskrat continued to scold him.

*"Get up! Don't play dead! If you've hurt Katherine and Lily, I swear I'll stop at nothing to avenge them!"*

Toad reached up, stretching his arm ever further until he swiped his hand across the cocoons. He opened his mouth wide, anticipating their fuzzy and sticky coatings as much as the juicy insides when he bit down.

His tongue snagged one toward his teeth, but before he could eat it, the muskrat children begged him to stop. Then their father said—

*"What did you do, monster? Eat them? I went up to the cliff and there's nothing there. Not even bones!"*

Toad did not swallow. He pushed the cocoon against his right cheek and told the children he would keep it warm inside his mouth.

Toad's world shook. He felt a jab in his back that made him turn over and spill the muskrat family into the water. He clawed at whatever had attacked him. Father Muskrat and the children were gone. No amount of calling or summoning brought them back. But he heard Father Muskrat's voice bubbling up from the water, followed by a sudden stab of pain in his side.

Toad howled, almost spitting out the cocoon. But he knew keeping it safe was too important, so he nestled it again in the pocket of his cheek before leaping out of the water. He stared into the pool as a man rose out of it, armed with a broken push pole, its tip a jagged splinter.

"You dare attack Toad, King of the River?"

But Toad retreated, agony overwhelming him in waves. The man came ashore and Toad recognized him. He had tried to steal Toad's treasure.

*"Where are they, monster? Why were you buried under leaves? Were you trying to hide?"*

"Toad only hides with Anna."

The man froze for a moment. *"Why did you say that name?"*

Toad tried to answer but started coughing and the cocoon fell from his mouth. He saved it with his tongue and repositioned it.

*"What's wrong with you? Are you injured? Did Katherine manage to get in one good hit before you killed her?"*

Toad swayed, only just keeping on his feet. Where was he? The pool was gone. He somehow wasn't anywhere near where he'd been. The trees held no memory for him. He knew nothing at all except the lingering coldness in his skin and the searing edge of Mother Isobel's dagger in his stomach.

"Anna was here—"

*Not Anna*, Toad thought. *Lily. And Toad is Toadam. No Toad is not Toadam Toad is another.*

He probed the lining of his gum for the cocoon. Where was it? He couldn't have eaten it. Not after making his promise to the muskrats.

Toad turned his black eyes toward the man as if he might know, only to have the man jab him with the sharp stick. Toad wasn't able to dodge the strike, and the spear struck him in his left shoulder, slicing the skin. Black blood poured from the wound, and he dropped to his knees. As he sank, Toad received an internal stab from Mother Isobel's blade and this sent him into a scream of rage and exhaustion. Where was the cocoon? Where was Anna? Why had she left him here?

*Lily, not Anna. Lily. Lily. And Toad is Toadam and Toadam is—*

Where was the cocoon? He couldn't have eaten it. His tongue probed all along his mouth—and found it. Almost in the back of his throat. He roped it back into place. The cocoon tickled against his gums as if there were movement inside it.

He saw his black blood running down his skin and saw the leaves stuck to him. He remembered how Anna—*Lily*—covered him before she left him to go find...to go find...

The man with the sharp stick stood staring at him.

"I don't want to hurt you anymore, but you must tell me where you took Katherine and Lily."

The end of his stick was wet and black. Toad looked between it and the wound in his shoulder.

"Anna," he said.

"Yes, you keep saying it. You were calling Lily that, weren't you?"

"Toad knows Anna."

"What about Katherine and Lily? Where—"

"Anna," Toad said.

The man trembled. His mouth formed words to himself as his eyes shifted back and forth. Then he said, "Veronica, Sarah, Rachel. Do those names mean something to you?"

"Toad finds Anna and then she hides again."

"*How* does she hide?"

"Toad finds Anna and brings her to Mother Isobel and then Toad gathers rocks and Mother Isobel makes the tombstone so Anna can hide again."

"So together you and the witch *do* kill them! Was Lily to be your next victim?"

The man jabbed him again. Toad snarled, mustering his strength. He bit the spear in half and then clawed at the man's face, only just missing. The man took off running. This made Toad grin despite his suffering. "Toad is King of the Forest!" he shouted and gave chase. How Toad wished he had even a bit of his usual strength. He'd already be ahead of the man, lying in wait. He'd play with him to teach him a lesson. He might use the summoning song to lead him into the water and watch him drown, but the summoning song was beyond his power now. The agony in his belly spiked if he even thought of trying to use it. His body had become lumbering and stiff. He couldn't stretch himself like he was used to doing.

They went deeper and deeper into the woods. The cocoon kept tickling Toad's cheek. He thought of the time of stone and how it felt to be flesh again. Maybe cocoons were times of stone for the fuzzy worms. Anna said she liked the flying leaves. *Lily* liked them. Maybe Toad should too.

The man stumbled. Toad heard him panting, gasping. He raised his hands over his face.

"Kill me if you want. Just tell me Katherine and Lily are safe. It's all I ask."

Toad started to answer, but the cocoon moved again. It tickled him more than ever and he laughed. He put both hands over his mouth.

"What amuses you? Did you do something to them? Are you gloating?"

The man kicked his way along the ground, rolling, scrambling. Toad followed, still trying hard to keep his mouth closed against both the tickle and the urge to scream his rage.

"Listen to me...I'm not your enemy. I don't have to be. I don't *want* to be. Whoever—whatever—you are, Lily cares for you. So does Katherine. And I care for them. *Please.*"

The woods opened up ahead. Toad could tell the man was heading for it with all his strength. The sensation inside his mouth had become maddening now. The cocoon rolled from one side of his mouth to the other, back and forth, back and forth.

"Made it," the man said, almost too winded to talk. "Look...please, look...we're alike...we're the same..."

Toad stopped. How had he come to be on top of the cliff? The tombstones were all there. But he'd ripped them up and thrown them at Mother Isobel to protect Anna.

*Lily.*

And there were no trees atop the cliff, but he saw trees everywhere. He looked at the man.

"I made this place to honor them," he said. "To honor her—Anna."

"Lily."

"*What?*"

"Anna is Lily and Toad is...Toadam is..."

He bent over. Lily's voice echoed in his mind: *We're brother and sister. Lily and Adam.*

"Adam, Adam, Adam, Adam," he said.

He touched the first tombstone and the next. Anna. Anna. Anna.

*Lily.*

*Christian has a sister named Anna.*

*Toad is not Christian.*

*Toad is Adam.*

*Adam has a sister named Lily.*

He sank down as the cocoon gave one final wriggle and split open in his mouth. The tickle couldn't be contained now and he raised his head, mouth open wide. The butterfly flew out, its wings as blue as the sky. It sped away from him like the summoning song, as delicate as wind among flowers. The butterfly lit upon the back of the man's right hand and they both stared at it in shared fascination. Toad inched closer, wincing as he went, until they sat beside each other. The butterfly's wings fluttered but it did not take flight.

"It's beautiful," the man said.

"Adam," he said, touching his chest. "Adam's name is Adam."

"Mine is Harold Goodman. I'm a friend of Lily's. That means I'm your friend too. We—"

The butterfly took off as a new sound came into their hearing, followed by the sight of many people moving through the woods. Adam watched his new friend Goodman get up and stagger to the edge of the clearing.

"It looks like a whole army and they're marching toward New Vineland. But why?"

A new voice answered from the woods behind them. *"Fancy meeting you here, Harry."*

As a man on horseback came into the clearing, Adam tried to stand in case his new friend needed protection. He felt another cut from the dagger. When was his stomach going to overcome it? What if it couldn't?

He collapsed and lost consciousness.

# Chapter Fifty-Eight

*Nightcamp, Nightcamp,*
  *Where have you hid?*
  *I seek your aid*
  *Show me the path*

Just the hint of the girl's voice brought Nightcamp awake and made him jerk his head up against the tether's quick limit. He snorted, confused by the darkness, at a loss for time or even the day. But awareness soon returned. Of course, he knew the day, if not the date. Hobbs neared completion of the statue. Pike and the army would be in a position to attack that night. These twin clocks of fate were preparing to chime together on the hour of decision, an hour that wouldn't resolve itself until dawn. The sun would rise on broken bones and broken stones and perhaps, if their plan failed a broken world. Having suffered through his morning beating under the crop of Evan Vines, Nightcamp had taken his hopes and fears into the sanctuary of an exhausted sleep. But all of his considerations and worries fell away, replaced by his attention to the girl's voice as he wondered where she was and why she sought him.

Her words were cast out like seeds on a wind, riding a melody that approximated the summoning song, but cruder–a product of raw ability rather than refined skill. Nightcamp could not help but be impressed, and he sent his thoughts back along its course, seeking her mind.

*Nightcamp hears,*
*He calls you to follow*
*Have no fears*
*Have no sorrows*

Though he'd never fished, he had a memory of watching his first owner sit on the bank of a lake, waiting for a pull on the string he'd cast into the water. When the fish was hooked, the line played out and the rod dipped. It was almost possible to feel the unseen force on the other end of the line. That's what Nightcamp experienced now. His song had found the girl and she'd seized it. He couldn't tell quite how far away she was, but it seemed a fair distance, at least a few miles. The direction of her response surprised him. She was not coming from the eastern river but from the southern woods. His first impulse was to think some tragedy had occurred, but he tamped down this fear. The child was adventurous, headstrong and no doubt missed her father after so many months of absence. Wasn't it just as possible that she'd run off in search of him and gotten lost?

Nightcamp summoned Wormwood, though he had no expectation of him arriving soon. If it were still the middle of the day, he would be busy minding Vines, attending to every whim, keeping the fantasy of his reign over New Vineland concrete. One hour passed. He heard no more songs from Lily but her presence remained, the connection stronger, nearer. Another half hour passed and Nightcamp felt her drawing very close. Concern grew in him. She was wearied, aching, and breathless. Even her thoughts consisted of pain and panting, too chaotic and scrambled to even make out a word.

A few more minutes passed. It seemed clear now the girl would arrive before Wormwood. How Nightcamp wished he could greet her with his head held high, projecting an image of strength and security. The girl needed that more than ever, and she'd find instead a pathetic, beaten animal that seemed more in need of help than herself.

She stumbled toward him out of the dark, collapsing on all fours. In her complete exhaustion, she didn't even seem to notice him. For a second, Nightcamp found himself wishing she wouldn't. He could just see her in his right eye, covered in grime, her clothes ripped, her shoes gone. What had happened to her? She had been running for her life, not out on some escapade to find her father.

She lifted her head and said, "Oh," in the most pained way before crawling over to him. She kissed his head and massaged his neck. "Thank you, Nightcamp. Adam and I were a lot further away from New Vineland than I thought. I wouldn't have made it here without you. I wasn't sure if you'd even remember me."

*Nightcamp remembers kindness*
*Recalled compassion never succumbs*
*To deafness or to blindness.*

She tugged at the tether and freed him. Before he could lift his head, however, Nightcamp found her arms hugging his neck with all their strength. "I have to find my Papa. So much has happened. My Mama, she's...the witch turned her to stone and...I've found my brother. I never knew...the witch stole him away..."

Nightcamp strained to understand as the girl's speech dissolved into choked sobs. She was carrying enough traumatic experiences and revelations to last a lifetime, but she'd acquired them in just a few hours. That much was obvious. His full attention was riveted on one thing—the found brother. In her present state, Nightcamp doubted she'd be able to explain what had transpired in the level of detail he needed. A more direct communication was needed.

He nuzzled her face.

*Time is too short*
*For questions long*
*Open your mind*

*To Nightcamp's song,*
*Think of a river*
*Your thoughts are flowing*
*From you to me*
*Until I have knowing.*

The connection between them strengthened as they looked into each other's eyes. Nightcamp felt her mind opening. All the thoughts she had tried to put into words washed into his mind, a series of images as clear as any painting yet shimmering like mist. He saw an enormous pumpkin, stone animals, a creature deformed and piteous with eyes as black as his very coat. Something was happening between Nightcamp and the girl he had not intended. The river of thought was supposed to flow from her to him, but there was a countercurrent just as strong that brought his experiences to her. Nightcamp felt her receiving moments from his life just as he received moments from hers. He heard her groan and felt himself flinch as he found himself inhabiting her body.

He was running across the plains like he so often did in his dreams, but now the running took place on two legs, so awful in their slowness. The world was so much larger, everything so much further away, with no hope of ever reaching a destination. His lungs took in such meager amounts of air and his bones felt like a collection of fragile twigs. He looked ahead and found he wasn't running toward a mountain, but a man. He recognized James Hobbs, who waited on his knees, arms wide open. Nightcamp ran into the mason's embrace, with the words *Papa, Papa!* screaming through his mind. The man changed in the middle of the hug, transforming into the deformed creature he'd seen before, a body of cold, blubbery flesh. Now Lily thought *Adam!* and *Brother!* They plunged into the water together and swam to the cliff. He felt a powerful song surge through him, unlike anything he'd ever experienced. An immense power came out of him, all too brief, all too desired. He saw a woman with her eyes closed, a woman Lily's mind identified as *Mama.* She was dead, drowned, and then—*Life.* Could the girl have such abilities? He sensed her elation, her confusion at this brief taste of her abilities. Then they flashed to the top of the cliff where Mistress Isobel stabbed Lily's mother with a dagger and turned her to stone.

*If I'm experiencing her life, then she must be experiencing mine.* Afraid, he tried to stop the exchange. In the end, however, Lily herself did that, standing up and moving away from Nightcamp just as Wormwood entered the tower.

"What is this?" he said. "Why is she here?"

Nightcamp gave a sharp snort, bidding Wormwood to be silent. Then he focused his gaze on Lily. The girl returned it, so brave despite her obvious confusion and her growing sense of betrayal.

"I saw you," she said, her voice small and solemn. "With—*her.*"

Nightcamp remained still.

"I didn't just see you," she continued. "I *was* you. You—I—we did so many terrible things. I think I saw Papa aiming a pistol at us. But it was dark and raining, and he didn't have a beard. Then we ran away...a fat man with a baby...and then we saw Evan Vines, and..."

Her eyes widened. A horrified look entered her expression, so alien to her face that Nightcamp had to force himself not to try nuzzling it away. He dared not attempt making such amends now. Her eyes teared up. She had every right to see him as a monster, a creature that deserved nothing but scorn and loathing. Maybe she'd even seek out Evan Vines's crop and hit him too. She deserved to strike him as much as anyone.

"That baby was my brother," she said. Her voice took on a stillness far beyond her years. "You helped that man take him from Mama and Papa. Then you helped Evan Vines give him to the witch. She called you her most valuable servant!"

That awful night from twelve years ago had never gone stale in Nightcamp's thoughts, but now he realized he'd never understood just what transpired there. It had not been just another mission to bring Mistress Isobel her *bread.* She'd taken the child and transformed it, not into a statue but something unlike Nightcamp had ever seen. *I will send forth my own son to destroy your tormentor.* Her words stormed into the forefront of his thoughts.

The girl shook her head. "Why? *Why?* I can't believe you *helped* her—"

*Nightcamp had his innocence*
*Sacrificed to arrogance*
*Guilty of obedience*
*Guilty of cowardice*
*Assisting evil and avarice.*
*Sorrow in my heart*
*Atonement in my bones*
*My soul is at your–*

He stopped. The girl's fresh trembling was so tangible he felt it in his hooves. She wiped her eyes, unable to keep up with the new flow of tears.

"You all tricked me," she said, pointing at Nightcamp and then Wormwood. "You and you...and Mr. Goodman...and even Papa..."

Wormwood now marched forward to place himself between them. "Girl, how do you know any of this?"

"Nightcamp showed me!"

He lowered his head, unable to meet either of their stares. More pieces of Lily's life were being realized in his mind just as pieces of his were in hers. He saw years pass through her eyes. Saw her family farm, saw the crops, and endured the endless chores that tethered her to monotony. A lonely life in many ways, colored by moments of strange happiness, friendships forged with chickens and cows and inanimate objects. Her true joy centered around moments in her father's workshop and long, eager talks with something called...*Fat Jack.*

A pumpkin? He could not fathom it at first, but the gourd grew in his mind until he could see nothing else because *she* could see nothing else. This bright orange globe had become her confidant and best friend. Nightcamp lived out lengthy periods when Lily left the supper table and ventured into the middle of the crops to sit beside Fat Jack until her mother called her in for the night. The pumpkin talked back. There was no mistaking its hearty, friendly songs, just as there was no mistaking the voice itself. He *knew* that voice from twelve years ago, and after Evan Vines killed the man, Nightcamp never dreamed of hearing it again.

For the first time in his long life, his back legs buckled, and he collapsed. Lily cried out and ran to him as he tried to stand. Wormwood joined them.

"Are you hurt?"

Hurt? Nightcamp didn't know *what* he was just then. He felt as wobbly as a newborn foal. He shot his thoughts into Wormwood's mind—

*A confluence of events*
*Beyond comprehension*
*Broadens my outlook*
*And apprehension.*

"What does confluence mean?" Lily said, and Nightcamp and Wormwood both looked at her.

"You heard his thoughts?"

The girl nodded.

"How can this be, Nightcamp? What's special about her?"

*Exposure to the summoning song*
*Or natural ability*
*I cannot think of any other*
*Likely possibilities.*

Wormwood grunted and Lily repeated her question.

"Confluence is when things come together and merge."

She cocked her head. "My papa's being here is part of that, isn't it?"

"Clever girl."

"I need to see him."

Wormwood shook his head. "As Nightcamp can explain, that's impossible. The *confluence* of events we've spent so long trying to achieve will begin in a few short hours. Your father is behind schedule."

"It can't be his fault!"

"I don't say it is. But even an imperfectly threaded needle can stitch a seam. He must be allowed to work uninterrupted for as long as—"

"I'm trying to find him now! If you won't help me, then I'll go myself."

Nightcamp moved in front of her.

*Do that, Lily, and all is lost,*
*Worthless despite the dear-paid cost.*
*Seek not your father until it's night.*
*I will say when the time is right.*

Obvious distrust and doubt showed on her face, but how in the world could he expect otherwise from her?

"But what about Adam and Mama?"

*Wait you must*
*It won't be long*
*Patience first*
*Then right the wrong.*

But Lily wasn't having it. Nightcamp kept matching her movements, blocking her every attempt to dart away. Wormwood was sneaking up behind her, but even with so much at stake, Nightcamp couldn't conscion the idea of her being restrained. Yet if Lily found and interrupted her father now, seizing these last few hours to perfect a statue that *had* to be as perfect as possible, their precarious plan faced doom. Should one little girl be allowed to interfere with all their efforts?

*No,* he thought, he saw another option besides crude force. He dropped to his knees in front of her.

"I don't understand," Lily said. "Are you going to take me to Papa?"

Wormwood laughed in a scornful way that Nightcamp regretted. "Child, your father wouldn't recognize you even if you stood in front of him tugging on his shirt."

"That's not true!"

"He is possessed by his vision. The rock has carved him as much as he has carved it."

"Papa would never ignore me!"

Wormwood gave a dismissive wave. "Nightcamp has offered you his back. You'd be wise to accept."

"I don't trust him."

*Why should you, knowing what you know?* Nightcamp thought.

"He gave his back in service to the witch. Now it's the essence of his free will. If he's offering you his back, he's offering you everything else he has to give. His strength, his speed, his determination...and his cleverness. You could do worse than put your faith in all of these things."

Nightcamp looked straight into Lily's eyes and dipped his head.

"How can I believe any of you? You all tricked me."

"That includes your father," Wormwood said.

The girl wiped her eyes, but she couldn't dry them. Nightcamp whinnied to her and projected his thoughts.

*Your father committed all his skill*
*To bring an end to this evil*
*A sacrifice of mind and heart*
*To dedicate his precious art*
*And you too must play a part.*

"That's right," Wormwood said. "We didn't have a choice unless it was choosing not to act at all. Your father understood the greater purpose. You had a role to play. If you were older, and if time were on our side, he'd have told you. There have been many sacrifices to bring us to this moment. Tricking you despite the pain it caused him was a sacrifice your father made. Get on Nightcamp's back. *Trust* him. He can take you anywhere you want to go except to your father."

The girl sat stock-still for a moment, still wiping her eyes. But she did rise and come to Nightcamp, getting onto his back.

"Take me back to my brother," she said.

# Chapter Fifty-Nine

Nightcamp felt Lily's weight shift again and knew she was looking back at New Vineland as she had several times since the trip started. She did not speak to him, and her silence was a harsher rebuke than any whipping from Evan Vines.

She didn't have to direct him at all. He retraced the steps he'd relived in memory, moving a few miles south through the dense woods and then keeping to the riverbank. He felt the child's growing worry and tension as they neared the spot. Nightcamp slowed, careful of the mounds of leaves that seemed to be everywhere. An unpleasant odor, faint but distinct, pulled him toward the west, but Lily spoke up and told him to stop.

"Adam? Adam, it's Lily!"

Nothing answered, nothing moved.

"I'm sure that's the spot," she said, directing Nightcamp to a particular pile of leaves. He went closer. Yes, the air here was stamped with a stronger impression of the same putrid scent, which was more than just damp, rotting foliage. He dipped his head near to the ground and sniffed.

"I don't understand," Lily said, her voice tearful. "I left Adam right here. These are the leaves I put over him to keep him warm. He was so tired and sick. I don't think he could get up and move on his own."

Nightcamp sniffed along the leaves and the ground. There was a second scent of human sweat, almost undetectable among the mix of fouler odors.

*Someone came,*
*I know not who.*
*Their trail leads west.*
*Let's follow through.*

Nightcamp didn't wait for her answer. He broke into a trot, winding around trees that became more familiar to him. His knowledge of them wasn't based on any experience he'd gained from sharing Lily's thoughts. He'd been in this part of the forest with Goodman, helping to realize his dream for a shadow cemetery, even if he couldn't fathom what the tombstones on the cliff meant or why Mistress Isobel would countenance them or why they all repeated the same name. Clearing the trees had felt like a small redemptive act, unimportant and unrelated to their greater plans. But that wasn't true. He picked up his pace, careful to keep Lily safe but pushing right to the edge. Nightcamp's thoughts raced far faster and covered the vaster territory of memory. He saw the deformed creature, Lily's brother, hurling tombstones at Mistress Isobel. He saw the two siblings playing together in the icy night, alone by the massive pumpkin whose voice he knew. When he looked down, Nightcamp did not see the ground or the forest. He found himself navigating a latticework of bone, flesh, and stone, covered thick in the tangled vines of lives and intrigues that stretched back as far as Mistress Isobel herself. Perhaps she thought herself the gardener, the planter of these vines. Or maybe she counted herself the masterful architect of the framework that was always destined to transform into the tower.

If so, Nightcamp was encouraged more than ever by a growing hope that she was neither gardener nor architect. Like all of them, she was herself a vine, though he doubted her ability to even consider such a possibility. It mattered not. The only concern was whether the true gardener or architect, whoever that might be, saw fit to let her succeed.

He stopped. His flanks were racked by a shiver.

"What is it?" Lily said.

How could he explain the self-disgust that had brought him to a dead halt? How could he explain the dangers of giving yourself over to a wild, almost blind faith? Only the desperate sought hope in patterns and only the paralyzed and impotent grasped at coincidences. Nightcamp knew better than to surrender himself to such nonsense. Yet he'd almost done it.

Was his dread of the battle ahead so overwhelming? Was his confidence in their plan so infinitesimal?

"Nightcamp," she said. "Do you hear that?"

He stirred out of his troubled rumination. No sooner had he noticed the new sound when he saw several men coming toward them, their rifles raised and ready. They wore black forage caps, and their single-breasted blue jackets were trimmed with gold braid and brass buttons.

"Girl," their leader said. "What are you doing here?"

"I'm looking for my brother."

"How old is he?"

"I...don't know."

Nightcamp saw the men exchanging glances. They looked too nervous for his comfort. He wasn't afraid of their bullets, but he worried for Lily.

"Where did you come from?"

With perfect innocence, she said, "New Vineland," before Nightcamp could warn her. The tension in the men ratcheted and they aimed their guns. Nightcamp thought he had mere seconds to react. He considered rearing up, but without the saddle, Lily would be thrown to the ground. The forest was too dense for him to bolt at any good speed, and he couldn't pivot and run from them. They'd just fire after him, leaving Lily exposed to every pursuing bullet.

*"What have we here, lads?"*

Nightcamp's ears perked. His dark mood lifted in an instant as Pike came into view on a brown mare. They made eye contact. Except for the slightest hint of a grin, Pike's expression stayed inscrutable.

"Sir, this girl says she's from New Vineland."

"And a possible spy," Pike said.

"I'm just searching for my brother," Lily said.

She spoke in a plaintive tone, but Nightcamp knew she understood the game and Pike's role.

"So you say," Pike said. He pulled a pistol and aimed it at Nightcamp's head. "You'll come with me now. Men, you did very well. Resume your patrol of the perimeter and detain anyone else you come across. No one in New Vineland must know we're here until the cannons start firing tonight."

The soldiers saluted and left, moving off in silence. As soon as they were out of sight, Pike put the pistol away and grinned.

"Good to see you, my friend."

Nightcamp snorted and whinnied.

"You're that man from the dock," Lily said. "I remember you."

"And you're one of the bravest girls in the world. One of the sweetest, too."

Nightcamp and Pike rode forward.

"Where are we going?" Lily asked.

"You said you're looking for your brother. He's not far."

That much was true. They reached the clearing in only fifteen minutes. There were no soldiers here. Pike must have ordered them all away.

"Adam! Mr. Goodman!"

Nightcamp felt Lilly getting ready to jump off while he was still in motion and came to an immediate stop. He saw Goodman sitting by the tombstones, trying to comfort a pale creature who lay stretched out on the ground, a pool of spilled milk the dirt refused to drink.

Toad.

Adam.

The boy from *that night.*

Seeing him through flashes of Lily's experience did little to prepare Nightcamp for the reality of this creature. So many of his features resembled the telltale marks of Mistress Isobel's artistry, the rounded head and mounded body. Much like Wormwood, he possessed no hardness, no edges. His skeleton seemed to have dissolved inside the flesh, leaving an ever-fading echo of structure. The overall impression was a person sculpted by the hands of a baker rather than a mason.

*And I'm responsible for his fate*, Nightcamp thought, his head and heart heavy as he watched Lily run and put her arms around the creature's neck. As Harold Goodman got up, she hugged him too. Hugged him and thanked him for watching over her brother. They began to trade stories, tales of their horrors and adventures. Nightcamp lowered his head, feeling more like an unwelcome stranger intruding on a family reunion—or worse: an intruding stranger responsible for all the family's woes.

"Adam was dreaming of Lily."

"I've been thinking of you every minute I was away. I wasn't able to get to Papa, but I had to get back here to see how you are."

Nightcamp turned away only to find Pike standing there, his expression a little wistful. Pike put his hand on Nightcamp's right flank.

"I've missed you, friend."

Nightcamp nodded.

"I stumbled upon Harry and that...creature...a few hours ago. It's a good thing Jackson and the bulk of the army were already moving into position at the time. They might have shot on sight. I kept the vanguard troops away from here. I imagine they'd take one good look at him and opt to open fire. Harry explained it all as best he could. The poor thing."

*How would Pike react if he knew my role in the* poor thing's *creation? Doesn't he know he's talking to the real monster right now?*

"You want to be alone?"

Nightcamp nodded again.

Pike gave his flank a light slap. "Wanting to think for a bit, eh? As if you're not already ten miles ahead of us. I'll leave you be, but I'll have to be moving ahead soon to join Jackson at the front. I tell you, Nightcamp, the people of New Vineland may be creatures of rock, but they'll never meet anyone harder than Old Hickory."

Pike left, going over to Goodman, Lily, and her brother. Nightcamp looked south through the trees. In his mind's eye, he saw the Hobbs farm and the pumpkin. Fat Jack. His fellow conspirator, his fellow criminal whose great crime was never completed because Nightcamp's own efforts to intervene got him killed.

He lowered his head, thinking harder about the man and what happened on that night of darkness and storm. He remembered his joviality and his confusion about the man's character. How had such a person heard and answered Mistress Isobel's summoning song? How could he be willing to commit such a black deed? Nightcamp's memories of the man began to succumb to Lily's experiences with him in his transformed state. How had it come to be? What force ordained it?

Once again, the concept of the latticework overwhelmed him with notions that everything that had happened, everything that was happening or *about* to happen, had some purpose beyond his understanding. His uneasiness with the idea was no less than before. Even if tomorrow found them victorious, the notion they were meant to win and were always going to succeed gave him no succor.

*Nor should it, old horse,*

*Trapped in philosophy's stall.*

*Because that means our choices,*

*Our very voices,*

*Were never there at all.*

He whinnied at the sudden song. The ground shifted beneath his hooves. The talk going on behind him faded away, as did the surrounding trees. In a flash, he stood in the middle of the crop row, looking at Fat Jack. But the pumpkin was not there. Nightcamp saw the man as he last remembered him, beaten down by Evan Vines, his mouth bloody, his front teeth missing. He reached a feeble, trembling hand toward him, but they were just far enough away that touch was impossible, and Nightcamp could not will himself closer.

*Look at the bed I've made for myself.*
*Here I've laid this entire time.*
*Bring me a bunkmate so I can sleep.*
*Bring me Evan Vines.*

Nightcamp tried to make a sound. When he found he couldn't, he nodded his head. As soon as he did, the man lowered his hand and gave a sickly grin. His mouth opened and shut. Nothing sing-song came from his lips. He managed one word in a voice that was almost as deep and croaking as Adam's.

"Tonight."

Nightcamp experienced another flash. He found himself back in the clearing with the tombstones. Pike had gotten onto his mount with Lily and Harold looking up at him. Adam Hobbs still rested on the ground. Nightcamp thought his posture looked very similar to Fat Jack's.

"Nightcamp," Pike said, adding a hearty laugh. "Glad you could join us again. What new scheme have you dreamed up for us now?"

Nightcamp wished he knew.

# PART SEVEN

# HEART

# Chapter Sixty

Lily watched Pike disappear into the woods as Mr. Goodman finished helping her and Adam get settled atop Nightcamp's back.

"I like him," she said, and Nightcamp whinnied.

"He's a rare one," Mr. Goodman said. "As rare as your father, I should think."

Lily smiled. "Can I see him now?"

She saw Mr. Goodman look to Nightcamp and added, "Adam and I are done letting other people make decisions for us. If Nightcamp won't go to Papa, then we're getting off him."

"Easy, Lily. Trust me."

"All of you keep asking me to do that."

"And we haven't earned your trust," Mr. Goodman said, nodding. "I know."

She leaned close to Nightcamp so he could see her. The song they shared had gone very low but never ended. Lily called upon it now to bridge their minds.

*Nightcamp, decide what you will do.*
*Take us where we want to go.*
*If you won't, then–*

Adam, sitting behind her, slumped forward, his weight driving her against Nightcamp's neck. Mr. Goodman reached up to steady him.

"He seems badly hurt. We'd be better off finding a doctor instead of James—though what doctor would see to Adam, I don't know."

"Adam wants Adam's papa."

"See, Mr. Goodman? He'll get better when he sees Papa. It may be the only thing that can help him."

She implored Nightcamp again and prepared to jump off and start running. The horse had been able to block her in the stable, but she had the advantage in the woods. Nightcamp must have realized that. He started forward and Mr. Goodman fell into step beside them.

"*Now* we'll go find Papa."

Mr. Goodman let out a long sigh. "You're not going to give us much of a choice in the matter, now are you, Lily?"

Lily shook her head. Adam put his arms around her waist, and she held them together as the jostling of Nightcamp's steps threatened to spill his weight against her. Lily glanced back to see her brother's head bobbing. His black eyes were open but she couldn't tell if he was awake. She patted her fingertips against his hands and said, "Soon, Adam. We're going to get to Papa and then he's going to figure out how to save Mama."

The sun had almost set when New Vineland came into view. The great town was ablaze with light, glittering everywhere and white like pieces of quartz in Papa's workshop. The only part of the city that didn't glow was the tower, whose darkness made it blend into the sky until it didn't exist at all.

Pike, still on his mount, sat watching as they came up to him.

"The army's almost in place now. Jackson's split them into a western and northern attack force. But only the west-positioned cannons will open fire."

"Why?" Mr. Goodman said.

"A ruse, Harry. The northern army is much stronger, and it'll be stronger still if the western assault draws away whatever counterforce

New Vineland has to offer. Then the Northern guns will let loose. The western artillery is made up of light cannons, 6 and 8-pounders. The north has all the heavy artillery. If that tower can hold up to almost a hundred 24-pounders blasting away at it, then all we can do is tip our hats to the witch."

Lily heard Mr. Goodman let out another long sigh. "At long last, it's happening. When will the shooting start?"

"We're less than twenty minutes from the President's signal. I must get to him now."

Pike started to move west as Lily called out, "But what about Papa? He'll be out of the way, won't he?"

The look on his face gave her the answer. Even Mr. Goodman acted like he'd never considered the question.

"Lily, your father has another task to do—"

"*Where* is he? You can't start shooting until he's safe!"

"I'm sure James—"

Lily rocked herself atop Nightcamp, urging the horse forward. When he wouldn't move, she kicked at him with her heels.

"Mr. Goodman, help me get down."

"It's too dangerous to go to your father now," Pike said. "He can take good care of himself. He's safest knowing *you're* out of harm's way."

Lily ignored him. When Mr. Goodman didn't move to help her, she began working herself off of Nightcamp's back. But even her determination couldn't quite overcome her fear of the drop. But Adam fell first and stretched his arms up from the ground to lift and settle her onto her feet. She felt the weakness of his grip, his failing strength.

"Adam can't go with you," he said.

"I know. It's okay. I'll go alone."

"Lily," Mr. Goodman said. "I can't let you do that."

She started forward anyway, giving a shout when he grabbed her, but in the next instant, she was free. Adam wrapped one arm around Mr. Goodman's waist and just managed to pull him back.

"What I mean," he added, "is that I can't let you go alone. Please release me, Adam. I'm on your side."

"Harry, if you're anywhere close to the tower when the northern artillery opens fire—"

"I don't care, Pike! We've used Lily enough. Put her whole family in jeopardy."

"Letting her run head-long into hell makes amends for that?"

"Allowing her to make her own choices does. Release me, Adam. I promise to look after Lily. I know just where your father is."

"Thank you, Mr. Goodman."

Pike moved his horse in front of them. "Damn it, you don't understand the danger you're putting yourself in. Artillerymen aren't sharpshooters. Cannon fire doesn't discriminate. For the love of God, at the very least let Nightcamp take you if he will."

Lily realized then the horse had been silent the entire time. She looked at him and found him staring into the eastern darkness, out and up toward the distant cliff. An orange glow blazed atop it.

"The witch," she said, and everyone turned to look east.

Pike scowled. "I must get to Jackson now. Whatever happens, good luck to you all. Here, Harry." He took a slim wooden case from his saddle bag and handed it to Mr. Goodman.

"What's this?"

"Fortune favors the well-armed."

He galloped away. Lily watched him go, then cast another weary stare toward the cliff.

"Nightcamp, what does it mean? Does the witch know what's about to happen? Does she know about Papa?"

Lily concentrated on the horse's mind and found a second song present, a bond much stronger than the one she shared with Nightcamp. It came from the light atop the cliff.

Adam pulled closer and Lily knew he could hear it too. More than just hearing it, he understood what was being said.

"Mother Isobel wanted Toad to kill Toad's papa. But Toad is Adam now and Adam has a different Papa."

Flashes of Nightcamp's experiences ran through Lily's mind, and as imperfect as her understanding was, she comprehended enough. "She wanted you to kill Evan Vines."

"Now Mother Isobel wants Nightcamp to do it."

Lily stood up. "Mr. Goodman, I don't think Nightcamp is going to be of any help. Will you still go with me even if we have to run?"

"Dear Lily," he said, flashing the kind smile she'd loved from the moment she met him. "I'll follow wherever you lead."

# Chapter Sixty-One

Something happened to Lily as soon as she got within a few hundred yards of the nearest building. The structure began to shimmer in the dark, and she found herself dazed and stumbling. Mr. Goodman grabbed her arm to steady her and said, "What is it? What's wrong?"

"I think I'm seeing New Vineland for what it is," she said. "What it *really* is."

She blinked, looking all around. All of the buildings vanished. The people who'd moved to and fro in finery and freedom became white statues standing on a desolate plain.

"I envy you, Lily."

"Why, Mr. Goodman?"

"Because all anyone can hope for is to see a thing for what it is, whether we like it or not."

"Don't we do that all the time?"

"Oh no," he said. "Hardly ever. I realize that now."

The sudden huskiness—even sadness—in his voice made Lily touch his forearm. She continued to look at the stark awfulness before her, knowing she was experiencing the truth as Nightcamp had seen it. The statues were falling here and there, close and far away, without any obvious pattern. Gargoyle creatures knocked them down and swarmed over each toppled figure, chewing on the bodies, defacing and disfiguring them. *Harvesters*, Lily thought, searching through Nightcamp's memories. *They're called harvesters.* Despite their terrifying appearance, she did not fear them. They showed no awareness of her or Mr. Goodman, who was saying, "Excuse me" and "Yes, just let me through" with unfailing politeness, though he spoke to hallucinations. She came to stand right over two harvesters as they finished chewing away the statue of a man, creating a sculpture as hideous as themselves.

The harvesters moved on to another statue, leaving Lily to contemplate the aftermath. Mr. Goodman said, "What are you looking at?" She found herself unable to answer him. The statue was beginning to move, neither quite stone nor flesh. It sat up and looked at her with eyes lit by a dim red glow. This startled Lily, but as the creature got up, she realized it hadn't really seen her at all. It turned toward the tower, which was so much taller in reality, more like the beanstalk Jack climbed in her imagination when Papa used to read her the fairy tale. The creature headed for it as if by instinct and Lily followed.

"James and his statue are on the western side of the tower," Mr. Goodman said. "We should go this way."

She saw him heading left like he meant to approach in a broad arc. The creature was cutting a direct path, however, and she followed it until the tower rose in front of her, rock yet more than rock. It throbbed like a heartbeat and swayed like a reed. The creature began to claw its way toward the top and Lily lost sight of it, but she knew what it was going to do. The tower was made from it and from thousands more just like it.

*"Lily."*

Mr. Goodman had offered his hand and she took it. As she did, the illusion of New Vineland reasserted itself. She saw the buildings and the bustling people. She felt the air of happiness and contentment. All of this made her shudder.

They came around the corner and she saw the statue of Evan Vines. The figure rose high above them, dwarfed only by the tower itself. It was Evan Vines rendered as a perfect titan. Papa had captured the man's smirk very well, and his large, blank eyes cast a hungry stare to the east. Another of Nightcamp's memories shot through Lily's mind, and she saw the statue as it had been weeks earlier, surrounded by scaffolding, with Papa climbing up and down as he chipped away at different levels and features. Now she saw the remains of the scaffolding, mere wooden beams that were scattered in a broken pile at the statue's feet, which were the only parts not realized in any detail. Evan Vines's legs rose out of two blocks.

Papa had found a new way to travel across the statue. Lily and Mr. Goodman stared up with identical looks of awe as they watched the statue's right hand, palm up, move with Papa standing in the middle. The motion was almost fluid and silent, as easy as flesh. All of Papa's sculpted animals seemed so crude compared to what Lily saw now.

"Papa!" she shouted, coming closer. "Papa, it's Lily!"

*He doesn't hear me*, she thought. It was the only explanation for why he didn't respond. She now heard his voice, his wonderful voice, singing through the air. Its strains reawakened old memories of hearing fleeting bits of song coming from within his workshop.

*Stona blednis*

*Stona sentos*

*Bikkoyas kerbos stona*

Lily shouted to him again to no avail. Papa pointed at a spot up and to the right on the statue, and the hand moved him to it. He placed his palms against the statue and sang even louder.

*Stona magios*

*Stona ne kwes agitas*

*Bikkoyas elanias stona*

The stone flashed a brief spark from somewhere deep within its body.

Lily stood on her tiptoes and using all the air she could muster, shouted, "Papa, please! You're in danger!"

"I think it's useless," Mr. Goodman said.

"It is," another voice said. Lily saw Wormwood moving toward them. "It's as I told you, child. Only the stone speaks to him now."

The hand dropped Papa level with the statue's left thigh. He placed his hands against the surface and sang again.

*Stona ne kwes*

*Bikkoyas stona kwano*

*Stona petnos*

*Stona dantos*

*He may not get lower to the ground than he is right now,* Lily thought, running to the right foot. Mr. Goodman and Wormwood both shouted for her to come back, but Lily ignored them and began to climb. The unshaped rock wasn't smooth and had plenty of crevices. *Just don't look down,* she thought as she reached the statue's ankle. The rock here was smoother and a little slick, but not polished. Her arms and legs shook as she tried to go higher, feeling for any place to insert her fingertips. Papa meanwhile swung to the right, still singing. She could see his face for the first time. His eyes had a glow to them as white as marble in sunlight. He touched the statue, put his ear against it, and sang. She shouted at him again, willing herself up another inch. She got a glimpse of the ground by accident and waves of dizziness began to overtake her. How had she gotten up so far? Mr. Goodman seemed small as he stood with his arms raised as if he intended to catch her.

She gasped, the ache in her fingers building. She lost hold with her left hand and dangled.

"Papa, I'm going to fall! I can't hold on anymore! Please help me, Papa!"

She dropped, plummeting, screaming. Stone flashed to her right. She hit the ground faster than she expected and then the ground lifted her high. Lily saw Papa kneeling beside her. His left hand was pointed at the sky and the statue's hand continued to lift them. The white light had left his eyes, leaving only the wonderful brown she'd always looked to in times of trouble. He hugged her with his right arm. His body radiated heat, almost as hot to the touch as Mama's wood stove after its fire was going strong. Lily wasn't about to pull away. It felt like they'd been apart for years and she began to sob.

The statue's palm came to a rest above its head and Papa helped Lily stand. She felt like she was at the top of the world.

"Why have you come? Did you sneak away?"

"No, Papa, I—"

"I never wanted you to see any of this, to know—"

"But I do. I know almost everything. Papa, I came to warn you. The army is here."

She pointed west into the dark.

"Army?" Papa shook his head as if he didn't understand the word. He squinted. "Oh, yes. I remember. I told them I was against that plan...I think I did..."

He swayed. Lily thought he was about to fall and put her hands on his leg, though she couldn't hope to catch him if he stumbled.

Papa put his right hand atop her head. "You know everything?"

She nodded.

"It seems I've fallen into bad habits. Your mother was right about my obsessiveness. It's dangerous. I don't even know the day. I can't remember the last time I ate. The air...it's colder than I remember it being. Lily, how long has it been since I left you?"

"It's October, Papa. I haven't seen you since—"

"*June.*"

Papa squeezed his eyes shut and screwed up his face in a way that made Lily hug him tight.

"It's okay, Papa. I know you did it to help everyone."

"Help," he said, as if he doubted it. "So much accomplished in such a short time. I've sacrificed so much, yet—we need more time. Another week. Another day. Even another hour, if I applied myself, I could—"

"Papa, the army is preparing to fire on us!"

"I don't remember anything about the army coming. Was I told? The past is a white wall to me now. Soldiers? Guns? Stone must battle stone. Do they not understand that? Did they doubt me?"

Lily felt his anger. All at once, his eyes blazed with white light again. The glow flowed across his face and made his features seem like granite. He gestured and the statue's hand moved them down to the level of its head. Lily could almost fit into the statue's eye sockets.

Papa reached out and touched the face.

"They were wrong to question us!"

"Papa!"

"*Stona dantos, stona petnos.*"

Lily called his name again but found it useless. Her despair rose. What could break his communion with the stone and return him to her?

"The witch has Mama!"

Papa became very still. The glow dimmed in his eyes.

"The same witch who took Adam."

"Katherine," he whispered. "*Adam.*"

"He's alive, Papa. The witch changed him, made him different, but he's still Adam."

Tears came down Papa's cheeks and all the remaining light seemed to drain out with them, leaving his eyes clear again.

"Adam is alive? You've met your brother?"

"Mr. Goodman has too. So can you—right now. But he's hurt, Papa. So is Mama. The witch hurt them both."

Papa lowered his head. "And I wasn't there for either of you."

In the distance, Lily saw a line of fire appearing out of the darkness from left to right. She shivered.

"I think they're about to shoot!"

She only just got the warning out when the first cannons boomed and the volleys whistled overhead. The artillery smashed into the tower. Lily held her breath and waited. Something was happening. The summoning song, so pervasive and steady that Lily had taken little notice of it, became a shriek. Pieces of the tower seemed to be raining from the sky. For a hopeful moment, she thought the cannons had done damage. But it was not debris. The creatures who comprised the tower were breaking free and marching toward the rest, pushed forward by the cry of the song.

"Papa, we have to leave. Bring the hand down so Mr. Goodman and Wormwood can climb on."

Papa nodded. The hand came to a rest in front of a stunned Mr. Goodman, who was waving his hands in the air, still clutching the pistol case Pike had given him. He threw himself onto the palm, but Wormwood refused.

"My duty is here. I'm needed for one final task—to keep Evan Vines from fleeing."

More shells exploded above them. Mr. Goodman cringed, hands over his head.

"Who cares what happens to Vines now?"

"Nightcamp does."

Nothing else needed to be said. Goodman shook the man's hand and retreated to the center of the statue's palm. Wormwood knelt before Lily and smiled.

"We've had an unfortunate relationship," he said. "Maybe in time you'll forgive me for—"

She smiled back. "I already have."

"Brave and generous girl. You've given me all the redemption I'll ever need. Go now, all of you."

Papa had the statue moving again. Stray bursts of cannon fire struck its back, making the whole structure shake. But Papa was right. The artillery did not harm them as the statue walked away from New Vineland with giant, thudding strides. Lily guided Papa to the spot. The cannon fire continued in the distance, joined by the shouting of men. Lily spun around to see a great clash of figures through the moonlight and smoke. It seemed almost like a battle of toy soldiers, something she and Adam might have spent hours arranging after they'd finished their chores.

"The army will be slaughtered," Papa said without looking back. "Bullets and bayonets have little power over rock."

Lily grimaced, but the battle raging concerned her less and less as she anticipated bringing Papa to Adam. She saw his small white form at the edge of the woods. He was resting across Nightcamp's back.

Papa stopped the statue and lowered the hand, with Lily pulling him off it before it had quite reached the ground.

"Adam, can you hear me? This is our Papa. Adam?"

Nightcamp turned his head.

*He is weak*

*And should not speak.*

"If he sees his papa, he'll get stronger."

Papa stood in front of him, just looking. For several long moments, he did not speak. Lily became fearful he saw only *Toad.*

Then Adam raised his head a little. Whatever doubts Papa had must have crumbled, because he held Adam's face in both hands and then leaned closer until their foreheads touched. They spoke so low Lily had to strain to hear them.

"Adam missed Adam's papa."

"And I missed my beloved little boy. Your mother and I both, and your sister, as well!"

Papa beckoned to Lily and she rushed forward into their shared embrace.

"How I've dreamed of standing with my son and daughter. Our family is almost complete again."

"Except for Mama," Lily said.

She felt Papa stiffen. "I'm going to take care of that now."

Papa kissed Adam on the top of his head and then did the same for Lily before pivoting toward Nightcamp.

"Take my children home."

"Papa, you can't send us away now!"

"I can't face the task ahead unless I know my children are safe. That means getting you back to the farm. Nightcamp will speed you there."

"But Adam and I are scared."

"We all are. But the witch and I have a reckoning. I swear I'll bring your mother back safe and sound."

"But you can't go alone!"

"He won't," Mr. Goodman said. Lily and Papa both turned to discover he'd opened the case Pike gave him and pulled out two pistols, which he now displayed with great solemnity. "Let's go, James. I, for one, am ready for a duel."

# Chapter Sixty-Two

*Dear Father,*

*This may be my last letter. If I perish tonight, I would only hope you believe I died, in the best sense, a Godly man. I assure you I'll die an Englishman. The night air is cold and crisp. The fire of war explodes behind me. Looking back, I see thousands of soldiers waging a desperate struggle. Cannons and flintlocks make ever-changing constellations on the dark plain. Meanwhile, I ride toward a battle I cannot explain on a mount I lack the words to describe. I stand shoulder to shoulder with a man whose genius surpasses my understanding. But I comprehend his rage. This is a night of duress and redress. No Bible verses come to mind at this moment, but Shakespeare is adequate enough.* Now bid me run, and I will strive with things impossible! *Certainly, New Vineland has confirmed Hamlet's rebuke to Horatio.*

Goodman allowed himself a grim smile as he finished thinking his letter toward the sky. Then he fixed his attention on the cliff face. He and James stood on the statue's left shoulder as it strode across the river like a grown man traversing a puddle. Each step brought equal amounts of courage and dread into his heart.

*The moment is here at last. Our strength against the witch's powers. May the side of good prevail.*

In all the years he'd spent dreaming of this moment, Goodman never imagined a scenario like this. He'd always envisioned a sneak attack where he alone, or perhaps accompanied by Pike, ambushed the witch and killed her in some undefined way. Memories of those fantasies embarrassed him more than he could say now that he faced the reality of the witch's power.

He looked back at the battle raging in New Vineland and hoped Pike was okay. Then he looked straight ahead again. The orange glow had become a raging fire that seemed to consume the entire top of the cliff. The flames sent out waves of cold rather than heat. Chilly blasts of wind almost knocked him off his feet. James put a steadying hand on his shoulder but did not look at him. His eyes shone with a bright white light that now blazed forth from the statue's eyes too.

A great rumble and cracking sound came from the cliff face. A chunk of rock as big as a house broke away and flew straight at them, striking the statue square in the chest. The force of the impact shot through the body, knocking Goodman off his feet and causing him to drop the dueling pistol from his right hand. He groped for it and picked himself up, risking a look near the edge to assess the damage.

"Not even a scratch, James! This proves you're more powerful than she is!"

The boast carried up to the witch and infuriated her. A hail of rocks assaulted the statue, forcing Goodman into the crook between the statue's shoulder and ear. James stood rooted in place, hands held out, fingers curling and uncurling, each gesture conjuring the statue to greater feats of fluidity and resolve. He and the statue appeared to be one being now, the stone imitating every motion of the flesh. The titanic reproduction of Evan Vines began swatting away the volleys of rock, even catching and lobbing some back, causing Goodman to shout and cheer.

The colossus reached the cliff and began climbing, its fingers gouging holes into the face with all the ease of a child raking through sand. The cliff face shook and buckled against them, but the statue's grip held firm. Their final assault seemed all but certain now, and Goodman's heart beat in wild anticipation of it. He heard a new sound behind them. Hundreds of people were running from New Vineland, streaming into the river, sinking out of sight. Goodman squinted. Despite all he knew about the illusion of New Vineland, he could not help believing he was watching some elaborate, horrifying suicide ritual.

Their heads rose on the other side. He saw men, women, and children crawling straight up the cliff at them, gnashing their teeth as they gained on them.

*"James."*

"I know. The witch has summoned her servants to defend her."

"Can they hurt the statue?"

"I don't know."

The swiftest people—Goodman wasn't sure what else to term them—leapt upon the statue's feet and clung to it. Goodman heard the most sickening noises, a mix of cracks and scratches, clicks and clacks that sounded like teeth trying to chew shards of glass. James did not stop the climb, but progress was slowed as he tried to shake free of the attackers. Goodman braced himself. Each shake sent dozens of people falling back into the water like fleas. Goodman found the sight of this no less horrific even though their appearance was an illusion.

The swarming continued, the gargoyles crawling over each other in a scramble to bite into the rock. None of James's efforts could free them of all the onslaught. Goodman saw men and women and children on their hands and knees gnawing at the rock. They looked like starved termites on a giant block of wood and they were eating very fast. Twenty or thirty were now feasting on the statue's right ankle. A severe cracking sound came from deep inside the block.

"We can't let them hobble us, James."

"We're almost at the top."

"What good will it do to reach it if the statue can't stand?"

*I have to try something,* Goodman thought. *I may be useless in the battle with the witch anyway, but if I can help James make it safely then I'll have done my duty.*

His hands shook as he took aim with the pistols. Pike had called them *good luck,* and if ever such a thing were needed, now was the time. *I, for one, am ready for a duel.* The bravado of his words struck a hollow note now that he held the weapons. What would Pike think if Goodman admitted he'd never shot a gun? Imagining the old sailor's expression gave him a flash of levity but it did not stop the tremble in his hands. Their shaking combined with the statue's lurching movements made it impossible to aim from this distance.

*I'm going to have to fire from point-blank range.*

Goodman glanced at James, found him absorbed in manipulating the statue, and started thinking of how he could descend to the statue's foot. Between the smoothness of the worked stone here and the movement of the legs, he saw no option. Grimacing, he looked at the cliff face as it moved past him. It was full of nooks and crannies, ledges and handholds. The statue's ascent was slow enough to let him leap and scramble for a hold. *It's not even that far a jump,* he thought. He need only dangle for a few moments and then drop onto the foot as it rose to meet him.

The plan might be madness, but he saw it transpiring with perfect clarity. He slipped the pistols into the waistband of his pants and inched along the shoulder to get as close as he could to the cliff face.

*Just a little courage now,* he thought, though courage and rationality were oil and water for him just then. The face of the cliff rushed by in front of him.

*I can't,* he thought. *Father, I can't do it. I'm useless. Faithless.*

The image of his father scowling back at him gave the needed push. He flung himself forward. For a moment, he felt himself suspended in the air. Then he hit the cliff wall and began to tumble. His clawed hands groped for leverage. The rock tore the skin off his hands but his fingertips found some miracle nook and he jerked to a stop and dangled. Exhilaration overcame pain as he held firm as the statue's right foot now rushed toward him. Goodman let himself drop and he landed among twenty people who were on their hands and knees gnawing away at rock.

*Not human. You know they're not human. See past the spell.*

Still, his hands shook as he placed the barrel of one pistol against a man's temple.

*Not human.*

He gritted his teeth. God help him, he couldn't pull the trigger.

"Please, stop," he whispered. "Please—don't make me—"

*Not human. Not a man at all.*

*"Fire, Harold. It's doing the Lord's work."*

He heard his Father's voice as if it were spoken over his shoulder. Goodman looked. Father wasn't there, of course. But what if the letter he'd thought out had been received? What if these words were his Father's simple reply?

Goodman closed his eyes and pulled the trigger. He expected a scream. None came. But the bullet had shattered something. He opened his eyes to a different scene, no longer deluded. The people were gone, replaced by creatures that resembled living gargoyles, misshapen, and monstrous. One stood up to face him. It had a chunk missing from the side of its head.

Goodman backed away, discarding the used pistol and taking out the second as the gargoyle came at him, its sharp fingers daggering at him. Its body was almost colorless except for its glittering eyes, which looked like two little rubies inserted into the sockets. As the gargoyle lunged, Goodman raised the pistol in both hands and fired into its right eye at point-blank range. The blast shattered the eye and sent a jagged fracture across the gargoyle's head. The monster stood still a moment, then staggered toward him a single step.

*It's not enough*, Goodman thought, looking behind him. He had nowhere else to go.

A cracking sound came from inside the monster.

It shattered into five large pieces at his feet.

Goodman shouted in victory, but his satisfaction was brief. A rumble came from overhead. The statue's right hand had reached the top of the cliff and its arms began hauling the torso over the edge, grinding it away in the process. The statue reached waist level with the top just as the gargoyles succeeded in chewing through the right ankle. Goodman heard the crack of separation as the stone shifted away from him. He tossed the useless gun aside and leaped. For a second time, his torn fingers found an outcropping of rock just large enough for him to grasp. He looked down to see the broken foot plunging into the river, carrying the gargoyles with it.

Above, the rest of the statue was disappearing onto the plateau. He judged himself thirty or forty yards from the top.

*No direction but up. Not too far. Keep your eyes skyward.*

His right toe wedged itself into a crevice and he pushed up. James and the statue were now gone. Goodman found himself in a world that felt empty. The only sound that reached him was the ongoing battle across the river. The cannon batteries fired volley after volley. Above that fray, he heard the frantic shouts of men and, sometimes, the unmistakable scream of the dying.

*Pike's okay. He must be okay.*

A cackling laugh from overhead made Goodman snap a look straight up.

*"Warlock, thy skill in stone impresses me. Thou can give life to rock. Very well. Here is thy wife. Make her breathe again."*

*Dear God*, Goodman thought.

He resumed the climb.

# Chapter Sixty-Three

Lily looked at Nightcamp as the statue carried Papa and Mr. Goodman away. The horse did not return her stare.

"The witch has been talking to you. I could hear it."

Nightcamp still refused to look at her. It was her turn to come and stand in front of him.

"Did she order you to do something? Are you going to betray us?"

The horse shook his head.

Lily sighed and put her hand against his right flank, feeling the puckered scars.

"Share your thoughts with me. Please? I'm scared."

A song rose between them. She felt the fullness of the bridge between their minds.

*To the farm you must go*
*But Nightcamp must stay here.*
*Give yourselves to the river's flow,*
*Allow yourselves no fear.*

"You want us to go by boat?"

She followed Nightcamp's gaze as it landed on Adam. He lay very still on the ground. His breathing was steady with his moans.

*He's faster in the water*
*Than even I on land.*
*Obey your father's order*
*While I obey Mistress Isobel's command.*

"What has she ordered you to do?"

*Evan Vines must die tonight*
*She's given me this task.*
*I will fulfill this fine request*
*But not in the way she asks.*

A sinister air surrounded Nightcamp now, and for the first time, Lily felt afraid of him. She backed away and knelt beside Adam. His skin was so cold and dry.

"He's weak. I'm worried about him."

*Water is his element*
*This river is his soul.*
*Strength he will find again,*
*The river makes him whole.*

"Nightcamp, I think...water may be my element too. I think I can help him in the river. Adam, are you ready?"

"Adam can't move."

She caressed his head. "Not even a little?"

His body shifted no more than an inch, then went still.

Nightcamp knelt next to them. Lily pulled and tugged Adam's heavy body across his back as best she could, an effort that took several minutes. Nightcamp carried them both to the water and entered the river until the water lapped at them.

Across the way, Papa's statue began its climb. Lily watched in fascination until Adam groaned.

His voice was stronger.

"Papa? Lily?"

"I'm right here. I'm—"

Adam lolled to the side. Lily felt him slipping over and clung to him all the way into the river. His weight seemed to triple in an instant. He began to sink.

"Adam, no!"

She slapped at the water, begging for the power of its song. Panic made her mind spin into chaos. She heard the river's melody.

But felt nothing.

Lily clung to Adam as his sinking body pulled her down. Her lungs burned and colors burst across her vision. The river's song became a cold, ghoulish shriek, and then—

Toad rocketed her to the surface. She coughed water as he held her, his black eyes alive as never before.

"Adam feels better now."

Lily laughed, hugging him.

*Go now*
*Back to the farm*
*Away from here*
*Away from harm*
*Before this night*
*Finds its end*
*We may be rejoined*
*Family and friends.*

Despite the hopeful promise of his voice, Lily found the same air of darkness surrounding Nightcamp. What fate did he intend for Evan Vines? She feared guessing.

Adam splashed her, and all her grim thoughts ended. Even Papa and his statue lost meaning for her.

"Adam will take Lily home."

"It's your home too."

He wrapped his arms around her. "Adam can go faster by swimming under."

"Don't forget I can't hold my breath as long as you can."

"Adam won't forget."

Lily gulped air until her cheeks were puffed out and then she and Adam submerged. She remembered the speed they'd gone upstream but that was nothing compared to now. She could only compare it to the feeling of sledding down a steep hill in winter. It was as if some great force pushed at their backs, propelling them ever faster. Forgetting everything else in her excitement, Lily shouted, her glee coming out in bright, silver bubbles.

They surfaced and Lily gasped. She had no idea how many miles they'd put behind them. Nightcamp had been right. As fast as he might be, her brother was faster. After submerging a second time, it seemed mere minutes before they reached the dock. Adam helped Lily climb up and then sprang onto the planks with a somersault. He landed groaning, though, and clutching his stomach.

"In the river, Adam forgot the hurt," he said.

"Do you want to get back in the water?"

"Adam wants to be with Lily."

"I can sit on the dock. It'll just be the two of us talking."

"Adam wants to be with Lily on land."

She helped him walk off the dock and up the path to the farmhouse. Something moved in the grass. Lily thought it was a rabbit, and it was—*almost.*

"One of Papa's statues," she said.

"Adam remembers."

"Don't worry," Lily said. "I'm sure it won't hurt you. It knows you now."

The stone rabbit nuzzled against Adam's foot.

"When Papa and Mama are back, he'll make many more animals for both of us. Then he can teach us. He's shown me a little bit but I'm not very good."

"Adam wishes they were here now. Adam's scared for them."

"Papa will know what to do. And he has Mr. Goodman with him. Together they'll kill that awful witch."

Adam grimaced again, almost doubling over. Lily frowned and caressed his arm.

"Let's go someplace where we can wait together and not be alone. We'll go see Fat Jack. You remember him, don't you?"

"Adam thinks so."

They veered into the crops. Lily shivered. She hadn't been cold at all in the river but the chilly fall air against her wet skin threatened to make her teeth chatter. She'd see Adam seated safe and sound next to Fat Jack, and then she'd run inside to fetch blankets.

She stopped short, spying an orange glow through the crop rows. So many times she'd seen Fat Jack in the light of day and thought of him as a lounging sun. Now he had his own true brightness. Lily led Adam toward Fat Jack on cautious steps. Soon she realized blankets would not be needed. Fat Jack was sending off waves of heat as well as light. It was as if he were on fire.

Adam slumped to the ground. As she knelt to attend him, she heard a boisterous voice.

*Lily, Lily, sweetest girl*
*Help your friend in this time of need.*
*I've paid dearly for my greed*
*And now I long to leave this world.*

"Fat Jack," she whispered.

*Nightcamp you know,*
*And I know too.*
*We were together long ago*
*And stole the baby who–*

"I know," she said, dropping her gaze. In her shared memory she could see the large man who Nightcamp had helped in the witch's final bargain. Her hands balled into fists and she looked straight ahead into Fat Jack's light. The pumpkin was gone, replaced with the man himself.

He stood looking at her, bruised and battered, bloody. The front teeth were missing from his smile.

"Why did you do it? Why would you make a deal with *her?*"

"Stupidity and hunger," he said. "There's no evil quite like greed, Lily. It's only fitting I was killed by a man who shared the same appetite."

She closed her eyes, experiencing some of Nightcamp's confusion as he stood in the storm watching Evan Vines kill the man.

"Nightcamp wanted to help you," she said. "Wanted to save you."

"He might yet—with your help."

She saw the fat man's front teeth go flying and land in the soupy mud. She knew now just where she was standing, and she looked at him again.

"You betrayed me," she said, near tears. "I thought you were my friend. I talked to you. I trusted you."

"I didn't know who you were. Until very recently, I didn't even know who I was–or what I had been. My memories consisted of blackness and silence. Then there were two sounds. Your young voice and the tapping of your fingertips, as if on my forehead. I felt myself expanding. Maybe that's all life has ever meant to me. Getting bigger. I knew I had a hollowness in me. I was surrounded by thick walls and the only thing that could penetrate them was your sweet voice—your wonderful song. I felt filled by them and I wanted to give back the pleasure and joy I received. I swear to you I didn't know my own past until *he* came. I heard the witch's song coming from him and it woke me. I began gathering strength, reaching out beyond myself. The song that connects me to your brother also connects me to the horse."

"Nightcamp."

"Yes. At long last, I found him and made contact with him. He's going to help me get my revenge on Evan Vines."

"You're a pumpkin. What can you do?"

He touched his cheek and his broken mouth.

"Give me back my face."

*"Face?"*

"Only you can do it."

"How?"

Fat Jack did not answer right away. He seemed distracted, looking north.

"What is it?" Lily said.

"I hear Nightcamp."

Lily turned to look north too. "He's coming?"

"Not just yet. But soon. Oh, he's a clever creature. We've both suffered and we both brought our suffering on ourselves. We're looking for the same redemption."

"I don't know how I can help."

A sly gleam flashed in Fat Jack's eyes. "I know your papa's taught you to carve. You've told me all about it many times."

"A little," she said. "But stone."

He answered with a laugh as big as his belly. "Can my shell be harder than rock? Hurry, Lily! Carve me my face and make the mouth wide and fierce!"

Fat Jack's human form faded, leaving her to stare at the glowing pumpkin. She stood still for half a minute, dazed.

Tools. She needed tools.

She ran into the house and sought out Mama's sharpest knife. Unable to decide, she gathered all seven of them. When she returned, she found Adam groaning and holding his stomach. His eyes were orange from Fat Jack's glow.

"Hold on, Adam," she said. "Let me get started, and then we'll get you back to the river."

She took the first knife, the one Mama used to remove fish and chicken bones, and placed the tip against Fat Jack's shell. His broiling heat sent a stinging sweat dripping into her eyes. She realized she was panting. Her hand trembled so much that she had trouble holding the knife. Despite everything she now knew, after all the years of keeping Fat Jack safe, the idea of stabbing a knife into him sickened her.

*But I have to do it.*

She pushed the blade only to find it bending—and snapping. Lily gaped at the broken knife. Turning, she picked up the second and the third. Both failed to make the slightest scratch on Fat Jack's shell. At last, she picked up Mama's cleaver and brought it down with all of her strength. The blade ricocheted back as if she'd tried to stab a boulder and the recoil forced her to drop the knife.

*Hurry, Lily, carve my face*

*Nightcamp comes*

*No time to waste.*

"But you're as hard as a...rock," she said.

*If he's like a stone, then maybe I need to get Papa's tools.*

Lily sprinted toward his workshop.

# Chapter Sixty-Four

Concussive jolts rocked the entire cliff with their force and threatened Goodman's grip as he summoned one final burst of strength and heaved himself up over the edge. The fires that had seemed to burn and race across the plateau had receded into a tight globe of power encircling the crone's crooked silhouette. Her long, thin, shadowy arms were raised above her head. James had brought the statue to its knees in front of her, joined the hands into one massive hammer, and rained blow after blow against her protective bubble. But the witch's defenses did not falter and the force of the strikes shook the ground. Goodman had to dive forward as the ground near the edge gave way and tumbled into the river.

"Scholar of stone, magister Mason, surely our paths have crossed for a greater purpose than this fight. We need not be enemies. How can we be when we each hear and sing the song of stone? Thy melody is strange to me, but we are bound by common cause. The world proclaims it from its rocky core."

James responded with another fruitless strike. Goodman grimaced to hear a sharp, explosive crack from deep inside the statue's hands. The pieces fractured and crumbled, undone by their own force. James seemed to be hugging himself, as if willing the statue to hold together. But the fissures spread and the towering sculpture of Evan Vines shattered and fell into a heap. Gray dust rose from the collapse, clouding Goodman's sight as he got to his feet.

*"James?"*

No one answered. Goodman waved his hands ahead of him as he searched. The cloud of debris was as thick as a London fog and made him cough. The orange glow around the witch persisted and he was reduced to approaching it like a moth to a flame.

A hand seized his forearm. He saw James there, his hair and beard aged gray with dust. They stood in silence as the air began to clear. Two figures stood facing them in the rubble. As the light around the witch receded, revealing her, Goodman realized the second figure was a statue. He recognized its features at once.

"James, it's—"

"I know."

"Thy wife's voice cries out still. Do thou hear it, Mason?"

"I do."

The witch gave a laugh so nasty and superior it provoked Goodman to attack her. Only James's grip on his shoulder kept him from lunging more than two steps.

"She's *praying.* Another tedious follower of the Christian banner."

"That's a fair deal better than whatever god *you* worship!" Goodman said. James squeezed his shoulder again and pulled him back.

"Do thou know the Parable of the Sower, Mason?"

"I do," James said.

"A tale of amusement for somber nights, told from ignorance. My Lord seeks out stony ground to cast his seed. I am his crop, and I did not rise at speed. Far from being rootless, my roots are stronger for the testing. Now the knowledge of sowing has been granted to me. Behold the garden I have suffered to rise across the river."

Goodman shook his head. "You don't hear those explosions? The cannon fire? That *garden* of yours is being plowed over by—"

Goodman gasped, rising on his tiptoes as the point of a dagger forced him up. He'd not even seen the witch move, but she now stood in front of him, her dark eyes gleaming.

"I will turn thee to stone a piece at a time, starting with your tongue."

"*Wait,*" James said. "He is a bystander. Let him be."

"Do thou seek a bargain, Mason?"

Goodman heard James's low chuckle. "You have my wife hostage in stone. You hold my friend at knifepoint. What can I offer?"

"A test of talent and skill, our abilities matched."

"That sounds like a contest, not a bargain."

"There will be no contest."

"You should have more confidence in your abilities."

The witch laughed and took her knife away from Goodman's throat. She pointed it at a broken piece of the statue's leg.

"That block of stone will serve as thy proving ground."

"But I don't even have a chisel."

"Mock me not, Mason. Thy hammer and chisel are but props. Thou have my blessing to use the full scope of thy powers."

"And what will I be judged against?"

"My own talent," the witch said, gesturing to Katherine's statue. "The end result of this block of stone against thy own. Since thou are young and still in thy apprenticeship, I will forsake the carving song and limit myself to a single tool."

She tapped her dagger's black blade against Katherine's stomach.

"We will see which of us can conjure the best new shape from our stones."

Goodman looked at James and found him resolute and grave. With his hair and beard still white from dust, he seemed like some image of Zeus. He stayed silent for so long that even the witch arched her frayed eyebrows and said, "Well?"

"You took my son and changed him. Now you'd take my wife and mutilate her? What would you hack away first? An arm? Her head?"

The witch again put the dagger to Katherine's face. "Most splendid ideas, Mason."

"Wait!" James said. "There's no need to prove your power. I accept it. I bow to it. You said there was no need for us to be enemies. I agree. If you want a real bargain, I'll make it with you now."

"Yes?"

"Turn Katherine back to flesh and let her and Harold walk away."

"I fail to see the bargain in this, Mason."

"The bargain is my submission."

"James, *don't*—"

"What a prize I'd make, locked in stone for your *amusement*. Where will you place me in the world you're about to conquer? Will you build a palace and place me beside your throne? Will you place me facing east in a garden so I can watch the sun rise upon your kingdom for all eternity? Or will you throw me face down on the floor in a dark basement and let the spiders crawl over me?"

The witch's excitement became palpable to Goodman. He saw calculation in her eyes and imagined she was conceiving of all the ways she could betray the agreement after it was struck. How could anyone make her keep her word? With James trapped in stone, why couldn't she turn and do the same to them in an instant? What would stop her from going after Lily?

He imagined the Hobbs family imprisoned in statues that the witch arranged in a circle so they could stare and lament each other's fate from the depths of their stony confinement.

*Don't do this, James. You must realize the mistake. She'll never act in good faith.*

"I agree to thy terms, Mason. Our pact is reached. Come and stand before thy mate."

James did.

"As I return thy wife to flesh, I will bring thee to stone, that both may witness and know the transformation of the other."

In a sing-song voice, the witch began her chant. Goodman thought James seemed fascinated by it at first until the first signs of life from Katherine made him wince. Goodman didn't know what he expected to see as the change took place. Would the stone pieces crumble away like a shell? The overall effect was closer to watching a bruise heal. The stone faded bit by bit, starting at her feet.

He saw James's legs hardening at an identical rate.

As the transformation crept up past their waists, Goodman saw Katherine start to bleed. James reached out to her just as the enchantment overtook his arms and froze them.

The witch clapped her hands.

"And now to understand the folly of thy bargain, Mason. My stone enchantment saved her life. Death is the antagonist of flesh, not stone. Death hungers, and now it will finish the meal my spell denied it."

"Save her!" Goodman said.

"No such requirement was in our bargain. Now, Mason, though the stone overtakes thy eyes, yet they will see your mate die. Thou will carry this knowledge into eternity. I will bring thee to the halls of my workshop and place thee in a special gallery of vanquished foes, where thou shall have pride of place."

Goodman caught Katherine as she collapsed. He tried to staunch her bleeding with his palms, but the blood seeped through his fingertips.

"Lily," she whispered. "Lily, Adam, I..."

She lost consciousness.

"*No.*" Goodman trembled and glared up at the witch. "Change her back before it's too late!"

"The bargain was struck, and I honor its terms. Pest, thou are free to go."

"James wouldn't have made the deal if he knew the truth!"

"So says everyone after the fact. Come, boy," she said, gesturing toward the edge of the cliff. She took several steps toward it. Goodman looked at Katherine. She was still alive, but her eyes were closed. How much longer could she linger? Was she past hope?

He got up and stood a few paces behind the witch. She did not turn as she started speaking again.

"A fine spectacle. An army of flesh against my servants of stone. Who shall wear the victor's crown at dawn?"

"If there's a God, then it won't be you."

"There are many gods, all with hearts of stone no matter their pretenses. My Lord simply celebrates reality."

"You know no pity at all?"

"Is there pity in stone? Is there pity in sunlight or in the river? If not in nature, where is pity found?"

"The heart! The human heart!"

"The heart is unnatural, lacking the stone's firmness, the sun's illumination, the river's nourishment."

Goodman shook his head. Across the river, the cannon fire was becoming sporadic. He could only imagine the army lines had been overrun, the artillery crews either put to flight or dead. Was Pike alive? Goodman found himself short on hope.

The thunderous sound of hooves made the witch draw her shoulders straighter. Goodman sensed her fresh pleasure.

"Ah, Nightcamp. The great stallion returns, which means Vines must be dead. The wearisome pact between us falls. It did not end in the way I foresaw, but once again the patience of stone proves its superiority."

They turned as Nightcamp appeared at the end of the trail. The rider was decrepit, old, and thin. Goodman could not imagine who it might be or why Nightcamp had brought him here.

"Witch," he said, his voice as weathered as his appearance. "What have you done to me? What is this?"

"Thou bargained for the fantasy in thy head. I granted it."

"New Vineland is gone! My city...my country...my flesh..."

Goodman laughed as he understood the man's identity. Vines glowered at him.

"Who are you—her latest fool?"

"She hasn't needed one since she found you. You've given her more than a decade of your life—"

"It hasn't been a decade—"

"You've spent *years* in a mindless dream and gave cover to her own plans."

"New Vineland was no dream!" he shouted, his voice cracking. "It was a perfect city, a place where no want wanted, where everyone—"

"A place where everyone praised and worshiped you. I know all about it. But it was never real. There was no city. Nothing but the tower and the horse you sit on now."

Evan Vines shook his wizened head and stared toward the west. "It can't be...it can't be..."

"Friend stallion," the witch said, and Nightcamp snorted in response. "Thou were thoughtful to anticipate my pleasure in this final meeting. But I did bid thee kill him. End my pact with this man and then I will ride thee at the head of a new army. Thou have suffered long under his banal and petty cruelty. Now avenge thyself."

The horse reared back as if to throw Evan Vines, who shouted in his shock. But Goodman could see Nightcamp hadn't come close to giving his full effort, and as he came down Vines seized the reins with all the strength he had left to him.

"Beast, she gave you to me. You're *mine* and you'll do as I say!"

Nightcamp settled.

"See, witch? I control him. Stay here atop this rock and rot, old woman. The soldiers will deal with you."

"Nightcamp, if thou betray me, thy reward will be an eternity in stone."

The horse turned tail and Evan Vines mustered a triumphant laugh. Goodman saw the witch produce another dagger from the folds of her robe. He grabbed for her wrist but she was too quick. The blade launched and Goodman found himself sprawled down on the ground, wincing in expectation of hearing Nightcamp's horrific cry. Instead, there was an odd *clink* and the witch reacted with a sharp hiss.

The statue of James Hobbs had moved. It now stood between them and Nightcamp's fleeing figure. With all the fluidity of flesh and muscle, the statue bent to retrieve the dagger. Goodman saw James's eyes glow with bright white light as he stepped toward them.

"You are short-sighted, witch," James said. "Stone is no punishment to a man obsessed with its secrets."

"This cannot be," the witch whispered.

"In a way, I must give you thanks. This experience has given me an understanding of rock I never thought possible. I hear the songs of mountain crags. I hear melodies from subterranean caves. Beautiful and powerful. Your screams will not drown them out."

The statue seized the witch by the neck, lifting her high in the air. She flailed, choking out a garbled chant. James laughed at her as Goodman got to his feet, though he could do nothing but observe. James's statue was changing.

"Turning me back to flesh in a last chance to save yourself, is that it? What would your *Lord* say to such a betrayal? Perhaps he's already abandoned you. Perhaps he never had any more substance than the fantasy you fed to Evan Vines."

He gave her a savage shake as the witch's words faded. Her head lolled to the left and Goodman thought she must be dead. It seemed she had completed her spell with her last breath because the hand and arm that lowered her to the ground was flesh and bone. So stood James in his entirety, though in that moment Goodman had trouble seeing the man as anything less than a god. They exchanged a quick glance before James went to kneel beside Katherine, who made the faintest murmur.

"*James.*"

"Just be still."

"But Lily...Adam..."

"They're safe."

Goodman went to the witch and felt her neck for any evidence of a pulse. He found nothing. The sound of hooves sent him turning around. This time several riders appeared on the plateau. Goodman grinned to see Pike. He sat next to a tall, rigid man with graying, swept-back hair. By his sheer bearing, Goodman knew this must be Jackson. His eyes were dark and seemed to hunger. Both men, as well as the other riders and their horses, were covered in cuts and grime, bloody and bruised.

"Pike!" Goodman said. "We need a doctor. James's wife is badly hurt."

The tall man barked an order, and the other riders dismounted. Pike maneuvered his horse to the right and motioned for Goodman to follow.

"Where's the witch, Harry? Did she escape?"

"There," Goodman said, pointing to the dead body. "James killed her."

"Mr. President," Pike said, gesturing. Goodman watched Jackson and two soldiers stand over the body. Jackson drew a saber and said, "For Charles."

"He'll take no chances," Pike said, climbing down. He put an arm around Goodman and turned him from the scene. "The whole fight was a near-run thing, Harry. I wish we'd fared better, but we did just enough. It's over."

"Not yet, Pike. Evan Vines escaped on Nightcamp."

"Escaped, you say? Perhaps. Come and let's get you a horse. You and I have one last ride to make this night."

# Chapter Sixty-Five

Lily threw aside the hammer and chisel in frustration as she fell back from Fat Jack and settled next to Adam, who moaned and held his stomach.

"Nothing will work," she said, wiping her brow. "Fat Jack, your shell is harder than stone."

*Evan Vines is coming soon*
*I have no face to meet him.*
*Without a face he'll know no doom*
*And death won't come to greet him.*

"I wish Papa were here. *He* could carve your face."

Adam groaned. "Lily has to do it."

"But I've tried everything! All of Mama's knives, and every tool in Papa's workshop, and none of them even made a dent."

Adam coughed and black blood dribbled from the corners of his mouth. Horrified, Lily got up. "We're getting you to the river. I don't care about Evan Vines or Nightcamp or Fat Jack."

"Adam wants Lily—"

"I don't care. You're more important to me than any of them. You're hurt and the water will make you better."

She tried to put her hands around him and pull, but he was so heavy and lifeless.

"Lily must carve."

"I've already told you nothing works."

"Adam can help."

His body began to thrash and contort in a way that made Lily shriek by reflex. Adam seemed to be trying to fold himself in half, every contortion bringing a fit of hisses and whimpers. The blood now came out in a heavy flow. Something appeared in his mouth. Adam coughed, gagged, and spat, his contortions wilder than ever. He flung himself onto his stomach and gave a final heave—

The witch's black dagger fell to the ground.

"Adam knows it will work," he said, his voice reduced to a faint wheeze. He collapsed and his white body seemed whiter than ever despite the black stains of his own blood.

*"Adam?"*

The faint groan he made gave her strength enough to pick up the knife and wipe the handle dry on her clothes. The blade shook in her grasp. It sang to her, sending an insistent melody up her arm. She felt it in her muscles and bones, in her blood. In her heart. Her mind flashed with shapes and figures she'd never seen before. The song drew her hand to lift the dagger and use it to trace their forms in the air.

*A carving song,* she thought. She'd never heard anything like it and felt equal measures of fear and thrill. The dagger now seemed merged with her palm. The blade belonged to her arm and her heart belonged to its song. The impulse to carve would have its say. Lily's pulse went wild as she brought the dagger and touched it to Fat Jack's shell. The pumpkin responded with a fresh burst of heat and internal light. Yes, the dagger would penetrate him, and the carving song showed her the face she would cut for him.

Lily cried out, both hands on the handle, and stabbed the knife into the middle of Fat Jack's enormous body. Boiling hot juice spurted from the wound, scalding her skin, but no amount of pain could separate her from the dagger. The song called to her and she found herself singing it, overtaken by its rhythms and passions. The words were beyond her comprehension but the song demanded her voice and she gave it. The clever blade gave Fat Jack his eyes and they glowed with bursts of hellfire.

*Make the mouth wide and fierce. Make the mouth wide and fierce.*

Oh, she did. Wide, gaping, toothed, an oven of fire. A tongue of flame shot forth to lick her flesh. This made her shout and drop the knife as she fell back before a massive, sinister face that seemed to wink at her. Fat Jack could not control the fury within him. The new mouth bestowed and blew fiery kisses at her. She looked down and saw the bottom of her filthy skirt had caught fire despite still being wet from the river. She bent to beat the flames out with her hands but the fire only grew. The ground rumbled from the approach of thundering hooves. She heard Nightcamp urging her away. His voice and the fire consuming her clothes became one thing. Lily got up, struggling toward the river. She fell. The fire felt like it was consuming her legs. She screamed and tried to rise, only to fall again—

Adam caught her. Somehow he'd summoned the strength. He bled worse than ever but he scrunched up his face and bolted into the air, a bound more powerful than any she'd ever seen from him. He had launched them toward the river. For a moment, it seemed they were floating and suspended at the top of an arc. The farm—the whole world—lay far below them. Fat Jack's blazing face. Nightcamp racing toward it. Evan Vines's cries reached Lily even in the air. *"Where is this place? Damn you, beast, where have you taken me? I command you to stop!"*

As they began their d, Nightcamp entered the crops, charging straight at Fat Jack. Just as he reached him, Nightcamp came to such an abrupt halt that it sent him into a vicious roll that would have broken any other horse's legs. Evan Vines was pitched from the saddle and launched straight at Fat Jack's hungry mouth. Lily saw a fireball erupt as the two heads met, and the only sound louder than Evan Vines's screams was Fat Jack's jubilant song—

*Revenge is delicious*
*I am at ease*
*You gave me my face*
*You gave me my peace*
*Atonement I ask for*
*Forgiveness I seek*
*Your heart can bestow it*
*I beg you to speak!*

"Yes!" Lily said. "Oh Fat Jack, oh Nightcamp, yes, yes I forgive you both—"

She hit the water.

# EPILOGUE

It was dawn when she heard Papa's footsteps on the dock. Lily knew he was coming. Nightcamp told her he would bring Papa back but she didn't say a word to him at the time. She just sat on the end of the little pier and stared out at the river, giving her sorrow to its slow and steady current.

She'd not been alone for some time. Mr. Goodman and Pike arrived two hours earlier, but they could do little except survey the aftermath and try to guess what happened. Mr. Goodman sought to comfort her but she had no interest in him. After a while, he'd quit trying.

"Lily?"

She swallowed at the sound of Papa's voice. Her shoulders shook. It was impossible to stop the dry sobs as Papa sat beside her. He let his left arm drape across her shoulder.

"Your mother is going to be okay. The doctors were able to save her."

She nodded.

"I learned from Nightcamp what happened here. About Fat Jack. About—"

"Adam's dead," she said.

She waited for him to answer. Any answer he gave would have been terrible, but she didn't reckon on Papa saying nothing. That was worse.

"He used all of his strength to get me to the river. I clung to him. I thought the water would make him strong again like it did before, but...but..."

"I see," Papa said.

"He told me that he loved me and you and Mama. Then he told me he had to go. He said, 'Adam was King of the River, and now Lily is Queen of the River.' And then he floated away from me. He just let go and floated. The current took him and—he was gone."

"Not gone," Papa said. "Look here."

He touched her chest. He touched her forehead.

Lily cried then. She'd thought the tears were all dried up.

"Here," Papa said. "Lean forward. Let your tears fall into the river. That way they'll find Adam, no matter where he is. We'll send our love together."

They sat beside each other for a long time, and somehow Lily felt better. Papa helped her to stand, and they walked back to where Goodman, Pike, and Nightcamp stood waiting next to the charred remains of Fat Jack. There was no sign of Evan Vines.

"Is it over?" Lily said.

"In some ways, yes," Papa said. "In other ways, never. But the threat is gone. The witch is dead. New Vineland is destroyed."

"I almost thought this day wouldn't happen," Mr. Goodman said.

Pike clapped him on the shoulder. "What do you do now, Harry? Go back to England? Head west for more adventures?"

"No, Pike, I think I've had enough of traveling. I'm going to settle here and see if we might build a proper town where New Vineland stood. They'll need a church, and a church will need a pastor. Maybe I'll fit the bill."

"Suit yourself, young man," Pike said. "Me and Nightcamp have decided to chase the sunset, haven't we?"

The horse whinnied, and Lily came forward and patted his flanks. He nuzzled his head against hers.

*Your courage, child, surpasses all,*
*Your equal none can be.*
*Your sorrows are a present pall*
*But joy is your destiny.*

"I think it is too," she said, smiling. "For all of us."

# ABOUT THE AUTHORS

**Sean Eads** is a writer and librarian living in Denver, Colorado. He is originally from Kentucky and has a master's degree in literature from the University of Kentucky and a master'sdegree in library science from the University of Illinois. His first novel, *The Survivors*, was a finalist for the Lambda Literary Award. His third novel, *Lord Byron's Prophecy*, was a finalist for the Shirley Jackson Award and the Colorado Book Award. His fifth novel, *Confessions*, was also a finalist for the Colorado Book Award. His favorite writers are Ray Bradbury, Herman Melville, Cormac McCarthy, and Ernest Hemingway.

**Joshua Viola** is a Colorado Book Award winner and Splatterpunk Award nominee. He co-authored *Legacy of Kain: Soul Reaver – The Dead Shall Rise*, an official prequel to the beloved video game series, which became the fourth most funded graphic novel of all time on Kickstarter, raising over $1.4 million. He edited the *Denver Post #1* bestselling horror anthology, *Nightmares Unhinged*, and co-edited *Cyber World*, named one of the best science fiction anthologies of 2016 by Barnes & Noble. He co-authored the comic book slasher series *True Believers* with Stephen Graham Jones, featuring official cameos from icons like Jamie Lee Curtis, R.L. Stine, Jeffrey Combs, and Barbara Crampton. As a producer, he has contributed to films such as *Aliens Expanded*, *The Thing Expanded*, *TerrorBytes*, *Shelby Oaks*, *Shrine of Abominations*, *Deathgasm II: Goremageddon*, and the recent *Deathstalker* reboot directed by Steven Kostanski (*The Void*, *Psycho Goreman*), starring Daniel Bernhardt (*The Matrix*, *John Wick*) and produced with Slash from Guns N' Roses. In 2024, he founded Bit Bot Media with musician Klayton (Celldweller), a multimedia company focused on original and licensed IP, including *The Terminator*, *Legacy of Kain*, *Evil Dead 2*, and more. Bit Bot also collaborates with Canadian film studio Raven Banner Entertainment on film productions, merchandise, and distribution, including titles like *The Autopsy of Jane Doe* and the documentary *Hate to Love: Nickelback*. Joshua's video game development includes work on titles such as *The Rocky Horror Show, Pirates of the Caribbean: Call of the Kraken, Unioverse, The Smurfs, TARGET: Terror*, and others. He is the owner and chief editor of Hex Publishers and resides in Denver, Colorado, with his husband and son.

# THE END?

**Not if you want to dive into more of Crystal Lake Publishing's Tales from the Darkest Depths!**

Check out our amazing website and online store or download our latest catalog here.
https://geni.us/CLPCatalog

We always have great new projects and content on the website to dive into, as well as a newsletter, behind the scenes options, social media platforms, our own dark fiction shared-world series and our very own webstore. Our webstore even has categories specifically for KU books, non-fiction, anthologies, and of course more novels and novellas.

Readers...

Thank you for reading *Servants of Stone*. We hope you enjoyed this novel.

If you have a moment, please review *Servants of Stone* at the store where you bought it.

Help other readers by telling them why you enjoyed this book. No need to write an in-depth discussion. Even a single sentence will be greatly appreciated. Reviews go a long way to helping a book sell, and is great for an author's career. It'll also help us to continue publishing quality books.

Thank you again for taking the time to journey with Crystal Lake Publishing.

You will find links to all our social media platforms on our Linktree page. https://linktr.ee/CrystalLakePublishing

Follow us on Amazon:

# MISSION STATEMENT

Since its founding in August 2012, Crystal Lake has quickly become one of the world's leading publishers of Dark Fiction and Horror books. In 2023, Crystal Lake officially transitioned into an entertainment company, joining several other divisions, genres, and imprints, including Torrid Waters, Crystal Lake Comics, Crystal Lake Games, Crystal Lake Kids, and many more.

While we strive to present only the highest quality fiction and entertainment, we also endeavour to support authors along their writing journey. We offer our time and experience in non-fiction projects, as well as author mentoring and services, at competitive prices.

With several Bram Stoker Award wins and many other wins and nominations (including the HWA's Specialty Press Award), Crystal Lake Publishing puts integrity, honor, and respect at the forefront of our publishing operations.

We strive for each book and outreach program we spearhead to not only entertain and touch or comment on issues that affect our readers, but also to strengthen and support the Dark Fiction field and its authors.

Not only do we find and publish authors we believe are destined for greatness, but we strive to work with men and women who endeavour to be decent human beings who care more for others than themselves, while still being hard working, driven, and passionate artists and storytellers.

Crystal Lake Publishing is and will always be a beacon of what passion and dedication, combined with overwhelming teamwork and respect, can accomplish. We endeavour to know each and every one of our readers, while building personal relationships with our authors, reviewers, bloggers, podcasters, bookstores, and libraries.

We will be as trustworthy, forthright, and transparent as any business can be, while also keeping most of the headaches away from our authors, since it's our job to solve the problems so they can stay in a creative mind. Which of course also means paying our authors.

We do not just publish books, we present to you worlds within your world, doors within your mind, from talented authors who sacrifice so much for a moment of your time.

There are some amazing small presses out there, and through collaboration and open forums we will continue to support other presses in the goal of helping authors and showing the world what quality small presses are capable of accomplishing. No one wins when a small press goes down, so we will always be there to support hardworking, legitimate presses and their authors. We don't see Crystal Lake as the best press out there, but we will always strive to be the best, strive to be the most interactive and grateful, and even blessed press around. No matter what happens over time, we will also take our mission very seriously while appreciating where we are and enjoying the journey.

What do we offer our authors that they can't do for themselves through self-publishing?

We are big supporters of self-publishing (especially hybrid publishing), if done with care, patience, and planning. However, not every author has the time or inclination to do market research, advertise, and set up book launch strategies. Although a lot of authors are successful in doing it all, strong small presses will always be there for the authors who just want to do what they do best: write.

What we offer is experience, industry knowledge, contacts and trust built up over years. And due to our strong brand and trusting fanbase, every Crystal Lake Publishing book comes with weight of respect. In time our fans begin to trust our judgment and will try a new author purely based on our support of said author.

With each launch we strive to fine-tune our approach, learn from our mistakes, and increase our reach. We continue to assure our authors that we're here for them and that we'll carry the weight of the launch and dealing with third parties while they focus on their strengths—be it writing, interviews, blogs, signings, etc.

We also offer several mentoring packages to authors that include knowledge and skills they can use in both traditional and self-publishing endeavours.

We look forward to launching many new careers.

This is what we believe in. What we stand for. This will be our legacy.

Welcome to Crystal Lake Publishing—Where Stories Come Alive!

www.ingramcontent.com/pod-product-compliance
Lightning Source LLC
Chambersburg PA
CBHW070556300726
48975CB00006B/1604